Spy Another Day

(The King's Rogues Book 3)

by Elizabeth Ellen Carter

© Copyright 2020 by Elizabeth Ellen Carter
Text by Elizabeth Ellen Carter
Cover by Wicked Smart Designs

Dragonblade Publishing, Inc. is an imprint of Kathryn Le Veque Novels, Inc.
P.O. Box 7968
La Verne CA 91750
ceo@dragonbladepublishing.com

Produced in the United States of America

First Edition February 2020
Print Edition

Reproduction of any kind except where it pertains to short quotes in relation to advertising or promotion is strictly prohibited.

All Rights Reserved.

The characters and events portrayed in this book are fictitious. Any similarity to real persons, living or dead, is purely coincidental and not intended by the author.

ARE YOU SIGNED UP FOR DRAGONBLADE'S BLOG?

You'll get the latest news and information on exclusive giveaways, exclusive excerpts, coming releases, sales, free books, cover reveals and more.

Check out our complete list of authors, too!

No spam, no junk. That's a promise!

Sign Up Here

www.dragonbladepublishing.com

Dearest Reader;

Thank you for your support of a small press. At Dragonblade Publishing, we strive to bring you the highest quality Historical Romance from the some of the best authors in the business. Without your support, there is no 'us', so we sincerely hope you adore these stories and find some new favorite authors along the way.

Happy Reading!

CEO, Dragonblade Publishing

Additional Dragonblade books by Author Elizabeth Ellen Carter

Heart of the Corsairs Series
Captive of the Corsairs
Revenge of the Corsairs
Shadow of the Corsairs

King's Rogues Series
Live and Let Spy
Spyfall
Spy Another Day
Father's Day (A Novella)

Also from Elizabeth Ellen Carter
Dark Heart

★★★ Please visit Dragonblade's website for a full list of books and authors. Sign up for Dragonblade's blog for sneak peeks, interviews, and more: ★★★
www.dragonbladepublishing.com

Acknowledgement

Thank you always to my beloved husband, Duncan, who is always happy to discuss the intricacies of character developments and to help me untangle plot knots. Thank you to Scott Moreland, the world's best editor (even he says so) and Kathryn Le Veque, the world's best publisher (who doesn't say so, but is). And to Shawn and Kris for keeping me on track.

Author's Note

On long road trips, my husband and I play a game – the alternative view of history.

In this game, we pick a pivotal moment and unpack how the future of the world might change as a result.

What if the South had won the American Civil War? How would that have affected the mills of Manchester, the expansion of the British Empire, and the growing of cotton in Australia?

What if Edward VIII had not abdicated? How would that have influenced the British response to Hitler's expansion across Europe?

That brings me to The King's Rogues.

The series started after coming across the fact that Napoleon actually did canvas the idea of an airborne invasion of England by hot air balloon. There were real attempts at such an incursion, the belief being that once a small detachment of troops landed, the citizenry would rise up and overthrow the monarchy and the government.

Funded by the Louisiana Purchase, Napoleon could throw money at any scheme to conquer England. And by all accounts, he did. There is an amazing etching of a three-windmill powered paddle wheeler said to be able to carry thousands of troops. There was a plan to tunnel under the Channel. And then there were hot air balloons.

In the end, Aeronaut Sophie Blanchard warned him of the impracticality of the scheme (no one had successfully flown from France to England, but there had been a successful balloon crossing from England to France a decade or so earlier).

Finally, the outcome of the Battle of Trafalgar put paid to invasion plans as Napoleon concentrated on taking Europe instead.

But what if plans for a troop insertion by hot air balloon were more advanced than we now know to be true?

If hot air balloons could not travel east to west, then what about travelling west to east? And what is west of England? Ireland. Which side did Ireland favor? France.

What if the United Irishmen had secured Napoleon's funding and were prepared to trust him again with a better plan?

What if the spies who thwarted the scheme were lost to history?

I hope you enjoyed playing this alternative history game with me, and fell in love with each one of The King's Rogues as much as I enjoyed researching and writing them.

– Elizabeth Ellen Carter

The face is the mirror of the mind,
and eyes without speaking confess
the secrets of the heart.

– St. Jerome

Prologue

1 January 1806
Outside Charteris House
Truro, Cornwall

"MR. BASSETT, IS there nothing we can do?" His apprentice, Joe, face soot-stained, looked at him with wide mournful eyes.

"Get one of our horses from the stables and race as fast as you can to Sir Daniel. Tell him the fire was no accident. Someone set it by the back door, poured turpentine all over it before lighting it – and stayed long enough to watch it go up."

Bassett spun round to look at the shopfront, suddenly remembering. "My God! The key!"

He took off at a run back toward the burning building without a second thought.

"Mr. Bassett!" the youth called out.

"Follow orders, Joe!" Bassett yelled back. "Go to Sir Daniel!"

One week later

ADAM HARDACRE PUT a black-gloved hand on the shoulder of the young man before him.

With red-rimmed eyes, Bassett's apprentice stared straight ahead at the coffin laying before the altar, manfully holding back tears in public that he'd allowed himself to shed in private.

It had been hard for the lad. Young Joe had lost everything – his home, his work, and a man who, by all accounts, had become a good friend to him.

Even though Adam didn't know the deceased that well, his own throat constricted when one of the mourners gave a heartfelt eulogy. How was it that such sentimentality had been opened up in him?

Beside him, his wife, Olivia, squeezed his hand.

Sir Daniel Ridgeway, head held high, posture erect, led the pall-bearers two-by-two, to their positions. Joe made up the sixth at the end.

It had all the occasion of a military funeral, although no one in St Mary's Church wore decorations. This was a decidedly civilian affair.

Each one of the twenty mourners rose to their feet and bowed their heads as a mark of respect as the coffin passed.

Adam remained standing even after the others had filed out to begin their graveside vigil.

"You can't blame yourself."

He looked down at Olivia and drank in her loveliness. The warmth of her brown eyes made him grateful to the good Lord above that this woman was his wife and was prepared to stand by his side come hell or high water.

He saw no pity in her face, just understanding and a silent promise of steadfastness he sorely needed right now, although he would admit *that* to no one but her.

The truth of the matter was he *did* feel responsible. How could he not? He even had it in writing – a note from Harold Bickmore.

This is not over.

It had been a threat and a promise rolled into one.

And it took the form of arson, an action designed to put The King's Rogues out of business. As a result, a good man lost his life.

Adam squeezed his wife's hand and nodded to indicate he'd heard her. He wasn't sure he could form the words to tell her so. They left the church hand-in-hand.

At the grave, he watched his friend and employer closely. Sir Daniel carried the twin responsibilities of clandestine spymaster and pillar of the Truro community. The strain showed on his face – a man who'd had had too little sleep and burdened with too much to do.

Yet Ridgeway performed his public duty without flagging, sparing a word or two of comfort to the mourners. Adam knew how much the devastating fire had cost him financially, too. After all, he had owned Charteris House. Shopkeepers on either side of their little headquarters would require compensation for their losses.

Adam's nerves jangled despite his outward calm. If it was just him alone, he would have saddled up and searched under every rock and in every hell hole from here to John O'Groats for that bastard traitor, Bickmore, but he'd been under orders to stay close.

"You have a job to do, Lieutenant," Sir Daniel had told him in no uncertain terms. "I can have a hundred operatives around the Kingdom alerted and searching before you've even left the county. Bickmore will show his face again, mark my words. Our best chance of finding him is in the material we already have."

Alas, marking time was not among Adam's preferred pastimes. Nor could he bear a burden of distress he was powerless to relieve.

"I'm going to have the carriage brought around," he told Olivia.

She simply nodded and moved to stand beside Joe who, as the coffin was lowered into the open earth, could no longer contain his tears.

ON THEIR WAY back to Sir Daniel's home of Bishop's Wood, they passed what remained of Charteris House.

On this crisp winter's day, Adam could smell the strange combination of damp and ash. Everything which could be salvaged from the rubble had been – but alas not the clocks. Not a single one of Bassett's beloved timepieces survived the conflagration.

Such a waste. Poor Joe couldn't even bring himself to look.

"I've ordered the site to be cleared tomorrow," said Sir Daniel. "There will be no trace that The King's Rogues were ever here."

"Have we heard from Nate and Susannah?" Olivia asked.

"I hope Abigail will have received word while we've been out," Sir Daniel answered before directing his attention to Bassett's apprentice. "Chin up, lad, you did as much as any man could. I'm proud of you."

Adam pulled himself from his stupor. There was too much to do – starting with how the hell Harold Bickmore escaped Naval custody.

"We're *all* proud of you, Joe," Adam added.

THE LETHARGY THAT accompanies funerals was absent at Bishop's Wood. The Ridgeways' country residence was a fine Georgian manor surrounded by the woods for which it had been named. It was a peaceful retreat, generally, but now it was also a temporary place of business.

Lady Abigail Ridgeway sat at her desk in the morning room to receive the first post of the day. She liked this room. It captured the best of the winter sunlight, but that was not why she favored it particularly today.

In truth, she needed respite from their unexpected houseguest.

She was untroubled to confess that she was not a very compassionate woman by nature. Even as much as she loved her adopted daughter, Marie, Abigail also accepted she was not a particularly maternal creature either. Thank goodness the girl had Daniel to guide her upbringing in such things.

As a result, the role of a kindly nurse was not one that fell on her shoulders easily. Indulging an invalid stretched the limits of her patience – especially when she suspected the party in question was making somewhat of a meal of his current situation.

She turned her attention to the pile of correspondence that Musgrave, the butler, had left on her desk.

The first was a letter from Susannah Payne, which she recognized by her neat cursive hand. She and Nathaniel ought to be enjoying their honeymoon as newlyweds. Instead, they were now preparing their inn, The Queen's Head on the western Cornish coast, to be the new headquarters for The King's Rogues.

> *"… do let us know what special arrangements are required and we will endeavor to have everything in place for your arrival at St. Sennen. We were horrified to hear of Bassett's…"*

Abigail skimmed the rest of the letter. The Queen's Head would be ready for their arrival in five days' time. That was all she needed to know. The letter was put to one side.

She opened the next. It was from Admiral Sykes, direct from the Admiralty in London and addressed to Sir Daniel.

> *"We regret the escape of the prisoner, Harold Monteagle Bickmore, from our custody on tenth of December.*
>
> *"The prisoner, in concert with three accomplices whom we have not identified, overpowered the guard escorting him to the first hearing of his court martial. The search is continuing for the prisoner who has since been tried and found guilty in absentia based on the strength of evidence supplied by you and Lieutenant Adam Hardacre.*
>
> *"As the prisoner has openly professed his treason, our resources have focused on the coast closest to France in the expectation the man will attempt to make his break across to enemy territory.*
>
> *"As your letter made plain, we were remiss in letting your company know of developments in a timely fashion and we deeply regret the losses you've suffered.*
>
> *"We remain confident that, in time, we might recapture…"*

Abigail set the rest of the letter aside in disgust.

Useless! Completely useless!

The Admiralty had allowed its plans for Admiral Horatio Nelson's state funeral to completely overshadow their responsibilities.

It was just as well that she sent her *own* agents out last week. They would have more solid leads on the whereabouts of the traitor before Whitehall could finish writing the orders.

Abigail gritted her teeth to prevent very unladylike profanities crossing her lips.

Fools to a man!

No doubt, Daniel would have stronger words than that to say when he returned home.

Movement caught her eye.

Through the trees beyond the window, she spied the carriage returning from the funeral.

She looked down at the last piece of correspondence, this addressed to Lady Abigail Houghall at an address in Bath.

Oh my, she hadn't resided there in twelve years, not since before she wed. The time before Daniel seemed a lifetime ago. She smiled at the memory of their unusual first meeting, then turned over the envelope.

There was a return address.

The Honorable Alexandra Gedding
Stannum House
Cornwall

Alexandra? Felicity's daughter? The last time she'd seen the child was as a babe in arms.

She heard Musgrave at the front door and left the letter unopened. Old family connections could wait for a more opportune time. There was much to do before they relocated to the village of St. Sennen.

She met Daniel in the hall and greeted him with a kiss, but did not ask about the funeral. There was nothing good one could say about them.

Besides, as with the letter from Susannah Payne, she knew already all she needed to know. The elderly man had been found in the apartment above his shop in Charteris House. The flames hadn't even reached his quarters. The old gent was apparently overcome by the smoke even as he slept.

"How's our patient?" Daniel asked.

"As his hands are bandaged, he insists on me feeding him, except he spends most of his time looking at my bosom instead of the spoon."

"I can't fault the man for his taste."

Abigail accepted her husband's compliment with a coquettish wink.

"We'll see if he's on better behavior later. I threatened to have big Billy from the stables see to his care instead."

For the first time in a week, Daniel cracked a smile. That gladdened her, for she knew how her husband worried – but it disappeared as quickly as sunshine in winter.

"Any word about Bickmore? Adam is champing at the bit."

Abigail glanced to Adam and Olivia Hardacre who had just entered the entrance hall with Joe Browne, Bassett's apprentice.

"There is. And from Nate and Susannah, too." she said, opening the drawing room door.

Inside was a small man seated on a wingback chair as though holding court between two servants – a footman and a maid. His face was red and his burned hands were bandaged in white linen.

"If everyone's here," said Lady Abigail, "we might as well join Bassett in the drawing room."

Chapter One

November 1805
Stannum, Cornwall

THE POOR DEAR...

Her docile acceptance should have been her twin brother's first clue that she was up to something. After all, when had Alexandra Gedding ever accepted Phillip's instruction meekly?

"Come on, girl, he'll be here soon," she said, wheeling her dun-colored mare about. She urged the mount behind a stand of elms that would hide them both.

Allie chose the spot deliberately. It afforded her an unimpeded view of the crossroads where she waited for her twin.

She ought to feel embarrassed that a woman aged three and twenty was sneaking about to spy like a child but, truly, the man had given her no choice!

Even now, she recalled their conversation this morning with irritation.

Over breakfast, Phillip had announced he was going out after lunch and to not await his return. Allie forced herself to pretend disinterest in his business and told him that she might ride also. She did not object when he warned her not to go further than the village alone. It did no good to remind him she was the eldest by five minutes since he, as the male, had inherited the title of squire and the responsibility of Stannum.

There was no question that Phillip strove to be understanding, all the while reminding her that she was a young lady of *quality*. Long rides were out of the question; there was no groomsman at Stannum House to escort her. In fact, there were no groomsmen at all – just old Harry Watt, who tripled his duties as butler, footman and groom.

The only other servant they had was Mrs. McArthur, their housekeeper.

When she left the house, Allie had informed him she intended to simply ride along the mile-long stretch of Stannum Beach.

Let him think she took no interest in his comings and goings, although nothing could be further from the truth. She was genuinely anxious about her brother. Phillip had been acting secretive for weeks now. Yet any attempt she'd made to draw him out had been firmly rebuffed.

Might well he scoff at her concern but, as his twin, she *knew* in the fabric of her being that he was hiding something from her.

Allie brushed the sleeve of her mazarine blue riding habit and waited for Phillip to ride up the road from the village.

If he behaved as he had done on the past three occasions, he would leave Stannum House no later than three o'clock, probably to arrive at his destination before nightfall. This limited the number of places he could go.

And, wherever it was, he would be gone overnight but always back in time for a late luncheon.

She had not followed before. But this time, she determined to be at the crossroads when he passed. If Phillip headed south, it would most likely be to Bodmin. If it was to the southeast, the destination was Camelford. If it was more directly east, Launceston was the place.

At the sound of approaching hooves, Allie leaned forward to pat her mare's neck and hide herself more fully in the foliage. She recognized the gait of Phillip's dapple-gray stallion. Nephel heard it, too. Her ears twitched back and forth at the familiar sound.

The horseman was, indeed, Phillip. He looked the very model of a fashionable young buck. His dark green riding jacket fit perfectly across his broad shoulders. Today, he elected to ride without a hat and his glossy black hair shone in the early November sunlight.

She held her breath as his horse, Lightning, passed before her. The beast snorted. Nephel raised her head. Allie continued to stroke the mare's neck in the hopes she wouldn't whicker and give away their position.

The jangle of the bridle indicated Phillip had pulled at the reins to exert greater control over his mount as he came to the crossroads. Allie counted to thirty, hearing the hoofbeats recede, before urging her own horse out from their hiding place.

Lit by the late afternoon sun, she watched her brother take the southeastern road.

Camelford it was then.

She toyed with the idea of trailing her brother for the twelve-mile journey but decided against it. If Phillip spotted her – and no doubt he would – he would be furious. Then he'd become even more secretive. She wouldn't risk deepening a rift in a relationship already under strain.

She refixed a pin to hold back a strand of her own black, curly hair and waited until Phillip was out of sight before urging Nephel to take the road west into the setting sun toward home.

No sooner had she reached the weathered pillars and the rusted gate that marked the entrance to Stannum House, the thought of spending the rest of the afternoon alone with no one but Mrs. McArthur for company was unappealing despite her fondness for the Scotswoman.

Allie directed Nephel onward, continuing down the road that led to the village of Stannum. On the hill to the south, a tower of gray stone cast a long shadow down the yellowed grassy vale toward the village and the sea beyond. The engine room of Wheal Gunnis Mine was once the center of their fortunes. Its closure three years ago cast a greater shadow still over their community.

Where there was no work, there was no money. Where there was no money, families who could afford to, moved away. Those who could not, survived hand-to-mouth and prayed the seasons to come were more favorable.

So far, prayers remained unanswered.

Allie's journey took her across a ridge. To her right, a road led down to the ancient stone quay of Stannum. She paused and took in the view. The afternoon sun bathed the stone cottages in a weak pale gold light, the landscape around it shadowed in a blue-purple cast.

More than a third of the cottages were unoccupied. Her counting out of their misfortunes continued.

With no work, there was no rent. With no rent, there had been no money to repair the cottages, so even if there *was* work to be had in Stannum, there were no houses fit for people to live in.

Another cycle of a downward spiral of economic depression made worse by the war with France.

Before the narrow road curved, Allie could see the flickering fire from Clarrie Prenpas' blacksmith forge. At least their former mine foreman had managed to find work.

The only other business to keep its doors open was the little tavern, owned for generations by the Angove family.

Allie felt the weight of responsibility for Stannum as keenly as her brother. She desperately wished there was more she could do but, in truth, her own circumstances were not much brighter than those of the villagers.

When the mine petered out, so too did the family's main source of income. There were the rents on the cottages, of course, but how could they demand rent to be paid when there was no work to be had?

Although she had not been privy to the meetings that Phillip, as their late uncle's heir, had attended with solicitors and creditors alike, she knew well enough the dire straits they faced.

Suddenly, a galloping ride along the sands lost its appeal.

Her attention turned to the pale stone path worn over the centuries that ran along the edge of the cliffs. It led to a solitary cottage on the headland on the other side of Stannum Cove.

She knew it well and found herself drawn to it, even against her better judgment.

Should she go?

Living there was the only person she could talk to, although Allie wasn't sure what *he* would have to say about her unexpectedly showing up on his doorstep.

No, that wasn't the truth. She knew exactly what he would say – little of it would be pleasant, but at least it would be honest.

With a decisive snap of the reins, she urged Nephel into a canter. She might as well call on David Manston unannounced. It wouldn't be the first time.

DAVID SWUNG THE axe and felt it bite into the heartwood. A shock of pain sparked at his wrists and traveled all the way up his arms.

Dropping the axe with a mild curse, he sought to ease the ache by stretching out his limbs and breathing deep for a count to ten. He looked out at the sea beyond his home, the glare from the sun intense enough to make his eyes water. It took his mind off the ache, now settled in his shoulders.

When he bought the two-story cottage overlooking Stannum Cove, he was told it had once been a smuggler's hideout.

To his disappointment, he never saw any evidence of secret passages or hidden storerooms. Likely, only its proximity to the beach – down the cliff face via a precipitous path – accounted for the myth.

He vaguely recalled the admonishments of his drawing master –

"don't just see, *observe*" – and he took a moment to do so now, but only for a minute.

In the five years he'd lived here, David never tired of the view. It would catch him unawares at different times of the day – early in the morning when it was impossible to tell where the sea ended and sky began, where the towering clouds heralded the approach of ferocious storms.

Or there would be days like this one – mild autumn days full of color – with the turning of the leaves from green to red, the orange of the ripening pumpkins, and the gold-tipped waves of the sea at sunset, as he observed tonight.

Then he saw color of a different sort. The pale gold of a mare and her rider dressed in blue galloped along the cliffs in his direction. There was only one person who it could be – the *Honorable* Miss Alexandra Gedding.

David wiped his brow and turned back to his work once more, ignoring the impending visitor. He was not a man of leisure. There were chores to be done before the sun fell for the night.

He retrieved his axe and adjusted his grip before throwing his whole weight into a downward strike onto the stump. David felt the wood split with some satisfaction.

The hoofbeats sounded closer. He tried to tell himself that Alexandra's arrival was an annoyance, an inconvenience, but he couldn't quite bring himself to believe it.

In the time he'd lived in Stannum, he'd cultivated somewhat of a reputation as a hermit and that suited him just fine. People left him to his business and he left them to theirs. Any inquiry about his health or his doings beyond the most superficial of social niceties was treated to his mask of bland indifference.

It didn't take too long for people to get the hint.

Alexandra Gedding was *not* most people.

But he liked her, and he wished to God that he didn't.

He picked up another lump of wood and set it on the block. He listened to the sound of Allie dismounting while he lined up his aim. A gentleman would aid a lady down from her horse, inquire after her health and offer her refreshment.

He chose not to be a gentleman, even if he did own the title once.

This lump of wood cleaved cleanly.

He waited for Allie – hell, he couldn't even help thinking of her by her familiar name – to greet him, but she did not.

In the end, curiosity got the better of him. He looked around to see what she was up to and found her at the chicken coop, gathering his half a dozen hens into the safety of their enclosure.

Without so much as a "by your leave", she then opened the kitchen door of *his* cottage and entered, before walking back out with a bucket of millet and a scoop.

If she said nothing, then neither would he – after all, it was *she* who was trespassing on *his* property. He turned back to his task and continued watching her out of the corners of his eyes.

The hens clucked their appreciation at being fed. Allie went to the pump and worked the iron handle until sufficient water vomited into the empty bucket. She re-entered the cottage and still hadn't said a word to him.

David shook his head and gathered the freshly-cut timber to stack in the lean-to opposite the kitchen before he joined Allie – *Alexandra, if you don't mind*, he instructed himself – inside the cottage.

"Would you mind telling me why you're here?" he asked, making sure he added the right amount of exasperation to his voice.

Really, he ought to object more strongly to this woman making herself at home in his cottage, but he wouldn't mind a cup of tea and that was what she was making – stoking the fire, pouring water into a battered kettle, hanging it on the hinged iron rod, positioning it over the flame.

She shrugged. "I was taking a ride, and I thought I would stop by."

He used the rest of the water in the bucket to wash his hands and face. "And you didn't consider that I'd be too busy for visitors?"

She flashed a smile, which he hated because it made a pleasant face even prettier and the last thing he wanted was to think of Alexandra Gedding and her pretty face.

"You *were* busy, that's why I rounded up the chickens for you."

"Did you have another fight with Phillip?"

Her smile sputtered and died like a candle's flame in its death throes.

Ha! He was right.

"I didn't intend it to be a fight," she said, pulling down two cups and a small tea chest from the dresser. "I simply asked him where he was going for the third time this week. He told me to mind my own business and called me an interfering busybody."

It took all of David's willpower not to laugh. Instead, he folded his arms and leaned against a wall. "An accurate assessment, if you ask me."

Alexandra did worse than smile.

She *laughed.*

It was a rich melodic expression of mirth, not the tittering of drawing room ninnies, nor the bray of tavern wenches. And it seemed to him that the color of her eyes had just deepened to an emerald green.

"Be that as it may, I'm still concerned about him," she said. "He's not his usual jolly self. Over the past three months he's become withdrawn. He won't talk to me like he used to. Since about two months ago, he's taken to staying out overnight and not telling me or Mrs. McArthur where he's going, what he's doing, or when he's coming back."

It was growing pleasantly warm inside the cottage. David shrugged off his threadbare work coat. He hung it on a peg behind the door beside his oilskin coat and took a seat at his small kitchen table. The cozy domesticity of it wasn't lost on him.

Which only leads to dangerous thoughts.

"Did you ever consider a man doesn't want to have to answer to his sister and a servant?" David asked.

"What's the harm in just telling us why he's going to Camelford?"

"If he refused to tell you where he was going, how do you know he was going to Camelford?"

"Because I followed him."

David groaned and dropped forehead first on the table, splaying out his arms in dramatic fashion. He looked up. His theatrics had been a wasted effort. Her back was to him, preparing the tea.

"Tell me you didn't."

"Of course, I did," she replied, as though it were the most normal thing in the world. "Not as far as Camelford, of course. Only to the crossroads, just far enough to know he wasn't heading to Bodmin or Launceston."

She removed the steaming kettle from its hook with a cloth and poured boiling water into the teapot.

"And is that significant?"

"Well, yes. Our solicitor and banker are in Bodmin, so I know he wasn't going there," she said.

Alexandra brought the teapot to the table along with two mugs and sat opposite him.

"Perhaps the man has needs that can't be met at home," David said boldly, before turning his attention to pouring the steaming brew into a cup. He savored the piquant aroma as the amber liquid filled each mug. Tea was an expensive indulgence of his – a vice to be sure, but at least it was one of the safer ones.

Alexandra took a sip, drinking it without milk or sweetening – not that he had either to offer.

"Like what?" she asked. "Phillip can entertain at Stannum House any time he wishes, and if he wants to drink at a tavern, I can think of at least three within five miles of here, so why does he need to go to Camelford?"

David lifted his head and gave her a hooded look.

It took a moment, but he knew the instant the answer dawned on her. Alexandra's face glowed a very appealing shade of pink.

"Oh."

He found himself watching her mouth as she brought the tea to her lips once again. If he was a gentleman, he would change the subject and spare the blushes of a gentle-born young woman, but something perverse in him reared its head. He quite liked seeing Alexandra – *Allie* – unsettled.

And yet, a moment later, she waved a dismissive hand.

"There have to be willing barmaids by the dozen at those taverns he frequents. What's so special about Camelford?"

David could make a guess. Sometimes one needed a professional to do the job well...

"I know you're concerned, but just let him be for a while," he answered. "Let him blow off steam in whatever way he sees fit. Phillip is a sensible young man, but he's got a lot to sort out. Your late uncle made a right mess of the finances for Stannum."

"It wasn't all his fault, you know." Allie's defense of her uncle was halfhearted. "Sometimes one cannot help bad luck."

Bad luck, or bad judgment? Dear old uncle George Nancarrow ought to have known Wheal Gunnis was close to being worked out.

David remained silent. He'd made his opinion on the matter clear to the Gedding twins from the beginning. He knew Allie agreed with him, but her loyalty to her relative was a credit to her.

They sat in silent companionship, enjoying the tea while the light through the window faded from gold to a mauve hue, and the fire provided the only real light in the room.

Out of the blue, Allie leaned across the table, put her hand on his and squeezed it. "Thank you," she said softly. "You've always been very kind to me."

The sound of loneliness in her voice touched him deeper than it ought.

Oh no, he could not be having that. Sentimentality led to a tenderness of feelings, and he knew only too well where that path led.

"Kind?" he sneered. "Dear God, call me anything but *kind*, please."

Allie touched a hand to her chin and regarded him as though he had offered the wittiest bon mot.

"Not kind?" she said, the humor in her voice plain. "I fully understand, Mr. Manston. I shall make sure your secret is safe with me."

She patted his hand with exaggerated condescension and rose from the table.

He stood also. He reached her just as she put a hand on the kitchen door handle. She paused.

They were so close now. He could detect the faintest scent of orange water on her skin. His hand slid across hers over the doorknob and held it there.

"You shouldn't come here alone, Allie," he said, *sotto voce*. "Have a care for your reputation."

He watched her eyes widen a touch. Her tongue wet her bottom lip as she searched his face. Despite his best efforts, he felt the stirring of arousal.

"Is my reputation at *risk*, Mr. Manston?" she asked, voice husky. "We've known each other five years and never before have you objected to my visits."

Damn! Did she know what that tone of voice did to him?

"Then your recollection is very different to mine," he answered gruffly. "Haven't I told you to go away each time?"

"You tell *everyone* to go away."

"And they have the good sense to go."

"But you don't mean it. Not with *me*."

She rose on tiptoes and leaned toward him. He felt the brush of her breasts against his chest as she planted a soft kiss on his lips.

The act caught him by surprise. Apparently, it showed on his face because she wore a rather enigmatic smile.

"There, I think that is proof enough I'm safe around you," she said.

She moved her hand to turn the door handle. David kept his hand firmly over hers to prevent the knob from turning.

There. That surprised *her.*

She thought she knew him so well... a spoiled, privileged young woman too safe and too comfortable in this small little world that was Stannum.

He pulled her into his arms before he could second-guess himself. He plundered her mouth before she could utter more than a gasp.

He'd wanted to do that for the past two years.

He waited for her to pummel his back with her fists, but she did not. Instead, she wrapped her arms around his neck and returned the aggression of his kiss in equal measure.

In the end, it was he who broke off. His breathing was ragged, as was hers. To his dismay, she seemed to recover from it faster than he.

He let go of the door handle. She turned it. The last of the late afternoon autumn light spilled into the kitchen, and she walked out into it, calling to her horse.

David held a safe distance, but still close enough to assist her to mount if she needed it.

She did not.

She climbed the mounting block and gained her seat on the horse like the accomplished horsewoman she was.

But the glance she threw his way before she set off was unsettled.

Good.

Perhaps Alexandra Gedding had finally learned her lesson.

He was a dangerous man.

And his darkness ran deep...

Chapter Two

EVERY GIRL DREAMED of her first kiss – the tender pressing together of lips, a charming prince who would sweep her off her feet, the culmination of so many fairytales.

Allie didn't consider herself a naïve woman. She understood the mechanics of the act of love, only to realize that to know from reading was not the same as to physically experiencing. She'd played with fire when she kissed David on the lips, but only knew how hot it burned when he commanded it and turned its heat back on her.

Little wonder that she slept ill last night.

David's touch reached even into her bedchamber and into her dreams. It left her restless, wanting more of the dangerous passion that seemed to lurk beneath his obvious breeding as a gentleman and his mask of a gruff recluse.

Such a delicious contradiction, coupled with the fact that David Manston was uncommonly handsome – refined features, dark eyebrows over intense blue eyes, and a keen intelligence that was not afraid to challenge hers.

Allie shook her head to clear it and concentrate on preparing batches of spicy, syrupy parkin cake to serve at tonight's Bonfire Night feast.

She glanced over at Mrs. McArthur who worked with her on the task. If the woman thought she was out of sorts, Allie knew the housekeeper would never dream of mentioning it.

And that suited Allie just fine. She needed to be busy. If she was busy, she couldn't think. If she was busy, there would be no time to worry about Phillip who hadn't returned home yesterday. If she was busy, she could not think too much about David Manston's kiss.

Oh, who was she kidding? Allie muttered to herself as she grated another lump of fresh ginger. To think of one thing was to think of the other.

She brushed a dark curl from her forehead with the back of her hand. Perhaps David was right in his advice. Perhaps she fussed over her brother far too much – after all, she was the eldest, if only by minutes.

She knew Phillip struggled with the responsibilities that came with being late Uncle George's heir. Not only was there the care and upkeep of Stannum House to see to, but also responsibility for the community that bore the name of the house that once made its wealth in tin mining.

But that fortune was long gone.

Allie added the treacle to the mixture of flour, oats, and ginger and gripped the wooden spoon tightly. The batter was thick and difficult to stir, but the result was worth it. She sniffed at the half-dozen parkin cakes already halfway through baking. They made her mouth water.

Bonfire Night was one of the highlights of their community before the darker days of winter settled upon them. It marked the end of pilchard season which was usually additional reason to hold a *troyle* – a celebration. If their share of the catch ran to it, then there might be enough spare funds from their sale to purchase the dried fruits and spices for the Christmas puddings.

Baking parkin cake for Bonfire Night and the puddings for Christmas had been a custom shared with Mrs. McArthur ever since she and Phillip had arrived at Stannum House. That had been ten years ago, following the deaths of their parents and two younger brothers from typhus.

She and Mrs. McArthur would make one hundred and twenty of the round, plump puddings, one for every soul in the village. The gesture was little enough, but it was something to supplement meager diets over the leanest months.

The sound of half a dozen young feet running to the kitchen door brought Allie out of her own thoughts. A moment later, there was a banging at the door.

Mrs. McArthur opened it and six boys jostled for position. Between them, they carried a straw-stuffed effigy of Guy Fawkes.

"A penny for the Guy! A penny for the Guy!" they called.

"If I didn't *knooow* any better, I'd say ye smelled the parkin cake right from the village," she said in her thick Scottish burr.

The housekeeper was an imposing woman, tall with wiry black hair streaked with gray. Allie had to own that she was frightened by her on first sight, until discovering that her gruff presentation hid a heart of gold.

Allie smiled as the boys protested their innocence.

"Och, well I'm sure Miss Gedding'll have something for ye," the housekeeper answered before turning back to her with a wink.

"Sit yerselves down for a wee bit of my cake, while ye wait."

Allie greeted the boys and wiped her hands on her faded floral apron before making her way up the servants' stairs to her bedroom.

A house the size of Stannum should have a dozen servants but there were only two – the loyal Mrs. McArthur and Harry Watt. If anything was needed for the house that the four of them couldn't do, they hired people directly from the village to help.

She counted out six farthings from her reticule – a generous penny-ha'penny for the Guy – and was about to return downstairs when through the window, she caught sight of Phillip and another man riding into the yard.

He's back!

More than that, Phillip looked happy!

She returned to the kitchen to find the boys had eaten their cakes and were more than delighted to each receive a copper coin.

"Is there enough timber for the bonfire?" she asked, but did not wait for an answer. "Why don't you go out to see Mr. Watt in the stables? I'm sure he has some broken furniture pieces you can take back."

And the whirling dervishes, fueled by cake and excitement, tore out of the kitchen just as Phillip and his riding companion walked in.

"Master Gedding! Ye're back!" said Mrs. McArthur.

"You didn't think I'd miss Guy Fawkes Night, did you?" answered Phillip. He offered Mrs. McArthur a winning smile. "And I hate to impose at such late notice, but I have a guest staying for a few days. Could you please prepare the green room?"

Allie stepped forward. "You go ahead, Mrs. McArthur. I'll keep an eye on this batch of cakes."

Her eyes fell to the other man in the room.

"Allie, I'd like to introduce you to Mr. Julian Winter. Julian, my sister, Alexandra."

The man before her was mature, aged early-thirties at a guess – about David Manston's age. He had an open, pleasant face and his light brown hair contrasted agreeably with the color of his gray eyes and a riding habit of dark claret.

She bobbed a curtsy and once again wiped her hands on her apron. How shabby she must look in an old washed-out dress of gray. What must he think of them?

"You will have to forgive our informality, Mr. Winter," she said. "Bonfire Night is one of our biggest events here in Stannum. Everyone is involved in its preparation."

"Only if you forgive my unannounced arrival, Miss Gedding," he answered easily, with a smile to match. "After all, it is for the Bonfire Night that I've especially come. When Phillip told me about it, I was reminded of my boyhood, and I thought I'd like to relive the memory."

She smiled in response while she sought Phillip's eyes. Her brother was studiously avoiding making eye contact. *And well he should. Really*, it wasn't the thing to do to bring a guest into the kitchen. And wasn't he always the one trying to keep up appearances?

So, unless they were planning to don aprons themselves, all they were doing was cluttering up the place. It was Mr. Winter who recognized the dilemma first. He shifted his weight back onto his left foot and played with the brim of his tricorn hat.

"Oh, ah, if you'll excuse me, I'll go see to the horses."

Allie let out a long breath after the other man had gone.

"Are you still mad at me?" asked Phillip. He skirted around the other side of the table from her, eyed a slice of parkin and popped it in his mouth, looking for all the world like one of the boys from the village instead of a grown man with an estate to run.

"Mad? For arriving with a guest?" She shook her head. "No, of course not. This is your home. Of course, you should entertain. It's been far too long since we've done so."

She picked up a cloth and pulled out a rack of baking tins from the oven. She put it on the bench to cool the parkin and reached for another rack.

"I thought you might still hold a grudge after the fight we had before I left," he continued.

"Don't be a goose!" Allie pushed in the rack and closed the oven door. "When have I ever held a grudge? I... I just came to realize that perhaps I have been coddling you a little, and that you needed time in masculine company, away from your sister and your housekeeper."

She turned in time to see Phillip's dark eyebrows lift and a grin rise along with it.

"Who have you been talking to? Because that doesn't sound like you."

Allie found herself blushing and hoped that if Phillip noticed, he believed the cause to be the heat from the baking.

"After you left, I went out for a ride and ended up visiting with David Manston," she said. "And he suggested, in his none-too-subtle way, that I ought to cut the apron strings."

Her brother nodded and cut a couple more slices of the cake. Guessing his intent, Alexandra put a kettle on the stove to prepare afternoon tea.

"I don't think it's a wise idea to see Manston alone."

She bristled at the advice, despite the fact that David himself said the same thing to her.

"Why on earth not? He's a friend of the family."

While Phillip pulled down a platter from the top of the dresser, then brought out plates and cutlery from the butler's pantry, Allie quickly washed and dried a China teapot, cups and saucers, and placed them on a tray.

"Come on, Allie, you're not an ingenue. You know exactly what the society gossips would make of it."

She felt her face flush once more at the memory of the kiss but was glad to have her back to her brother, because she would *not* turn her back on the man who had been their only friend.

"*What* society?" she retorted, looking down at the tray. "We've kept to ourselves for years. I can't remember the last time we were out in *Cornish* society – let alone anything grander. Besides, you were grateful to have David's help when you had to close the mine."

She swept out with the tray into the dining room. Memory of that time was as fresh as yesterday.

The lode at Wheal Gunnis was petering out even before Uncle George's death. Allie readily acknowledged it was to Phillip's credit that he managed to keep the mine going for another two years before its inevitable closure, but it had been costly.

That was a horrible day, indeed. Allie had never forgotten it.

Phillip called a meeting of all the miners and the *bal maidens*, the girls whose job was to sort the ore from the stone.

Unlike other mine owners, who left it to their foremen to deliver bad news, Phillip attended in person. The entire village came, some three hundred folks in all. The closure of the pit, the mainstay of the community for one hundred and fifty years, was everyone's business.

What would they have done without David Manston that day? Although David was not that much older than she and Phillip, there was a gravitas about him that seemed to command respect – something her brother had yet to master.

With his aristocratic bearing, David had reminded her of a knight of old – tall, handsome and capable.

The men at the mine had been frustrated. They blamed Phillip's inexperience and questioned his competence. None would listen to him or the engineer's report that proved there was not enough tin to keep the mine open.

The men had become so angry, she had feared for her brother's life until David stepped forward and volunteered to mediate and arrange some kind of settlement against delayed wages.

Was it any wonder she fell a little in love with him on that day?

Phillip followed Allie into the dining room with a tray of his own, and he seemed inclined to continue their *discussion*.

"That's a low blow and you know it. This has nothing to do with Manston personally. I *like* him, and I *am* grateful for the help he gave us when we closed the mine."

Alexandra folded her arms and glared at her brother. "Then what *is* it about, then?"

Phillip's expression shuttered. It was clear he knew more than he was telling.

"It's about you, and finding you a suitor. You've already missed out on a debut and –"

"– now you're going to auction me off like one of the mares we sold this summer?"

Phillip set the salver down on the table with a bang. The plates on it rattled ominously. "Why do you have to misunderstand everything I do, Allie? Why should I even bother?"

"Hello?"

From the kitchen, Julian Winter's voice called out. Phillip cast a spare glance her way before disappearing down the hall. She could hear an indistinct conversation between the two men.

As she set the table, she caught her reflection in the mirror over the fireplace. No doubt, he was apologizing for the hellion mare's appearance.

Her dark curly hair was loosely tied back; she wore an old apron over an even older dress. She looked more like one of the servants than the mistress of the house. In fact, come to think of it, even back when Uncle George was alive, the maids dressed with more care than she did.

Brother dear, you have your work cut out for you if you think that any respectable man is going take your sister off your hands. You'd better get used to having her around.

The voices came closer. She quickly shucked off her apron and bit her lips to add some color before going to the windows to draw back the threadbare curtains and allow the mid-morning light to spill in.

No, she chided herself, none of this was Phillip's fault. The least she could do was be pleasant to his guest. She fixed a smile on her face and waited for them to enter the room.

"Forgive me if I don't join you and my brother, Mr. Winter," she said, bobbing a polite curtsy. "I do need to help Mrs. McArthur in the kitchen. I shall leave you in Phillip's company. But please do not hesitate to call if there is anything you need."

The man offered a winning smile. "Again, it is my doing for arriving unannounced. I certainly don't want to disrupt the household."

She found a genuine smile of her own. "Any guest of my brother's is most welcome here."

Mrs. McArthur was already back in the kitchen when Allie got there. The batter she had been mixing was now poured into baking tins and about to go into the oven.

"I put yon Mr. Winter in the green room. T'were Master Phillip's suggestion." The housekeeper spoke with a brisk efficiency which belied her age. "I've taken up the dust covers and opened the windows for an airing but I've not done the bedding nor the dusting. There's still everything to do for the *troyle* tonight."

"You have more than enough on your plate," Allie assured her. "I'll see to preparing Mr. Winter's room."

She went upstairs with a sinking feeling in her stomach. She knew *exactly* why her brother had placed his friend in the green room rather than the rose room, one further down the hall. The green room was opposite *hers*. How convenient it would be for them to simply *bump* into one another.

She hoped their guest would know better than to fall for such an obvious matchmaking ruse.

But the fact was the green and the rose rooms were the only two spare bedrooms suitable for habitation. Of the ten bedrooms Stannum House boasted, less than half were habitable. Six rooms had their furniture sold off and remained locked ever since Uncle George's death.

Phillip had claimed the master suite, and she had taken the blue room, which faced west with a view to Stannum Cove and the sea beyond. The green room faced south. Its view was of the pasture and farmlands and, at its center on the hill, the Wheal Gunnis engine house.

Equally tall beside it was the smokestack attached to the boiler. Lit by the bright sun, it stood like the trunk of a dead tree struck by bad luck instead of lightning. When in operation, smoke and steam would rise from it, bringing to life a great mechanical beast pumping air down to the miners and water up from far below the surface.

Now the beast was silent. With the window open, all Allie heard was the sea and the calling of gulls.

What she wouldn't give to see Wheal Gunnis up and running again with their little village prosperous once more. However, with the mine exhausted, it was a vain wish. She sighed and turned to look around at the room.

Despite Mrs. McArthur's claims that she'd barely had time to touch it, it seemed presentable enough – a bed, a washstand, a wardrobe, a desk, and a chair. What more could a man need for a stay of a day or two?

A quick dust, sweep, and mop, along with fresh linens for the bed, would be enough to satisfy their guest.

Where had Phillip met this man? Allie was sure she knew all his friends. Was he someone he'd encountered at some... *place of entertainment* in Camelford?

Julian Winter certainly looked respectable but there *had* to be more than just a wish to see how their little community marked Guy Fawkes Night.

"Oh, forgive me, I thought Phillip said I was to take the green room."

She started and turned to the man who stood in the doorway. Julian offered an embarrassed smile and moved the saddlebag from one hand to the other with an appealing uncertainty.

She ought to know better than to judge people on empty speculation.

"No, you are quite correct, Mr. Winter," she answered smoothly. "We're a bit short-handed as you can see, so I give Mrs. McArthur assistance with the housework."

She watched him as she said the words. Would he pity them in poverty? Would he treat them with contempt?

Instead, he stepped inside the room as though he'd hadn't heard her explanation and headed straight for the window.

"That is an excellent view of Wheal Gunnis," he said. "We rode around the hill on the way here, but we didn't stop. Tomorrow, perhaps, if the weather holds."

Curiosity got the better of her. "May I ask what interest an abandoned mine has for you?"

He turned and regarded her thoughtfully.

"It's complex to explain right now but, if you're interested, I would be only too delighted to monopolize your time at some future date."

Was he being patronizing? She didn't know him well enough at such brief acquaintance to know whether or not his invitation was sincere. Perhaps it was wise not to examine such things too closely.

She bobbed another curtsy. "I shall leave you to settle in. We leave together as a party at six o'clock."

Chapter Three

ALLIE SAT AT her dressing table and stared at her reflection. She touched a finger to her lips.

That kiss.

She dabbed a small amount of rouge on them until they turned the color of strawberries. The color she felt they must have been after David's kiss.

The memory of it was still arousing.

He'd never done *that* before despite the fact there'd been an undercurrent between them for quite some time.

Did he simply do it to teach her a lesson? She closed her eyes to recall his ragged breath on her cheek, the look of surprise that mirrored her own.

Then again, she *had* kissed him first.

If she'd stayed, would he have kissed her again? Would she have let him?

She was less sure of the first answer than she was of the second.

There was no question David had her heart – and had done ever since that day three years ago when he stepped out of the crowd of angry and upset mine workers to negotiate a peaceful solution.

Although barely acquainted then, she'd discovered in time that David was a man with the rarest of gifts – he was equally comfortable amongst the rough miners and fishermen of the village as he would be with the wealthy inhabitants of a fine drawing room.

And the folks of Stannum were comfortable enough with him that he had become the man they sought to read and write letters on their behalves.

More than that, at their darkest hour, David proved himself honest and fair, turning an impossible and potentially violent situation into something that everyone could live with. *That* was no small task.

Allie knew of other families like her own for whom bankruptcy was compounded by riots and arson by men driven to helpless desperation.

Every day for six weeks, David had arrived at Stannum House to thrash out a deal to pay the workers their due, but one which also gave Phillip relief from *his* creditors. Without that, there would have been nothing to pay the families of the miners.

It meant closing down two floors of Stannum House and selling a great deal of furniture and treasured belongings including most of the jewelry she had inherited from both her late mother and uncle.

Allie pinned up her curly black hair into a manageable chignon secured by plain wire pins. How nice it would have been to still have those gold ones topped with pearls to secure her brown velvet hat.

Beggars couldn't be choosers.

At least she and Phillip still had a roof over their heads; that was something to be grateful for at least.

At the end came the delicate matter of a fee for his services, but he'd dismissed any notion of it, claiming that just to sample Mrs. McArthur's cooking was payment enough. And once the job was done, David returned to his cottage on the headland to continue his life in semi-isolation.

Was it any wonder she felt a sense of obligation as well as attraction?

And yet, he seemed to want for nothing and for no one. To the best of her knowledge, he'd never received a visitor from outside Stannum in five years.

After a while, Phillip had ceased to press the case for David's payment, happy to have the whole unpleasant affair behind him, but she could not so easily forget. And she was far more stubborn than her brother, perhaps even more so than David Manston himself.

She ignored his gruff manner and continued to pay him the occasional call. Bringing a basket of delicacies from Mrs. McArthur was usually enough to gain grudging admission into his lair.

Oh, she teased him and tried to draw him out. After a while, she simply enjoyed his company over a game of chess whenever he deigned to share it with her. Even now, he was the only one who would listen to her and take her thoughts and questions seriously.

She was a fool to think she was a *little* in love with him. It was more – *so much more* than that.

In all that time, his behavior toward her had been above reproach. He never touched her, apart from commonplace courtesies such as helping put on her cloak or assisting her into the saddle – mannerly things which seemed so ingrained in him that it suggested that his social status ought to be equal to, if not greater than, her own.

And yet she knew nothing more about his past than she did three years ago…

Without a lady's maid to dress her, Allie managed for herself, adept now at reaching behind and adjusting the stays of her gown. Tonight, she wore her warmest dress in a dark blue and shrugged into a pelisse of forest green, trimmed with brown fur. She gave herself one last critical look in the mirror.

Perhaps a kiss changes everything.

ON STANNUM BEACH, the last of the soft November sun shone on the unlit pyre of driftwood, deadfall, and broken old furniture piled twenty feet high. On top of it was a scarecrow figure. Made of sacking and filled with straw, it represented a crudely created figure of a man well known to them all. Black hair and boots and a blue torso which, at a distance – a very great distance, Allie decided – might be said to resemble Napoleon Bonaparte.

Dotted around were smaller fires designed to light the coming night, to warm the villagers, and cook a meal. People moved from brazier to brazier to greet friends and search for stray companions.

Allie smiled to herself as she observed figures here and there slip away into the darkness for a tryst.

Would David be here? The half-light, half-dark would suit him. She looked south to the headland where his cottage stood overlooking this beach. It was too far to tell whether a lamp burned in the window.

Having long lost Mrs. McArthur and Phillip, Allie joined a group of older women by the fire. They discussed hopes for the herring catch which, thus far, had been only fair at best. Without a better run of fish soon, the coming winter was going to be bad one.

The longer she listened, the heavier the weight of expectation lay on her shoulders. After all, *she* was the one living in a big house in a world of plenty. It was her responsibility to help those without.

Little did they know their circumstances were not so different…

The ghost of Wheal Gunnis loomed over them all, and she and Phillip had no solutions to offer. The only thing that kept them in good standing with the villagers was the fact they were still here and had not abandoned Stannum to retreat to the likes of London, Bath, or Harrogate, never to return. Other prominent families in other places had done so.

Still, the situation could not go on.

Allie made a promise to the Widow Greene to visit her ailing son in the morning and see what could be done to help them both.

Distraction came from the sound of an accordion. The note rose mournfully at first until it was joined by a flute and the first bars of a lively tune were played. Soon, a fiddler added to the melody.

Villagers gathered and danced around one of the braziers on the hard-packed sand.

Phillip's guest approached her, seeming relieved at finding a familiar face. "I do have to say that your housekeeper's parkin is the finest I've had since boyhood," said Julian.

"And where is home, Mr. Winter?"

"Yorkshire."

The answer was a surprise. Allie would have said London, for he hardly seemed to have the inflection from the region.

"Really?" she said. "I would not have picked it."

"Ah, my accent?" he asked. Allie nodded.

"Father sent me away to school to make sure I mixed with those with the *right* accents."

"I see," said Allie. "Is that where you got to know Phillip?"

She kept her voice light and waited for his response to see if he would lie to her. She knew all Phillip's school friends, even those he referred to only in passing and not one of them went by the name of Julian Winter.

"No." Then he paused. "Phillip and I are more recent acquaintances."

The next question was on the tip of her tongue when two of the village girls, aged about fourteen, bounded up to them.

"Ye must dance, Miss Gedding! And yer friend, too, if he's a mind to!"

Allie found herself tugged along, so too Julian, irrespective of whether "he was of a mind" or not. She glanced back to see how their visitor took to being manhandled.

The girl who had tugged his arm giggled as Winter picked up his pace until *he* was the one leading. On his way past, he grasped Allie's hand before breaking out into a near run. The other girl squealed, then giggled as Allie firmed the grip on her hand until the four of them formed a chain.

She burst out laughing and allowed herself to be carried along. They all deserved to have some fun, did they not? Was there any harm in forgetting their troubles for a while?

The moment they neared the other dancers, they were brought into the dancers' circle. Allie threw herself into dancing, her spirits lifted by the joyous faces of her neighbors who, for this moment in time, had put away their own cares, too.

Soon, more people joined in and the circle grew larger until she had lost track of whose hand she held.

The music become faster and faster. The pounding of feet broke up the sand, making it soft and unstable underfoot for some of the revelers – or perhaps that was more to do with the cider which flowed freely.

The music built to a crescendo just as the first of the dancers fell, bringing half a dozen down beside her. The dance ended in a roar of laughter and everyone clapped except for the hand that still held hers.

She turned to look up into the eyes of David Manston.

She blushed.

He grinned.

"Do you wish to dance again?" he asked.

Allie, still trying to catch her breath, shook her head. "I can't!" she gasped.

"Good. Let's walk instead."

They strolled side-by-side several hundred yards along the beach, their hands almost touching, but not quite, until the sound of revelers faded beneath the sound of the waves lapping at the shore.

"I want to apologize for my boorish behavior a couple of days ago," he said.

"Your apology is unnecessary," she answered. "If you recall, I kissed you first."

The fact that David had been thinking about their kiss warmed her inside.

He huffed and shook his head. "What I gave you in return is *not* what a respectable young woman should expect from a kiss."

They continued their walk silently for a few yards farther. The warmth from the exertion of the dance ebbed. The night chill away from the bonfires started to bite. She drew her pelisse closer about her.

"What if it was what I wanted?"

"Then I fear for you."

"Of whom should I be afraid?" she asked lightly. "You?"

He didn't answer. A frustrated exhalation was enough to reveal his thoughts.

"If I were such a respectable young woman, I should not have teased you in that fashion. In fact, I shouldn't be in your company alone."

"Haven't I been *trying* to tell you that for the past two years?"

Was that mild exasperation she could hear?

"You have," she answered. "And I choose not to listen. Oh, I'll grant that your kiss took me by surprise, but I don't regret it."

David stopped. She searched his profile. The moonlight highlighted only portions of his face, bringing them into sharp relief.

"Don't tell me that *you've* had a fit of the vapors over it?" she challenged.

She caught a flash of bared teeth before he turned away to stare out at the sea. The moon lit the little whitecaps before the waves tumbled onto the shore.

"For the love of God, you're either stupid or hopelessly naïve," he offered at last.

Allie squared her shoulders.

"Perhaps I'm neither. You *might* allow me the notion that I knew *exactly* what I was doing, although God knows I'm questioning my judgment right now."

Even in the darkness, she could see the tension in his shoulders.

"Get out of here, Allie. Go find some lovestruck swain to make calf-eyes at you and make you a proper proposal."

The man was a stubborn fool! More stubborn than *she* was and perhaps no less foolish.

"If only you knew how much you sound like my brother at present," she said, and started walking away. She got no further than a couple of steps when David answered.

"Phillip? It's about time he did his duty by his sister."

She paused. "Yes, well, he's brought a prospect home with him today."

David suddenly closed the gap between them. "Just the one? What about the others?"

"What others?"

"Old Prenpas told me he saw Phillip talking to a group of four gentlemen on horseback at the Camelford crossroads this morning. He was under the impression they were all heading to Stannum."

Allie shrugged her shoulders and continued on. David fell into step beside her.

"No, it's just the one," she said. "But after telling me there's four lurking about, I don't know whether to be disappointed at being introduced to just the one, or dismayed by the thought my brother plans to spring another three! What on earth would I do with four?"

Out of the blue, a memory recalled itself and she laughed.

"I do, however, remember being told the story of my wicked second cousin, Lady Abigail Houghall. She was also my godmother, don't you know? They said that, on her eighteenth birthday, she was found with a man not her fiancé, between her –"

Beside her, David groaned. He pulled her into his arms and kissed her. Not with the savage passion of their kiss two days ago, but still, not to underestimate the intensity of it.

She was completely aware of him – the strength of his arms around her, the feel of his lips on hers, his tongue tasting hers, and the sensation of the late evening stubble on his cheek.

This was what she wanted. His honesty. The truth that the attraction she felt for him was not all one-sided.

He broke off the kiss but not the embrace. She savored the feel of his arms around her and the sensuous awareness those hands brought her.

"You talk too much," he said. "And that appeared to be the most effective way of shutting you up."

She gave him her most triumphant look. Oh yes, he *wanted* her – despite his words to the contrary.

They retraced their steps back to the *troyle*. This time, he kept his arm around her and she was grateful for the warmth as well as the embrace.

Ahead of them, men with flickering torches threw their lighted offerings onto the pyre. The kindling caught immediately. Orange and gold flickering flames grew higher and higher until they reached the unfortunate effigy on top.

Even though they were about fifty yards away, she could hear the cheers from the crowd. Soon, the entire bonfire was alight, dwarfing the light and heat of the smaller fires around it.

She and David came to a stop at the edge of the shadows, close enough for Allie to feel the warmth of the fire at her chest. David stepped behind her, his body protecting her back from the chill. His hands were at her waist, just above the flare of her hips, and he held her to him, shielding her from the jostling of the half-inebriated, whose faces were flushed with drink as well as the bonfire's heat.

It was a possessive hold, a confident one; the touch of a man who knew his way around the feminine form.

If anyone else had touched her in such a fashion, he would know her displeasure, and in no uncertain terms. But she wanted this from him – his kiss, his touch, and so much more.

For years, she had waited for David to express an interest in her above neighborly regard and, yet, he had not.

She was sure he'd wanted to. She saw the way he observed her when he thought she wasn't looking. The attraction was there without a doubt but, until two days ago, he'd held himself back.

Why?

Still, he was not above teasing her. He leaned forward until his lips were near her ear. His breath sent shivers down her spine which had nothing to do with the cold.

"See the group where your brother is?" he asked after a moment. "The third man along to your right in the light brown coat? Do you recognize him?"

She forced herself to follow his question. She found the man he referred to. He was tall and thin, but the flickering firelight made it difficult to discern anything particular about him.

"No, I've never seen him before."

"And what about that one? He's got his back to us now. He seemed rather comfortable holding your hand while you danced."

"Ah, *that* one I do know. His name is Julian Winter. He's the one Phillip brought home today. Are you *jealous?*"

He chuckled. Even the sound of his laughter was arousing. *What was wrong with her?*

"If I thought you had any genuine interest in him, I would let you fly safely into his arms, little bird. Then I could return to my happy, solitary life. But I'm not to be rid of you so easily, am I?"

Chapter Four

FROM THE MOMENT he had held Allie in his arms at the door of his cottage, David had known he was playing with fire – a fire that would burn hotter than the bonfire before them now. Yet, despite his promises to keep himself apart, he could not seem to help himself when it came to this woman.

He cursed himself for it, then cursed the even worse luck that she seemed to like him, too.

That's why he had acted like a satyr that night. It was right that she should ride off, if not in horror, then at least disquieted by his brutishness. But the satisfaction had lasted only as long as the walk back into his cottage where the only sound was the fire in the grate, and before him, the mocking reminder of his solitude in the form of two cups on the table instead of one.

He thought here, at the Guy Fawkes Night with the whole village in attendance, he'd be safe from his baser desires. But the moment he saw her dancing, the carefree joy on her face drew him into her orbit.

He could have left, he supposed, except there was nowhere else to go.

David shook his head. He shouldn't have even come here tonight; except he was curious when Prenpas told him about the strangers that Phillip seemed acquainted with.

Even though the Gedding twins were only a few years younger than him, he felt responsible for them in some odd way. When Wheal

Gunnis had closed, David felt their helplessness and he became the friend they desperately needed.

The type of friend he wished he'd had for himself all those years ago...

The irony wasn't lost on him that, in another life and under different circumstances, he and Alexandra might have met at a soiree at some fine house party in the district. After all, they would have moved in the same social circles.

And if he had married, as his parents wished, and to whom they wished, it would have been an unhappy state of affairs. Worse still was the knowledge that there was no guarantee he wouldn't have still felt this visceral attraction to Allie if their paths had crossed.

How different she was from Claire...

God, what a disaster that would have been! There would have been no disguising his disgrace then. And if Allie knew what his family believed of him now, she would run a mile. As she should.

As any sensible woman should.

He shook his head. His thoughts should not go *there*. The movement must have caught Phillip's attention for he appeared to excuse himself from his companions and walk toward them.

The first stranger he'd pointed out walked away. The other one, this Julian Winter, glanced their way; rather, glanced Allie's way. After a slight hesitation, Winter followed a pace or two behind her brother.

David removed his hands from Allie's hips but, judging by the look on Phillip's face, he'd seen enough.

"Manston."

"Gedding."

If Phillip wanted an explanation or an apology, he'd be waiting for a long time.

Allie was quick to evaluate the situation. She left his side.

"Gentlemen," she said, giving them all a knowing look, "I'm going to find Mrs. McArthur."

Phillip looked as if he were about to say something to his sister but she strode off and did not look back. Gedding covered his disconcert by introducing David to Winter.

The man immediately stretched out his hand.

"It's an honor to meet you, Manston. Phillip has told me about the help you gave when the mine closed."

David looked at the man's hand a moment then took it. The shake was firm and no-nonsense.

"As a neighbor, I was happy to help."

Winter glanced back to where Allie walked.

"A good friend to the family, I'm sure."

A pointed remark? He'd file that one away for future reference.

"I invited Julian because he thinks there may be chance to restart the mine," said Phillip.

That was a surprise.

"Are you sure? The surveyor's report said there was no possibility of finding any more ore."

Phillip's face showed some kind of restrained enthusiasm. "That is true for tin; not necessarily so for *copper.*"

Excitement bloomed within David. But he tamped down his instinctive interest. There had been far too many disappointments over the years.

"What makes you think there's any up there?"

The blunt question didn't seem to deter Phillip. He actually grinned.

"We won't know until we take a look. But see here – I've never forgotten how you helped us. And I'm not a man who forgets his debts. If there's something there, enough to make it a going concern, I want to make sure you get what you deserve."

Another pointed remark? Two in one night had to be some kind of record.

"Will you join us at Wheal Gunnis tomorrow?"

Before David could answer, Julian Winter spoke. "I intend to spend a couple of weeks here to get a better understanding of the geology and take a look below ground. If there is nothing there, then I've had a couple of weeks away from my family's mine in Yorkshire and enjoyed the pleasures to be found in the West Country."

That was one pointed remark too many.

"I'll join you," David said decisively. "I appreciate the invitation."

Winter grinned and slapped him familiarly on the shoulder. Phillip was a little less exuberant.

"Why don't you go on ahead, Julian? There something I need to talk to Manston about."

"Right you are then!" Julian affably saluted and went off in the direction Allie had gone.

David didn't hide a wry smile. There could be any number of reasons why Phillip wanted to chat – but he'd bet that it would only come down to one subject.

"Alexandra."

And there we go.

"I don't feel comfortable about you spending time in her company alone."

David let out a frustrated breath. "I've done my level best to discourage her from my company for the past three years. Perhaps *you* should have a word with her – she's *your* sister, after all."

The look Phillip returned told him exactly what he thought about his chances.

He continued to stare the other man down. Phillip gamely held his look for a moment, but only a moment. Any fight Allie's brother had in him was gone.

"I suppose you have a point," he conceded. "But Allie won't entertain the notion of anyone else if you... *encourage* her interest. Look, I know you have reasons to keep to yourself, but I do have high regard for you. Could you..."

The younger man paused. This conversation was awkward for the both of them but David was not about to fill the other's silences.

David's stomach pitched a moment. Did Phillip *really* know the reason for his self-imposed exile? Or was it simply an empty platitude? If it was the former, it was a surprise the man hadn't run him out of Stannum, and locked Allie away from him. Perhaps this was the conversation they *should* be having.

Phillip continued at last.

"Look, we're men together, we know what we're about, but Allie deserves more than being someone's harmless little flirtation. She's my twin. Her happiness means more than I can express. Allie deserves a chance at happiness... to marry into a good family, to marry someone she can be content with, and who can give her everything she deserves."

It was on the tip of David's tongue to say something. But what was there to say?

May the best man win?

Well, that wouldn't be him. And they both knew it.

David nodded in the direction Allie and Winter had gone.

"And you think Julian Winter is the man for her?"

Phillip shrugged. "Maybe, maybe not. Time will tell."

"Time will tell," David echoed.

Any hope that Allie's brother would walk off after saying his piece was dashed and that left him in the awkward circumstance of giving him an answer.

"You have my word."

The look of relief on Phillip's face was almost comical.

"Look... it's nothing personal. I have the highest regard for you as a man but –"

Dear God, don't let the conversation take this turn.

"– It's nothing," David interrupted before the man could say more to destroy the tentative friendship between them. "I will make it perfectly clear to Allie that any tenderness of feelings she possesses are not returned in anything other than the most platonic considerations."

Phillip thrust out his hand to seal the agreement.

"Thank you. Once again, I'm in your debt."

HE'D KISSED HER *again*.

Allie smiled.

Twice in two days – well in three days, actually, but who cared?

Of course, it didn't mean he was necessarily in love with her – Allie was not so green as all that. Yet the fact was plain that he desired her. It truly was an encouraging development... despite his protestations to the contrary.

Oh yes, she was being terribly forward, but what was a girl to do when the man she wanted would not hurry in his attentions?

She savored the memory of the latest kiss and the feel of his hands on her waist. Perhaps that was all the prompting David Manston needed to take up the pursuit.

Was it any wonder she was wide awake while the rest of the household slept?

She made her way downstairs and found sanctuary in the library. It was the one room where she could close the door and imagine Stannum House in its former glory.

The two walls of books from floor to ceiling had once been the envy of every scholar within fifty miles. Uncle George enjoyed nothing more than showing off his collection of books on Greek and Roman mythology.

She opened the stopper on a brandy bottle and poured herself a half-measure. Apart from one small barrel hidden away in the cellar and a dozen bottles, it was the only alcohol in the house.

She sat at the writing desk and looked about the room.

She was grateful the library had not fallen to the fire sale. She enjoyed Greek and Roman mythology. And that was not all the intriguing reading to be had in the library. When she was thirteen years old, she'd come across a small volume of sketches featuring Greek mythological characters in very *carnal* situations.

Never did she read the stories of Deianira and Hercules or Psyche and Eros in quite the same way again.

She smiled at recalling the horror her governess expressed when she'd discovered those books in her charge's room. Allie had been refused unsupervised access to the library for some weeks after. She supposed the sketches had been returned here but, certainly, they hadn't been put back where she'd found them.

She'd looked.

Ah, her governess! The woman had also been her aunt's governess and was full of tales about the wickedness of the male sex and the pitfalls that awaited young women who gave in to their wanton desires.

Second cousin Lady Abigail was frequently the object of these lectures – the poor woman was trotted out like the Guy on the bonfire tonight, the weight of sins heaped upon her shoulders as a lesson in "what not to do".

That such a woman was chosen to be her godmother was a mystery for the ages.

From everything she had been told about her uncle's cousin, it seemed Abigail was a woman who'd known how to get a man's attention and keep it.

I wonder whatever happened to her?

The last tale Allie had been told was that Abigail had been banished to see out her days in seclusion and disgrace at Bath under the watch of George's eldest cousin, a formidable creature by the name of Philomena.

She dismissed the addendum to the tale that Abigail's isolation was at the behest of the Prince of Wales himself. That was an embellishment too far.

Still, ever since, Allie had it in her mind to cheer on this *adventuress*. No doubt, she could have offered some sage advice about winning David Manston.

Perhaps she still could…

Alexandra set down her brandy and pulled out a piece of paper from the top drawer. She flipped opened the silver lid of the ink bottle and primed her nib, aware that the spirit was going her head.

Lady Abigail Houghall
Bath

My lady, forgive the presumption in writing to you, but we do have a family connection and I wish to beg your indulgence.

My name is Alexandra Gedding. I am the niece of George Nancarrow, who was cousin to Philomena Fitzroy-deVries who is your aunt.

I do not wish to press on any claim other than to make myself known to you as a relative, even if our ties are somewhat tenuous.

Stannum House is now in the hands of my twin brother, Phillip, following Uncle George's passing. I have spent many a – Alexandra moved her hand away from the paper and onto the blotting pad, until she could think of just the right word – *an **entertaining** hour being informed of your exploits.*

If only a small portion of it is true, then you have in me a devoted admirer.

You will always be welcome at Stannum House.

Your faithful goddaughter,
Alexandra Gedding

Before she could second-guess herself, Allie prepared an envelope and wrote the address.

She wafted the letter, waiting for the ink on it to dry. It might have been an act of tipsy caprice, but now done, Allie wondered more about her cousin. If nothing else, it would be nice to have someone to correspond with. Perhaps as a poor put-upon spinster, Lady Abigail, too, might enjoy the occasional letter from a young relation.

She dropped the letter into the tray for outgoing correspondence and drained the rest of her brandy. It really had gone to her head.

The thin silver gleam from the crossed swords mounted on a cartouche on the wall beside the door caught her eye.

She pulled the epee from its mount and performed an advanced lunge, just as Phillip's fencing master had taught the both of them.

She hadn't thought of old Gough for years. He was such an eccentric bird, tall and thin – almost painfully so – but one would underestimate him at their peril.

Given there had been no one to act as a suitable practice companion, and that Alexandra was the same height as her brother, she trained alongside him. In turn, Phillip was to be her partner for the dancing master.

Allie sized up her invisible opponent.

Feint, deflect, a lateral parry, then lunge.

She made her way to one side of the room and saluted, raising the blade high in front of her face.

Her opponent didn't have a name, but in him was embodied all the woes and calamities that had befallen Stannum. He would be a tall brute, sunken-faced, just this side of being a caricature of Death.

Feint, deflect, parry, lunge. Then a series of remises as her imaginary foe stepped back and further back.

Feint, deflect, parry, lu –

"Oh! Oh, my!" Alexandra pulled back the steel before it ran through actual flesh and blood.

Fortunately, the man was also fast enough to dodge her blade.

"Forgive me, Mr. Winter!"

The man laughed. "No, it's the second time in a day that I should apologize to you, Miss Gedding. I saw the light on and I thought your brother might still be awake. I didn't mean to intrude on your… duel."

Alexandra returned the fencing sword to its place.

"I'm afraid Phillip has already retired," she said. "The truth of the matter was I couldn't sleep. But I do beg that you excuse me. Now that I've dispatched my foe, I think I shall retire also."

She picked a spill from the mantel, lit it by the fire and then relit her candle to take her up to bed.

"Please, don't feel obligated to do the same. The library is at your disposal."

Winter entered and picked up a book seemingly at random – certainly he didn't look at it, only at her.

"Then something to read me off to sleep then."

The situation was disconcerting. She moved herself to the door and bobbed a curtsy in passing. She crossed the hall and ventured up the main stairs quickly.

There was something odd in the air. She recalled what David had told her of Prenpas' news. Phillip met with another three men on the road in addition to Winter. Should she have asked.

By the time Allie entered her room, the coals in the grate there were red and glowing. She began to undress, then wondered about locking her door. Did she really think Winter might enter her room? Not really, but all the same… to lock or leave unlocked?

If she overslept and Mrs. McArthur came looking for her, she would find it odd that the door was locked and that would raise awkward questions.

She would compromise, locking the door while she undressed and unlocking it as she retired. If she moved her dressing table chair out a little more than usual, anyone entering would have to move around it and tread on a squeaky floorboard which was bound to wake her.

She kept listening as she brushed her hair and, sure enough, a few minutes later, she heard footsteps on the stairs and the squeak of the door opposite opening, then closing.

She put down her hairbrush with a sigh. Tomorrow, she would seek answers from her brother.

Chapter Five

DAVID WALKED ALONE on the beach. It was a more direct route home than going through the village and along the clifftop. The moon, very nearly full, guided his way along the sand to the winding path upwards over rocks that became boulders which in turn became part of the headland itself.

His little cottage sat cold, gray, and bleak. He regretted not putting a lamp in the window for a small cheer of welcome.

But what good would that have done? For a start, it would have been a waste of lamp oil, not to mention foolhardy to leave a flame unattended. More foolish still to live under an illusion that someone was there to welcome him home.

Before he opened the door, he looked away from the sea up to the hill behind. Moonlight bathed the old mine engine house tower in silver.

David frowned. Was that mist that clung to the tree line? Or was it smoke?

He shook his head. It was an illusion – like so much of his life.

He closed the door behind him, pleased to find his little abode warm. He glanced at the part-finished chess set he had started to carve a few weeks ago.

A packet of correspondence on his drafting table sat unopened beside it where it had been ignored for a full week while he whittled the form of the first of sixteen pawns. He could guess what was in the correspondence.

Dear Mr. Manston,

We regret that we have not yet sold your still life series but we remain hopeful. In the meantime, we wish to commission another set of illustrations –

Yes, another commission for a very *particular* type of artwork. After he sent the last lot back, ready for the engravers, he found his heart was no longer in it.

Had it ever been?

He indulged in an open-mouthed yawn. The letters would wait another day.

Upstairs in his bedroom, he coaxed life in the embers in the grate and set a bed-warming brick by the fire.

He undressed.

How odd that he should think of Claire tonight when he hadn't for many years. But there was something about tonight that brought back the memory of his past with a freshness such that it seemed just yesterday.

"Claire Wickham."

Saying the name aloud conjured her image in his mind's eye. She had been the most beautiful girl he'd ever set eyes on – and he'd decided *that* when he first saw her at the age of seven. The Wickham family had been friends with the Manstons going back generations. Also among this set of friends was the Owen-Jones family.

It seemed that every high day and holiday was spent with these families, which suited David well since Thomas Owen-Jones was his best friend in the world.

As they grew up together, Claire only became more beautiful. She was like a goddess brought to life – a nymph, a sprite. She was petite with light brown hair. When she turned her large brown eyes toward him, he wanted to be a knight, the hero who slayed the dragon for her.

To his young heart, she was as perfect as any woman could be. So later, when his father suggested a match with Claire, he was overjoyed.

The very first person he shared his good news with was Thomas. If only he had recognized then why his friend greeted it so tepidly. It wasn't until Claire and her family attended a lunch hosted by his mother and father that he had discovered the truth.

David wrapped the now-warmed brick in a cloth and rubbed it over the sheets before placing it at the foot of the bed and climbing in after it.

That had been ten years ago.

He dropped into a deep sleep almost immediately and, all of a sudden, he was twenty-one years old and filled with delight that his father, the Viscount of Carmarthan, had recommended an alliance with a girl he had been in love with since childhood.

Lunch had been a trial. Four sets of eyes watched everything they did, so it was a relief when Mrs. Wickham suggested that he take Claire for a walk about the garden of Abevan, their country home. They would be within sight of the house, but it would still afford them privacy to talk.

There had been so many signs, if he hadn't been so moonstruck. Then he might have noticed the girl, who once followed him and Thomas gamely around their country estates during those summers, now faintly trembled at his side.

David had continued on, talking about his plans to attend a fine art school in Italy, to elicit a reaction from Claire.

The sound of the gravel crunching underfoot was the loudest sound, not even the sound of the spring birds or the beautiful pink roses in bloom could elicit a murmur of response.

They rounded a hedge out of sight of the house. Claire gravitated toward a sun-dappled bench and started to sob. The natural response of a man was to try to comfort the afflicted, but no sooner had he put a gentle hand on her shoulder than she cried out as though he'd struck her.

"Claire? What's wrong? I... I'm sorry, but I don't know what I've done to upset you so."

"Oh, David, you have been nothing but kindness itself!"

"Then help me understand."

"I... I do not w-wish to marry," she whispered.

The words fell leaden in his chest. He sat down beside her. Claire rearranged her skirts so not a single thread touched him.

"Do you mean that you do not wish to marry at this time?" he asked, making sure his voice was even. "Or is it that you do not wish to marry *me*? Is there another?"

He asked the question as gently as he could. Given his limited experience with the opposite sex, he did know that a woman confronted by a slight on her character would become angry.

Not Claire.

If possible, the girl paled even more.

"I have been aware of your... affection for me for quite some time," she said. "And I wish there was some easy way to tell you."

Pretty brown eyes filled her face, imploring him.

"Please, believe me when I say it was never my intention to toy with your affections. We've grown up together. I love you as a sister loves a brother."

He felt a sickness in his stomach. He also hated the fact that his first thought had been for his mother. It was widely known that she did not get on well with his father, so an agreement that seemed to suit them both so well, for whatever reason, brought a long-desired peace to the Carmarthan household.

"You didn't answer my question," said David, trying to keep his voice steady. "Is there another who has claimed your heart?"

More tears welled in the eyes of the beautiful girl before him.

It was clear that the one who had *his* heart lived in despair of their union.

Her tears spilled down her face and David was lost.

It would be ungentlemanly of him to press her further to name the fellow, so he didn't.

Although each word was a stab to his own heart, he spoke them. "I won't wed you if you do not wish it."

The young woman's face, which had been so pale before, now flushed becomingly.

"Thank you! Oh, thank you, David. I am forever in your debt."

He couldn't bear the sight of how denying what he wanted most brought unalloyed joy to her face, so he lowered his eyes as he might do to avoid looking directly at the sun.

"Our parents will not be pleased," he whispered. "I know our fathers have already shaken hands on it, and our mothers are already planning the nuptials. We will need to tell them together."

To his surprise, Claire clutched his arm, and her hand seemed ice cold, even through his jacket.

"I *cannot*! I am so afraid of making Mother angry. And she *will* be angry. No, it is you who has to refuse *me*."

In the length of time it took for a dozen heartbeats to pound away, his mind had already imagined his father's reaction. David swallowed the growing horror.

"How?"

"You are the man, are you not?" Claire's voice gained a little strength. "It is your responsibility."

The disregard for his feelings stung, sending a tiny drop of poison into his veins that would eventually kill any kind regard he had for her.

He wasn't sure what expression showed on his face, but Claire's lip trembled.

"Please, David. Talk to Thomas. He knows I have no desire to wed."

Thomas. It was Thomas.

And David, his heart sinking, had agreed – a fateful decision that was at once the ruin *and* the making of him.

Would he have made the same decisions if he had to do it over again?

He wasn't sure that he wouldn't but, by God, the cost had been high…

ALLIE PATTED NEPHEL'S mane, waiting for Phillip and Julian to finish saddling up. The huff of the mare's breath was visible in the chilly morning air.

The sound of hooves announced the arrival of the fourth member of their party. She led her mare to the riding block and climbed up unaided before she acknowledged him.

She admired David Manston's seat on his horse. There was an insouciant manner to him as though he didn't care whether his clothes were fashionable, just functional, and yet he looked more put together than any of the young bucks she had encountered in Truro.

David, too, appraised her openly and she sat up straight in her saddle knowing it showed her silhouette to its finest advantage. He grinned a split second before she did, a private, unspoken joke between them. It was a caress, even though a good three yards separated them.

Julian's horse carried saddlebags and, across the man's back, a wooden tripod was attached to some kind of brass contraption that looked something like a small telescope.

"I thought the lode was underground." David called. "So why the surveying equipment?"

"Sometimes what we see above ground is just as important as what is below," said Julian. "I've been talking to an interesting chap by the name of William Smith. He's a mineral surveyor. I've been corresponding with him about his work on creating a geological record of Great Britain."

"Is that a fact?" asked David, sounding genuinely interested.

Julian nudged his horse over to him, barely giving Allie a nod of acknowledgement. Phillip returned Allie's sidelong glance. Now that Julian had an audience, it seemed he was not prepared to let it go.

"Smith was working at a coal pit in Somerset. He observed that the rock and the seam appeared laid in predictable patterns," said Julian.

The twins let the two men start off on the easy ride to Wheal Gunnis while they followed behind.

The truth be known, Allie was pleased to have her brother's undivided attention for the ride.

"It feels like I never get to see you anymore. I miss my brother," she told him.

"I know, and I miss you, too," he said. "And I've realized that I haven't told you how much thanks I owe you. You've been working so hard as the mistress of Stannum House and for the village, too. You might think I don't notice, but I do."

Allie reached out her hand. She grasped Phillip's own outstretched one and squeezed it before putting her attention back to her ride.

"Do you really think Winter can find something out with that contraption of his?"

"I don't know. But we're going below, too, so you might be a bit bored up there just waiting about."

Allie shook her head.

"I shouldn't mind. Someone ought to remain topside."

"You won't be alone," he said after a moment. "Manston will be with you."

Allie said nothing, sifting through the words to try to uncover Phillip's true feelings about that fact and coming to no conclusion.

She remembered what David had told her at the Bonfire Night and wondered how to broach the subject of the other three men Prenpas was supposed to have seen with Phillip and Winter. Then it occurred to her that she still knew nothing of Phillip's acquaintance with this man.

"How did you and Julian meet? I don't recall you mentioning him from school."

There – that was phrased innocently enough.

"I met him at a… a club I've joined in Camelford."

"A club."

"Yes, a gentleman's club."

She waited for him to tell her more. He didn't. And with memories of their argument of a few days ago still fresh, she thought it wise not to press him further.

And still, she had dozens of questions. How did he know Julian had the qualifications to bolster his claims? What if he was a fabulist? What if his optimism was misplaced? What was the plan to keep Stannum afloat if the mine could not be reopened? There was only the value of Stannum House estate and if they sold off their land, would the villagers be forced to leave their homes, too?

She'd given a great deal of thought to these questions and considered what she might do in Phillip's position. She had not come up with any answers.

They had fallen behind David and Julian who appeared to be in deep conversation ahead.

It was nice to see David in their company. If anyone could help steer her and Phillip to the right decision it would be him.

Why did all the men in her life have to be so mysterious? David was obviously born for a life much better than the one he lived. He could be a doctor, a solicitor, or even an army officer. Just look at his ability to marshal people to a cause. And yet he lived here, in the middle of nowhere.

"What do you think of him?"

Alexandra was startled out of her musing and turned to her brother, unsure which man he asked her opinion of.

"Julian," Phillip continued. "He's a very solid chap. His family is from Yorkshire but he has a house in London."

Allie nodded but as the silence stretched on, it became clear she was expected to answer.

"Yes, he appears to be a pleasant man." She agreed because it was true and she didn't know what else to say.

The large brick building that housed the pump engine and machine room loomed before them. Another two hundred yards would have them at the mine head. The road before them grew steeper as it approached the crest. It had been more than two years since Allie had last ridden up here. Over that time, grass had reclaimed the ground around the workings.

Instead of heading directly to the top of the hill, Julian and David took a lesser path that forced them all to ride single file around the back of the mine to its southern face. The men moved slightly ahead as Allie looked about.

Here, the landscape was gray, not green, overwhelmed by the sheer amount of rock that had been extracted from underground. Tons of tailings had turned the dell into a gray stone quarry.

It was in the lee, so the wind that howled in from the sea was quiet. She heard the conversation that went on before her.

"The old mine manager passed away last summer," said Phillip. "Tis a pity we didn't know about the possibility of copper. It would have given old Ross a measure of cheer."

"No one knew the history of the mine and what she was able to produce better than he," David added.

"We'll just have to trust the old maps and records are enough to give us a starting point," Phillip concluded.

Allie breathed in deep, then frowned.

There was a faint smell of smoke, just as there had been when the mine worked. It brought to mind those familiar sounds – the *chuff-chuff* of the pump and the clack of the pistons, the occasional ground-shaking grumble of an explosion to expose a new seam, and the singing of the *bal maidens* as they worked side-by-side on the tables, breaking the rock into smaller pieces to extract the ore.

She shook her head. It was clear she was more taken by the idea of the mine reopening than she had been prepared to admit. A seed of hope started to take root.

Oh, what a difference it would make to the folks of Stannum! Money in their pockets, bellies full. Perhaps even some folks returning to take up residence in the abandoned cottages. How wonderful it would be to see some of the old craftsmen return.

If enough families came back, the church could reopen once a month and the children could go to school.

On the brow of the hill, they stopped, the mine head at their back. Before them was the fall to the sea, the rising sun from the east catching the cluster of pale gray stone buildings that made up the village below.

The light glinted on the water, turning some of the waves silver. Out to sea, small fishing vessels, sails full, made their way back to the shore – hopefully with a successful night's catch.

Perhaps this *was* the beginning of good times returning to Stannum.

Chapter Six

DAVID DETECTED THE faint smell of smoke as they rounded the back of the mine. So, it hadn't been mist or a figment of his imagination last night – there really had been a small fire up here.

Yet nothing seemed out of order.

One part of him argued it could be travelers passing through who had stopped for the night. Another part of him knew different. One had to go out of the way to get to the mine. If they were travelers, why didn't they continue on to their destination or go the few miles from the crossroads down to Stannum and find a bed for the night there?

Without a single shred of evidence, his gut told him that the men Prenpas had seen with Phillip were the ones camped up here. But why? Did Phillip know who they were?

"I'll get this equipment set up," Julian announced.

The party dismounted and entered the machine room. It was largely empty. The equipment it would have housed had been sold off to pay the workers.

The squat building opened to the engine room and the shaft that went deep underground.

"How far down do you intend to go?" David asked.

"If the water table hasn't risen, we might get a good indication on the gallery at the eighth level," said Phillip. "That's where we made the call to abandon the mine after the last blast revealed nothing."

"It's been three years. Shouldn't we have more men here to shore up the supports?"

Phillip shook his head. "I didn't want to get the men's hopes up. I don't have any concerns about the timbers, they ought to be in good condition, but we won't take any unnecessary risks."

Allie seemed uncharacteristically silent during the discussion, simply chiming in with an offer to set the lamps.

Phillip slapped Julian on the arm. "Help me check whether the ventilation shaft is clear."

David joined Allie in one of the long outbuildings where the *bal maidens* had worked. He smiled at the memory of Allie herself being among them in the last, hard six months of the mine's operation. Anything that could get what little ore there was to market.

It had proven fruitless in the end, although it did serve to break down the reserve between the girls from the village and *"'er from the big 'ouse"*.

At one time, one of the short walls of this shed would be filled with lanterns for the men who worked below ground. Now there was only a dozen of them on a lower shelf, forgotten and abandoned.

Allie picked them up and put them on the table. She managed to find a cloth from somewhere to wipe the lenses clean.

David smiled to himself, pleased he had his back to her. Most young women of her station wouldn't deign to do physical work. Indeed, they were dismissive of anyone who toiled with their hands for a living – his mother in particular was one, and Claire another.

Yet Allie rolled up her sleeves, literally, and set about the task diligently and without complaint while he set a fire.

There was tension in the set of her shoulders and David knew that the trip underground was only part of its cause. After a few minutes of working in silence, she spoke.

"I thought about the men Prenpas saw with Phillip. Do you think they could still be hanging about? I could smell smoke on the way up and I'm sure I didn't imagine it."

"I smelled it, too."

"Maybe they were here and have moved on."

"That could be so," David said noncommittally, coaxing life into the fire. He wanted to take a good look around the site before he'd be willing to pronounce judgment one way or the other.

When he stood, a dozen lamps with thick sturdy candles were primed, ready for the flame.

"Let's see if Phillip and Winter are ready for us."

He found Winter outside with a sketchbook in his hand. The man peered through his theodolite and made notes before adjusting the instrument and making some more.

Phillip emerged from the main building.

"I'm satisfied everything is as safe as it can be," he said. "There's a bell at the entrance to each gallery. I'll ring it once for each level we're on. We'll head straight down to gallery eight and work our way back up. Manston, do you have a watch?"

David shook his head. Phillip pulled out his silver hunter from his waistcoat pocket, glanced at it and then gave it to him.

"It's twenty minutes to ten," he said. "Ring the topside bell on the hour."

David nodded in acknowledgement.

Winter joined them. "I don't expect to get more than two galleries examined today. But if we start with the lowest section, it will give us an indication whether it is worth continuing."

David felt a degree of trepidation. Without question, mining was dangerous work. Descending into an abandoned mine was more dangerous still.

He wondered how Allie felt. The answers didn't show readily on her face. Quietly, without fuss, she brought the lit lamps and set them before the edge of the shaft, handing the first one to Phillip.

"There are more candles in the bag beside you as well as a flint and striker," she told him.

Together, she and David watched the two men descend rung by rung on the iron ladder until they were swallowed by the darkness. After what seemed like ages, but in reality was no more than five minutes, they heard the bell at the entrance of the uppermost gallery and the flare of a light piercing the gloom.

After another ten minutes, David heard another bell. He glanced at the pocket watch, got to his feet and rang the bell overhead. He saw Allie wince and cover her ears at the sound. She caught him grinning and stuck out her tongue at him in a most unladylike manner.

There! That was the woman he wanted to see, the one with spirit, not one succumbing to fear.

He built another fire in a brazier to take the chill from the air. The promise of a clear morning disappeared, replaced by cold, flat clouds and a misting drizzle.

"Stay here and listen out for the next bell," he said, glancing again at the watch. "I'm going to check on the horses."

ALLIE NODDED BUT kept her attention on the shaft below, listening for the echoing voices as her brother and his friend descended further below the surface.

She heard the sound of another bell. They were down five levels. She was expecting the sound of a sixth when David returned.

"Any sign of our erstwhile visitors?" she asked, keeping her voice as light as possible. If she expressed worry, he would clam up in a misguided attempt to protect her.

He hesitated as if evaluating the worth of doing just that.

"I found a spot where the ashes were still warm," he said. "But no other sign. I imagine they simply camped here overnight and left at first light."

Allie sat up and stretched, conscious of the ache of tension in her neck and shoulders. Then she stood, folding one of the horse blankets and placing it on a stump to use as a seat.

"What do you think of Phillip's new friend?" she asked, tilting her head to look up at him.

David shrugged. "He seems to know what he's talking about. I think his interest in Wheal Gunnis is genuine. Why? Do you have another sense of him?"

Allie shook her head.

"No, he's seems like a perfectly decent man."

His laughter was not a response she expected.

"Why, Miss Gedding, you sound disappointed."

She fixed him with a look. "Well, if he were a reprobate at first sight it would be easier to tell my brother I don't wish to accept his attentions."

"I think that would be a mistake."

The words were not unexpected, but they were not the ones she wanted to hear. She refused to believe he had no feelings for her – especially not after their kisses. Would he really let her go into the arms of another?

"It would be a greater mistake to marry a man I did not love because…" She breathed in deeply and looked down to compose herself before looking up at him directly. "My heart lies elsewhere."

She watched his expression closely. They had flirted together too often for there to be any misunderstanding on the matter. His arms remained crossed at the chest. A tic at the corner of his mouth showed there was no disinterest there, but something else.

"Allie…" Her name was a drawn-out sigh on his lips. "We can't."

One part of her wanted to approach him. One touch and she knew he would take her into his arms. But this time, she stayed where she was.

She shook her head ruefully. "If I believed you meant that…"

"Is my word on the matter not enough for you?"

There could only be one reason why a man would refuse something so freely offered. The thought struck her with cold clarity, turning her heart to ice.

"Then at least tell me who she was. This woman who broke your heart and trampled it to dust so that you refuse to accept the –" The word love was nearly on her lips, but she refused to say it until she could be sure that David was prepared to meet her halfway.

The spark of surprise that was swiftly hidden behind his reserved expression told her the arrow had hit the mark.

It had only been a guess, of course. Never had she regretted a correct guess in her life.

After a long moment of silence, Allie dropped her eyes from his.

"Forget I spoke," she told him.

Above the sound of drizzle from the open door of the engine house came another ringing of the bell far below. David broke his gaze away from her and reached for the pocket watch. He looked at it and rang the topside bell.

Phillip and Julian had been below ground for two hours. That meant it was noon. Sometime in the next hour they would be on their way back up to the top and Allie could puzzle through this contradictory man that she had the cursed luck to be in love with.

She wished she had something to do with her hands. She didn't knit well. Her embroidery, she was once told, was "adequate".

Although the building they were in was large, far larger than David's little cottage, it felt oppressive.

She stood up and stretched her legs, determined not to look at him. Then she heard a deliberate, put-upon sigh given for her benefit, no doubt.

"Her name is Claire."

Her stomach plummeted. She squeezed her eyes shut a moment. If this paragon had a name, then she was real. And David spoke of her in the present tense.

The tense of the living.

In her mind's eye, Allie had already determined that this woman was the most exquisite creature who ever lived. Elegant, refined and most certainly not a hoyden.

"Well... aren't you going to ask more questions?" David asked.

She glanced back to see the rigid form of his posture, the faint lines around his eyes, the set of his jaw that had thinned normally full, kissable lips. They told her one story. But it would be in his eyes where she would learn the truth.

And there she found it in the unflinching honesty that had been a part of their friendship for the past three years. Her heart tumbled a few beats. She bitterly regretted opening this Pandora's box.

At least Pandora was left with hope. I don't even have that.

Allie shook her head.

"Strange, you're usually so full of questions."

She would normally offer a witty rejoinder at his tease. Instead, she took a deep breath of her own.

"I know you too well, David Manston. Whatever else there is between us, I know you wouldn't lie to me."

"After Claire... I..." He paused, clearly choosing his words carefully. "I'm sorry, Allie. There's no future for us. I can't be your husband; I wouldn't make a suitable husband for anyone. You cannot know how sorry I am."

The flatness of his delivery only added to her feeling of falling.

She fought for control of that part of her which cried out at the unfairness of it. They were attracted to one another and, as far as she knew – *had assumed* – he was free from attachments.

I can't be your husband.

Oh my, that explained so much. He and Claire were man and wife living apart, never to reconcile, never to be free to love again.

She struggled to find a smile and, at his tender expression in return, she knew she had succeeded in finding one of her own that was bittersweet.

"You have won," she said. Her voice was firm. It didn't shake as she thought it might. All-in-all, she was rather proud of that. "I shan't tease you anymore nor press for things you cannot give."

David *ought* to look pleased. After all, hadn't he told her time and time again – and sometimes in language not at all pleasant – that she was a pest, an annoyance and to leave him the hell alone?

And then he'd kissed her. Twice.

But he didn't look pleased.

If she wasn't mistaken, he looked as bereft as she felt. He opened his mouth as though about to say something when a sound caught both their attentions. As David turned, two figures rushed in, seeking shelter from the rain outside.

She recognized the two graying, middle-aged men instantly. Clarrie Prenpas, the blacksmith who was as broad as he was tall. With him was his friend, Francis Foggett, a man who was half Prenpas' size and build.

"I told old Foggett here that I weren't mistaken," said Prenpas, breathlessly. "I heard that mine bell toll and then we find ye two up here alone. And to be sure, he thought it were the ghosties."

The smith eyed both of them with sly interest.

Allie looked away. If she blushed, he might get the wrong end of it.

"Gedding is down below with a friend of his," said David.

That sharpened both men's attentions.

"Why do the lad want to do a fool thing like that? Going below?" asked Foggett.

David glanced to Allie then back to the two men before him.

"They want to see if there might be something more than tin down there to mine."

SPY ANOTHER DAY

"Ye mean copper, pr'haps?" asked Prenpas.

"Perhaps," David agreed. "But don't breathe a word to anyone else. There's no point in getting people's hopes up until we know more about it."

The smith nodded his agreement. "Aye, it's a point well-made, Mr. Manston. Tis a pity we don't know more. The village could do with some good news."

"How fares the fishing?" Allie asked Foggett.

"Not as well as we'd hoped, Miss. T'will be a bleak winter, indeed, until something do change."

The misting rain became a persistent drizzle and the gray sky darkened further, leaving the building illuminated only by the lamp. The echoing sound of the bell made its way up from the mine below.

David checked this watch and announced the hour as half-past four.

While Alexandra lit more lamps, Foggett stirred up the fire. After a while, Phillip's voice echoed up from below, calling that they were on their way up.

Peering down into the void, David could see their lamps perhaps a hundred feet below, swinging about as they climbed the rungs. Finally, Phillip and Julian emerged shivering and stumbled toward the fire. David hadn't appreciated how cold it was below ground.

After a moment regaining some warmth, Phillip acknowledged the two new arrivals.

"Well, this is quite the party," he said.

"Hopefully, the beginning of good times again, Master Gedding," said Prenpas in a not-too-subtle fish for information.

Allie settled a warmed blanket over her brother's shoulders. "Far too early to tell, old man," said Phillip. "Julian here will need to consult with a few more people."

"Aye, we're sworn to secrecy as Mr. Manston here told us."

David accepted a thankful look in his direction.

"We're doing everything we can for Stannum," Phillip added.

"Aye, we know ye are, Master Gedding."

David busied himself working with Prenpas to re-lay the timbers that covered the mine shaft, hating the way he was so conscious of Allie's presence.

At every point, he knew where she was and what she was doing, and he made sure he would not have to look her way as he went about his own tasks.

After such a long time of companionship with her, it felt so wrong.

But he was doing the right thing. He was sure of it, just as he was sure of his own name. So why didn't that bring him any comfort? Why was it he felt like a cad?

Because he'd lied – albeit by omission – to a woman he respected, whom he considered a friend and, as a result, she thought less of him.

It was better that he be hanged for a sheep as a lamb.

But it pained him so to feel her withdrawing from him. Instead of the bright liveliness she seemed to bring to everything, she was uncharacteristically quiet as they readied the horses for their miserable return journey back to Stannum in the rain.

He deeply regretted having to hurt her that way, but what choice did he have?

Should anyone recognize his family's title, rather than the historic family name, then there would be no hiding his disgrace and ruined reputation from her.

Better to have her think he was married or, at the very least, still in love with Claire.

Hell, whatever romantic notion she wished to put on it would be fine by him – just as long as he could retain some measure of the respect he had earned here in Stannum. That would be enough for him.

And if Allie accepted the limitation of their relationship and still wished to remain his friend, then he'd consider himself a fortunate man, indeed.

Right now, the sooner he could retreat to his cottage, bolt the doors, and return to his hermit life, the better for his own sanity.

He should never have evoked Claire's name and summoned a ghost that lurked in the recesses of his consciousness.

David was startled by a slap on his back.

"You will come back to the house with us, won't you?" asked Phillip. "Julian brought some other equipment with him. We'll use the samples we brought up today to test for copper."

He nodded just as Allie crossed his vision, bringing two of the horses to the building. Already the shoulders of her riding habit were wet. She ought to be inside and dry before she caught the ague.

They left Prenpas and Foggett to walk the narrow and precipitous path back down to the village – a shorter distance than the main roads they would travel on horseback.

The drizzle was teeming rain by the time they'd reached the stables. Harry Watt accepted his equine charges and directed their riders to the house.

"Bleak day, indeed, Master Gedding!" exclaimed Mrs. McArthur. "Och! All of ye in wet clothes. Well, the fire is lit in the library and in the bedrooms and ye –" She pointed to Allie. "– had best get upstairs, Missy, before ye catch yer death."

David waited for Allie to make some bright remark, but she didn't, simply excusing herself and going up to the floor upstairs via the servants' stairs off the kitchen. Julian soon followed – that stuck like a burr to his skin.

Irritating, but he could live with it.

"We're about the same build," said Phillip to him. "Borrow something of mine while your clothes dry."

He followed Phillip up those same stairs and down the hall. He heard movement in rooms opposite each other along the hall.

So, Phillip hadn't wasted any time placing Julian Winter in Allie's path, it seemed.

Stannum House had an air of ghostly resignation. It smelled dusty although all the surfaces he had seen were scrupulously clean.

"You'll have to forgive us," said Phillip. "When it's just Allie and me…"

Phillip opened the door to the master suite. It was a large room that once would have been fit for royalty, but now only half of it seemed inhabited – very much like the house overall.

Phillip opened an oak armoire and pulled out a drawer.

"There's something I should tell you," said David. "I had a word with your sister. I think you'll find she's over her infatuation with me."

Phillip turned and regarded him a moment. "You're a sport, Manston, a true friend. Thank you. I knew I could count on you to have Allie's best interests at heart."

David nodded and accepted a shirt and breeches from Phillip.

How come it felt like *her* best interests no longer felt like his own?

Chapter Seven

MRS. McARTHUR CAST them a leery look when Julian returned downstairs with a wooden box and set it upon the kitchen bench which Phillip had hastily cleared.

Allie stood at her brother's shoulder just behind Julian – and as far away as possible from David. She glanced at him from the corners of her eyes. It was strange seeing him in her brother's clothes – familiar but different.

She forced her attention back to the box that Julian was opening. What she had taken for a plain writing box was, in fact, a little laboratory.

Julian pulled out a small spirit burner and an equally bijoux mortar and pestle.

On the table were envelopes marked one to eight.

"Copper is a very easy mineral to test for," said Julian. "So, we can at least see if we're wasting our time in short order. Phillip, will you roll out the map?"

Her brother did so, holding the parchment in place with four large rocks.

"We collected samples from each level and made sketches of the rock strata. I don't know if this will tell us anything but I thought there was no harm in trying a small test sample before I return to Somerset."

"How exactly does this work?" David asked.

"We crush a small sample of the rock and mix it in a glass bowl with this." He held up a bottle of clear liquid. Its paper label read *Nitric Acid*. "Then we heat it until the rock is dissolved and add some ammonia. If there is copper in the ore, the solution will turn a dark blue."

Allie instantly put a hand to her nose when Julian pulled the cork from the ammonia. She stepped a few paces away from the pungent odor and brought an edge of a shawl up to cover her nose and mouth. David saw her and offered her a tight smile. No doubt he was trying hard not to breathe in, too.

He also moved further around the table to allow her to remain at a distance and still see as Julian added the ammonia to the first sample. It remained stubbornly clear.

"One down and seven to go," said Phillip, unable to hide his disappointment.

"It's all about patience," muttered Julian, grinding another sample to dust.

Long minutes passed, then an hour, then another, as the experiment was repeated another five times.

Then she saw it.

Like alchemy, clear liquid in the glass was now turning blue.

"Is that –?"

David and her brother stepped in closer behind Julian.

"It's a result. It's not strong but it's a chance," said Julian.

"Where did that sample come from?" said David.

"Gallery seven," Phillip answered. "Should we try for number eight?"

"Nothing ventured, nothing gained." Julian reached for the ore sample and prepared the test once again. And, again, the clear liquid turned blue, a darker hue than before.

David leaned back and gave a show whistle.

"You've got to say *that's* promising," Phillip added.

As the aroma of ammonia faded, Allie removed the shawl from her nose.

"Then what do we do now?"

"I still want to see William Smith, the geologist, and get his opinion, but it seems to me that we should go back down to galleries seven and eight," said Julian.

"We'll need to find investors," mused Phillip. "We need money for blasting powder and to pay the workers we'll need to excavate. But without a definitive seam to show, we'll only attract speculators."

"Or me."

The atmosphere became leaden as all eyes turned to David.

"If Mr. Winter and this geologist Smith says it's worth exploring, I'll put up one hundred pounds in exchange for a thirty percent stake."

Allie was startled. She found herself looking into her brother's eyes, green, the same shade as hers.

"You're as poor as a church mouse," she declared to David. "Where on earth are you going to put your hands on a hundred pounds?"

The words were past her lips before she considered the wisdom of speaking them.

She shut her mouth at David's baleful look in return. And she heard rather than saw Julian rise from the table.

"Ahem... I'm sure this is something I'm not needed for, so I'll go to my room and write my report."

Tension remained heavy in the kitchen after he had gone.

Phillip, too, looked uncomfortable. "A hundred pounds is a lot to wager on an uncertain bet."

David shrugged off the warning. "Nothing in life is certain – not even life."

Phillip looked unconvinced. Allie knew him well enough to know he was torn. It was one thing to be promised a small return in consideration of past services rendered, another to ask a major partnership.

"Think about it and come back to me," said David, as though he'd offered a cigar instead of a small fortune. Allie found herself under his scrutiny momentarily.

Thoughtless words. How she wished she could take them back. Especially today.

He turned to her brother.

"Thank you for the loan of your clothes; I'll return them. But I should leave now before it gets too late."

Phillip thrust out his hand.

"Thank you… I'll consider your offer carefully."

David accepted it with a nod, retrieved his coat hanging by the fire, still damp, and opened the door. The rain had eased and the breeze brought with it the tang of salt from the sea.

From the kitchen window, Allie watched David head out to the stables.

She turned to Phillip and saw him mesmerized by the sapphire blue-colored solution in the glass.

For the first time since the weight of responsibility had fallen on his shoulders, she saw hope in his eyes, and she was not so caught up in her heartache that she did not feel it herself.

Even so, she and David still had unfinished business between them. Before she could talk herself out of it, Allie ran out to the stable.

David had his back to her. In the lamplight, he worked the girth strap around his horse, a large, black creature she'd dubbed Noir, although Allie was unsure whether that was his name. She'd never heard David give it one.

Another thing she didn't know about David Manston.

Had she ever known him? Was he ever only a prince in her dreams, built on nothing more than her gratitude for his steady, calm authority when all about them had been in turmoil?

Noir acknowledged her presence with a turn and a slight nod of the head. The master did not notice. Indeed, he was unlikely to have heard her approach.

"Get back inside. I won't be responsible for you catching your death."

For a moment, she wondered if he spoke to his horse, although it struck her as a strange thing to tell the animal.

She stepped further inside the stable and out of the draft.

David sighed, straightened up from his task, and looked at her. "Allie, do you actually have the brains you were born with?"

"I didn't think you were aware of my presence."

"You have no idea how aware of you I am."

The words quickened something inside her. Did she detect a note of longing?

"Then why do you hide things from me – your wife, your past, your living? Because you must have a decent living if you can offer my brother *one hundred pounds* on a speculative venture."

She saw him grit his teeth as though it were a superlative effort to keep his anger under control.

"Have you ever considered it's none of your goddamned business?"

She folded her arms and planted her feet, the heat of her own rising temper expelling any chill she felt.

"Oh no, you've made it my '*goddamned*' business – even more now that you've proposed a partnership with Phillip."

"What does my past mean to you or to anyone if I make good on my word in the present?"

She had no good answer to that – only that she wanted to know the whole man, *all of him*, certain that the good she saw in him outweighed any of his possible past failings. But David seemed determined to put a brick wall between them.

"Then what about your future?"

"That's something you and I have no control over."

"I don't believe that and neither do you."

Now she had David's full attention.

"Oh? Tell me how so, madam philosopher?"

"You have to believe in *some* better future, otherwise you would never have made the offer of a partnership to my brother. In fact, you've wagered on it."

In the flickering shadows cast by the lamp, she saw David work his jaw as he considered her words. She was right. He *knew* she was right.

She felt a flare of triumph. It must have shown on her face because David's expression changed. It was calculating. He stepped closer.

"Perhaps I consider it payment for something else."

"Like what?"

Her body instinctively recognized a desirable man on the hunt, and part of her wished very much to be his prey.

He didn't answer as he stalked her. He'd tried to frighten her off once before with a sexual display. How could she possibly tell him that what she desired more than anything was for him to take her?

Despite this, she retreated a step or two until her back was against the stable wall. Now he had her trapped, his powerful body against hers. Curse him for making her want him all the more.

"What do *you* think?" he replied at last.

She giggled.

"You think my brother has sold me off for a hundred quid? That's a more foolish bet than the speculation on there being copper in Wheal Gunnis."

She lowered her voice and pressed herself forward. Did she feel evidence of his desire against her? She raised herself on tiptoes and ran her hands over the waxed cotton of his coat until she reached his shoulders. She slid her hands across until they met at the nape of his neck and dropped her voice.

"Besides, why do you imagine I'd want payment?"

With the slightest pressure from her hands, he lowered his head and slowly leaned into her. His body didn't lie; she felt his hardness.

She sighed her surrender and waited for his kiss. Instead, he pressed his lips close to her ear.

"Maybe I consider you and your brother pitiable charity."

Anger tainted the desire that thrummed through her. Warning pounded in her ears.

She pulled her hands from his neck and pushed his shoulders to put some distance between them, but he was as immovable as granite. He pressed against her more firmly still, his hands on either side of her waist, trapping her to him.

"You're surprised I feel sorry for two hapless orphans?" he continued, his voice rasping against her ear. "I've tried to be pleasant about it. I've tried being gruff about it. You think I'm a gentleman, Alexandra? Then think again.

"I'm a beast, a ravening beast. You think you can turn me into your lamb? I'm a wolf in sheep's clothing. I only do what pleases *me*. Do you understand?"

A lump in her throat released itself as a sob at the same time as her hand connected a slap, hard, across his cheek.

David pulled away, cold air filling the void between them. Her knees nearly buckled but she forced herself upright against the stable wall.

"I hate you," she whispered.

He backed away further until he reached his horse. He swung up into the saddle and looked down at her, his expression tormented, as she knew hers to be.

"Good."

His voice was hard, filled with an emotion she could not decipher.

"You *should* hate me."

Chapter Eight

December 27, 1805

"**I**'M PLANNING A trip to Camelford."

Phillip's casual remark caused Allie to lift her head from her book at the breakfast table.

"Would you like to go with me?"

Camelford, the place of his secret assignations. Now he had her full attention.

Phillip continued.

"I mean, it's probably too late to order a gown for Winter's party or anything – not that we've got the money for that sort of thing – but there might be some ribbons or something you can do to one you've already got I suppose."

"You have some business there?" she asked innocently.

"You've caught me out."

She made sure Phillip could see her expectant look. Her brother merely laughed at the expression.

"Stop looking like a goose. It's been a long time since I've had a day outing with my sister but, since you ask, I have a meeting arranged with some potential investors. You'll be free to roam the market in peace."

"Am I not invited to this investor's meeting?"

"What on earth for?"

"I do have a stake in Wheal Gunnis, too, you know."

"Don't you trust me to represent both our interests?"

"Of course I do. It's just that –"

Phillip placed a hand on her shoulder and squeezed affectionately.

"Look, let's not argue, it's too nice a day for that. On the ride over, why don't you tell me your thoughts to make sure I've not overlooked anything? In fact, I challenge you. Interrogate me like a potential investor."

It was a compromise Allie was ready to accept. In truth, she knew that her presence would actually put her brother in a worse bargaining position. It would be as David had so bitterly pointed out to her – less of a sober business proposition and more of an act of charity.

The memory of David's barb cut deep.

"Agreed!" she said, forcing a brightness into her voice. "And be certain I do *not* intend to let you off the hook."

He smiled.

"I wouldn't expect anything less from my sister."

It was a fine day, possibly the last before winter truly bit. She slowed Nephel to a stop and wheeled her mount about.

From the elevation of the road, she could see for miles. To her left, about four hundred yards away up on the plateau was Wheal Gunnis. Today, its tower cast a morning shadow down the narrow vale, pointing to the village. Its tumbledown collection of low-set buildings clinging to the side of the hill until it met the expanse of yellow beach at the cove.

Beyond it, the sea was light blue close to the shore, but grew deeper in hue as the sea itself deepened. About a hundred yards or so out was a rocky islet. At low tide, rocks emerged from the water like jagged teeth, disappearing again as the tide rose.

The locals knew those hazards well. Their small fishing vessels followed the deep channels on either side of the shoal without incident. A larger ship would not be so fortunate, so it was just as well that no large ships ever passed there. Their course was always farther out to sea to pass around the headlands that buttressed Stannum.

Also, at this elevation, about a mile to the south on the opposite headland, light caught the rectangular whitewashed shape of David's cottage.

She had not seen him since the day he told her he was married and claimed his interest in her was borne of pity.

The words had stung even though she was sure he didn't mean them. Despite being a curmudgeon on occasion, they were friends. Never had he suggested charity as the reason he'd helped and befriended her and Phillip.

No, she was keenly aware that he only brought it up after she revealed her interest in him had bloomed into a romantic attachment…

"Are you going to sit there and look at the view all day!" Phillip called to her.

She shook her head to clear her mind and nudged Nephel into motion to catch up with her brother.

Perhaps she was a fool for forcing her attentions onto a man whose words said one thing but whose actions said another.

Whatever demons tormented David Manston, they were not hers to vanquish.

DAVID WAS GRATEFUL for the steady, hard work of plowing his small field with his horse, Jack, in harness. The task left him alone with his thoughts.

They wandered here and there, never settling into one location for too long. It brought to mind a caterpillar he had once watched in his little walled vegetable garden. Every morning, he saw it moving about so aimlessly, and considered removing it from the mulberry leaves. But he ignored it as other chores called to him more urgently so, by the evening, he had forgotten.

By the time it formed a chrysalis, he didn't have the heart. Besides, after surviving his gardening, and the sharp eyes of birds looking for prey, he felt the creature deserved the miracle of its metamorphosis. Besides, he wanted to see the type of butterfly which emerged. No one loved the caterpillar, but they certainly loved the butterfly.

Why was that? Were they not the same creature?

One morning, he happened upon the creature struggling from its cocoon and, tempted though he was to help, he knew from his school lessons that the fight to be reborn was necessary to strengthen its wings.

Eventually, the butterfly emerged. Iridescent blue wings pulsed slowly in the sunlight, growing in strength in the sun's warmth.

When it flew away, it made him unaccountably happy.

If an insect could rise from its low state, perhaps there was hope for him as well.

David looked about the field as he directed Jack and the plow. After the winter, he would see if he could get a crop to flourish, then it might bring a little more food and hope to the people of Stannum.

That he was considered an eccentric by some of them did not concern him. It just gave him another excuse to keep himself to himself.

Yet perhaps, like that butterfly, it was time for him to emerge from his cocoon. After all, it had been ten years since he took the fateful step of ruining his own reputation on Claire's behalf. Was there anyone left who actually cared what the young Baron of Carreg had done? Would Allie care?

He smiled wryly to himself as he turned Jack for another achingly slow return down the field.

What would she say if she ever happened to learn the poor hermit of Stannum was the son of a Welsh viscount? And a man with a reputation as a libertine who indulged in the most debauched practices?

He reflected on what he had done for Claire and Thomas.

No. He thought too poorly of himself to be a caterpillar. A worm was more apt.

HE RECALLED CLEARLY the day Thomas Owen-Jones had pulled him aside at a dinner party several days after his ill-fated walk with Claire.

"Claire says she spoke to you, that you agreed to end your engagement."

"She does not wish to wed me, and I would not wish to marry a woman against her will," he had replied evenly.

Thomas continued to look grave. "We've been friends for a long time, haven't we?"

The tone in his voice had sounded caution. David merely nodded.

"There's something I need to tell you," Thomas continued. His friend couldn't even look him in the eyes as he spoke. "Claire told me that she didn't – that is, *we* didn't realize – that you had a *tendre* for her. It makes what I'm going to tell you, so much harder... we're in love."

Though David already knew it, hearing the words from his friend's lips struck him with the force of a blow. It hurt worse than the blows his father had rained on him as a child.

"It happened last summer at the Pettifers' house party," Thomas continued, "I –"

"It truly doesn't matter when it happened, does it?" he gritted out, looking off across the room but not seeing it. "Why didn't Claire put your name forward?"

"She *did*, but her mother in particular wouldn't hear of it. She said she wishes her daughter to one day be the Viscountess Carmarthan when you inherit your title. I have no grand title to give."

"Well, my parents are certainly in favor of the match, *and* I've already indicated my willingness. I can't see them changing *their* minds. So, what are we to do?"

Thomas looked nervously at him. "The only thing I can think of is to make you unmarriageable."

David barked out an incredulous laugh. "Thank you very much! How do you propose to do that?"

"If words will not do it then deeds will be required."

"Such as?"

Thomas glanced about then reached into to his waistcoat pocket and fished out a card. It was plain white with just three words on it: *The Olympus Club*.

"A club?"

Thomas touched a finger to the side of his nose.

"A *special* club. Here…"

He followed Thomas out into the garden. "A scandal, that's all. Just a minor one that wouldn't raise an eyebrow amongst the fast set, but would add to Claire's claim that she couldn't marry you."

David burst out laughing.

"Don't laugh! All you need to do is make sure you're seen coming out of the place."

How young he had been then, and how easily persuaded to go down this path. If only he could go back to the past as one might flip back the pages of a book. He would warn his younger self to not listen to Owen-Jones but instead just walk away and find some other means to deny himself, and give Thomas and Claire what they wanted.

But what was once seen could not be unseen – even now, years after the fact.

David had agreed to the plan. Thomas had told him it would be best if *he* didn't accompany David to The Olympus Club. Instead, he would go in the company of Thomas' older cousin, Douglas. The man had once been considered one of the major matrimonial catches, but now had a reputation of being utterly dissolute.

Behind the green-painted door of the very respectable townhouse was a world unlike any David ever dreamed existed.

In an alcove just off the main hall was the first naked woman he had ever seen outside of a painting or statue. Living and breathing, she lay supine on a chaise longue. Her lips were painted carmine red, a contrast to her pale skin but which picked up the hue of red nipples standing high and proud on her breasts. The black silken blindfold that covered her eyes echoed the dark thatch of hair between her legs which were spread invitingly.

So enraptured was he by the vision of womanhood laid before him that David didn't notice her bonds at first, not until Douglas and his cronies shoved him and laughed at his youth and inexperience.

"Get on her before someone else has a go! She can hardly say no, can she?"

"Ah, leave him alone Matthewson, he knows better than to drop his breeches for the first whore he sees."

Emboldened, though still somewhat embarrassed, David looked at the girl bound arm and leg to the furniture.

"Well, at least touch her, so you know what to expect."

He hesitated.

Douglas huffed his impatience. "Go on! That's what she's there for."

Fortunately, his drunken companions were soon taken with their own garden of delights further down the hall, where more naked women posed in tableaux. David was not nearly as green as Douglas and his friends imagined, but it was one thing to lift the skirts of a tavern wench after a few pints, and quite another to enter a place like this.

In terms of the pleasure of the flesh, it was as though that up until this moment, he'd simply assuaged a hunger. Here, it was intended that he banquet on the daughters of Eve from a lavish feast of flesh laid out for his delectation and to sate desires he had not known existed before this moment.

It was *more* than a brothel; he knew that now. No other gentleman's "club" required the guests to wear masks.

With identities concealed, inhibitions were abandoned, and there were nearly as many men disrobed as women.

Some made gluttons of themselves cavorting with two, sometimes three women at a time; others paid particular attention to just one chosen girl – and they almost always looked young, his own age perhaps.

David's erection bulged in his breeches. He wandered through the viewing rooms half in disbelief of what he saw, watching others take their pleasures in a variety of ways. The smell of sex, tobacco, and heavy incense clung to the back of his throat, giving him a headache. He found a parlor where a bored but clothed man handed him a gin when what he really wanted was a beer. It seemed only spirits were served here and he downed three glasses of the clear spirit in quick succession before he felt the effects of it.

He stumbled off into another room, quieter than the others. It was occupied by a man and a woman. They sat together on a chaise positioned precisely in the middle of the room. Her hand lay in his lap.

Like the girl at the beginning, she was naked and blindfolded. Her light brown hair was mussed around her face. The man, older, judging by the white hair at his temples, still himself mostly dressed, lifted his head in a wordless invitation to enter.

David did so without really knowing why he obeyed. The other man gave him a knowing look and stroked his companion's hair.

"Tonight, I have something different for you, my pet," he told the girl, drawing her to her feet. "I should like to watch my new friend here attend to you."

David looked at the man uncertainly.

"You're a newcomer to The Olympus Club, I see. New to the way we do things here? I think it will do you both good to learn the taste of discipline…" He drew the girl a few paces away from the chaise. "Daphnis, you will remain standing here and still until I tell you otherwise. Do you understand?"

"Yes, Master," came her breathy reply.

"Denial of pleasure can be a pleasure in itself, my dear. That is the lesson you will both learn today."

The man turned to David. He gestured at some cords on the chaise.

"Tie her wrists behind her," he ordered, "and I will instruct you both…"

DAVID DIDN'T SEE the stone flicked up by the foreshare until it hit him on the cheek. He dropped the reins, cursed and dabbed the back of his hand to his face. It came back with a spot of blood.

Even the ground he worked seemed to condemn him.

David shook his head, ready to return to his plowing, when a thin column of smoke rose from near Wheal Gunnis.

Again? Those squatters once more. He never did find out about the strangers who were with Phillip Gedding on the crossroads.

Perhaps it was time to investigate and put the rumors of ghosts to bed for good.

Chapter Nine

St. Sennen
Cornwall
18 January 1806

LADY ABIGAIL RIDGEWAY put her hand in her husband's so he could assist her down from the carriage. She looked up at the squat three-story building before her.

It had taken ten days but The King's Rogues were back in business here at The Queen's Head.

She was tired; they were all tired – Sir Daniel, the wounded Bassett and his young apprentice, Adam and Olivia Hardacre. For a day at least, she welcomed someone else taking care of the little details.

Nate and Susannah had given up their honeymoon to set up their new base of operations. As Abigail herself well knew, sometimes the opportunity for love had to be taken whenever the chance presented itself.

First to greet them was Susannah's former housekeeper, now business partner, Peggy Pascoe, a woman close to Abigail's own age. She glanced up the road from whence the carriage came, as though anticipating someone in hot pursuit.

Alas there was no one. It would be much easier if their arsonist *did* make himself known, Abigail considered. But, according to her sources, Harold Bickmore was still laying low somewhere in London.

Peggy curtsied formally, betraying the class difference between them.

"If it be pleasing to you, Sir, Ma'am, we have the south rooms on the third floor prepared. You'll be sharing that floor with Lieutenant Hardacre and his wife. You can be rest assured, my maids are discreet. They know not to be talking out of turn to anyone. They won't be saying nothing to nobody about why you're here. Your man Bassett is here, Sir. He and his apprentice have made themselves right at home on the second floor. Now, when would you and your ladyship like tea?"

Did the woman ever take pause for breath? Abigail wondered.

Daniel turned to her as though seeking counsel when, in fact, she knew he was doing his damnedest not to laugh. For a fleeting moment, she considered dropping her husband right in it, but had a last moment change of heart.

If one had to seek romance where one could, so too could the same be said for humor and maintaining a gracious sense of it.

"Thank you, Mrs. Pascoe," Abigail said, keeping her own voice even. "We could not wish for a finer welcome. We certainly don't wish to disrupt the smooth running of The Queen's Head. After all, it's our desire to be as inconspicuous as possible."

Peggy curtsied once more, turned, and abruptly yelled at the top of her voice, making Abigail start. "Sam! Bags!" A young fellow came at a run to see to the new guests' belongings.

It was still early, so the bar and dining room of The Queen's Head was empty. Abigail could hear voices in the kitchen. Manners normally dictated that she greet and thank Susannah Payne, their hostess, but there was work to be done – a mountain of correspondence from her network of spies and informants that needed to be read, answered, and actioned.

It brought back old memories of when she and Daniel were on the run, not knowing who they could trust. The fact they were now in England, instead of France, only slightly lessened the undercurrent of tension.

She reached the landing of the second floor and saw through an open door a room occupied by two tables placed side by side. Young Joe sat at the makeshift drafting table. Bassett hovered over and behind him, observing his work. Bassett's hands were still bandaged but, thank God, recovering well.

"I hope we're not interrupting," said Abigail. Bassett raised his head and instantly bestowed on her the look of adoration that she'd come to ignore.

"My lady, Sir Daniel, we're up and running as you can see. Hardacre and Payne have managed to get us some large wall maps. They're in the room next door along with some desks. Mrs. Hardacre is working in there at the moment."

Before Abigail could approach the door, Olivia Hardacre emerged looking every inch the governess she had been before she wed Adam. Hair tied back and plainly dressed, the woman even sported a pencil behind her ear as well as that owlish look of someone who has been so long at a task, the real world about them was more like a waking dream.

She greeted Lady Abigail and Sir Daniel. "I've spent the past few hours on translations of the correspondence taken when Bickmore was captured. Adam and Nate are not expected back until tomorrow. They took the *Sprite* out yesterday morning to try and narrow down the area where Bickmore was supposed to be headed before his arrest."

"You've done well, my dear," said Daniel, taking the woman's hand and giving it a squeeze. "I know this has been a trying time for all of us. When they return, I suggest we take a day to catch our breaths."

Young porter Sam appeared stooped over with one of their two trunks on his back. He looked between Abigail and the staircase to the top floor expectantly.

She climbed the stairs behind the young man while her husband continued to talk business with Olivia. Sam led the way through the open door of a room which contained a small double bed, a wash-stand, and a couple of mismatched wooden chairs. Not unacquainted with sparse comforts, Abigail felt the room would do nicely.

Sam deposited the trunk against a wall, bowed to her uncertainly, and then bounded back downstairs with the energy of one who was only a little older than a youth. Within the minute, he was back with the second trunk. Another shy bow and he was off, clattering down-stairs.

After half a day in the carriage, the small bed looked as inviting to Abigail as the one in their master suite at Bishop's Wood. She sat on the edge of it with a sigh. A knock on the door put paid to the fleeting idea of a nap.

"Lady Abigail, it is good to see you again."

Abigail threw off her tiredness as she might with an old cloak and rose to greet Susannah Payne with a kiss on each cheek.

"My dear, you've excelled in making this place our headquarters," she said, noting the pleased blush on the younger woman's face. "I do hope that Bassett has not been too demanding."

Susannah may have lost much of her prior reserve, but Abigail was aware Nate's wife still exercised a great deal of caution in her words.

"It's been no hardship at all, my lady," she said formally. "Not only did I wish to bid you welcome, but also to let you know my private parlor downstairs is also at your disposal."

"I shall take you up on your offer. And if you'd oblige with a large glass of sherry, and get your young groom to bring through my writing box, I shall be quite set."

Alone in Susannah's parlor with the closed door muting the sound from the bar and kitchen beyond, Abigail opened her writing box and withdrew the first of the letters that awaited her. She scanned the information from an agent assigned to watch one of a number of London boarding houses.

A man fitting Bickmore's description had left these particular premises and was on the move, but not to the east coast. Abigail frowned. They were all agreed it would make sense for Bickmore to hide out somewhere near the English Channel – Kent or perhaps further north to Whitby – but instead the man had been followed only as far as The Swan With Two Necks coaching inn at Cheapside, still within London.

From that stop, a man could board a coach going anywhere from Southampton to Manchester.

Abigail considered the intelligence while finishing her sherry, then she locked her writing box and went up to the second floor. Joe found the timetable for that particular inn. Abigail took it through to the room where the maps were.

Andover, Axminster, Basingstoke, Bath, Bury St Edmonds, Camelford...

She looked over the hung map featuring the coasts of England and Ireland, and traced the road that came from the east.

Bickmore was heading back to Cornwall. The man was not intending to escape to France at all; he intended to slip over to Ireland. She *knew* it. She scanned the map thoroughly. He would want to arrive close, but not too close to his ultimate destination across the Irish Sea. It would need to be a place large enough to blend in, but not so large as to come to the attention of the authorities.

She tapped the map with her index finger.

Camelford.

Only a few miles from the coast, and there was a lot of coastline where one might hide out.

She traced her finger along until she found St. Sennen. A little further to the north, a smattering of ink spots denoted the village of Stannum.

A larger dot had something written next to it. Abigail peered closer to see the words *"Wheal Gunnis"*. The letter she had received from that relative of hers – Alexandra Gedding.

Stannum House, Cornwall.

Abigail vaguely recalled being made the child's godmother and, indeed, only God Himself knew why. She suspected at the time that the child's mother had done it to spite wretched old Aunt Philomena.

If she recalled correctly, the house at Stannum had quite an excellent library – an indulgence of the head of the Nancarrow family.

That might come in handy, but the location even more so. Stannum was but twenty miles away from St. Sennen, not at all too far to pay a long-neglected visit to her beloved goddaughter.

THE WEATHER CLOSED in, bringing endless days of rain. To Adam's surprise, he didn't find himself chafing with the inactivity, instead he enjoyed the semblance of a normal life. Mornings waking up slowly next to his wife with no need to rush into the day, time spent in the company of people he now considered friends... he could almost ignore the drumbeat of war and imagine that Harold Bickmore and his betrayal were nothing more than a bad dream.

But then there was an entire floor of The Queen's Head which gave lie to all of that, as well as the time his wife spent puzzling through the letter that brought Nate Payne to their attention in the first place.

He dropped a kiss to the top of her head as she bent over another piece of paper. He read it over her shoulder, even though he was already well familiar with its contents.

Dear Aunt Runella,

Your nephew has been remiss in writing, but the Gorgons have been insistent on having their way.

Iris reports Aristaeus has three hundred and Phorcys brings another hundred to his aid.

Ares has taken to the skies. Eurus brings his usual bad luck, Apheliotes might be prepared to cooperate.

Adrastus should be aware of betrayal. Pyroeis wanders closer.

Deipneus still plies his trade.

Thanatos draws closer, too, so this letter will be my last.

Your faithful nephew,
Delas

With his fingertips, he captured a strand of his wife's light brown hair that had fallen loose from her chignon and drew it over her ear.

Olivia sat up straight, rested her head back against his chest then looked up at him.

He loved this woman and he showed her with a soft lingering kiss.

"I thought we decided that it was all nonsense," he said, nodding at the letter before them.

"I don't believe it is, but at least I've managed to identify who all the ancient Greek deities are – and I think there might be something there. I want to present what I have to Sir Daniel and Lady Abigail."

Soon there was six around one of the tables in the dining room of The Queen's Head. The Ridgeways took the head of the table while Adam and Olivia sat opposite Nate and Susannah.

"The letter has always puzzled me," said Olivia. "If Felix went to so much effort to concoct it, then there has to be more than just creating something memorable to get our attention."

"Felix was the man closest to Joseph Fouché's inner circle," Sir Daniel conceded, leaning forward to rest his arms on the table. "But after the ordeal he went through, we should take what he says with caution. His mind may have been tormented as well as his body."

"Still, it couldn't hurt to take a look at what Olivia has discovered," Adam countered.

Sir Daniel nodded. "Then we are all ears."

Olivia took in a deep breath and looked down at the document.

"We know what it says, but we don't necessarily know what it means," she said. "I know we will all have our own views, and this is what I want to throw open here. Say anything that comes to mind. It might spark a new line of thinking."

Sir Daniel nodded but was otherwise silent.

Nate stretched his back. "I remember every line in that letter; shall I recite it?"

In receiving no dissent, he began: "'Your nephew has been remiss in writing, but the Gorgons have been insistent on having their way. Iris reports Aristaeus has three hundred and Phorcys brings another hundred to his aid'."

Olivia raised her hand to stop the recitation.

"The Gorgons are monsters, like Medusa."

Lady Abigail laughed. "One should never underestimate the effectiveness of the female of the species."

"I want to focus on the second sentence," Olivia continued. "Iris represents the rainbow; she was a messenger of the gods. What comes to mind?"

"Rainbow... rainbow," Adam mused. "'You're as likely to find a pot of gold as you are the end of a rainbow'."

Nate burst out laughing. "You're kidding!"

"Yes. No... maybe," Adam shrugged, "but we know Ireland is the key to this."

Lady Abigail arched an eyebrow, a play of a smile on her lips. "Maybe Napoleon has an army of angry leprechauns massing on the coast?"

It was clear Olivia intended to ignore the banter and chose to read the next line herself.

"'Aristaeus has three hundred'... all I've been able to find out is that Aristaeus is associated with beekeeping."

There was silence for a moment. Lady Abigail suddenly looked thoughtful. "Bees are on Napoleon's coat of arms."

"Go on, Olivia, tell us what else you've found," Adam encouraged.

"Phorcys, who 'brings another hundred to his aid', was a dangerous sea god more ancient than Neptune."

"If we take Aristaeus as Napoleon then who is Phorcys?" asked

Susannah.

"If we're to make the assumption that Napoleon is planning to supply three hundred troops to Ireland then it makes sense that the other one hundred might be supplied by the Irish," said Nate. "Ancient sea god... an ancient family perhaps?"

"Lord Edward FitzGerald?" Lady Abigail asked her husband.

"He was executed five years ago, but the United Irishmen are still a force," Sir Daniel answered. "Thomas Emmet? He's the brother of Robert Emmet who staged the uprising against Viscount Kilwarden a few years ago. We know he's in communication with Napoleon because the man *was* supposed to provide troops for the rebellion."

"That makes sense," Nate conceded. "It bolsters our reasoning that Ireland will be the staging point for the invasion. And Ares... even I know he's the god of war, so that is self-explanatory."

"Well, here's something else, Eurus is the god of the east wind."

"And Apheliotes?" Susannah inquired.

"I'm not sure... something to do with the wind as well..." Here Olivia hesitated. Adam reached out for her hand and held it. "I really thought we were on to something here. But wind, rainbows, and bees? The more we go on, the more I fear we're overlooking something, or neglecting something that would be a greater benefit."

Sir Daniel nodded thoughtfully. "Do continue, Olivia."

"Well, there is Adrastus. He was a legendary king of Argos during the war of the Seven Against Thebes. And whoever he is was to be aware of betrayal. Next is Pyroeis. He seems to be related to Ares, but there also a connection to fire and shooting stars."

"Congreve rockets?"

Adam was not the only one to look expectantly at the peer.

"They're a new weapon developed by Sir William Congreve. I've only ever heard of them. I've not seen them in action," said Sir Daniel. "A form of them was used against us by the Mysore Kingdom in India – hundreds of them set off at once. I imagine they would look like shooting stars. Congreve has been working on perfecting their range and he's convinced he has a reliable weapon that can be quickly launched on land *and* on sea."

"What's the range?" Adam asked.

"He's claiming up to two thousand yards."

Nate offered a low whistle. "And raining down fire on ships and coastal villages – all from the safety of a ship out at sea."

"Well, God help us if Napoleon has perfected them before we have."

What had begun as an amusing exercise, a parlor game on a rainy afternoon, became serious.

"We're nearly at the end," said Olivia. "Deipneus was a demi-god associated with breadmaking. The letter says he stills plies his trade."

"Well, that's the easiest one of the lot," Lady Abigail announced. "That's Gustav, the baker at Fort St. Pierre who helped Nate escape."

"Do you think he knows more than he's been able to tell us about what Felix had uncovered?" Susannah asked.

"We can always inquire."

"Is there anything else, Olivia?"

She shook her head. "Just that Felix knew he was dying when he dictated his message to Nate; Thanatos is the Greek god of death."

"Excellent work," said Sir Daniel. "But I don't think we should overthink this too much. We should believe Felix wanted his words to have the plainest meaning.

"If we run with that, the invasion, or at least some spearhead, will come from Ireland. There is a connection between the Emmet family and Napoleon. The threat will come from the east. Perhaps the king who ought to be aware of betrayal is our own king, and there are some of his own men who cannot be trusted."

At last, there was silence. The only sounds to be heard were of the rain against the windows, the crackling fire in the dining room and noises from the kitchen.

"Thomas Emmet cannot be too pleased Napoleon didn't support his brother with promised troops," said Susannah softly.

Adam nodded thoughtfully. "We weren't at war with France then… but I wonder, now that things have changed?"

"It's a pity we don't have a man on the inside, someone who knows some of the Irish rebels," added Nate.

"It might be arranged."

All eyes were on Sir Daniel Ridgeway. He leaned back in his chair and looked up at the ceiling, clearly thinking out loud.

"There's a young major-general by the name of Arthur Wellesley who has not long taken his seat in Parliament," he said. "Wellesley just happens to come from an aristocratic Irish family who are loyal to England. Through him, we could arrange to have someone placed in the Bermingham Tower in Dublin Castle where the remaining ringleaders of the 1803 uprising are being held."

"Who are you thinking of sending, my dear?" Lady Abigail asked.

"I'll go." Sir Daniel brought his attention back to the table. "It's not fair to separate our two pairs of newlyweds."

Adam gave Nate a deliberate look which he returned.

"Do we trust the old man on his own?" said Nate.

"No, I don't think we do. All three of us will go."

Now it was Sir Daniel's turn to exchange a look with his wife.

"It will mean being away from home for at least three months," he warned. "Gentlemen, I do not ask this of you. You have a duty even higher than that to your king and that is to the women you love."

Chapter Ten

March 1806
Stannum House

ALLIE HID AN indelicate yawn behind her napkin before smiling
benignly at Miss Lydia Stonely's inane chatter. She thought
about how nice it would be to take Nephel on a run along the beach
instead being stuck indoors.

But she'd promised Phillip she would make more of an effort to be
sociable in the hopes of attracting fresh interest and new investors in
Wheal Gunnis. However, the truth of the matter was their genteel
poverty had made her as much of a recluse as David Manston.

She listened to cutting gossip about other girls in the district in
silence, admiring in her hand the scalloped form of the Worcester
teacup with its band of cobalt blue and decorated with gilt foliage.
Allie had actually forgotten they had such finery in the house, so used
had she and Phillip become to dining with Mrs. McArthur and Harry
Watt in the kitchen, and using the servants' plain earthenware settings.

Being so long out of the active society, Allie could contribute nothing to this conversation, even if she had a mind to gossip – which she
didn't. No doubt, the trio attending this little gathering – Lydia, of
course, Julian's Aunt Harriet Erskin, and her daughter, Margaret
Erskin – would gossip about *her* the minute she was out of the room.

Oh, the things she did for her brother... and for Julian, too, the
truth be told. She liked him. Not in the same way she felt for David –

more in the same way she cared Phillip. Julian treated her in the same teasingly affectionate way. But there was no frisson of danger or desire.

But David had become a stranger to her. Christmas had passed and since January, she had seen him less than a handful of times. In each case, he was there to see Phillip.

But today was the day for the test blast at Wheal Gunnis that would prove whether there was enough copper to reopen the mine.

Two hours ago, there had been a mild tremor that did little more than rattle a teacup. Allie suspected her guests hadn't even been aware of it.

Yet every tick of the clock was another moment she didn't know whether the blast would bear fruit. It left her with nothing to do except entertain these ladies.

Honestly, she had no idea why these women accompanied Julian to Stannum today. She resisted the temptation to look out of the window, not that she could see the mine from it anyway. How she would rather be up at Wheal Gunnis instead of being stuck here with these wittering ninnies.

Now, Julian's aunt had taken command of the conversation. Harriet Erskin was one of those women who ruled her household; no doubt her husband bent to her dictates if he knew what was good for him.

Allie shuddered. Surely not all marriages were like that? What happened to David's marriage? Was his wife a scold? She couldn't imagine David in love with someone like *that*.

And why should the fact he was married, but separated from his wife bar him from polite company? Why, in London, any number of members of the *ton* had abandoned their vows and lived separate lives from their spouses.

Since gossip was the currency of this particular society, perhaps she should drop in her two penn'ethworth.

"Do you know of a Claire?" she asked the gathering of women. "One who is separated from her husband?"

She hated the question as soon as it was out of her mouth. It only served to prove she was no better than the rest of the silly gossiping hens. But it did seem it was a useful way of finding out information.

Lydia leaned forward. "Oooh, that *is* an intriguing little tidbit!"

"Claire?" said Mrs. Erskin. "Surely you can't mean Claire Owen-Jones; she and her husband are devoted to one another. Absolutely inseparable since they married eight years ago."

Allie took mental notes of the name but made sure she looked thoughtful. "No, I'm pretty sure her surname started with the letter 'M'."

In truth, she had no idea whether Claire still carried David's name.

She watched the three women sit back and look thoughtful for a moment.

"The only woman I know who is estranged from her husband is Lady Georgina Kennedy. She barred her husband from entering the house after she caught him with his latest mistress in the marital bed. At least she was far more discreet with her own affairs," offered Lydia.

"Are you sure you're not getting confused with Marchioness Claudia Penghillis?" Margaret asked. "Although she didn't so much separate from her husband as he put her away in one of those awful asylums."

The young woman leaned forward in a conspiratorial whisper.

"I heard the footman caught her having a conversation with the wrens in the garden; she told him she'd trained them to fly to Westminster and advise the Prime Minister on how to conduct the war."

Allie forced down a snigger at the poor unfortunate soul and managed to conjure up a grave expression.

"Oh, dear," she answered.

The three other women went off on a tangent, discussing another female who appeared to be in this season's crop of eligible young misses. Very little of the commentary was kind, but as Allie didn't know these people and cared for the society even less, she sat and feigned interest.

What an utter bore. She'd gladly wield a hammer on the stones up at the mine herself if she was brought good news.

The minute hand on the mantel clock seemed to slow to a stop. She wondered whether there was some polite way to excuse herself, a headache perhaps, when she saw three men on horseback gallop past on the way to the stables.

All gossip stopped there. Lydia preened herself in anticipation of Julian's arrival. She hid a smile. Lydia had been making calf eyes at him for months now. The poor man hadn't failed to notice, but was doing his level best not to offer any encouragement.

Alas, it would not be enough for a determined young woman – and she should know.

Allie looked at the girl with her blonde hair, clear fair skin, and good figure. Lydia Stonely was not unattractive in her physical appearance, but it would be a hard life indeed for a man to be wed to a woman whose only serious discourse centered on what was the current mode.

And the current mode was not going to be three grubby miners.

The men were going to be absolutely blackened – hardly ready to take tea and cake with the ladies in the drawing room.

Allie fixed a smile on her face and excused herself. As soon as the door into the hall closed, she ran to the back of the house and to the kitchen just in time to see three filthy males tumble through the door.

Phillip slammed down a football sized rock onto Mrs. McArthur's kitchen table.

"Feast your eyes on that beauty."

Allie stepped closer. It was one of the most unusual specimens she had ever seen. Through the dirt, she could see parts of it were a lustrous blue-green with gold-like flecks through it. It wasn't like tin ore which looked almost silver.

"Copper?" she asked hopefully.

"Better than that," answered Julian. "It's a type of ore *especially* rich in copper. If it is what I believe it is, well... this is about the purest I have ever seen."

"And there's *loads* of it," said Phillip.

Her eyes fell to David and her heart tumbled at the sight of him. He, too, looked elated. Even dirty and disheveled, the grin on his face made him look younger, more carefree. Their eyes met and held.

Allie lifted her chin.

"I've heard what these two have said, but I won't believe a word of it until I've heard it from your lips as well," she said.

David gave her a level look, but his blue eyes sparkled like gems in his dirty face. He paused dramatically, letting the seconds tick away.

Allie held her breath. How dare he be so handsome? How dare he tease her like this?

"Congratulations," he said. "With further investment, Wheal Gunnis is back in business."

Tingles ran through her. Allie brought her hands to her mouth to break off a sob that threatened to spill over. Her eyes never left David's and his expression softened. For a moment she thought she saw a yearning in his face.

Or perhaps she was just seeing what she wanted in those eyes, instead of the reality of it.

Mrs. McArthur bustled into the kitchen.

"Och! What ye be doing to my kitchen, ye grubby little urchins! Shoo! Get back out to the stables and wash yerselves there before coming back into my kitchen!"

Phillip reached out for the ore on the table. Allie slapped his hand and took the rock for herself.

"After spending the past few hours with Julian's relations, I've earned the chance to bask in this moment, too. I shall wash it –"

The rock was taken from *her* hands.

"*I* will wash it," the housekeeper announced. Allie shot her a smile.

"– and have it on the table before me to look at whenever their conversation bores me. My goodness, Julian, your Miss Lydia…"

The man's face sobered.

"She's not *my Miss Lydia* anything. *I* don't wish to speak ill of any female but…" Here, his eyes pleaded with her. "Can I please ask the greatest of favors?"

Allie hid a smile, but Phillip and David were not so sensitive to Julian's discomfiture – they grinned.

Imps.

Julian took a deep breath. "Would you pretend to receive me favorably… feign an attachment with me? I know it is cowardly of me to not speak directly to Lydia and her mother, but… and I think I speak for all of the males here when I tell you that it is sometimes hard for us to speak our minds and express our wishes when we know the subject will disappoint or otherwise injure a lady's feelings."

Allie couldn't resist teasing. "And men have no such compunction to express themselves plainly to other men? Even at the risk of injuring *their* feelings?"

"Men will sort themselves out with a punch or two," said Phillip. "We'd never do that to women, so we rely on the fairer sex to have mercy on us."

Allie glanced to David who had yet to make a comment. Those blue eyes continued to sparkle so she paid attention to his mouth and the sardonic curl of his lip. And still he said nothing. Would he be jealous? The vain part of her hoped so.

She gifted Julian with her most fulsome smile. "Well, then… a lady to rescue the fair knight from a ferocious dragon? I can hardly refuse, can I?"

Julian visibly breathed out in relief.

"You're a good sport, Allie."

"Well, now that ye've made yer schemes, out of my kitchen with ye," said Mrs. McArthur, sluicing the rock in the sink with water from a bucket. "I've enough to do without ye cluttering the place."

The three men left the kitchen with the same enthusiastic energy with which they entered.

Mrs. McArthur toweled the rock and handed it to Allie. "I wouldn't think ye're a grown woman showing off that thing like a gel in a schoolroom."

"Ah, but this is not an ordinary rock," she said. "This is the rock that will repair Stannum's fortunes!"

Chapter Eleven

March 1806
Bermingham Tower
Dublin Castle
Ireland

"HOW DO YOU fare?"

Adam worked to keep the concern from his voice.

The man seated on the scarred and battered chair beside him was no longer Sir Daniel Ridgeway, English peer. He was Danny Fitzgerald of Roscommon, arrested on a charge of criminal conspiracy.

"Well enough," said Ridgeway, keeping his voice low to prevent the guard outside the cell from overhearing. "It's taken a while to gain their confidence but Mackenroth seems to accept my bona fides."

Ridgeway, normally so immaculately groomed, looked worn and haggard. His reddish hair had grown shaggy. Three-day-old darkened whiskers studded with white made the lines on his face look even more pronounced. His clothing was faded and stained.

Adam's own guise was no less outlandish. He wore the black cassock of a Catholic priest, present to hear the confession of the political prisoners. A light bandage over his right hand disguised his crossed anchors tattoo.

The two men sat knee to knee, a large Bible open in front of them even though it was near to impossible to read in the dim light that filtered through a tall, narrow aperture high up on the wall.

"Mackenroth accepts that I know you and that you are willing to help us," Ridgeway continued, "but he wants to talk to you himself before he trusts you with making contact with anyone from the outside."

"Any message for Bassett or Lady Abigail?" Adam asked.

He felt a tap on his knee and shifted the book in his hand and accepted a sealed letter from Daniel. He slid it across the leather and slipped it in the pages in the back.

With that accomplished, Sir Daniel's expression seemed to lighten.

"How does Bassett like his new headquarters on the *Sprite*?"

"Nate threatens to throw the man overboard every second day, but Bassett is complaining less and is only seasick once per voyage."

"I want Bassett to make a copy of everything Mackenroth gives you before you pass it on."

Outside, they heard the sound of a door being opened and shut.

Adam closed the Bible and held some rosary beads in his hand. To anyone looking in, they would see a priest and a penitent.

He spoke in a voice loud enough now to be overheard.

"God the Father of mercies, through the death and resurrection of His Son, has reconciled the world to Himself and sent the Holy Spirit among us for the forgiveness of sins. Through the ministry of the Church, may God give you pardon and peace. I absolve you from your sins, in the name of the Father, and of the Son and of the Holy Spirit."

"Amen," Daniel responded.

Adam rose to his feet, catching a glance at the door. The hatch was open and a pair of eyes peered through.

"God has forgiven your sins, go in peace."

Daniel rose also. "Thanks be to God."

Walking with more confidence than he felt, Adam approached the door which opened before he got to the other side of the room.

"I would like to see the other prisoner now please, my son."

He didn't know how thick he should be laying on this priestly performance but he figured he ought to keep it simple. The guard looked at him and frowned.

"Where's yer pyx?"

Pikes?

"Ye know, the little box thing for Communion?"

Adam forced a serene expression on his face, although his heart was pounding. "I prefer to hear confession first, so our sinners can prepare their hearts," he answered. "I will return in a couple of days for Communion."

Which he had no intention of doing. The part he played seemed blasphemous enough without compounding it further.

But the answer seemed enough to satisfy the guard who led the way down a narrow passage at the top of the tower that led to another cell.

The man in this cell was closer to his age than Ridgeway's. Tension was thick in the room. The man seemed to radiate with it.

"Time to confess yer sins, Mackenroth," the guard mocked.

Mackenroth gave a gap-toothed sneer at the man and presented Adam a hard, knowing stare before looking beyond him to the guard who still remained inside the door. In a thick Irish burr, he began.

"Bless me, Father, for I have sinned, it's been three months since my last confession."

The guard closed the door behind them. Adam approached and indicated the man to sit on the bed while he pulled across a chair.

Mackenroth's voice became a low grumble. "I need someone to get a message out for me. Are ye the man to do it?"

"You got the letters from your family, didn't you? And fresh clothes?"

"It's always been easier to get things into a prison than out. Haven't ye ever noticed the doors only open one way in this place?"

Adam dropped his beatific façade. "You either trust me and Danny or you don't. Either way, it's all the same to me."

The change in his demeanor served its purpose. Mackenroth seemed to be more at ease.

"One more test before I willingly put my neck in the noose."

"What is it?"

"Go to Duignan's Inn and tell them ye've got a message from John for Collette."

"Then what?"

"Then ye wait. They'll check ye out for me. If they like what they see, they'll have a message for ye to give to me."

"And if they don't?"

"Then no one will worry about ever seeing ye again."

Adam straightened slightly in his seat. That was very unequivocal…

"Anything else?"

Mackenroth bowed his head in an act of piety for the benefit of the guard who, no doubt, still watched. But Adam saw the man's grin.

"I'll let ye know… *if* I ever see ye again."

Adam rose to his feet, refusing to be unsettled by the man, although he knew well he ought to be cautious. He ended the interview by giving a benediction just as the guard opened the cell door.

"Have courage, my son," he added, flashing a sarcastic grin that only Mackenroth would see. After all, *he* was the one who was free to leave.

FOUR DAYS LATER, Adam walked into Duignan's Inn. He scanned across the room. It was about half-full – decent numbers for noon. He recognized two men at one of the tables. Although they appeared to be engrossed in a game of dominoes, he knew they were aware of his presence.

Nate and Bassett made no acknowledgement. Good. That was the prearranged signal that nothing was amiss.

Adam ordered a pint at the bar and returned with it to a vacant table that gave Nate a clear view of anyone who took the seat opposite. Instead of the golden amber hue of his preferred ale, this was darker and reddish in color.

He took his first swig and held it in his mouth a moment to identify the flavors. It was slightly sweeter and nuttier in taste. All-in-all, if nothing else came from this meeting today, it will have been worth it for the beer alone.

Several people came in and out of the pub without paying him the least bit of interest.

How long was he supposed to stay here?

When he'd given Mackenroth's message to the landlord, he was told to return on this day at this hour and nothing more.

One pint became two as the hours passed and, damn, if his bladder wasn't near full. There was nothing to be done about it. He rose from his chair and passed Nate and Bassett on his way to the privy out the back.

He had no choice but to have his back to the yard, unbutton his breeches, and aim at the hole in the ground.

There were few times in a man's life when he was completely vulnerable, and this was always one.

Adam listened intently to the sounds about him, hoping he wouldn't be caught short, so to speak. When booted foot falls came up behind him, he wished to the Heavens above that his bladder would empty quicker.

He finished his business and buttoned himself up, sensing that the owner of the footsteps lingered somewhere near, waiting.

"Ye've seen Mackenroth."

The voice was a whisper from the deep shadows.

"Do you always come up behind a man when he's taking a piss?"

"I couldn't risk speaking to ye in the inn. Ye never know who's an informer."

"What makes you think I am not?"

"Because Mackenroth gave ye the words to say."

"I'd prefer to see who I'm talking to."

There was silence for a moment. Adam stepped forward. Had the man gone?

"Follow me."

The hunched figure moved quickly from the shadows and headed behind the privy to a small gate that led out into the back alley.

Adam glanced back at the inn. If he didn't return soon, Nate and Bassett would come looking for him, but there was no choice but to follow the man.

THE DOOR LEADING into the warehouse closed behind him, momentarily plunging him into darkness. He blinked rapidly to adjust the gloom.

"Ye're Adam Hardacre, aren't ye?"

The disembodied voice echoed in the space, making it difficult to pinpoint where it was coming from. He was growing impatient, not to mention nervous. If Nate and Bassett had followed him, now would be a good time for them to intervene.

"Look I've followed you halfway around this bleeding city," he called out, even as he crouched down to cautiously remove a knife from his boot. "Now, are you going to come out and speak to me or am I going to have to tell Mackenroth that you've gone soft in the head?"

Adam heard the first of half a dozen foot falls. In a shaft of light from the high transom windows stood the silhouette of a lone man, wiry to the point of being described as skinny. Adam cupped the blade of the knife in the palm of his hand so it appeared he was unarmed.

"Truly, I'm sorry for leading ye all this way. This warehouse is the only place I could think of that we could speak in private."

The man sounded young, in his early twenties. Adam remained where he was but watched him walk to a bale of wool and drop himself down on it.

"He's had yer every move watched since France," the man said.

"Who?"

Adam was afraid that he already knew the answer.

"Harold Bickmore."

The name of his former friend, now his sworn enemy, should have come as more of a shock than it did. Still, he approached the stranger cautiously – he knew both Adam's name *and* he knew Bickmore.

"All right then. My name is O'Brien – and I tell ye now I'm a loyal Irishman who wants to see his homeland free of foreign rule."

"I admire your sentiment," Adam said softly. "I'm here for nearly the same reason – to prevent France from ruling England. That's *all* I'm here for."

"Aye… it be one thing to fight for yer own sovereignty, it's something else to bend the knee to another just to be rid of an enemy."

Now satisfied there was no one here but the two of them, Adam sat on another wool bale nearby. He saw little of the features of the man before him. His head was bowed, giving a view only of his black hair and his workman's clothes.

"How did you identify me?" Adam asked.

"I was an able seaman in the Royal Navy until last year. Everyone was talking about ye and the way ye stood up to the Admiralty. It's a shit shame how they treat a working man and deny him what's rightful, just because he weren't born with a silver spoon in his mouth. Anyway, just over a year ago, Harold Bickmore came here with letters from Thomas Emmet and a plan approved by old Boney himself."

"An invasion plan?"

O'Brien raised his head – sharp cheekbones on either side of a sharp nose, a wide expanse of forehead, and a thin, pointed chin.

"A plan, as far as I can reckon, would not help Ireland a jot.

Mackenroth and the others can't see the United Irishmen are simply being used by the French."

"What is the plan?"

A shake of the head was O'Brien's response. "I don't rightly know, but there's talk of bringing over three hundred Frenchies to join a hundred of our boys."

"That's barely a complement for a single frigate."

"And do ye see any frigates? Do ye see any ships at all?"

"An invasion force of four hundred *and* no ships. What's the plan? *Fly* them across the Irish Sea?"

O'Brien shrugged. "I have no answers for ye now, but I will in a few months. There's an odd eccentric, Dermot Flannery. The old man's a tinkerer, likes to build things."

"Like rockets?"

O'Brien shrugged. "I suppose so. Rockets, mechanical bits and bobs. Ye give him a plan for something and he'll make it. Mackenroth's ordered me to take Flannery to France for a meeting."

Adam nodded thoughtfully. "Do you know with who?"

The man shrugged. "I can give ye names – Fouché and Blanchard – but they don't mean nothing to me. My job's just to deliver him safely there, then come back here with whatever instructions they give me."

Adam's heart pounded wildly. What he wouldn't give to see those instructions *and* those plans.

"Does Bickmore know the plans?"

"I don't know, but he always looked like he knew more than he was saying."

"What you're offering won't come cheap, I'll wager."

For the first time during this strange meeting, O'Brien showed a flash of emotion. He jumped to his feet and poked a bony finger at Adam.

"Ye think I'm just a fekking turncoat, a traitor against my own people! I won't have it!"

Tempting though it was to match O'Brien's rise in emotion, he forced himself to remain calm. Besides, he still had his knife if things got too out of control. O'Brien closed the small distance between them.

Adam kept his voice as calm as possible. "Then what is it you *do* want?"

"Get me and my girl to America with enough to get us started in New York or Boston."

"I can arrange that."

In truth, he wasn't sure if Sir Daniel Ridgeway's influence extended to keeping such a bargain, but that was *his* problem.

Adam stood, hid the knife up into the lining of his coat, before holding out his right hand. O'Brien stared at the hand a moment before reluctantly taking it.

"What's the message you want to give Mackenroth?"

"Tell him that Iris is looking forward to seeing him again. He'll know what it means."

Iris… Iris represents the rainbow… a messenger of the gods.

He pulled out a pouch from his belt and poured a handful of Irish silver ten-pence tokens into his hand, watching O'Brien's eyes widen. Despite the protestations he was doing this for the love of his country, a man still had to eat.

"Here," said Adam, indicating that he should cup his palm. He did so, and the silver coins spilled into it. "Consider this earnest money for your new life in America."

Chapter Twelve

June 1806

A LLIE LET NEPHEL walk along, keeping pace with the twenty or so men and women from the village.

It was market day at Camelford and it seemed all of Stannum was on the road. Once upon a time, a good number of merchants used to come on their monthly rounds, but the money to be made in the village dried up when the ore dried up. When Wheal Gunnis finally closed, the traders stopped coming.

Now, as inconvenient as it was, the villagers made a day of the journey to Camelford and back.

Today, Allie and Phillip traveled with them. Phillip made himself popular amongst the youngsters, lifting them up onto his horse and cantering ahead for a hundred yards before trotting back to pick up the next child and repeating the process until the party had caught up to them.

"There's going to be a bad storm tonight, Miss Alexandra," said Freda, the wife of Prenpas the blacksmith. "Feel it in my bones, I do."

Allie reined her horse to a stop and dismounted to walk beside the stout woman.

"I'm inclined to agree."

And she did not say so just to be polite. The blue sky above gave lie to what the barometer reading told her before they'd left the house. Moreover, she felt the change in wind direction early this morning, a howling gale that seemed to shake the very stones of Stannum House.

She was a child of Cornwall, not fooled by a day that started out bright and clear. She knew only too well that a storm lurked beyond the horizon.

"Let's hope we have fine weather at least until we get home again."

She looked ahead at Phillip, happy to see him looking so carefree.

It was strange how hope could so much change a man. The idea of Wheal Gunnis back in operation had put a smile on his face. And that, in turn, had put a smile on hers.

How she prayed it wasn't a misplaced hope. That would be worse than having no hope at all.

Had that been David's misfortune?

She fell back from the blacksmith's wife and waited until the last of the villagers had passed her before she drew Nephel close to a tree stump that would allow her to remount.

She rode along with gritted teeth. How often had she promised herself not to think of David? And yet, here she was doing it again, another month on from their last meeting. At least she'd kept her promise of not "just popping by" his cottage.

A girl had to have some pride, after all.

How was it that was harder on her than it obviously was on him? She told herself it was because she missed playing chess with someone who could still best her. The last time Phillip had beaten her in a game was when they were both thirteen.

She also told herself she missed discussing the events of the day with someone who give his opinion frankly and didn't try to patronize her because of her sex.

Julian Winter was returning soon. Now that the weather was warming, they would make a further blast to determine if the small seam would lead to a bigger yield. Surely David would be there for that. His pledge had been enough to get them started, but they would need another ten investors just as generous before they had a hope of reopening the mine.

"Come along, slow poke!" Phillip called back to her.

That was the spur she needed to shake off her brooding.

"We'll see who the slow one is," she called over the cheers of the villagers on foot as she urged Nephel forward into a gallop.

THE RIDE TO Camelford was a pleasant diversion but, in the end, with no errands to run and no spare coin to buy fripperies, Allie set back to Stannum on her own. How nice it was to ride such a distance without heed to anyone else.

She gave the mare her head. Nephel seemed to enjoy the run also, her legs stretched out in a headlong run.

The stone pillars that marked the entrance to Stannum House flashed past and, before Allie knew it, she was riding along the cliff path. Here, she felt the buffeting winds on the exposed headland. If she breathed in deeply, she could taste as well as smell the brine of the sea and the dark earthy promise of the storm.

There! Out to sea, just as Mrs. Prenpas predicted in the morning, large billowing clouds now banked on the horizon. The impending weather gusted across the headland. In a few hours, those pristine white clouds would darken and bring drenching rain onto the coast.

Once more, Allie cursed herself a fool for being attracted to a man who said the only interest he had in her was pity. Well, she hadn't seen any pity when they brought back that large lump of ore. David missed her as much as she missed him. If she had a hundred pounds herself to wager on that fact, she would.

As she approached his cottage, two strange horses tethered outside piqued her curiosity.

Allie frowned. Normally at this time of the afternoon, the chickens would have full run of the yard and David's black stallion would have the entire field in which to roam. She saw neither.

She spurred her horse forward at a trot. As she reached the front door, two men emerged from around the side of the building.

One was a rather good-looking chap with light brown hair who quickly recovered his surprise at her being there. The other – older Allie guessed – was rough-looking, tall and scrawny with a pinched, pockmarked face, and eyebrows that seemed to come together in a permanent frown. A moustache covered his upper lip.

Both looked travel-worn, but their clothes were well made and relatively clean. She slipped her unused crop from the saddle and held on to it firmly.

Her appearance was clearly unexpected. They regarded her a moment before one of them, the good-looking younger of the two, stepped forward.

"Good afternoon, Miss," he said cheerily. "Someone from the village suggested there were cottages to rent in this district."

Allie wheeled her horse around to give herself a chance of a quick escape if needed.

Cottages to rent? Of what interest could this place have for anyone? Even if it were so, why didn't someone from Stannum direct them to the house?

"You are far out of your way, sirs," Allie replied. "And this house *is* occupied."

"This is the third time we've been here in a month," the older man challenged. "Don't look like there's anyone's here."

"*I* am the owner of this cottage," she said.

She spoke the lie with confidence and matched the look of the man, raising her chin defiantly. She waited for him to call her a liar and firmed her grip on the crop for reassurance. He took a step forward but the better-spoken younger one raised his hand to halt the advance.

"Would you consider renting this place out for three months since, as my assistant pointed out, the cottage does seem deserted?" he asked.

"Your assistant?"

The man's expression changed to one of fulsome apology. "Forgive me, Miss. I've been rambling for weeks in these parts with only Bert here for company. I've almost forgotten my manners. I'm Peter Silsbury." He bowed slightly. "I'm a naturalist working on a paper on the nesting habits of the coastal birds of Cornwall. This house would be the most perfect place to base ourselves, considering its proximity to the cliffs and to the hill up to the old mine there."

She looked him over. His clothes looked suitable for walking, and she supposed that any equipment such a man might need would fit in the saddlebags that their horses carried.

"For three months, you said?"

"If we get favorable weather. Otherwise we might need to extend out stay in the area for another couple of months."

The man seemed rather confident of himself, as though he had already won her favor.

"I will need to consult the current tenant," she said, "to see what his plans might be for the future. I shall send word to you. Where are you currently staying?"

She noticed the assistant shift his steely gaze to Silsbury. Silsbury's attention remained on her.

"We're staying at the Red Lion in Camelford, Miss... I do apologize but you do seem to have the advantage of me."

"Miss Gedding."

"Gedding? A relation to the Geddings who own the abandoned mine?"

"You're misinformed, sir. The mine is not abandoned. My brother intends to reopen as soon as we've secured enough investors."

A significant look passed between the two men. She shifted position in the saddle; Nephel walked forward a couple of paces. Allie reined her in. There was something about the men that didn't sit well. She had no evidence for it, only an unsettled feeling down to her bones that these two men were not who they claimed to be.

Perhaps Mrs. Prenpas was right; maybe the impending storm was making her feel out of sorts.

The Silsbury fellow gave her a bow and, belatedly, his "assistant" did also.

"Thank you once again, Miss Gedding. We shall await your reply. Come, Bert. We should be on our way before the weather turns on us."

She backed Nephel away a few paces as the two men approached their horses. They mounted and rode away along the path that would take them to the road to Camelford. She made sure she watched them go and saw this Bert character look back at her just the once before they disappeared behind a hillock.

She leaned forward to stroke Nephel's neck and silently counted to one hundred just in case the men returned. They did not.

At last, she dismounted and tethered her mare to the rail where the other horses had been a moment ago. The riding crop remained in her hand. She was not too proud to admit she was afraid. Afraid and angry by turns. These were *her* lands. She had been riding them on her own for years and never before had she felt fear.

She pushed at David's front door. It was locked. So too was the kitchen door to the side. She peered at the lock. Were there scratches at the escutcheon? It was difficult to tell.

She wandered around the back of the building; the structure exposed to the elements. The *boom* of waves crashing on the rocks below was louder here. Wind whipped her skirts and threatened to pull her hair from its pins. Her curls would be a tangle as it was.

All the windows were intact. Those not shuttered were salt crusted, as though they hadn't been washed for months, not weeks.

She had been leery of the men's claim that the cottage seemed deserted for surely it wasn't. There were a dozen signs of its occupancy, were there not? Then she realized the place *did* feel deserted – and she was alone. The jangling edge of fear, alien to her experience of this place, struck her anew.

Foolishly, she thought of calling David's name, as though the very act of saying it could conjure him up. She circled around to the lean-to that served as a stable for Noir. It was deserted, absent of tack and equipment. All the chickens had gone also.

She cast her eyes about again and approached the low stone wall connected to the house that formed a little walled garden, sheltered from the weather. There were small pots of vegetables and herbs. But the ground was fallow, and the potted plants were brown and dead.

She stood at the wall and looked about, just to reassure herself she wasn't being watched. Then she went to one capstone in particular and eased it out of its place. She searched a small cavity beneath with her fingertips, reaching for the spare key she knew was hidden there.

David had shared the location of it on one occasion years ago when she persuaded him to let her look after his animals while he made a trip to London. Was that where he was? London? If that was so, why did he get rid of his chickens? She would ask if anyone in the village had seen him and acquired the poultry.

There! Now she felt the key, kept in a pocket of waxed cotton to prevent the iron from rusting.

She was mindful of her movements, haunted by the idea of being watched by the two "naturalists" – or some other entity she did not know.

An involuntary shudder went through her, then she laughed. Mrs. McArthur would have her believing in the *piskies* and the ghosts of Wheal Gunnis if she carried on like this.

Still, it did no harm to be cautious of the real and living...

She glanced around before inserting the key into the kitchen door lock. After a bit of work, necessitating her to drop the crop and use both hands, the key turned. The hinges protested with a squeal as she opened the door. Dust motes danced in the shaft of light let in through the door.

"David?" she called. She stopped to listen. There was no sound of a crackling fire in the hearth. No comforting tick of the clock. She stepped into the main room of the cottage. The small clock over the mantel had stopped at twenty-five-past ten on some morning – or perhaps evening… it was covered in a thin layer of dust.

David was a neat and tidy man, perhaps even more house proud than she was. This was the clearest indication yet that he had been gone a long time. But how long? Since the day after they had done the test blast at the mine?

She took a careful look about. No possessions were missing as far as she could tell, so he couldn't have packed up and gone for good. The chess set he was carving was still there, half-completed. His shelf of precious books didn't look disturbed.

The table in the middle of the room caught her eye. There was something about it which was unexpected; something she had never noticed before. The only reason she caught sight of it now was because of the light cast through the open door.

The front edge of the tabletop glinted gold. She approached and ran her finger along the gleaming strip and felt indents at regular intervals. It was a piano hinge.

Something else she had not previously noticed was the raised lip that ran along the top of this edge but was not replicated on the other three edges. It was a most unusual table, indeed.

She stood back momentarily to take it all in. The table was perhaps three feet wide on the long front and two feet deep. It was made of walnut and featured four fluted square column legs. A foliate inlay of beech surrounded three drawer fronts, each being no more than four inches deep. The center one had a lock but the two on either side were not locked and had simple round brass knobs.

She pulled open the drawer on the left. It contained a couple of inkwells and a simply fashioned casket containing an assortment of pens and pencils.

The other drawer was empty.

On each of the short sides of the table were slides that pulled out, one stained with ink, the other with telltale marks of wax.

Still, there was nothing that revealed where David was and how long he had been gone.

The only other room in the cottage that remained unexplored was the bedroom.

She opened the door without hesitation or second thoughts about propriety. The room was dark, the window shuttered. She crossed to it, opened the window and unlatched the shutter to let in some light. She turned back to the room. David's bedroom was a surprise.

She thought it would be as bleak as the rest of the cottage. Instead, dominating the room was a large four-poster bed, one that ought to grace the master bedroom of a fine house. Its blue and gold damask curtains were tied open with gold cord to reveal a neatly made bed, a wool tartan blanket neatly folded at the foot.

Also at the foot, standing on the floor, was a large canvas-clad wooden trunk with the initials D. G. M. upon it.

Her heart tumbled at the sight of it. They were his initials. No matter where David was *now*, he intended to return.

She approached the brass lock and gave it a tug or two to confirm it was locked.

Thunder rumbled in the distance, a warning… or an alarm. What if something had happened to him? What if he'd gone down to the beach and been swept off the rocks? She took a deep breath and pushed the thought from her mind – it didn't explain why his chickens and horse were gone.

She let out a huff of frustration and looked about the room. Apart from a chair and washstand, there were no other pieces of furniture.

There was another long, sustained roll of thunder. She relatched the shutter, closed the window and closed the bedroom door after her, then kicked herself for leaving the kitchen door open while she explored.

The light streaming through it now had taken on a golden-yellow cast.

She glanced at the bookshelves once again. She supposed she could go through the books to see if there was any documentation hidden amongst their pages.

There was another rumble, as though definitely warning her to mind her business this time. As it was, she'd already taken tremendous liberties.

Her eyes were drawn to the table once more, her decision made.

Chapter Thirteen

I F IT *WAS* a drafting table as Allie suspected, then the top would rise from the back at an angle about the hinge.

She felt around, looking for the knob that would release it, and found an iron button on one corner. She pressed and held it with one hand and tugged at the top with the other. It opened effortlessly on toothed iron rods rising from a hollow in the back legs. When she felt it reach its maximum, she released the button and the surface locked in place to sit at a thirty-degree angle.

She looked underneath it around the side. Now there was a disappointment. She had hoped the lid would reveal a secret compartment.

Maybe it still does...

She went to the side and pulled out the slide there, then around to the other. Where they had rested when closed, revealed nothing. Opened, they exposed a two-inch-deep void beneath.

And it was not empty.

Inside were two plain looking, card-bound sketchbooks.

Why on earth would David hide these here?

She pulled them both out and placed them on one of the slides while she drew over a chair to sit at the drafting slope. A breeze through the open door tugged at her skirts. She took a deep breath and could smell the first hint of rain.

She considered closing the door but needed the light it provided. Allie took the first book, rested it on the slope. It sat securely, propped on a raised lip intended for this purpose. She sat down before it and opened the red and green marbled cover.

The first few pages featured sketches of familiar landscapes. She recognized Stannum, the streets of Camelford, the imposing engine house of Wheal Gunnis. These were very good; excellent in fact. Did David do these? Yes. In the corner of each were the neatly scribed initials D. G. M.

She turned over page after page of landscapes and botanical studies in pen and ink as well as watercolors. They were exquisite.

One was of three fishermen on the beach pulling a small rowboat back onto the shore, the figures small against the surge of water pounding on golden sands.

On the next page was a view she knew well: a flat rock partway down the cliffs, popular with lone anglers, but dangerous as it was frequently battered by the sea. The attention to detail was superb. She could see the sliver of white spume as it slithered down the crevasses. The picture was so alive, she felt if she concentrated hard, she would even hear the gulls overhead against the bright blue sky.

How was it that she had known David for all this time and she never knew he was an artist? Why did he not tell her? Why did he hide it away?

She looked at the second book. This had a plain blue cover.

The first page took her by surprise. Unlike the first book of landscapes, these were pen and pencil sketches of naked limbs, detailed works – the long line of a leg here, an extended arm there – almost scientific in their exactness.

The next page featured a full-length nude, a male standing with his back to the artist. At first, Allie thought it might have been a sketch of a Greek statue, but the more she looked, the more she saw the aspects revealed the model as flesh and blood, the muscles and tendons defined beyond that which would be required of a study in marble.

As with any other well-bred young lady, the subject matter ought to make her blush, but it didn't. She found it compelling. Once again, the D.G.M. monogram in the corner suggested that the artist was happy with his work.

She turned another page over. It was a female nude in repose, her arms stretched over her head. The model's back was slightly arched, her mouth open as if mid-sigh. It was beautiful, sensual. Something within Allie recognized the look and what it represented.

Clearly, this depicted a woman well-satisfied by her lover; his touch bringing her to ecstasy.

Allie's throat became dry as something more within her identified with the model on the page. She wanted to experience that sensation for herself. She wanted David to be that man.

Who was this woman in the picture? A little voice whispered to her. *Was she David's lover or simply a model?*

A new thought struck her.

Was this Claire?

She stared at the woman's face – the high angled cheekbones, the suggestion of light-colored hair. Would she recognize her if they ever encountered each other face to face? She feared that she would.

Of course, she told herself, artists were under no obligation to sleep with their muses. Even if David did, this woman could be one of...

No, imagining he had multiple models and multiple lovers instead did not bring any comfort either.

She flipped over the page before her imaginings could give root to jealousy.

On facing pages was another male nude. This one did not have his back to the artist. He was as naked as the day he was born – a David, an Adam, an Adonis, Narcissus with the most perfect of physiques. The face of the model was in shadow but his body was fully exposed to the light for anyone to gaze upon.

Over the page, another female nude regarded her with a coy yet knowing half-smile that suggested she had been privy to the content on previous pages and knew the reaction of the viewer.

Allie traced a finger across the nymph's exposed foot. Her gaze swept across the entirety of the image, taking in how shadows guarded the hidden delights of the flesh.

She couldn't stop herself from turning over yet another page. She paused. Naked lovers embraced. The woman's legs were wrapped around the man's hips which could only mean they were somehow in the act of love. The woman's face, she could see over the man's shoulder, was open-mouthed, her eyes closed in a state of bliss.

The sketch was so realistic and the expression so raw, Allie thought she could hear the ragged breath of the couple in congress, only to realize the sound was her own harsh breathing.

It was too much. She intended to close the book but, fumbling, another page fell open. Good grief! The man's head was now between her thighs!

She swept the page aside and it was almost a relief to find the next spread of leaves blank.

But it wasn't empty.

A folded letter had been tucked between the pages.

The more prudent part of her cautioned that she really ought to close the sketchbook now, replace both books in the drawing table, and pretend she had not seen a thing.

How on earth would she ever face David again, knowing he…

Then the letter slid from the book onto the floor, spilling with it something the size and shape of playing cards. Kneeling, she gathered them up and turned them over only to be confronted by luridly colored lithographs of…

Good God! She had no idea that one could… and *that!*

Oh, my! There were two men with a woman in that image!

She dropped the cards and her eyes fell on the open letter.

Dear Mr. Manston,

Thank you for your most recent artworks. I must say that Mr. Wood and Mr. Sheehan were most impressed.

As you may be aware, we do not offer advances on fine art consignments but we do completely understand your requirement to earn an income.

In addition to being fine art specialists, we are translators and distributors of French literature designed to appeal to particular discerning gentlemen.

Based on the quality of your work, and your sympathetic portrayal of the human form, we believe you might wish to consider entering a contract for the supply of works similar to the ones we enclose.

If you agree, we can come to some mutually beneficial arrangement regarding consignment sales of your fine artwork. Otherwise, with the most profound regret, we will have to pass on representing you.

Yours etc, etc

The letter was dated five years ago.

Allie returned the cards to the letter and replaced it between the blank leaves.

Then, standing before the portfolio, she turned over another page.

Here it seemed like the work of a different hand. Instead of the sensuous and, dare she say, *loving* portrayal of the naked form, the pen strokes were short, sharp, savage reproductions of the cards from the letter. The nib had bitten into the paper, scoring it in anger.

There followed page after page of the most salacious couplings, many of them featuring men and woman bound, some gagged, others looking oddly elated even as their lovers flogged them.

They looked like scenes from a brothel!

After a while, the nudity and the outrageous sexual positions no longer had the power to shock her, neither was she aroused by these cartoonish images. There was something else she noticed – the enervated facial expressions of the figures in the sketches. Despite their open eyes and open mouths, there was no passion, no life or sensuousness – certainly not compared to the earlier compositions.

And, unlike those pieces, these were not signed.

Was this how David earned his living? Was it the reason he hid himself away from society? He was ashamed of his work?

She glanced across to the red and green-covered book that held the beautiful seascapes. Why, a man with such a talent should be well received everywhere! So why wasn't he? Not for the first time, she wondered why a man of such education, giftedness, and refinement was living a hermit's life in an isolated hamlet in Cornwall.

The golden sunlight that spilled through the dirty windows and the open door turned silver and then suddenly darker still as sweeping clouds obliterated the last of the spring afternoon.

She put the portfolio containing the botanical sketches back in the secret compartment of the desk and picked up the other to hide it away, too.

At that moment, a gust of wind filled the room, slamming the kitchen door closed and plunging the cottage into darkness.

Startled, she dropped the blue folio and cursed under her breath. She felt her way to the fireplace in the dim light, carefully searching for a flint and striker with which to light a spill of paper that provided enough illumination to find a candle stub.

The shutters rattled as the wind howled. Thunder grew louder; a sharp crack and the sound seemed to tumble from one horizon to the other.

One candle was enough to illuminate the floor in front of the drafting table. She groaned with dismay. The thin spine of the book was broken, loose pages peeked out from the cardboard cover. When she picked it up, an entire stitched section fell out and the folded leaves scattered.

She gathered them up and set the folio on the angled top of the drafting table. Then she picked up the letter and the cards and searched for the place where they had originally lain.

She turned to the last page to ensure she had not lost anything when her eyes fell onto a sketch more similar in tone to the ones in the beginning of the book than the ones that appeared later.

Had she misordered them?

She flipped back a couple of pages and forward again. No, she hadn't.

In the candlelight, she looked at the sketch.

It was a female nude seated on a dining chair. One long limb touched the floor. The other leg was crossed over it at the thigh, the foot pointing down in almost a dancer's pose, a match for her elegant posture.

The crossed arms covered the breasts, and the act itself seemed more alluring, more sensuous than the open display of flesh on the preceding pages.

Unlike those illustrations, there was animation in this model's expression. David had caught a light in her eyes, character in the slight upturn of her mouth, and then there was the wild, untamed mass of dark curly hair that spilled down her back and highlighted the pale skin of her shoulders.

This was by far the finest work she'd seen. She felt like she knew this woman, that she was as flesh and blood real as she herself was.

A flash of lightning illuminated the room brightly for a moment, drawing her attention to a notation she hadn't noticed. In truth, she thought it was simply David's signature. She drew the candle close.

Indeed, there were the initials D.G.M. but beside them another word.

Alexandra

The flame flickered as her hand shook.

She looked at the illustration again, particularly the face.

Slowly, belatedly, she recognized it as her own.

Chapter Fourteen

Adam Hardacre felt his mood lighten once they crossed the bar and entered the calmer waters of the River Pengellan. He already anticipated his wife in his arms. He glanced at Nate at the helm of the ketch, masterfully bringing the *Sprite* back home and idly wondered what his Susannah would make of the beard he'd started sporting.

He'd give it two days before his friend was clean-shaven once more.

For the two of them, the time away from their wives had been relatively short, a week or two at a time. For Sir Daniel Ridgeway, the homecoming was months in the making.

The man had looked exhausted when he was finally "released" from prison. As far as Mackenroth was concerned, "Danny Fitzgerald" had been taken from his cell and executed as a traitor to the crown.

Indeed, Ridgeway had looked like a condemned man by then, disheveled and wan, so it was understandable he spent the day and a half voyage home asleep in the cabin below.

At least Adam presumed the man slept.

Bassett, for all of his wicked ripostes, was a terrible sailor. He, too, spent most of his time on this journey below deck, banished there by Adam after Nate had threatened to toss the little man overboard following one complaint too many.

Up the quiet tributary, the three-story stone inn sat like a sentinel in the fields. Home, at least, for the present.

Movement flashed across the field. It was Susannah's dog, Prince. Following up behind was the slower lumbering figure of Clem Pascoe, local ironmonger, and husband to Peggy, Susannah's business partner.

Overhead, Nate released the line that dropped the sail. Adam furled it, then tossed the anchor and secured the lines as was his custom on their return to The Queen's Head.

"Hey-ho! 'Tis a fine sight to see!" Clem called from shore. "Welcome back!"

Prince showed no such restraint. The hound, part pointer, Adam seemed to recall, bounded across the jetty and launched himself onto the boat.

The dog paused before Adam a moment, wagging its tail in acknowledgement before jumping up around Nate's feet with canine enthusiasm.

"How's everything here, Clem?" Nate called.

"Right as rain, don't you be worryin' about any of that. My Peg's got a feast prepared tonight that will put them big fancy London houses to shame."

Ridgeway and Bassett emerged on deck. The rest seemed to have done the aristocrat a world of good. Now clean-shaven, he looked ten years younger than the man who had been held prisoner in Bermingham Tower.

The same could not be said for Bassett, who looked gray and somewhat feverish. A few thin strands of his black hair were plastered to his forehead.

Adam found it in himself to feel just a measure of sympathy for their forger and quartermaster – a recreator of documents and *sourcer* of equipage, as he would have it – but only a little bit. The man might be small in stature but he had a sharp tongue. He and Nate had been subjects of his acerbic remarks too often to underestimate the man's fortitude.

"Hallelujah, give thanks to the good Lord above, we're saved," sighed Bassett who more or less stumbled from the boat to the jetty that led to the boathouse. "Dry land at last."

He glanced back, speaking to no one in particular. "Be sure to get my satchel and bring it inside."

Adam, Nate, and Ridgeway glanced at one another before Sir Daniel shrugged and went below decks and returned with a leather holdall.

"Gentlemen," he said after a long sigh. "I'm looking forward to a drink, a proper bath, and spending some time with my wife. I don't want to see your ugly mugs for at least two days."

THREE DAYS LATER The King's Rogues came together over beers and Peggy's Burgundy pie.

"Whatever is being planned, Mackenroth is adamant it will be launched from the Saltee Islands off the Wexford coast," said Sir Daniel.

"It still doesn't answer the question of '*what*'," said Nate. "It can't be an invasion by sea, not after Trafalgar."

There was a moment's silence before Ridgeway proposed a toast to the memory of Admiral Horatio Nelson.

"If we're agreed that Napoleon no longer has the resources to launch a naval invasion directly on England, then it has to be something else," Ridgeway speculated. "Less direct but equally crippling to the war effort."

"I think we're looking at all of this wrong," said Adam "At the risk of sounding obsessed, understanding Bickmore *is* the key. The man's clever. He hasn't wagered his life on battles and armies he has no control over. Everything he does has been strategic and effective."

"And whatever this scheme is, it's important enough to involve

Napoleon's inner circle," Nate added.

Olivia had listened, silent up until now. "What do we know of him that goes to the man's character? If we don't know what he has planned, we might learn what motivates him."

"Bickmore didn't turn traitor in an instant," said Nate. "It's perfectly bloody clear he was a bad apple for quite some time. You knew him best, Adam. What do you think? Can you recall anything that might give a clue as to what's planned?"

A conversation back in France came to mind. Adam had turned it over in his head many times before with no satisfactory conclusion.

"Do you remember a shore leave two years ago? We stayed at a tavern in Corsica and we caroused with one of the local men."

"We were dicing as I recall."

"You won a particular bet."

"Did I?"

"I'm sure with a proper incentive, I'm sure I could make you remember."

And that was the problem. Adam *couldn't* remember, no matter how hard he tried, nor what he did to try to help him to remember. Worse was the notion that Harold's words meant nothing at all and only served the purpose of making him doubt his own resolve.

He pushed his plate aside; talk of Bickmore always ruined his appetite. Beneath the table, he felt Olivia lay a hand on his knee, grounding him.

"Despite his privileged background, the man's a Jacobin," he said. "A zealot with as much righteousness as any Methodist."

Lady Abigail approached. Ridgeway made room for her to join them at the table. "If that's the case, he cannot be stopped by reason."

"He feeds on discontent," Adam added.

Ridgeway nodded. "Sadly, there is a lot of discontent to feed upon. War raises prices and causes scarcity. People can only feast on their patriotism for so long. The Poor Laws need a damned good overhaul."

Nate nodded. "Remember the Revolt of the Housewives ten years ago? Women forced through desperation to riot to get food for their families. It makes me appreciate the good fortune we have here at St. Sennen; we're pretty much self-sufficient."

"Other places aren't so lucky," said Ridgeway. "Especially those built around the mines. Those which have not been worked out have become too unprofitable to work."

The conversation and the meal came to an end. Nate excused himself from the table to join Susannah, who was serving customers. Ridgeway and Abigail chose a place by an open window where they opened a game of chess.

Olivia remained at her husband's side and put her hand in his. She gave it a squeeze.

"You cannot hold yourself responsible for this man," she said.

"I should have seen through him."

The woman before him shook her head, gifting him with a small smile.

"If he could fool you for so long, then his powers to deceive were well honed from the beginning."

Adam accepted that she was right. He raised her hand to his lips and gave a lingering kiss to each knuckle.

"Perhaps we're looking at this all wrong," he said. "Perhaps there isn't a large invasion to fear. What if Bickmore's job was simply to stoke the fires of discontent within Britain's own borders? If Napoleon can arrange for riots to foment in England, it would weaken us considerably. A weakened England would mean that there was no one to stop his march through Europe."

Olivia nodded thoughtfully, clearly to encourage him. "So is the plan to arm rebels?"

Would an Englishman willingly use rockets against his own people?
Rockets could be used to lay siege.

That Napoleon had managed to get his hands on and perfect the Indian rockets as Congreve had done was simply speculation.

Adam regarded his wife, grateful that she stood alongside him, a North Star, a constant that no matter how far he went, she was there to guide his way home.

"We won't know anything more until O'Brien returns from Brussels," he said.

"It's a pity we can do nothing until then."

Once more, he kissed her hand, a promise of intimacy to come as soon as they were alone. "I'm sure there is something we can do to occupy our time."

Adam was rewarded with a becoming blush from his wife's cheeks.

LADY ABIGAIL GLANCED down at the letter in her hand and approached the threshold of their bedroom. She watched her husband pore over his correspondence through his newly acquired silver-rimmed spectacles.

"I think we should take a drive in the country."

Sir Daniel slowly raised his head from the correspondence. He had not mistaken her tone of voice and, after many years together, it left him understandably cautious.

"For a pleasure jaunt, or did you have something else in mind?" he inquired. Ridgeway's face might look stern, but there was a tic of a muscle by his mouth that suggested otherwise.

"There's no reason why it can't be both."

He took off his glasses and laid them on the desk. Now she had his full attention.

"We know Bickmore may have been sighted at Camelford, but he's not been seen since," she said. "I would like to take matters in our own hands and look at some of the places where he may have gone to ground."

"I take it you have somewhere specific in mind?"

"Stannum. It's about ten, fifteen miles away from Camelford, less than half a day's travel from here. It's a small village on the coast with a disused mine."

Abigail waited for her husband to consider what she'd told him.

"And you think it won't arouse suspicions if we just wander in unannounced?"

"Not unannounced." Abigail held up the travel-stained letter from Alexandra Gedding. "Invited."

She entered the room and sat on a chair opposite, smoothing her skirts, knowing the delay in giving a fuller explanation would pique her husband.

"And?" he drawled. Abigail bestowed him a full smile.

"My goddaughter, Alexandra, wrote to me more than six months ago. She lives in Stannum with her twin brother as I recall, although it's been more than twenty years since I've seen them, but she was obviously enough up to date to write to me in Bath under my maiden name. Apparently, she had spent 'many an entertaining hour being informed of my exploits'."

Now it was Daniel's turn to grin broadly. "*All* of them?"

"Only the most scandalous ones, I expect," she replied airily.

"And what's her reason for writing to you now, after so long?"

"I imagine she wants to know if half of them are true before she falls into her dear godmother's footsteps."

"I suppose we shouldn't disappoint her." Then Daniel's face grew serious. "And it certainly wouldn't do any harm to look about the area."

Chapter Fifteen

ALLIE TURNED HER face up toward the sun and closed her eyes. She caught, for a moment, the glint of sun on a pane of glass on David's cottage.

Last night, she had the most disturbing dream. David had been about to kiss her when the two men she had seen lurking about the cottage yesterday peered through the windows and started hammering on the windows and doors, demanding entrance. Then somehow, she knew David was dead, feeling the dread terror of it down to her bones. She was alone in the cottage and no matter which door she tried, all opened to the edge of the cliff and storm-washed rocks below.

The heat of the sun reminded her that it had all been a dream. Allie sighed and urged Nephel back along the sand toward the village. Catching sight of Phillip on his horse ahead, she encouraged more pace from her mount.

The more she thought about the two men she caught lurking about yesterday, the more concerned she became.

Surely, Phillip must know where David was?

But she had given her word that she wouldn't visit David's cottage, so if she told him about the two strangers, then he would know she had broken her promise.

Allie wrinkled her nose, still pondering how she might broach the subject of David's absence when her brother called out.

"Race you back home!"

Phillip urged his horse into a gallop before the words were out of his mouth.

"That's not fair," Allie called, but Nephel didn't need much encouragement to follow Phillip's dapple-gray stallion.

They raced across the hard-packed sand on the beach, more than a mile of glorious coast on a fine summer's day. Last night's rainstorm washed everything, making it seem fresh and new. Children were crabbing around the rocks by the cliffs, their excited young voices competing with the sounds of gulls who were doing some fishing of their own.

They cantered in the softer sand across the dunes until they reached the path that took them into the village.

Allie reined in her own competitive spirit and let Phillip lead, pushing thoughts of David and the strangers from her mind.

In the distance, like a lighthouse in need of whitewash, was Wheal Gunnis. Getting investors to fund the reopening of the mine was a slow process. Three months and not even a tenth had been subscribed, although Phillip and Julian worked so hard.

Yet it was a step in the right direction. *Soon.* Soon the mine would reopen, bringing prosperity back to Stannum. On days where they needed encouraging, Julian was there.

The past three months had marked the end of the longest winter she had ever known, one that stretched out years. Spring brought with it the promise of better times to come for all of them. They had re-entered Cornish society again and, rather than use their still meager funds to replenish her wardrobe, Allie had spent much of her free time fashioning the gowns she had into something a bit more *au courant*.

She rather enjoyed having Julian as a counterfeit beau. It proved to be a felicitous arrangement. Phillip could hope matchmaking for his sister was bearing fruit, Julian could gently disentangle himself from any designs Lydia and her mother may have on him, and any wolves with lascivious intent were held at bay while Julian squired her about.

He had become a good friend and she enjoyed his company. In doing so, she managed to go for days at a time without thinking about David.

Until yesterday.

She fought the urge, once again, to look across the headland at his cottage.

Her mind's eye vividly recalled those erotic caricatures she'd found there. They were darker, more sinful than those she'd unwittingly found in her uncle's books on classic art years ago, but they did not consume her thoughts or her dreams as much as the more elegant pen and ink "life" sketches by David. They were what she had seen when she closed her eyes to sleep last night. They seemed to bring to life the emotion and the raw sensuality of the act of love rather than the mechanics of it.

Yet memories of those sensuous images, too, might have faded in time if not for the final page where David had given *her* face and *her* name to *his* fantasy.

It had triggered a physical reaction in her, a yearning for a completion, a *desiring* for him. Mind you, such thoughts were not aided by the motion of the horse she sat on, she thought ruefully.

And where was David?

Her concern for his mysterious absence was mixed with dread of his return. She thought she'd tidied up sufficiently; she'd put the key back in its hiding place in the wall. And she hoped fervently that when he discovered the blue book hidden in his drafting table was damaged, he might imagine it had already been like that…

Her brother's horse slowed on the road up the hill to the house. She shook her head and concentrated on the race.

Ha! Phillip was overconfident of his victory!

She urged Nephel to find a spurt of speed and galloped past the horse and rider to round the corner into the drive to Stannum House. But it seemed Phillip would not allow himself to be bested.

Yah!

Lightning's hoofbeats grew louder; Nephel's ears twitched in response. Allie leaned forward. "You're not going to let him beat us, are you?"

Nephel nodded once and found even more speed down the drive and toward the stable block. But as soon as they rounded the corner of the house, Allie reined in her mare abruptly. Phillip, who had rapidly closed the distance, slowed his mount when he saw what she saw – a large, elegant, black coach.

Allie glanced to Phillip and saw the same questioning expression on his face.

"I don't know anyone wealthy enough to have a carriage, do you?"

"I knew the debt collector was doing brisk business, but that's a bit rich, even for his tastes," Phillip joked.

There was no sign of the horses that would pull such a fine vehicle. Harry Watt must be seeing to them and the coachmen.

"Go on, dismount," Phillip urged. "I'll see to our horses. If we've got guests, you're in a better position to charm them than me."

No sooner had Allie dismounted than Mrs. McArthur came rushing out of the front door, her unruly black hair hardly at all contained under a starched white cap that she hardly ever wore.

"Och, Master, Mistress, ye'll be the death of me! Not telling me ye're expecting guests – and they be gentry no less."

Phillip looked down at her from his mount. "Don't look at me, I haven't invited any gentry."

"Neither have I," said Allie breathlessly. She inwardly cursed her own unruly locks and did her best to push loose pins back into place. She wiped the worst of the dust from her mulberry-colored riding habit. Oh well, even if nothing else in her wardrobe was the latest mode, she knew that at least her riding attire was.

Who could the visitors be? She racked her mind then swallowed. The letter she'd written to her godmother, Lady Abigail Houghall, last November half-tipsy on brandy and thinking of David…

What was it she'd said in the letter? Oh, no – a comment about her "exploits". But that was hardly an invitation to call in unannounced, was it?

"Did they give their names?" she whispered to Mrs. McArthur as she quickly wiped her boots and allowed the housekeeper to dust down the parts of her skirt she couldn't reach.

"Sir and Lady Ridgeway, they gave their names as."

That was a relief but it still didn't answer who and why.

"Have they been waiting long?"

"Not more than half an hour. I put them the drawing room and offered them tea. Thank the good Lord above ye hadn't gone racing off to Manston's place as ye usually do."

Allie swallowed again. She hadn't realized her regular visits to see David had been noted, but that consideration was secondary to the strangers at the door. She caught a glimpse of herself in the hall mirror.

The exercise had put color on her cheeks, her pinned-back hair served well enough. She took a moment to collect herself and strode briskly into the drawing room. A middle-aged couple rose to their feet.

She dropped a curtsy to them for, indeed, their very presence seemed to exude *quality*.

Her attention was drawn to the woman first, a fine-figured matron whose striking white-blonde hair was curled just so. She was dressed in an elegant day gown the color of cinnamon and embroidered in spots in a lighter thread that she thought might be ochre.

To Allie's surprise, the woman swept up to her with both arms out to take hers.

"My dear, you must be Alexandra! I wouldn't have known you if we'd passed in the street. If memory serves, you must have been about five years old when I last saw you."

This magnificent creature knew *her*? She turned to the man in a silent appeal for help. He bore an expression of faint amusement.

"I'm afraid you have the advantage, Lady Ridgeway, I..."

"Lady Abigail," the woman corrected her. "I had the title before I married."

The man turned to his wife. "Beloved, I told you we should have sent a message before dropping in on your goddaughter unannounced."

Allie felt a plunging sensation in her stomach.

"Nonsense! We're family," Lady Abigail replied.

"M...m... my lady," Allie stammered, "I never expected a visit. I mean, rather I thought a letter would be more than enough claim on your time."

"Tosh! We were in the neighborhood –"

"More or less," her husband added.

"– so it was no trouble to call on you."

"But we are sorry if we have put *you* to any trouble," the gentleman said kindly. "Your housekeeper does you credit."

Allie curtsied again, not knowing what else to do. The man was tall and broad across the shoulders. Imposing. There were strands of silver in his reddish-gold hair and sun lines around his eyes that hinted at his age – but surely no older than fifty, although he could pass for a good decade younger. He was as smartly dressed as his wife. Well-cut clothes did not need embellishments to demonstrate their wealth.

"Alexandra, I'd like to introduce my husband, Sir Daniel Ridgeway."

The man gave a polite bow. Allie found herself conscious of curtsying for a third time.

"Daniel, this is my goddaughter, Alexandra, a decision her grandparents rued from that day to this, I'll warrant!"

"Oh, I'm sure the tales were exaggerated –"

The words were out of her mouth before she could censor them. She waited to see if she had crossed a line and offended her erstwhile relative. Instead, Lady Abigail laughed gaily.

"I wouldn't be so sure of that! And where is that brother of yours, Phillip? Now there was a lad who was destined for mischief."

"Did I hear my name mentioned?"

Allie breathed a sigh of relief as Phillip entered the room behind her. At least between the two of them, they could split the attention of the couple. There was something about the two of them making *her* the subject of their attentions that left her feeling distinctly unsettled.

"Phillip! What a handsome young buck you've become," Abigail exclaimed. "Come over here and let me introduce you to my husband."

Phillip gave Allie a confused look.

"This is my godmother, Lady Abigail," said Allie, "You do remember her, don't you, Phillip?"

Recognition of the white-haired lady from their childhood dawned only vaguely on his face but he managed a convincing reply. "Of course, I do, dear sister," he said and advanced to the effusive embrace of Lady Abigail.

Allie smiled at Sir Daniel and excused herself to speak with Mrs. McArthur.

The kitchen was the domain of a one-woman whirling dervish. The housekeeper moved rapidly to and fro, and around the table, preparing food. Allie found a spot to stand out of the way.

"I've sent Watt to the village for a few lads and lassies to help us. Yer brother will have the room opposite ye and the lord and lady will have the master suite."

"I'm not sure Sir Daniel is a lord."

"Och, lord or king, it's all the same to me. The important thing is for Stannum House to present its best."

Allie felt the need to apologize profusely. "I feel horrible for putting you to so much trouble. Truly, I didn't know they were coming and –"

A clatter of pots and pans in the pantry left Allie uncertain the housekeeper even heard her. Mrs. McArthur emerged brandishing a large frying pan in triumph.

"Now ye hush then. This is the most excitement *I've* had in months. 'Tis about time this place had some liveliness about it."

"But what about..."

"Don't be worrying yer head about anything, lass, I have it all under control. But there's one thing ye *can* do for me. Ye and yer brother keep the gentry occupied and when supper comes, ye'll all be in for a treat."

ALLIE OUGHT TO have been more surprised than she was to find Phillip talking about the mine when she returned.

Sir Daniel and Lady Abigail seemed to be listening attentively or, at the very least, very politely. Allie cringed inwardly as Phillip suggested they look at Wheal Gunnis immediately.

"We'd be very much pleased," said Sir Daniel, "though I'm afraid I know very little about the topic."

Phillip looked positively giddy at the idea of speaking to another potential investor.

Lady Abigail cast an amused look Allie's way. Her catlike eyes appeared to miss nothing.

"Is something wrong, Alexandra?"

"No, nothing, except I feel my brother might be imposing or become a bore on the subject – especially for a lady. I don't want to presume –"

"Nonsense, after five hours in a carriage, the idea of stretching my legs has great appeal. Your mine cannot be any more than a mile or so." Lady Abigail rose to her feet. "Besides, I'm looking forward to renewing acquaintances with my goddaughter."

Lady Abigail tucked her arm in Allie's as they set off down the drive. Lady Abigail set their pace, letting Phillip and Sir Daniel stride ahead by a good ten yards.

"Well... do I live up to your expectations?" she asked.

"I... I have no idea what you mean."

Allie found herself under Lady Abigail's knowing expression. Tension rose in the pit of her stomach. What on earth had she let herself in for?

"I didn't come down in the last shower you know. The only reason one writes to a distant relative after many years is either to beg money or to have one's curiosity sated. Given that you write to an old address using my maiden name tells me you didn't know I had wed. That leaves the latter, especially since you expressed interest in my 'exploits' as you so charmingly put it."

"Was any of it true?" Allie blurted out before considering the appropriateness of it.

Her godmother laughed. "Now *that* is the right question to ask!"

But for the moment, it seemed the question would remain unanswered. They carried on in silence. Ahead, Phillip continued to chew Sir Daniel's ear off about the mine's potential.

Allie gritted her teeth. The mine was still a worked-out proposition when she had written to her godmother; they had had no idea then that it might be rich in copper. So she had a clear conscience that she hadn't written to beg for money. But now that the Ridgeways were here, well, it *was* a good opportunity.

But Phillip was doing it much too brown. If he didn't shut up, he could put the peer off completely. Unless the carriage and clothing were for show, the Ridgeways were not short of a penny or two, and they would know other people similarly flush in the pockets.

She turned to Lady Abigail, suddenly determined to have her question answered.

"Well, was it?" she asked, and had no idea what made her act so brusquely to a woman whose advice she sought.

Lady Abigail squeezed her arm. "I have no idea which part of the family you take after, but you appear to be a woman after my own heart. So, in answer to your question, yes. Some, if not a great deal you've been told about me and my scandalous ways is true."

Allie thought about it a moment and, emboldened by the woman's frank admission, offered an equally frank observation.

"You don't seem to be ashamed of it."

Lady Abigail smiled softly, seeming to recognize Allie's statement was also itself a question.

"Are you asking if I have regrets? My dear, if you don't have regrets, then you've not lived! But that having been said, I don't encourage anyone to make the same mistakes as me. I encourage them to make their *own* mistakes—" She patted the back of Allie's hand. "— they're much more satisfying."

Chapter Sixteen

WAS THAT THE answer to the real question Allie had been too afraid to ask? David's image came to mind and the flip-flop of her stomach suggested it was.

"Why did you come here?" she whispered.

"You invited me, did you not?"

No, thought Allie, *I didn't; not really*. But she went along with her godmother's reply. "Why did you accept?"

Lady Abigail shook her head; the spherical gold earrings at her lobes caught the light as they moved.

"No, I think that's enough questions for now. Why don't we enjoy a pleasant afternoon together, and we'll see if the answer presents itself in due course?"

They climbed the last four hundred yards to the engine house. It had been some time since Allie had walked up to the mine. She recalled the hikes from the village with the rest of the *bal maidens* to prepare for a day's work.

The four of them paused on the brow of the hill looking out to the sea beyond. It was a magnificent view across the hills and vales to the south. Sir Daniel took a few paces away until he found a spot to his satisfaction. From a jacket pocket, he withdrew a small spyglass.

Lady Abigail left Allie's side and joined her husband. As Sir Daniel pointed out various landmarks, Phillip drew Allie to one side.

"What do you think of our new relatives?" he whispered.

"I'm not sure what to make of Lady Abigail," she confessed. "I wrote to her on a whim. I expected her to *write* back. I never expected her to show up unannounced."

Was Phillip going to force her to apologize? No – his good humor remained intact.

"I'll leave you to enjoy the view, Sir Daniel," Phillip called out. "I want to take a look around and make sure we've had no trespassers."

Sir Daniel waved back in acknowledgement.

The twins walked side-by-side down the northern side of the engine house and toward one of the outbuildings.

In the lee, where the sea breeze didn't cut through, the air was warm.

"Well, I'm glad you wrote to Lady Abigail. Sir Daniel seems genuinely interested in Wheal Gunnis," said Phillip. "You know, he describes his occupation as investor. I think we could really make something of their visit here."

"Just as long as you don't frighten them off. I don't want Lady Abigail and Sir Daniel thinking we're trying to fleece them."

"Aren't we?"

Allie caught a smirk from her brother which she replied to with a glare and a wrinkle of her nose. They reached the sorting shed. Phillip grasped the lock and gave it a firm tug. It held. They continued their walk around that building and moved on to another storage shed. That too was locked tight.

"We'll invite Manston to join us for supper and –"

"He's not here."

Now it was her brother's turn to give her a considering look.

"Yes, all right," she confessed. "I went to his cottage yesterday. I haven't seen him in two months and I missed him. There – is that what you wanted to hear?"

She waited for a lecture about where she put her heart, but Phillip did not deliver it. In fact, he seemed surprised.

"I haven't seen him in weeks either," he said.

Allie frowned.

"You didn't know he was going away, did you?"

Phillip shook his head. "No."

They continued across the back of Wheal Gunnis.

"OUR LAST MEETING was two months ago. We agreed to reconvene when we might have enough investment to expose more of the seam. We thought twelve weeks would be a good length of time."

They walked through the cold shadow of the engine house. Allie fought an involuntary shiver and watched her brother's face carefully. "Then you agree that his absence is something to be concerned about?"

Phillip seemed to understand the real issue behind her question and gave her a dismissive shake of his head.

"The man has a life of his own, Allie."

Yes, and it shouldn't be a life without me. She pushed that thought aside and broached an issue which was more serious.

"I saw a couple of men outside his cottage. They claimed to be there looking for somewhere to rent, but there was something about them I didn't trust."

Now it was Phillip's turn to frown. "They didn't bother you, did they?" he asked seriously.

Allie shook her head. She would not mention how threatened she had felt by the man named Bert. "No, they didn't bother me," she reassured him.

"Thieves, do you think?"

"I don't know. They had a plausible enough story. The man who introduced himself sounded educated. He called himself Peter Silsbury. He said he's a naturalist and he did seem to know the area." Allie paused, considering. "Do you think they could be Wheal Gunnis' 'ghosts'?"

"It's possible, although, so far, I've seen nothing amiss here today. I'll see Prenpas and ask him to keep an eye out. Although I must say I don't mind fostering tales of ghoulies lurking about if it keeps the children from venturing up here, particularly at night."

They continued behind the workings and the slag pit below to circle back. Lady Abigail and her husband seemed fascinated by the view. They were in deep conversation, their voices low as though they wished not to be overheard.

Phillip started. He cocked an ear.

"Getting spooked about the ghosties of your own making?" Allie grinned. She was favored with a withering look.

Then Allie heard it, the sound of something tramping up the grass behind the engine house.

"It's probably a stray cow or goat," he told her. "I'll take a look."

Allie called out to the Ridgeways to alert them to her presence. She didn't want to intrude on what appeared to be a private moment.

Lady Abigail's serious expression livened as she looked up. "My dear, we were so enjoying the vista."

Allie doubted it. Although the scenery was magnificent in Cornwall, their little place here in Stannum surely wasn't remarkable enough to devote such rapt attention. Or perhaps, she was simply too familiar with it.

"What's out there, where the waves are breaking?" asked Sir Daniel. "A reef?"

"It's one of the reasons we don't have a bigger fleet fishing from here," said Allie. "At low tide, the rocks are exposed and only the smallest of boats can make it across the channels on either side. Even then it's treacherous."

Sir Daniel looked as though he were about to ask another question when something caught his eyes and he looked past her. Allie turned, expecting to see Phillip.

It was David Manston.

She couldn't help an expression of delight. And she felt her face flood with color at David's uptick of the mouth. *He'd noticed.*

"Forgive me," said David, a grin still hovering about his face. "I didn't mean to startle anyone. I saw a flash of light reflect off something and came up to investigate."

Hearing his rich voice once again warmed her from within. He appeared to be well and in good spirits. When had he returned? Late yesterday? Or this morning? And was he aware she had been in his cottage and seen his hidden artworks, the semi-nude portrait of *her*?

Heat filled her face. If anyone noticed, she would blame it on the sun.

The clack of Sir Daniel's telescopic spyglass being put away snapped her attention back to the present. The man regarded her thoughtfully; Lady Abigail plainly held in wry amusement.

"Forgive me. Sir Daniel, Lady Abigail," said Allie, "this is our friend and neighbor, David Manston."

"My lady, Sir Daniel," he replied, bowing to both.

"He's more than that," called Phillip who was emerging from behind the engine house. "David is also one of our partners here at the mine. He funded the exploratory blasts that uncovered the larger vein of copper."

Phillip joined them, slapping David on the back.

"Manston..." Lady Abigail began, thoughtful. "You wouldn't happen to be a relative of the Manstons of Carreg in Wales, would you?"

Allie noticed a look of surprise cross David's face and a shadow fall across his expression.

"A very distant relation, I'm sure," he answered flatly.

Not for the first time, Allie was conscious of how very little she knew about David's past. He never volunteered any of it, other than to say he had been a traveler abroad for a number of years and came to Stannum for the peace of the countryside.

Any curiosity she expressed in that regard had been firmly but politely rebuffed. And in light of the concerns that occupied her family, she hadn't the inclination to pursue the matter further. But now she wanted to know – especially since he seemed to earn his income by rather *unconventional* means.

"Glad to see you back, old man," said Phillip. "I was just telling Sir Daniel about our search for investors."

Good on Phillip, Allie thought. Whether her brother saw the tension between them or whether he had simply blundered in, she didn't know, but it was enough to break the spell.

"And you must dine with us tonight," Phillip continued.

And there it was, the mask which had taken her so long to penetrate was back on David's face. The pleasant expression it now wore was forced, though she suspected she was the only one who saw it.

"I'm afraid I'll have to disappoint you. I've only just arrived home and –"

"In that case, I insist you join us," said Lady Abigail. "You look like you need a good meal."

Allie and Phillip shared a glance. Lady Abigail had been here for less than half a day and she was acting like she owned Stannum.

A silent battle of wills was taking place in the gaze between David and the aristocratic woman. Her husband remained silent.

She wondered what a stalemate between David and Lady Abigail might look like. She caught his eyes. He seemed to silently plead for help, so she said the first thing that came into her head.

"We would be five for dinner; I'm not sure where we could find a sixth."

It was a weak excuse but she saw the relief in David's eyes.

"Oh, that's no bother," Phillip answered, completely oblivious to the undercurrent in the conversation. "You must have forgotten Julian was planning to join us."

Lady Abigail had her victory and the smile she beamed suggested she knew it. "Then that's our six then," she said. "We insist that we see you at eight o'clock to dine. I'm looking forward to getting to know my dear, sweet relations and their friends better."

Chapter Seventeen

FOR THE FIRST time in many years in her own home, Allie left the gentlemen to their brandy and cigars.

That left her alone with Lady Abigail. The woman she had been warned about and had wondered about was right here. And now she had no idea what to say to the woman.

Perhaps it was best if she didn't. She sat down at the spinet and smoothed the skirts on her soft green gown. She was pleased to see it wasn't too out of date if Lady Abigail's gown was any guide.

While not a musical virtuoso by any means, Allie knew several tunes well enough to give them a serviceable treatment, providing her a moment to catch her breath and reflect on the afternoon's events.

Following a promise extracted from David to return for dinner, the rest of the party returned to Stannum House.

Mrs. McArthur had shooed Allie away from the kitchen, telling her everything was under control for dinner, and Molly from the village would be here to act as lady's maid to both her and Lady Abigail.

Julian had arrived at six o'clock, taking in stride news that extra guests would be joining them for dinner.

There had been no time to apologize to David for her godmother's presumption, but he arrived at the appointed hour dressed as formally as Allie had ever seen him in a dark gray frock coat. She had no idea he even owned anything so fine.

Now the four men – Phillip, Sir Daniel, David, and Julian – were no doubt furthering the conversation which had taken place over dinner on the prospects of the Wheal Gunnis Mine.

But here in the drawing room, where a warm evening breeze through an open window brought in the aroma of honeysuckle in flower, Allie had no conversational gambit. They had no sherry either, but the older woman accepted the brandy and assured Mrs. McArthur she actually preferred it.

"Leave off your playing, Alexandra, and come sit beside me. Have some of this most excellent brandy," she said.

Allie did as Lady Abigail asked. She sipped from her glass and savored the heat of the alcohol running down her throat.

"My dear, dinner was superb; your housekeeper is a treasure," Lady Abigail added.

"I don't know what we would do without her," Allie answered in all truthfulness.

"It's been a difficult few years since the closure of the mine, hasn't it? Was that the reason why you decided write after all these years?"

"I suppose it was part of the reason," she answered. "I wanted to know from someone who had reached the highest pinnacle of society then had it all come crashing down, if there was reason to hope."

Those intense gray-green slated eyes under penciled-in brows regarded her steadily. "There is *always* reason to hope, Alexandra – but it all depends what you're putting your hope in, doesn't it?"

"You're not going to turn Methodist on me, are you?"

Lady Abigail laughed. "I'm too fond of drinking and dancing for that. But they're right in this – 'to everything there is a season'. Mind you, it doesn't make it particularly pleasant to go through at the time. If you're wise, you'll learn the lessons sooner rather than later."

The silence as Allie took in her words was marked by the ticking of the mantel clock and the soft crackling of the fire.

"How long have you and Manston had an attachment toward one another?"

Those remarkable eyes of her godmother returned her surprised look with a considering feline regard. She had plainly and astutely seen what passed between her and David up at the mine. There would be no use denying it...

At length, Allie answered. "It's been a one-sided affair for quite some time... at least I thought so."

She swallowed down another measure of brandy, lest she say too much and fearful it may cause her to do so.

Lady Abigail swooped on the comment like a hawk after prey.

"Darling, you must tell me *everything*! All of the people in my intimate circle are now happily wed, so I'm always intrigued by a fresh romance."

Allie found herself fiddling with her skirts once more. That's what she'd wanted, wasn't it? To talk to the most scandalous woman she knew, the one they said ruined a perfectly acceptable engagement when her intended caught her *indelicato flagrante* with another man, a woman who was a lover to viscounts, dukes, and apparently to the Prince of Wales himself?

And now, even though her life of adventure was over, it wasn't like she was a spinster stuck in Bath with old Aunt Philomena or had had to settle for a dull, fustilugs of a husband either.

Sir Daniel was a very handsome man and there was something about the two of them together that suggested the spark of romance hadn't gone out even though they were wed.

Whether it was the brandy that loosened her tongue, or simply having another woman to talk to, Allie told her second cousin once removed *everything* including the discovery of the semi-nude likeness of her in David's folio.

Lady Abigail leaned back slightly and gave Allie's figure a critical appraisal. "Well, the man can't be blamed... and yet you've never been lovers?"

Allie shook her head silently, knowing that to open her mouth again would force her to speak against the rawness of her throat.

"And you know nothing more about this Claire woman than you're sure she is Manston's wife?"

Once again, Allie shook her head.

"And you've never sought her out?"

She shook her head a third time.

Lady Abigail set down her glass on the small table beside her and leaned forward. The air seemed charged somehow, even though it was a perfectly clear and pleasant summer's night.

"All right, I'll make you a bargain," the woman announced "I'll find out about Manston and this Claire for you with *complete* discretion. But only on two conditions."

Allie straightened in her chair. What, exactly, had she expected from her godmother? Tea and sympathy, she supposed. Not someone who sounded like she was about to negotiate a business arrangement.

"The first condition is that you are prepared to listen to everything I find out on your behalf – for good *and* for ill. The second is I intend to share a confidence with you, and I demand *your* complete discretion. Nothing that Sir Daniel and I reveal while under this roof goes any further. You may only speak of it to your brother and no one else. Not even your Mr. Manston."

Allie blinked rapidly, trying to untangle the web of meaning behind her words, and warring with the embarrassment and shame in her own heart. Curiosity mixed uneasily with anger.

She wasn't sure if that's what Lady Abigail's manner – forthright to the point of abrasive – intended, but it served her now. Allie matched the other woman's tone.

"If we're demanding honesty from each other, then you shouldn't mind me asking what you and Sir Daniel were so keenly examining from up at the Wheal."

She waited to see an expression of affront on the aristocrat's face at her bluntness, but instead witnessed a gleam of interest in Lady

Abigail's eyes and a tightness at the corners of her mouth that suggested a suppressed smile.

"I *knew* I was right to take an interest in you," she said. "There is *so* much in you that reminds me of myself at your age. Lacking a little experience, mind..." She ended the comment with a shrug before pinning Allie with a stare.

"I shall ask you one more time. Are you sure you really want to know?"

This time, Allie was sure. She lifted her chin and picked up her glass of brandy from the table with confidence. She raised it in silent salute and brought the nearly empty glass to her lips to drain it. A twitch of a smile was Lady Abigail's response in return.

"Second things first then. Sir Daniel and I are spies in the service of His Majesty."

Allie nearly choked on her drink. Lady Abigail ignored it and dropped her voice.

"In answer to your question, there is a man we're looking for. We believe he may be hiding along this stretch of coast. I want you and your brother to be our eyes and ears."

Eyes watering, Allie waited for another smile, an amused grin to say the woman was joking, but her mien remained focused, serious. Instead Allie felt a tingle at the back of her neck and a little voice in her ear expressed caution.

"That is my bargain with you," said Lady Abigail. "Will you swear to keep our secret as I am prepared to keep yours, and will you hear out whatever I uncover on your behalf?"

The questions were grave, demanding an oath as solemn as one might make in a church or in a courtroom. Allie gave it without hesitation.

"I swear I will."

A moment later, the drawing room door opened so suddenly that Allie jumped. As for Lady Abigail, her face changed, as though the curtain had been raised and an actress was playing her opening scene. Her expression – no, her very *being* – seemed lighter, more vivacious.

She looked at each of the men as they entered the room, Phillip, Julian, David, and then Sir Daniel. The woman's eyes fell on her husband and Allie believed she saw not an actress but genuine softness in her expression for a moment.

"Darling! Alexandra and I have hatched the most ingenious plot!"

The brandy soured in Allie's stomach. Phillip looked at her with alarm, Julian with confusion, and David with sudden amusement, but Sir Daniel only had eyes for his wife.

"And what might that be, my dear?"

"We've agreed it would be a *grand* idea to host a party here at Stannum House. We will invite some friends who might be interested in investing in what I'm certain will be a profitable new venture."

If Sir Daniel was at all shocked by his wife's pronouncement, he didn't look it.

Phillip, on the other hand, looked positively giddy, so too did Julian. David's expression was reserved, however, thoughtful.

"Well, then Cousin Abigail," said Phillip, sounding breathless with shock. "I think this deserves a toast."

He waited until everyone had filled their glasses before lifting his. "To old acquaintances and new ventures!"

DAVID WATCHED PHILLIP lift Alexandra by the waist and whirl her about the moment the Ridgeways were safely upstairs to bed.

The sound of her laughter warmed him within. He thought two months in London with his publisher would be enough to keep her from his mind. But he had come to the awful realization that time and distance did not work.

He watched Allie accept a kiss on the cheek from Julian as the trio celebrated the chance to raise real funds to reopen Wheal Gunnis, and the strangest notion took him. He couldn't fault Julian for the liberty he took, and yet he couldn't bring himself to be jealous either. He rather liked Julian, who he had come to know as a solid, stand-up chap, a gentleman who deserved the honorific.

As for himself, the vile cad *he* was, he knew without a doubt this afternoon up at the mine that Allie still carried a torch for him. He saw it in her eyes, the way her surprise turned to tenderness, her look of delight.

One word of encouragement on his part would have her in his arms.

And here she was before him, smiling. In seeing her joy, something lightened in him, too, so when Allie held out her hand to him, he took it and let her draw him into their little circle.

"Well," said Julian who, frankly, still looked dazed. "There's a turn up for the books. You two having your own real-life fairy godmother."

"There's plenty to do yet," said David, who felt compelled to be a steadying influence. "The Ridgeways have kindly offered to help make introductions, but it's going to be up to us to sell the proposal to investors."

Phillip thumped Julian on the chest. "The Ridgeways have my room while they are here, so you and I are bunking in together. We can make a start tonight and flesh out the rest of the arrangements over the next few days."

The group made their way out into the hall and David shook hands with Phillip and Julian, bidding them goodnight. The two men started on their way upstairs when Phillip turned and looked down to his sister.

"Are you coming up to bed?" he whispered loudly.

"Soon," she answered. "I want to say goodnight to David and thank Mrs. McArthur again before I retire."

Phillip eyed them both. "Don't be long."

David and Alexandra watched the two men climb the stairs until they stood alone in the hall.

He turned to her. She seemed uncertain of him – something she had never been before. Now, *precisely*, why was that?

It occurred to him that, although they had seen one another several times over the past seven months, it had only been in the company of others; they were never alone.

And that was what he'd wanted, wasn't it? For the woman who was temptation itself to keep clear of him?

But she couldn't keep herself away, could she? And he couldn't bring himself to stay away from her…

It left them in a pretty little impasse.

His body reacted to her nearness, remembering the feel of her in his arms, the taste of her lips on his. The more he told himself to *not* think about it, the more vivid the images in his mind became. The second time, they hadn't even kissed, but their bodies pressed together and his knowledge that she felt his arousal… that the embrace ended with a stinging slap across his cheek had nothing to do with the liberties he'd taken, only with the words he'd used to drive her away from him.

She ought to hate him as much as he hated himself and, yet, she didn't.

"Thank you for coming tonight," she said. "It meant a lot to Phillip and Julian. And I knew if there was anyone with the gravitas to impress Sir Daniel, it was you. You were the one who believed in us when there was nothing to gain."

He drank in her beauty, the luscious black curly locks and figure that had been fuel for many of his nocturnal fantasies; the green eyes that sparkled like emeralds when she was angry and softened to the color of glass when she was content…

He took both her hands in hers. "You've given *me* something to believe in."

Those green eyes shone with unshed tears. The effect his words had on her surprised him. Hell, the words themselves coming from his mouth surprised *him*, and any resolve he had to hold himself apart from her dissolved in an instant.

A slight tug on her hand put Allie in his embrace once more. It felt good.

He knew he was a fool, but he might as well be a fool in the arms of a woman who loved him.

She nuzzled her head against his chest and held him tight.

"I missed you," he whispered.

"I missed you, too," she answered. "And I have a confession to make. I went to your cottage yesterday."

"I know."

"Oh…"

Did she shudder in his arms?

"You didn't put the hidden key in exactly the place I'd left it, and you're the only one who knows the key is there at all."

The sigh of her breath against his chest was like coming home; being home. And *that* was the danger – him getting too used to this. He looked into her eyes and nearly found himself lost there.

Damn, the need to kiss her was too much to resist.

The soft touch of his lips to hers was more than he had the right to expect, but her mouth opened under his.

After a moment, she broke off the kiss and rested her head against his shoulder.

"Would it matter to you that I know your secret?" she whispered.

Now it was his turn to shudder. Alexandra took advantage of his surprise to kiss him thoroughly. He gave himself to it, the carnality of the moment more potent than he imagined possible, all things considered – and he wanted more of it, more of *her* to bring a fantasy to life that was so compelling it spilled out of his dreams and onto paper.

"I want what I saw in your books."

Her words, temptingly whispered in his ear, only half-registered with him. He ignored the part of him that wanted to address what she said, and instead gave in to the feel of her body against him, the soft flesh of her breasts that he grazed with the pads of his fingers, the press of their mouths against each other's.

It was agony to leave.

Chapter Eighteen

"SO, WHEN DID you come up with the idea of holding a soiree?" Daniel asked as he extinguished the lamp and climbed into bed. Abigail snuggled up closer to him, resting her head on his chest. She didn't answer until his arm was around her.

"About a second before you walked into the drawing room," she said around a yawn. "It occurred to me we could waste weeks or months chasing after Bickmore. How much better if the bee came to the honey instead?"

There was silence in the darkened room, the ceiling dimly lit by the low fire in the grate. Abigail listened to her husband breathe, the rise and fall of his chest under her cheek. No doubt he was considering her words, reviewing them to see if the intuitive logic of her idea could withstand rigorous scrutiny.

She wondered if Daniel needed more convincing.

"That jumped-up little sailor destroyed our Charteris House. The things we've lost... and seeing Bassett in tears over the loss of his beloved clocks. I shan't have it! Bickmore took us by surprise once. I won't let him do it again."

Daniel soothed her with a stroke of her hair. "There's no doubt it's as much personal as it is political for Bickmore. His hatred for Adam is without question," he said.

"Yes. All the better to lure the man out – we want him well out of the way before O'Brien returns with his news."

Daniel turned on his side. Abigail could just see his face. "And you're happy to potentially put Olivia at risk? If you're going to make it a full party, then you'll have to account for Nate and Susannah, Peggy and Clem as well."

Abigail shrugged, unconcerned, "They're all grown-ups. They know the risks. And they'll be prepared."

"Alexandra, too? Is she one of your 'league' already?"

"She's a sharp one. I trust her to look after herself – and to keep her mouth shut."

"After only a day?" he frowned.

"I have good instincts about people and, besides, she's family…"

From his expression, Abigail knew Daniel was not prepared to accept her explanation at face value.

"What else aren't you telling me?"

She gave him her most coquettish expression and ran a finger down the center of his chest. Daniel growled, pulling her into his arms and holding her still there. After so many years, they knew each other so well.

"I've given Alexandra an incentive. She has a *tendre* for David Manston. If memory serves me, he has somewhat of a scandalous past, but I can't remember the particulars. I'll find out soon enough though. You know I always like to be aware of who owes whom."

There was silence again.

"You don't think I've overstepped, do you?"

The arms that held her tightly loosened and his hand rubbed circles on her back. Abigail snuggled up to her husband and her lips touched his chest through the opening of his night shirt.

"I can see how this plan could work," he admitted. "But if you only wanted to help your distant relations, you didn't have to go to this extent. You could have easily written out an order for five hundred pounds."

Abigail reached up and traced a finger along his jaw, giving a mock pout.

"But a party is *so* much more enjoyable."

Then she became serious. "No, money is not the solution to the Gedding twins' problems. But belief in them is. Let *them* make the case to reopen Wheal Gunnis. The cost of inviting a few friends and paying for a party is a small price that will pay big dividends all around."

TWO WEEKS LATER, Lady Abigail returned to Stannum House along with a woman she introduced as Peggy Pascoe, a cook, to discuss kitchen arrangements with Mrs. McArthur. While she was here, Lady Abigail insisted on seeing Allie's wardrobe.

Allie gritted her teeth as she led Lady Abigail upstairs to her room. She wasn't used to being ordered about by anyone, and she was becoming a little tired of it.

And yet, it was all for a good cause, she reminded herself.

Repeatedly.

However, if she kept biting her tongue as she had done all this morning, she was in danger of taking the whole thing off.

She had already picked out the gown she intended to wear and hung it up to air. She said nothing, instead simply pointing to it for Lady Abigail's judgment.

It was Allie's coming out gown. A soft apricot in hue, it had cost her uncle a fortune. Even though the color was not particularly her favorite, it was certainly the finest gown she owned.

Lady Abigail gave it a critical examination.

"This simply will not do," she pronounced – not to Allie's great surprise. At least she'd picked it up and glanced at it front and back before coming to a judgment.

"I know you've been rusticating, my dear, but surely you get *The Ladies Journal*, even out here?"

Allie bit the inside of her lip to give her tongue a reprieve and prevent a bitter retort emerging. Had the woman forgotten that the Gedding family as well as Stannum itself was impoverished?

It was safer if she merely shook her head.

Lady Abigail sighed and pulled open the doors to Allie's armoire as though this was *her* home.

"Don't give me that poor, put-upon look," the woman said, her back to Allie. "You're not the first woman to know the sting of poverty, and you won't be the last. Consider yourself thankful you have a way out of it, if you're prepared to put the effort in."

This was becoming intolerable...

Dress after dress was discarded upon a chair until the pile was too much. An avalanche of silks, satins, and muslins slid to the floor. From the pile, Lady Abigail picked up a gown of blue.

"There! This is something we might be able to work with. Put it on."

Allie could remain silent no longer.

"What? Now?"

"Yes, now!" Lady Abigail's brusqueness became a show of temper. "I'm not here for the good of my health. Your brother and his friends might be discussing business but don't underestimate the role you'll play. A bit of flattery here, a dash of flirtation there, and coming from an attractive young woman – it all serves to boost the egos and open the purses of the right people."

It was on the tip of Allie's tongue to sarcastically ask whether she ought to be taking notes when the next question was more kindly delivered.

"Now, do you have any of your mother's jewelry left?"

"Some. The most sentimental pieces because –"

"Where are they?" Abigail asked, cutting her off. Allie pointed to a mahogany casket on her dressing table, not trusting herself to speak. "That will help me make a final decision on your gown."

Allie picked up the gown thrust at her by Abigail.

It was in a shade called celestial blue – a rich blue a shade or two darker than the clearest summer sky. It had straight sleeves and was modestly square-cut across the bust. It was a pretty color, but the design of it was all wrong. As *rusticated* as she was, even *she* knew that.

She placed the garment on the bed and unlaced the lavender and white hail spot muslin day dress she wore. She slipped into the gown.

As Lady Abigail continued to rummage through her jewelry box, Allie looked at herself in the mirror. The color was becoming at least, she had to admit.

Abigail finally turned around and cast her eyes up and down. Her expression was not encouraging.

"You have a figure I can work with. And as for jewelry, I would say less is more. The pearl earbobs will be sufficient."

"There's a matching pearl necklace –" Allie ventured.

"Absolutely not! Not with that décolleté. Loosen the stays at the back." Her godmother approached and pushed the gown down until it sat almost off her shoulders. Then she tugged the neckline down until a generous amount of cleavage showed.

"There!" She turned her around to face the mirror, gathering the fabric at the back to make the bodice of the gown sit to her liking. "You will go to Camelford tomorrow for the sheerest organdie, lace, ribbon, and dye. I want you to recut the bodice so it scoops wide across your shoulders and shows just this amount of bosom. Use the organdie to make short puffed sleeves and the lace from under your bust to your hips. With your fair skin and black hair, you will have every eye in the room on you."

Allie blinked rapidly. She had been afraid Abigail would order her to make a new gown. There was simply no money for it, even if was only a remake of an existing garment. She could barely afford the lace and ribbon. How she was going to pay for the food and servants was another thing to consider.

"But organizing the soiree..."

"Tosh, there's nothing for you to do. I've arranged it all. I've already spoken to your estimable Mrs. McArthur –"

What? When?

"– and she's agreed to work with Mrs. Pascoe. She's part-owner in The Queen's Head Inn and one of the finest cooks this side of the Devon border."

Allie sank down on the bed, fearful that if she did not do so she might simply collapse. This was being put together with the precision of one of Nelson's naval campaigns.

"There's more to this than just helping two poor relations. What is it?"

Lady Abigail returned the pearls to the box.

"I already told you. Sir Daniel and I are agents of the Crown."

"And it has something to do with someone you're looking for who might be in this county," said Allie. "But I don't understand. Why not just bring in the army? There's a garrison not twenty miles from here."

In an instant, Lady Abigail's demeanor changed as though two personalities inhabited the one woman. This was the grave and serious one.

"The man we're looking for has a *fixation* on one of our agents," she said. "When Adam Hardacre shows up here, I'm betting this man won't be too far away. We intend to arrest him."

"And what is he?"

"Harold Bickmore is a murderer, a traitor, and a spy. And he may hold the secret to French plans to invade England."

Allie felt an unbidden shudder go through her. "Surely you don't intend to arrest him at the soiree?"

Abigail looked at her askance. "Heavens, no. Not unless we have to..."

It wasn't very reassuring. "It's a very expensive bet, the idea he'll show up, if you don't mind me saying so."

There was a shrug of the shoulders from her cousin. "The roll of the dice, the turn of the card – that's not where the gamble lies. The real stakes are about how well you can read another person, be it an enemy, a friend or a lover. I'm wagering a man's life and the security of England that I'm right. I don't intend to leave anything to chance – not even down to how you present yourself."

DAVID HADN'T INTENDED to vary his routine, but with the Geddings' soiree in a fortnight's time, he found himself fighting feelings of anticipation. He patted his black stallion on the neck and looked up at the engine house, the stone gleaming now that the sun had emerged following a morning shower.

In his imagination, he could hear the sound of the *bal maidens* singing as they occupied their day, and the steady rumble of the pump that removed the water and fed fresh air to the men who worked so far below.

He knew little about mining, despite being steeped in Wales' coal mining tradition, but even he could see the vein of copper exposed by the blast would spur Stannum's fortunes again.

He reached the crossroads and saw the trail of villagers making their monthly journey to Camelford for the markets. In the middle of the group was Allie who was speaking to an older woman. Ahead was Phillip, a child clinging on his back and laughing heartily as the man's horse cantered a few yards.

It felt good being part of something again, a community.

"Pleasant to have ye join us, Manston," called Prenpas. David urged the horse into a trot and then to a walk to keep pace with the blacksmith.

"I thought Jack could do with a ride today."

"So it be nothing to do with the Geddings' do-up at the house, then?" the old man teased. "With all them lords and ladies and like."

"Well, maybe," he admitted sheepishly. "I'll have to polish my manners as well as my boots."

That set the blacksmith into gales of laughter.

Allie looked back at the sound. She halted her horse, waiting for them to catch up.

David offered her a smile and, to his surprise, she blushed. She never blushed – at least not in all the time – oh…

He recalled the last time he'd seen her and her wicked admission.

How far was she willing to take this, he wondered? David eyed her deliberately, allowing himself to linger on the glimpse of an ankle, the line of her legs, and up to the shapely silhouette of her bust. Allie squared her shoulders, a smile flirted around her mouth, but she said nothing.

Oh yes, she knew exactly what she was about.

She thought she had him exactly where she wanted him.

We'll see if she feels the same after the party.

THE BANKER IN Camelford left him in the room alone with his small strong box. David unlocked it. It was the first time it had been opened in more than three years. Two pouches lay within. The first, made of red leather, contained a quantity of gold and coins, and was the reason for his last visit. The second was a smaller black leather pouch. It had been longer still since he'd opened this one.

This held something more important than gold – it contained his memories, his past. Now, they were to become his present.

He took a deep breath and untied the drawstring to remove a yet smaller black velvet pouch from within. He poured the contents into his hand and set them on the velvet one by one.

David picked up a pocket watch – a gold hunter. He gave the winder a couple of turns and brought the piece to his ear to listen to the cricket-like sounds from the escapement.

He'd put the watch in the lock box as soon as he'd settled in Stannum. There had been no call to wear such a piece and, besides, there was something liberating about letting the sun and the moon dictate his hours. The small mantel clock in his house was enough to keep track of the time and, even then, he let it wind down and stop more often than not.

He regarded the gold signet ring given to him by his grandfather. It carried the family crest, a griffin rising phoenix-like from flames. He set both the ring and the watch aside, along with a gold and sapphire cravat pin. He would dress as befit the Baron of Carreg, even if chose not to use the title.

He wondered how Allie would react. He didn't trust himself where she was concerned. She tested his self-control to the edge. But, if he was honest with himself, that ship sailed a long time ago. He wanted her in his arms and in his bed more than he'd wanted any woman in his life – including Claire.

But knowing Allie felt the same attraction didn't bring the comfort it should. She was not a woman he could simply tumble. She was worth more than that, *deserved* more than that. She deserved to be the Baroness of Carreg and, one day, to be his viscountess.

Let's see who of Lady Abigail's guests remember after so long. It may be their decision as to whether or not this phoenix rises from the ashes.

Indeed, this was to be his return back into society as much as it was to be Allie and Phillip's.

Screw your courage to the sticking place. And we will not fail.

David winced. The recalled words of Lady Macbeth gave him no comfort at all. They were meant to cajole and encourage her husband but their tale ended up a tragedy.

As this soiree could be.

Yes, very helpful. David told himself.

If gossip about him proved too corrosive to Allie and her brother, he would sell up and leave, this time for further shores such as America or Canada – even Australia would not be out of the question.

He shook his head clear of such grim thoughts.

Don't let's borrow trouble.

Also before him was a small collection of women's jewelry. Among the items was a pair of gold earrings. One day, he'd give them to his wife. They featured a polished bead of reddish-orange coral surrounded by seed pearls – given to him by his grandmother on his last visit. She was the only woman who believed in him, regardless of the rumors.

He smiled wistfully. *She* understood why he did what he did, even despite the sorrow it brought her.

While on her death, he'd received a note from his mother informing him of the news along with the ring he looked at now. It was gold with a sizable diamond in the center, surrounded by rich, green emeralds.

It was not the only women's ring he owned.

Glinting against the black velvet was a little gold ring with a ruby stone encircled by small diamonds. Passion, love and constancy – a message from the heart to the woman he'd pledged *his* to.

He'd bought it the day Claire's father told him he was in favor of their marriage. He'd intended to present it to her as a betrothal gift. It had remained in his pocket. Whenever he looked at it in the years since, it was a painful reminder of his folly.

No more. The next time he was in London, he would sell it. Putting the past aside and moving on was a course of action long overdue.

With new resolve, he placed that ring and his grandmother's back in the pouches and into the box. The rest he slipped into his pocket. He locked the box and called for a teller who escorted him back to the strong room.

He emerged out into the mid-afternoon sunlight, letting the heat of it soak into his clothes and warm his body after the chill of the thick-walled bank. He turned in the direction of the stables just in time to catch sight of Allie emerging from the haberdashers across the other side of the street. He allowed himself to admire the sway of her hips as she walked away. He was about to call her name when he observed another man taking particular notice of her, as well, just a few yards away from him.

He was tall, even taller than he by at least an inch or two, but the man was thin. Scarecrow thin, in fact. His light brown moustache only accented his sunken cheeks.

The way he observed Allie wasn't just the gaze of a man admiring the form of a pretty woman as she strolled by. There was something deliberate about his regard.

David looked ahead to see if Phillip or any other of the villagers he knew were around. There was no one, and the man was now across the street. He did not look in any of the windows. He clearly had his eyes on his quarry.

And Allie was now too far away to call out to.

David crossed the street at an angle to get just ahead of the stranger, took a few more paces after Allie, then stopped deliberately so the man plowed into his back. David turned and addressed him, using his most affable voice.

"My apologies, sir! I didn't see you there!"

The man grumbled an acceptance of the apology and tried to side-step him to the right. David stepped in front of him. The man stepped to the left, David to his right again, deliberately mimicking the odd dance of two strangers trying to move past one another.

The man's grumble became a small growl. David refused to break eye contact with him. The line of David's mouth hardened and, suddenly, so did that of the man before him.

There. They understood each other all right.

The mustachioed scarecrow curled his lip in a snarl, turned on his heel, and strode off the other way. David watched him until he turned a corner and disappeared down a side street. He looked back toward Allie and saw she had stopped in conversation with a woman from the village who had appeared. A moment later, they hailed another woman who had emerged from a shop.

Allie would be safe in company. This was Camelford, not London. Women could walk down the street in peace here without being harassed.

Hopefully.

He walked back down to the side street after the scarecrow man. There was no sign of him.

Who the hell was he? What was his particular interest in Allie?

Chapter Nineteen

ALLIE CLOSED HER eyes, squeezed them tight, and reopened them. She hardly recognized her own home.

A house which in recent years had been as quiet and empty as a tomb was now bright and bustling ahead of tonight's soiree.

Stannum House had been reborn.

She had forgotten how much work was required to bring a country estate to life. The kitchen had been out of bounds for the past two days, left completely in the hands of Lady Abigail's cook, Mrs. Pascoe, and the two maids she brought with her.

Meanwhile, Mrs. McArthur had reveled in her true role of housekeeper after the lean years of being housekeeper, cook and maid combined. Rooms which had been unused and unaired were finally reopened under her supervision. Decorative silver candelabras stored for years were strategically placed along the hall.

The chandeliers in the large drawing room were unwrapped from their cloth covers. Last night, they were lit for the first time in nearly a decade, and the freshly cleaned crystal shot sparkles of light across the floor and the walls.

When the maid servants and footmen spontaneously burst into applause, it was all Allie could do to stop from choking up.

Mrs. McArthur had marshaled a small army from the village. Every piece of glass had been cleaned until it shone, every piece of silver gleamed.

The six rooms that had not seen a living soul since Uncle George passed away were now clean, aired and waiting for visitors, replete with furniture brought in by a team of removal men hired by Lady Abigail.

The housekeeper had been so much in her element that Allie felt quite useless and told her so.

"Useless, ye say? This is how things *should* be in a grand house like Stannum," the woman had told her. "Ye be the mistress of the house, standing alongside yer brother, so never ye mind what happens downstairs. Ye just be upstairs in yer room making yerself look bonny."

All of this a gamble to revive Stannum's fortunes.

It left Allie nervous and humbled. She touched a hand to her stomach to settle the butterflies. She couldn't just sit in her room and wait until Molly was free to help her dress. She glanced longingly at the stables. It was still early afternoon. Would there be enough time to take Nephel for a ride before she was expected to get ready?

She envied Phillip and Julian. At least there was something they could do other than pester Mrs. McArthur over details she was well capable of taking care of by herself.

Julian had ridden down from Bath the night before, sheepishly admitting he was supposed to travel with Margaret and the family but couldn't bear the thought of spending two hours in such close quarters with Lydia.

And first up this morning, he and Phillip had ridden over to David's cottage to practice their presentation to the investors.

Lucky devils. Allie wished she had something to do to better occupy her thoughts.

No sooner had she decided to don a riding habit than a large carriage arrived with Lady Abigail, her husband, and their party.

She glanced at her day dress and decided it was suitable enough to greet visitors.

"Alexandra, my dear," Lady Abigail called. "I have some friends I wish you meet."

She was introduced to a handsome, tall blond-headed man with a military bearing whom she had already assumed was Lieutenant Adam Hardacre. His wife, Olivia, was an attractive-looking woman with brown hair and a pleasant smile.

The next couple was strikingly different. Nathaniel Payne was as tall as the lieutenant, but his hair was dark and his features sharper. His wife, Susannah, was a petite woman with light brown hair who seemed to carry an air of quiet reserve despite her friendly greeting.

Were they all spies? Allie considered asking the question of her godmother when Mrs. Pascoe appeared, walking at a clip down the hall.

She greeted the Hardacres and Paynes as long-lost friends.

"Duch!" she called out to Susannah Payne. "I hope you had a good trip up. Coo, you should see the kitchen, it's nearly double the size of The Queen's Head!"

Susannah and Olivia duly followed the cook, while Sir Daniel, Hardacre and Payne went back outside, leaving Allie with Lady Abigail in the hall. How was it that a woman two decades older than she could travel several hours today and still have more energy that she currently possessed?

"You're looking a little peaky," the woman observed. "I suggest you take a nap before dressing tonight. Before you do, I wish to speak to you in the library."

She strode off ahead, leaving Allie to trail behind.

Allie closed the door to shut out the noise of the servants at work. It was, by far, the quietest room in the house and she was all of a sudden conscious of the silence.

Lady Abigail peeled off her gloves and dropped them casually on the desk. "Have you reviewed the guest list?"

How was it she felt as if she were being examined on her lessons by her governess? Allie forced the thought from her head.

"I have," she answered confidently. "Phillip is going through it with Julian and David now. If only one-fourth of the men you've earmarked on this list subscribe, then we'll be able to reopen the mine in time for summer. And as for your *other* business, Stannum House is at your disposal for as long as you need."

Lady Abigail nodded her satisfaction.

"Then I shall fulfill my end of the bargain about your Mr. Manston. Are you ready to hear it?"

Was she?

Allie lost her nerve and lowered her eyes from Lady Abigail's. If she knew everything about Claire, would it make a difference? She might understand David better and, if he could never give her his full heart, then at least she would know why.

He wanted her, there could be no doubt of that. If he let her, would she give herself to him in spite of his being married? God help her, she quite possibly would.

She turned her eyes back to her godmother and nodded.

"David Manston is the Baron of Carreg. The *bachelor* baron," said Lady Abigail. "He isn't married. Has never *been* married."

Allie exhaled softly and lowered herself onto the sofa while her legs could still hold her.

Then why would he give her such an impression?

Her godmother strolled over to the table where the decanter stood and poured a small glass of brandy, returning to hand it to her. Allie's hand shook as she accepted it. She gripped the glass firmly in both hands and set them on her lap.

Allie looked up and forced the words from her lips.

"Is that all?"

Lady Abigail shook her head, the little silver-white curls around her temple jiggling. "There was a broken engagement ten years ago.

Allie's heart tumbled a few beats.

The woman continued, ignoring her goddaughter's discomfiture.

"There's something else you should know. According to my runners, Manston was involved in a bigger scandal just before that. It was likely to have caused the break of the engagement."

Lady Abigail's measured tone of voice warned Allie there was worse to come. She decided a sip of brandy might be in order and it turned into a larger swallow.

"Manston is disowned by his family. The details I have are little more than gossip. Some said he was a little *too* forceful in his wooing of his intended, but the greater rumor had it that he beat a prostitute so badly she never worked again."

No, the brandy was a bad mistake. Allie set it down on the side table, praying that the burning sensation she could feel coming up her throat would halt.

"I... I can't believe that's true," Allie whispered. "I've known David for five years; never has he shown the least sign of violence."

"I should also mention that the girl was not a run of the mill lightskirt either. She worked at a hellfire club called The Olympus Club."

She knew her face looked blank with lack of recognition. Was she supposed to know the name? Lady Abigail's mouth twisted to a sly smile.

"It's a club that caters to *particular* tastes that regular brothels do not service, if you gather my meaning..."

She would not have gathered her meaning if she hadn't seen David's sketches. The flush to her face was immediate and she couldn't blame it on the brandy.

"Then I shan't belabor the point." Lady Abigail sat beside her and put a hand on hers. "I *did* warn that you may not like what I found out."

For the first time, Lady Abigail looked at her with something that resembled sympathy. "These are rumors, my child. It is up to *you* to determine whether or not they have merit."

Allie bolted to her feet, unable to sit still. She wanted to run, scream, break something, but settled for pacing the library floor in agitation until the turmoil inside her erupted.

"How?" she demanded. "How exactly am I supposed to do that? How is one supposed to determine the truth of something which happened so long ago? Just walk up to him and ask matter-of-factly whether he beat a prostitute half to death?"

Lady Abigail was the very picture of calm, Allie resentfully noted. At this moment, she wished she'd never written to the woman.

"Hardly. Just check the guest list, my dear one," she said with exasperated affection. "Mr. Thomas Owen-Jones' wife's name is *Claire*."

Anger began to boil below the surface. All manner of curse words learned at the stables and at the mine threatened to burst forth. Allie forced a breath in.

"You *invited* them?" she bit out.

Lady Abigail shook her head indulgently.

"You want the truth of the matter? Look in Manston's eyes, look in Mrs. Owen-Jones' eyes. Then you'll have your answer."

Allie couldn't control the tremor that ran through her and struggled to assemble a coherent string of words to articulate her rage and horror. Visions of strangling her aristocrat cousin where she sat flashed before her eyes.

"Dear God, do you hate me so much? How could you do this? You invited *Claire*? You've ruined everything! David will never forgive me for this! If there's a scene, the evening will be ruined. *We* will be ruined!"

"*Calm* yourself, Alexandra!" Lady Abigail snapped, rising to her feet. "The guest list is *my* doing – you know that, Phillip knows that, and so does Manston. Heap the coals of blame on my head, if you wish, I don't care a whit, but say *nothing* to him and all will be well.

"After all, in society, there was always going to be the chance they would cross paths again. So, tonight it happens, and you have the chance to know the truth."

Allie swallowed down bile. Her anger had subsided; left in its place was nausea.

Lady Abigail tilted her head and regarded her closely.

"I was right. You *do* look a little peaky, Alexandra. Rest for a few hours; I'll send a maid up to help you dress."

DAVID WATCHED PHILLIP exhale slowly, a mannerism shared by his sister.

Gedding was nervous – as he should be. There was a lot riding on the outcome of this party tonight and, if David were truthful with himself, he was nervous, too – and not just about the business presentation.

"Did you want to run through it one more time?" Julian asked.

Phillip shook his head and tried to laugh gamely. "Ha! As it is, I'll be reciting it in my sleep."

"One more time can't hurt," said David. "If you like, we can set it to music and you can sing it in your sleep instead."

"Very funny," the young man replied and turned to discuss a point with Winter.

David reflected on the evening ahead. He had no qualms about his readiness to speak to investors tonight. He wouldn't have broken his self-imposed exile if he didn't believe the mine could be a success again. No, he had another reason to be nervous. Just a couple of hours ago, he'd seen the guest list.

Mr. and Mrs. Thomas Owen-Jones.

Tommy. His childhood friend, Tommy. His good *friend*, Tommy.

Did he and Claire end up marrying after that debacle? David had cut himself so completely off from the rest of the world, he didn't know for sure. He supposed they had.

Of course, the two of them could have cleared his name once they were wed, but they didn't. In ten years, they had said nothing.

Why would they? he thought bitterly. They could not say anything without confessing their own complicity in the whole ill-begotten affair.

So, Claire and Thomas would be at Stannum House tonight. Well, he only had two choices in the matter – retreat as he always did or raise his head up and weather what condemnation came his way.

After ten years, the pain of the wound had gone, but the scar on his soul left an eternal reminder. He'd loved Claire as deeply as he ever thought he could love another. Her rejection of him was a stab wound to the heart. The fact that she loved his best friend, and that he loved her in return, twisted the knife.

And then there was Viscount Carmarthan, his controlling father…

If only, if only, if only…

If only he had stood fast against the man until he'd attained his majority. If only he'd had the spine to stand up to him, but he'd pressed on David's love for his mother to bend him to his dictates, then he'd broken her heart anyway.

If only he had not fallen in with Thomas' idea of joining The Olympus Club. If he hadn't been so caught up in his own desperation and despair, he might have found another way out of the mess.

If only those facets of dark sex had not seduced and fascinated him as they did…

Although it had been ten long years, the image of a blindfolded Daphnis laid out on the bed, her hands and feet restrained, was etched in his mind. He saw her wine-stained lips open as he pleasured her according to how her watching master instructed. He heard her cries of pleasure.

It had become like a fever in his blood, a form of mental typhus.

He'd thought in exile he was over the excess of it, then the woman before him in his mind was the beautiful Alexandra, spirited and full of the passion he knew she innately possessed –

"Manston? Manston!" demanded Phillip. "Where the hell are you? Woolgathering? We're ready to leave."

David shook his head and gave a slight shrug.

Julian looked somewhat bemused, aware the cause of the tension in the room was more than just high expectations for tonight. "I'm ready to go when you are," he said.

Having accepted the invitation to dress at Stannum House, David gathered his satchel.

He tapped Julian on the shoulder and pulled him to one side while Phillip went outside.

"Are you still planning to be Miss Gedding's escort tonight?" David asked. "I can see you admire her."

Julian frowned. "Is that a problem? I know you and she –"

David shook his head to silence him – *and* the voices in his head protesting his actions.

"If there is any tender feeling on her part toward you, then I encourage you in the pursuit."

The look the man returned was one of surprise and suspicion.

Julian shook his head. "I cannot accept that on face value," he said. "I've seen the way you look at her and I know how highly she regards you. Miss Gedding is a lovely girl. Any man would consider himself lucky to claim her as a bride."

He dropped his voice and glanced toward the door, watchful for Allie's brother.

"I know a man in love when I see one, Manston, so why aren't you intending to plight your troth?"

David forced his inner turmoil down and spoke with a surprisingly steady voice.

"I wish I could. But it's impossible, and I'm certain tonight will make that plainly evident."

He could see that Julian had questions and plenty of them, but he elected not to give voice to any of them.

Julian frowned, perplexed. "I have a high regard for Miss Gedding. I don't wish her to be hurt."

"As have I," replied David, "which is why I am asking you to do this."

Julian looked at him doubtfully and went outside.

David followed and couldn't help feeling he was encouraging history to repeat itself.

Chapter Twenty

THE CLOCK STRUCK the seventh hour. Allie was pleased for the peaceful sanctuary of her bedroom. Never in all her years at Stannum House had she been witness to so much activity, for Uncle George never entertained so lavishly.

She looked upon her reflection in the long mirror and was forced to agree that Lady Abigail's changes to her gown had utterly transformed the garment. She had toyed with wearing the little puffed sleeves high up on her shoulders but they sat better grazing them, exposing the creamy skin across her bosom.

She had not been able to find matching ribbon for the trim, but the darker blue she had used worked better than she anticipated. In the light arrangement of curls around Allie's ears, her mother's pearl earbobs glowed in the lamplight.

Tonight was about performing for three audiences, she reminded herself.

The potential investors in Wheal Gunnis. Allie dabbed perfume on each wrist.

Lady Abigail's *personal* guests. Allie dabbed perfume behind her earlobes.

And Claire, David's lost love. Allie put a final dab between her breasts.

There could be no hiding from the past; it would be laid bare tonight. It was truly unfair of Lady Abigail to have done this. It would be only right to warn David. Then he'd know, wouldn't he?

Allie cursed her godmother once again as she put on her gloves and slipped over her wrist the ribbon holding a fan and her ivory tablet dance card.

With one deep breath, she opened her bedroom door. One of the girls from the village, dressed in the household uniform, bobbed her a curtsy.

"Oh, Miss, you do come up a right treat!"

"Thank you, Betsy," Allie smiled, her courage buoyed by the compliment.

If she had any lingering doubts, they were dispelled the moment she walked into the library which had been set aside for business.

A low, tense conversation between the three men there stopped instantly. Allie mustered an uncertain smile without looking at any one of them in particular; not to her brother, to Julian, or, least of all, to David. She walked past them and kept her attention on the desk. There was the large piece of copper ore unearthed from their first blast. Now thoroughly clean, it seemed to glitter like gold in the lamplight.

To one side was a large plan showing the mine workings.

Never before had she really considered how deep the men who worked underground went – hundreds and hundreds of feet below ground – to do dangerous, dirty, and uncertain work.

On the other side was a printed sheet that contained the going prices of copper and a certified statement by geologist William Smith that estimated the expected yield of copper by the ton.

She touched each piece in a half-prayer, half-wish for the success of tonight's venture before facing the men. Her eyes now fell to her brother who cut a dashing figure in his evening dress. He had shaved close and even had his hair cut, the mop of dark curls that marked the Gedding twins controlled by the liberal use of pomade.

"Pretty dress! It's new, isn't it?" he asked.

Allie shook her head. "I've had this one for years."

"Well it's come up all right, hasn't it?"

Julian burst out a laugh, his gray eyes twinkling. He stepped forward, picked up her hand in his, and bowed over it.

"Phillip, old man, you're also supposed to compliment the young lady *in* the gown as well," he said. "Allow me to do so on his behalf. The dress is without parallel and you are no doubt a diamond of the first water."

The compliment was hyperbolic – just the tonic she needed to banish her nervousness – and she responded in kind, tapping his shoulder with her fan.

"I do fear for the woman who is susceptible to your flattery, Mr. Winter."

"You wound me to the quick, Miss Gedding, when there can be no one here tonight who could come close to capturing my heart but you!"

"Ah, if only I could be certain that was true, sir, for I fear there may be another lady with a stronger claim than I!"

Julian put both hands to his cheeks in comedic open-mouthed horror "You haven't forgotten you're supposed to be my protector tonight, have you?"

"And from the wiles of Lydia Stonely, no less!" She patted his arm comfortingly. "Stay close by my side; I shall be your gallant."

The pantomime performance broke the tension in the air, giving them just the levity they all needed before the guests arrived.

Phillip, smiling, slapped Julian on the shoulder.

"Hopefully, we'll be too busy signing investors for you to have time to face the dragon," he said.

There was a knock on the door. Watt entered, resplendent in his formal butler's uniform, to announce that the first of the guests had arrived. Phillip followed him quickly from the room. Julian appeared to give David a significant look before he excused himself.

She was alone with David and finally gave him her attention.

Her breath quickened. If her brother's transformation had been remarkable, then David's was even more so. She thought him devastatingly handsome in his working clothes, but now, dressed in evening finest – a crisp black tail coat worn with white breeches and highly polished black leather shoes, a cravat expertly tied and fixed with a sapphire stickpin that was both elegant and understated – he looked positively aristocratic.

Every inch the Baron of Carreg. A stranger to her.

He bore her inspection without comment, but when she returned to his eyes, one brow was cocked in a rakish manner that made her weak at the knees. A flush of heat filled her. She wafted her fan to cool the blush she knew was on her cheeks.

Allie drew in a breath and exhaled slowly to steady her nerves. She could not let David be ambushed by Lady Abigail's stunt.

"There's something I need to tell you about one of the guests tonight," she said.

"Claire Owen-Jones?"

Allie started, disarmed. She nodded mutely. A mix of expressions crossed David's face in an instant.

"Your godmother is a hell of a woman," he said.

She didn't know whether that was a compliment or a condemnation.

"You are not married to her as you let me believe." It was less a question than a statement.

Allie kept her voice even, but could not hide the disappointment.

He nodded, his face a mask.

You want the truth of the matter? Look in Manston's eyes.

All she saw in them was defensiveness and hurt.

"Is what they say of you true?"

His face crumpled a moment as though he were in pain before he recovered himself.

"That's a hell of a question, Allie."

"Well?" It was the only word she could articulate.

David swallowed hard, then spoke, his voice flat.

"I shudder to think what that godmother of yours told you. What was it? That I abuse and beat women? That I had to flee in exile to the Continent for ten years? That my proclivities are so vile that experienced courtesans quail? Are they the questions you want answers to?"

Fighting for composure was difficult. She felt her face burn. Her chest was tight, making it difficult to breathe.

David straightened himself, his normally open expression shuttered from her. "If I denied it, I'd be telling a lie. If I admitted it, that wouldn't be the truth either."

"That is no answer at all," she whispered.

"A society so tightly connected as ours is also very unforgiving. You know this as well as I do. Where there are gossips, there is no absolution. If they remember what happened a decade ago, they will judge me as though it were yesterday.

"The only truth I know for certain is that I am the Baron of Carreg, and I can never go back to reclaim my title or my heritage."

The world was suddenly atilt. Allie closed her eyes tight, fearing if she did not, she would stumble or faint. She knew it was irrational, but she wanted her old David back, her *ordinary* David, the curmudgeon with a good heart who could never see it in himself. She would even accept a long-estranged wife if it meant he loved only *her*.

When she swallowed, her throat was raw in unshed tears, but she forced her head up and searched deep for a calm she knew she could possess.

How was it that the calm she found seemed so much like coldness?

"And Claire? Do you love her still?"

The woman who asked the question was a stranger to her, not the self she knew. The change had not gone unnoticed by David either. His expression was guarded.

"She will not have fond memories of me, and it won't be without justification either," he said.

"*That* was not my question," Allie hissed.

A flash of anger crossed his features but, before he could respond, a firm tap on the door broke the spell. The door swung open and Lady Abigail Ridgeway stood there, her plum-colored gown striking against her platinum hair, making her presence even more imposing than ever.

Allie stumbled some paces back and lowered herself onto a chair, panting as though she had run a mile. David recoiled from the woman as though she were a snake, then deliberately turned his back and strode for the decanter of brandy on the side table and began to pour himself a drink.

Lady Abigail's expression was steely. It was clear she missed nothing of the tension in the room. After a moment, she spoke, her voice even.

"Alexandra, my dear, your guests are beginning to arrive."

Allie stood, raised her head pridefully and headed for the door, catching David's glance as he hunched over the decanter, the stopper clattering as he replaced it.

"I look forward to greeting them *all*, my lady. I'm sure this evening will be *full* of surprises."

The majordomo bellowed his announcement. "The Honorable Mr. and Mrs. Thomas Owen-Jones."

Allie considered it a pity her courage lasted only as long as her anger.

She greeted the couple, hoping trepidation didn't show on her features.

Claire Owen-Jones was as delicate and as fine as a Dresden doll. Her brown hair was piled high, save for the array of ringlets falling around her ears. A gown of silvery-blue showed off a fine figure. In truth, the young matron was still a beautiful woman.

So, this was the woman who had captured David's heart all those years ago.

Beside her, she felt as gauche as a farmer's daughter.

She accepted the hand of Thomas, Claire's husband, who bowed over it in gallant fashion. He was of medium height with dark brown hair. He was dressed well – and fed a little too well if his paunch and a slight rounding of the face were anything to go by.

Almost belatedly, Allie remembered her role as hostess. "It is good of you to join us."

"It's very kind of you to invite us to your home," said Claire. "We've heard Lady Abigail's events are memorable affairs, but we've never before been invited to one."

I think you'll *definitely* find tonight memorable, thought Allie. She found a smile and hoped it was not a brittle one. "If I might confess, it is a new experience for my brother and I also," she said. "We've not had recent opportunity to entertain in the manner we would wish, so we're indebted to my cousin and Sir Daniel for their assistance."

She was rather pleased she could carry herself with confidence, regardless of how tissue thin it was. If she had learned any lesson at all from her godmother, it was that the performance was the key. And she possessed enough pride to see her through this evening.

Claire's smile stiffened abruptly as she glanced across the room. It didn't go unnoticed by Allie that the woman touched her husband's hand to attract his attention.

Allie turned to look and saw David looking directly at the couple. He had an odd expression on his face – sardonic... wry, perhaps. He saluted the couple with the glass in his hand and a nod of his head, but did not approach.

Allie looked back at her guests. Both wore expressions of surprise but they were quickly righted. Thomas Owen-Jones excused himself, leaving his wife at Allie's side.

"Are you quite all right, Mrs. Owen-Jones?" she asked solicitously. "You seem to have come over a little peculiar."

Before she could question her own actions, Allie put her arm through that of the petite woman and led her further into the hall. She noticed that Lady Abigail appeared to be deep in conversation with another guest. But she was not so engrossed that her eyes didn't follow Allie as she searched for a place for Claire to sit.

"No, no, I'm quite well," Claire protested weakly. "We've had a long journey, that's all."

"*Quel dommage!* A pity to be sure," Allie responded, leading her to two empty seats. "Come, do sit by me for a little while and tell me all about your family. They are from Wales, I understand."

The woman settled to the chair with apparent relief. "Why, yes, although Thomas and I spend most of our time in London and a little in Cornwall where he has some business interests." She frowned slightly. "But I'm afraid you have the advantage of us, Miss Gedding…"

Allie smiled. "Well, as it so happens, we have a friend in common."

The woman's sculptured eyebrows frowned in confusion a moment before her face colored. A reply seemed just on her lips when Lady Abigail appeared before them.

"Alexandra, my dear, would you do me the honor of introducing me to your guest?" The question was phrased impeccably, but Allie was not fooled by it. She gave her godmother a direct look which was returned in equal measure. Claire, meanwhile, seemed to have recovered somewhat and rose to her feet with Allie.

"Lady Abigail, I'd like to introduce you to Mrs. Claire Owen-Jones. Mrs. Owen-Jones, my godmother and cousin, Lady Abigail Ridgeway."

Claire bobbed a curtsy.

"I understand we owe you thanks for our invitation tonight as well as Miss Gedding."

Lady Abigail waved her hand, dismissing the gesture as nothing. Her brow puckered.

"Owen-Jones… would your husband's family be relatives of the

Tremayne family? I'm thinking of Warrick Tremayne in particular."

Allie inwardly shook her head. *Drury Lane should witness such a performance.*

The cautious expression Claire had worn ever since spotting David left her face. "Why, yes! He's my husband's youngest uncle. You know him, my lady?"

"We were quite bosom friends," the lady responded, although Allie noticed a sly twitch of her mouth. "We must talk later, but now I have to steal my goddaughter away, if you'll forgive me."

The look of relief on Claire's face was palpable. As she sat back down, Lady Abigail took Allie's arm for a turn around the room.

"Mingle, my dear!" she muttered under her breath. "You are hostess here tonight. Your role is to be charming and make people kindly disposed to you and your brother."

"You think I'm content to be an empty decoration in my own house?" Allie hissed under her breath. Lady Abigail gripped her arm tight.

"Foolish child! Don't be such a ninny as to ruin this evening for yourself over a jealous spat. I thought you were smarter than to make a scene."

Allie's cheeks burned as though the verbal slap was physical. She swallowed her resentment and anger to smile and nod at Olivia Hardacre, who was in the company of her friend, Susannah Payne.

"You forget we have a bargain," Lady Abigail continued. "You have two jobs to do tonight. One is to smile and grease the wheels so the gentlemen with the fat purses will open them and get Wheal Gunnis going again. The other is to keep this party lively, so my agents can do *their* work."

Lady Abigail's grip loosened and the look Allie received this time was one of sympathy.

"My dear, I promised you no easy answers, remember? Keep your eyes open and you will learn far more by astute observation than by fretting – and that also includes your Mr. Manston."

"I don't wish to speak of him."

"Then don't. Now, put on a good face because there's a couple over there I'd like to introduce you to. Lord and Lady Besche have just returned from Austria."

Resigned, she gave her evening over to her godmother's instruction. People who had simply been titles on a piece of paper a few hours before became flesh and blood and, as much as she resented Abigail's lecture, she had to admit the woman was right.

She listened to Sir Andrew Fullerwood talk about divesting his interests in a mahogany plantation in Honduras. The more questions she asked, the more flattered he became, so by the time he had been called away by some other guests, Allie knew enough to share with Phillip the best approach to take when discussing business with him.

Then there was there was the Honorable Mr. and Mrs. Strassner from Bodmin. They were a very jolly middle-aged couple. They seemed like salt of the earth country folk, their clothes ever so slightly out of fashion.

"They might look like plump pigeons," Abigail confided later on, "but a more shrewd couple this side of the Welsh border you are unlikely to meet."

Abigail tapped her with a fan to draw attention. "Ah!" the woman called out to another. "Lady Healey-Ray, there is someone I wish to make known to you."

Allie found herself in conversation with the rather dashing widow, then accepted a dance with Sir Andrew.

But all the while, her eyes followed the Owen-Jones' around the room, watching as they chatted pleasantly with other guests, but making great pains to avoid David.

If she did not know what to watch for and to watch closely, she might have missed it. But the more Allie observed the pair, the more they revealed.

Curse Abigail for being right.

The couple did not seem angry or disdainful, rather they seemed apprehensive, almost furtive. Why would *that* be? Had it not been Claire's honor that had been compromised?

As for what little she saw of David, his savage wash of anger in the library had gone and he appeared an impeccable guest – charming but not overdoing it.

Allie watched him invite Lydia Stonely to stand up and dance, and in doing so, caught her eyes. He knew she was watching. There was a particular look about him that told her the action was designed for her benefit. Did he think she'd be jealous? Perhaps *he* ought to be worried as the look of rapture on the silly woman's face suggested her attachment was not as solid as Julian feared.

Chapter Twenty-One

D AVID ONCE READ that to face one's fears was to see them shrink. *We are more often frightened than hurt; and we suffer more from imagination than from reality.*

Who was it? Ah, yes, Seneca. A classical education had not gone to waste.

Seeing Claire and Thomas being greeted by Allie was startling. He thought he might be transported back to his twenty-first year by seeing them but, to his surprise, he barely recognized Thomas at first. If he hadn't known better, he might have mistaken him for his father.

Married life – the life *he* ought to have had – appeared to have agreed with his old friend. His face was soft and round from rich food and an abundance of good living.

And, as for Claire, he expected his heart to pound on seeing her face once more.

It did not.

The advance knowledge provided by Lady Abigail's guest list had forearmed him to be sure, but it was a surprise to discover that Claire's soft beauty paled in comparison with Allie's vibrant coloring. And even more than that. Claire had always possessed a nervous energy like the sound of a long-sustained note on a violin string. Now, it had started to show on her face. Features striking in youth were now sharp and angular. How different she seemed compared to Allie's warm vivaciousness.

Then she looked his way, and her face froze. She tapped at her husband's hand and he looked, too, and was startled.

David smiled stiffly and acknowledged them. The hollow feeling of ten wasted years weighed in his gut and not even a glass of fine wine was enough to fill it.

But he wouldn't do anything that might ruin the chance the Gedding twins had of restoring their fortunes – his own interest in the matter not withstanding – so he turned away and watched the room.

He saw Sir Daniel in serious conversation with two guests he had arrived with. Hardacre and Payne, his memory supplied. He watched as one of them, Payne, he thought, broke away from the conversation, approach a pretty brunette woman to speak with her a moment, before slipping out a side door.

For a cigar perhaps? Somehow, he thought not. Interesting... there was an undercurrent to this evening that he'd missed, focused as he was with preparing the presentations and anticipating an unpleasant reunion with Claire and Thomas.

He really ought to make the acquaintance of Lieutenant Hardacre. He took two steps forward before he heard his name called elsewhere.

"David?"

He turned to find himself face-to-face with his former friend.

"Tom," he acknowledged.

The man tried to look him in the eyes but could not, instead seeming to focus on the end of his nose. "I... I don't know what to say after all this time."

"After ten years, we're beyond words, wouldn't you say?"

Apparently not.

The man didn't take his cue to leave. *Worse.* Thomas wanted to talk.

"When I suggested that you... that is, I never expected you to go that far."

David didn't know what annoyed him more – the half-baked apology or the memories it dredged up. He shook his head.

"Leave it," he said gruffly. "Though I wish to hell you and Claire had just eloped to Gretna Green."

At Thomas' shame-faced expression, David fought a wave of contempt wash over him. For too many years, he'd blamed himself entirely for his actions – in no small measure rightly – but he wished to God he'd had a true friend at the time who might have counseled him differently.

He walked away but not before his eyes fell on Allie, taking a turn about the room, arm-in-arm with Lady Abigail. Arguably, she looked like she was having a worse time than he was. Then her expression changed. It hardened a moment before a mask of the perfect country house hostess slipped completely over her face.

Before he could ruminate any further on that, Julian Winter attracted his attention, forcing David to ready himself for his own performance as mine owner.

I hope Lady Abigail enjoys her little theater. Damn, that woman was a piece of work.

A LITTLE OVER halfway through the evening, Julian approached to claim his dance.

Allie couldn't fail to notice an extra spring in his step and a mischievous grin around his mouth and couldn't help an answering smile in return. Julian was a true gentleman, delightful and uncomplicated, and fast becoming a good friend.

If she was honest with herself, there had been times over the past six months when she considered what it might be like to have him as a beau.

Charming and uncomplicated Julian.
Intense and complex David...

Julian deftly performed a turn step to avoid Lydia Stonely, who was just leaving the dance floor with a partner. He bowed as Allie got to her feet and offered her his hand.

"Pray tell, what brings such a smile to your face?" she asked with amusement, noting the slight scowl on Lydia's features as he led her out onto the dance floor.

"A promising business venture, an amusing evening with a charming dance partner in my arms, what man could ask for more?"

"Your flattery does you credit, sir," she rejoined. "You shan't have any difficulties in finding suitable young ladies to woo."

Julian leaned in and gave a stage whisper. "As long as it is not Lydia."

She managed to catch sight of the young woman glaring in their direction before a new dance partner said something to catch her attention.

"So how do the presentations go?" Allie asked.

"All business! No wonder you're a spinster," Julian teased. "It's not seemly to talk enterprise while dancing. You shall have to wait for afterwards."

The country dance began and she threw herself into it, letting Julian's levity buoy her own spirits. Then, as the dance progressed, her partner became Thomas whose face seemed more flushed than it ought to be for a man of his relative youth, but he continued on gamely.

Like iron filings drawn to a lode stone, she looked about for David and found him. The woman he held in his arms was Claire.

What a handsome couple they make.

She was as short as David was tall, her delicate build and pale features contrasting attractively with David's dark hair and tanned features. It came as no surprise, however, that they didn't seem comfortable together. Their dancing was stiff, lacking the energy she knew David to possess and the grace she expected from Claire.

It was a relief when the dance required them to change partners once more.

Eventually, she found herself in David's arms. It was as though she had found home. His touch was familiar, making her aware of how her body reacted to his movements. His expression, however, was closed off to her, as if warning her against questioning him here, surrounded by her guests. They danced without speaking.

When the dance came to an end, Julian found her and claimed her hand once more. He led her out to the garden, promising the news he had denied earlier. Across the way, she could see the brightly lit window of the study. She fanned herself in lieu of a breeze which seemed absent this evening.

They sat on a stone bench in the garden, close enough to hear the musicians start another lively country tune.

"Congratulations, Miss Gedding, you are well on your way to your family fortune being restored."

"Truly? You do not jest?"

He shook his head.

"We were hopeful of being nearly fully subscribed by the end of the evening. However…" He let his words to trail away.

She snapped her fan closed and tapped him on the shoulder.

"*However…*" she repeated, allowing a play of a smile to cross her features.

"We'll be happily and successfully *over*subscribed!"

She let out a squeal of delight, threw herself into his arms, and kissed his cheek.

Julian wrapped his arms about her and offered a squeeze of affection before releasing her.

"Tell me all! Spare no details," she pleaded.

He grinned. "Our guests were rather skeptical at first, particularly Strassner, but once they saw the independent report for themselves, he put himself down for two hundred and *fifty* pounds.

"And you were right about Sir Andrew. We did not mention Honduras at all, but his ears certainly pricked up when Phillip mentioned the projected return on investment. Did I tell you Manston has an excellent business brain? Lord Harper was asking some very probing questions. I know if it had been left to Phillip and me, we'd have made a hash of it. But Manston was completely up to the challenge."

Allie put her hands to her cheeks where she could feel the heat of them through her evening gloves. "I can't tell you how overjoyed I am," she said.

She became conscious of being scrutinized, and the heat on her cheeks remained. Julian seemed to be taking in her features before settling on her mouth.

He slowly leaned in for a kiss. It was a light touch of the lips, soft and sweet, yet it lacked ardor.

Julian looked rueful as he sat back.

"'Tis a pity that," he said.

"I'm afraid I don't know what you mean."

"You're a lovely woman, Alexandra, and *I'm* not considered an unsuitable prospect. On paper, we ought to be well-matched. I thought perhaps a kiss might cause a spark between us, but it seems it is not to be."

She considered not only his words, but also their tone very carefully. He was not disappointed. Regretful was a more apt description.

"Your heart belongs to David Manston – it did even before we first met, didn't it?" he asked softly.

She dropped her eyes and fidgeted with her fan.

"I'm sorry if I ever gave you cause to think... or that I'd dallied unkindly with your feelings... I –"

Julian's hand settled over hers and squeezed it.

"There is nothing at all to apologize for, no fault to be laid at your feet or my own. You would do me the greatest honor if you think no more of it. As I regard Phillip as a brother, I've come to see you as a sister, and – I hope – a friend?"

SPY ANOTHER DAY

His kindness was more than she had hoped for. "Oh, Julian, yes, of course. Likewise, you have become dear to me as my own brother. It's just that…"

She hesitated. Allie had spoken to no one about her feelings for David, though it was plain enough to Phillip and now Julian, too, where her attachment lay. Once again, Julian seemed to know exactly the right thing to say.

"I'll let you in on a secret," he said. "Your regard for him is not unrequited. I have no idea what prevents him from claiming your hand, but I hope one day you'll both sort it out."

Allie squeezed Julian's hand in return.

"As do I."

"But I do beg that you do me a kindness," he asked.

Allie kissed him on the cheek. "Anything, dear friend."

"Dance with me one more time – just to discourage Lydia."

As THE EVENING wore on, Allie was content to sit out the next set of dances. She watched Lady Abigail work the room with the efficiency of a Member of Parliament soliciting votes in the House of Commons.

She allowed herself to idly consider her godmother standing across the green carpet from Prime Minister William Pitt the Younger and smiled absently at the woman who took the seat beside her.

Where was Sir Daniel? And for that matter, where were Lieutenant Hardacre and Mr. Payne?

They'd set up no card room, although that may not have stopped some enterprising gents from finding a venue in one of the downstairs rooms. Still, midnight supper was yet to be served and judging by what she'd seen in the kitchen, they would be foolish to miss out on the dishes Mrs. Pascoe had prepared.

She frowned. Had they departed early? No, over there were Susannah and Olivia chatting with Mrs. Strassner.

"The guest you mentioned we had in common… you mean David

Manston, don't you?"

Claire's softly spoken words beside her – tentative, curious – were a splash of cold water over her musings.

"Has he..." Claire's voice was little above a whisper. Allie experienced a rush of resentment at having to lean close to hear her. "Does he ever speak of me?"

What an odd thing to ask.

Allie looked at her as she fidgeted with a lace-trimmed kerchief in her hand. The woman seemed to be an entire bundle of nerves. Had she always been like this?

"Is there any reason why Mr. Manston should speak of another man's wife?"

Claire's face sharpened a moment before sinking like a stone beneath an expression of sorrow.

"We – that is, Thomas and I – were once very good friends with David. We grew up together and we were little more than children ourselves when..."

The musicians performed a loud flourish and Harry Watt, relishing his role as butler, sounded a gong and announced supper was being served in the dining room. There was a smattering of applause and the hall started to empty.

Claire stood and looked about pensively. Searching for her husband? Or for David? Allie, too, looked around the room and could not see David. Claire's eyes settled on to her husband's as he conversed with some other guests and the nervous trembling of her shoulders ceased.

"'When' *what*, Mrs. Owen-Jones?" Allie asked urgently, rising beside her. "What happened between you that caused David to lose everything, most of all his good name?"

The woman shook her head, brown eyes looking up at her. "I can't speak of it," she said.

Allie fought the urge to shake the silly woman by the shoulders

SPY ANOTHER DAY

until better answers fell out of her mouth.

"I'm afraid I have to insist." Her voice was harsh, she knew it was, but she couldn't restrain herself any longer. "David has lived like a fugitive for the past ten years, accused of vile crimes. Are *any* of the stories true?"

The fragile creature before her looked ready to burst into tears. Allie looked up in time to see Thomas Owen-Jones breaking off from his conversation and trying to approach, his brows lowered as he observed his wife's distress but his progress in her direction was hindered by the flow of couples toward the dining room.

The time to talk would be over the moment Claire's husband joined them.

"Please, Mrs. Owen-Jones. I beg of you from one woman to another. If you know the accusations against him to be false, then *tell* me. Tell me the *truth*. It will be balm for your own soul if you do."

The last words hit a nerve, the brittle façade fractured, and the first of a line of tears fell down the woman's face.

"We took shameless advantage of David's love for both of us," Claire whispered hurriedly. "My parents insisted on a marriage with David, and there was no good reason to refuse other for my love for Tom. That was something they could not accept."

"Claire?" Thomas drew near.

"You must believe we did not know of David's plans until he had laid them in place on our behalf," the woman continued, "then it was too late to stop it."

Owen-Jones drew his wife to his side and gave Allie a direct look. She raised her chin, unapologetic for his wife's distress.

"Forgive us if we do not stay for supper, Miss Gedding," he said stiffly. "I'm afraid the evening has been too exhausting for my wife. I beg you to make our excuses to your brother."

"Leaving so soon, sir?" Allie worked to ensure her voice traveled no further than the three of them. "It seems to be a trait of yours to cut and run when convenient."

She watched the man's face turn puce with restrained emotion. Owen-Jones said nothing. Any retort he might have a mind to express left voiceless.

Allie felt no such restraint.

"Have you expressed your regret to Manston? Made your excuses to him? Ten years, sir, is a long time to carry the weight of another man's sins."

Just as Owen-Jones started to usher her away, Claire raised her head.

"David was a good man even back then, Miss Gedding. I'm sorry it took us so long to realize just how good he was to us."

Chapter Twenty-Two

DAVID HEARD THE jangle of bridles but ignored it.

It was the morning after the soiree. There had been a late briefing of the Wheal Gunnis Mining Company afterwards but today, he expected no one. More than that, he didn't *want* to see anyone either.

He turned his attention back to his latest sketch. He'd been slow in fulfilling his latest commission and his agent had written him a rather nasty letter threatening dire consequences if he did not send him *"in short order, high quality illustrations of a man and woman in a drawing room setting on the verge of coitus with prick and cunny clearly visible. Chaise lounge preferred. A second drawing of three naked women with garlands in their hair as to imitate wood nymphs dancing around a Grecian maiden who is indulging herself while in repose. And last, but not least, a semi-clad (showing breasts would be preferred) demimonde with whip in hand, ready to lash a bewigged gentleman on his bare buttocks."*

The threat meant nothing to him. He'd been slow in fulfilling his commission because he no longer wanted to do them. The demon that drew him into this debauched world had been sweated out of him like a fever over this past year, leaving him weak and listless.

And yet he was under obligation, suffering through the chore by telling himself that if he finished the task, he could tell Sheehan and Wood this would be the last. They would have to find themselves another artist.

An insistent hand beat at the door.

He glanced at it and counted to twenty beneath his breath in the hopes whoever was there would simply give up and go away.

Bang! Bang! Bang!

No such damned luck. He threw down his pencil and cursed.

The noise continued even as he laid a hand on the door. He pulled it open violently. The woman before him did not jump back in surprise. Rather, she folded her arms before her, a riding crop in her hand.

"Lady Abigail," he said flatly, finally acknowledging his caller.

"Well? Aren't you going to invite me in?" she asked, her voice just this side of peevish.

They stared at one another for a good long moment in a silent battle of wills, before David pivoted on his heel and walked away, leaving the door wide open.

He was not going to slam a door in a lady's face, but neither was he going to make her feel welcome.

He returned to his drafting desk and glanced at the outline sketch of the couple with a faint feeling of disgust. He closed the sketchbook and turned around.

"I'm a busy man. Say your piece and then leave."

Lady Abigail's gray-green eyes never left his. Indeed, her chin lifted a little in defiance as she walked further into his little parlor, found a chair – *his* good chair – and sat down.

"Are you a *coward*, Mr. Manston?"

"What the hell?"

"I ask because I've never seen anyone walk away from his reputation without a fight," she continued.

"My reputation speaks for itself – as you made it your business to know."

"I *do* know. And that is what puzzles me – because I don't believe a word of it."

He really ought to shut up now and say no more, but Allie's relative had gotten under his skin. He had no idea why he felt obliged to justify himself to her and yet here he was, doing so.

"You've heard the stories. Why do you doubt them?"

"Because I've spoken to Alexandra. Moreover, your Claire has spoken to Alexandra and has told her quite a different tale to the one she recounted to her parents and yours, all those years ago."

Past and present collided in that instant like being smashed against the rocks on the cliffs below.

Claire and Alexandra, as different as two women could be, and yet he could say that he loved them both. But one broke his heart so deeply that there was not enough of him left to give to the woman who deserved the best of a man – the whole of a man.

"Claire and Thomas would like to make amends," said Abigail.

Anger came like a volcanic force, the heat of it through his feet, up his legs, into his torso and arms. He turned and shoved his heavy oak drafting table with such violence it toppled over onto the floor with a thunderous noise. The bottles of ink shattered. Red ink flowed, reminding him of blood as it followed the cracks and the valleys of the flagstones.

There, what did she make of that?

His clenched jaw ached and his chest heaved. He turned back to Lady Abigail and glared at her. She thought he was not capable of violence? Of the things they said of him? Those things which *he himself* had written?

"*There!*" he roared aloud, pointing to the destruction. "Do you doubt me a violent man now?"

Lady Abigail never looked at the wreckage. Instead, her attention was on him, as though she saw something he could not discern for himself.

"That's furniture," she said. "It's not a woman."

The act of rage had left him drained. He pulled his drawing stool to him and sank down on it.

"Tell me all of it, David," she said, her voice gentle. "From the beginning."

"Why? What possible difference could it make now?" he demanded hoarsely. "It can't change what has been; it can't change the present."

"I need you to tell me."

He drew himself up and looked at Lady Abigail as if she'd become a serpent.

Her mouth twisted in a wry smile, as though she had already known his thoughts.

"Alexandra is in need of protection, although she doesn't yet know it –"

"Protection from what? Who –"

"– and the only man I trust to protect her is you. The only man she will listen to is *you*."

"Well that's hardly likely after everything she's heard about me, is it?"

"Nevertheless, it's true, unlike your past, and if I didn't think you were up to the task, I'd have called elsewhere," said Abigail, dusting down the sleeve of her riding habit. "So, if you've had quite enough of feeling sorry for yourself, I should like to help you in exchange for helping me, but I do need to hear the whole of it."

David cursed himself as a sliver of hope managed to pierce the darkness of his soul. The rawness in his chest revealed he must feel *something* at least. The chance to clear his name, to demonstrate he *was* the man Allie believed him to be was damned near irresistible.

"Why is this so important to you?" he asked. "And what danger is Allie in?"

Lady Abigail saw the exact moment of his weakness. He saw how she exploited it with a coy smile.

"Answer my question first and I shall be glad to answer yours. Do we have a deal, Mr. Manston?"

David glanced across to his dining table and the chessboard. A half-finished game with Allie stood on it from months ago.

Checkmate.

He drew in a breath and began.

"The letter my father received from the brothel keeper about the girl... I dictated it."

A look of satisfaction crossed the noblewoman's face as she sat back to listen.

THE WELL-DRESSED, HEAVYSET man leaned back in his chair and stared at him across the desk.

"A letter from me banning you from The Olympus Club? It's most unusual. Ordinarily, people write to *me*. I have many letters from men– *and* some women, too – literally begging for membership."

Despite the hundred and one misgivings that buzzed in his mind, David had pressed on.

He'd tried Thomas' idea to make himself a libertine. And it had led to an addiction as powerful as laudanum.

David had been seen leaving The Olympus Club. Not once; a dozen times, more. Word had gotten back to his and Claire's parents and it had done no use. They wanted this match.

Well, if they refused to break the engagement, there was only one thing for it. To make himself so *completely*, so *utterly* unmarriageable that Claire's parents would withdraw from the suit. They could not refuse her Thomas after *that*.

What did any of his life matter anyway, when the two people he loved best in the world loved each other more?

"The Olympus Club is also a place where no questions are asked, am I mistaken in that, too?" he had inquired of Zeus.

Zeus, who went by the more prosaic name of Reynold Chalmers

in his ordinary business dealings, leaned back in his chair.

"A letter will cost you," the man warned.

"And I'm prepared to pay handsomely – it's what business is all about, isn't it?"

Chalmers leaned forward across his desk and, with deliberate intent, pulled his writing box toward him.

"Then tell me the sad tale, young Ampelos. I know some of our *experienced* women will be sorry not to have had your pleasure."

David had rehearsed the letter over in his mind all afternoon, revising it over and over until he was satisfied it was shocking enough, because it would be the final curtain on a piece of theater to be performed by himself, Thomas, and Claire that night.

What could be enough to get oneself barred from the most notorious rakehell club in London? How about raping and scourging one of the girls with a savagery so complete that her mind and body were irretrievably broken?

David dictated the letter in fulsome detail, nearly sickening himself in the process. Indeed, Chalmers' own face settled into a grimace as his pen scratched across the paper.

"There'll be no hiding this once it gets out, you know. If your father doesn't cover it up, you won't be welcome in any club in the city, let alone polite society."

"I don't particularly care."

Chalmers slid the completed but unsigned letter across the desk. David read through it. He didn't think the roiling in his stomach could get much worse, but realized he was wrong as he read through his alleged transgressions laid out in black and white.

He nodded once, bitterly satisfied.

"Sign it."

"It'll cost you one hundred and fifty guineas."

He'd skewered the man with a look, but far from being quailed, Chalmers seemed surprisingly earnest. He'd threaded the fingers of his hands together on the desk before him and began to speak.

"One of my girls came to me this morning. I'd sent her to Mrs. Clementine last week to treat a certain condition, if you know what I mean. The girl thought she was pregnant and wanted to get out of the game. Never really wanted to be in it in the first place, if you know what I mean. She only did it to send money up north to her family.

"Turns out she hadn't gotten herself knocked up after all. She has cancer. Bad. Jenny's a good girl and she deserves a turn of fortune. It's fifty for me. One hundred for her. You see her tonight and we'll get her out of here by morning and not let any of the other girls know. It will be as if she disappeared. That'll get the tongues wagging, if that's what you want. And that letter will finish it."

He closed his eyes and considered what the man had told him and nodded once.

"Tonight then. I'll give the money to the girl directly."

There was no slyness to the man's expression. On the contrary, he looked rather relieved as he reached across, drew the letter back and signed it.

David stood.

"I'll be back at eleven o'clock for the rest of the night to complete our deal, then I'll leave. After that, if anyone comes to ask for me, tell them what's in the letter. Then send it by messenger to my house first thing in the morning."

Chalmers rose also. "It's a hell of a thing you're doing, Manston."

The ambiguity of the statement haunted him for ten long years.

ABIGAIL OWNED A moment of sympathy for the man before her but she tamped it down. She didn't have time for pity, and David wouldn't appreciate it either.

"Give me the full name of the girl if you know it and any other details you can remember," she said and ignored the askance expression he gave her. She rose to her feet and, with a nod of her head, drew his attention back to the ruined desk.

"You'd better fix that and get to work. I'll drop by tomorrow for the information. I'll see what my men can run down, but I make no promises."

"I don't understand why you're doing this."

"It's actually none of your business why I do this. Suffice it to say my own reasons are enough."

"That involve Allie."

"And Phillip."

"And now me."

"If you're prepared for it."

She could see the man sloughed off his own pity when Alexandra was involved. Excellent, that's what she needed – a strong, decisive, protective man.

"Then tell me *your* story, Lady Abigail," he pressed firmly. "And don't be stinting on the details."

"My husband and I are hunting down a dangerous traitor to the Crown."

"You jest."

"I wish I did," she said. "The man we're seeking is the key to stopping French invasion plans for England. We believe he and his gang to be in the area. We want to lure him to Stannum before he can carry out the next part of his plan."

"Isn't this the job of the army? Or the navy, or something?"

"One does not send in the army to catch rats, Mr. Manston. One sends in the rat catchers."

She watched him blink slowly, uncomprehendingly.

"*Spies*, Manston. Traitors who can blend in; those whom one would never expect. Our fighting men do well when they have enemy colors to address – not when the enemy can disappear like a will-o-the-wisp among their own.

"There is a ship departing France for Ireland in the next few weeks. It will be sailing by night close to our shores. There will be a man on the vessel that my husband and his men intend to capture. We also want to keep this person here in your cottage for a few days until it is safe to move him."

She saw understanding dawn in his eyes.

"Manston the hermit has his uses after all."

"You have few visitors and your home overlooks the sea. We can bring this man here and get him away without concerning the villagers."

Abigail watched him scrub his unshaven face with his hand as he took in what he'd been told.

"Tell me again how Allie is involved in this?" he asked.

"In addition to the man I mentioned, there is his gang we have yet to fully identify, but make no mistake, they're in the area. I'll be leaving in a couple of days, and I need someone I can rely on. That will be Alexandra."

"You're going to leave a young woman on her own to be your *spy*?"

Abigail raised her head and gave him a half-mocking look.

"She won't be on her own if she has *your* support."

"In other words, blackmail."

Manston wore the full force of her mockery.

"It's only blackmail if there's not a fair exchange involved," she laughed. "Your complete cooperation for the full exoneration of your name if your story checks out."

She rose to her feet and held out her hand to him.

"Do we have an agreement?"

The faint sneer on his handsome face softened until it became a chuckle. In that moment, he reminded her of Daniel not long after they'd met. She waited; sure she was not mistaken about this man, although he was one of the more stubborn of his type.

She had dangled enough incentive – the twin lures of his reputation restored and to aid the woman he loved – that he ought to give in.

He stood at last and took her hand firmly. She was ready to have him shake it in a businesslike manner. Instead, he turned their joined hands and placed a kiss on her wrist.

"I'll do it for Allie, as well as for king and Country, but I hold no expectation of my good name being restored – that ship has long sailed."

Abigail inclined her head. "Miracles have been known to happen, Mr. Manston. I wouldn't write off the chance."

Chapter Twenty-Three

Early July

IT WAS A messenger sent by Prenpas who first alerted David to the damage at the mine. For the past two weeks, the mine foreman and three of the villagers had spent half-days up at Wheal Gunnis working on renovating the outbuildings – the tool shed, the sorting shed, the site office.

The plan was to start extracting the first load of ore before the end of August, giving enough time for three months of mining before winter made it too cold to work.

He'd ridden up and just dismounted to speak with Prenpas himself when Allie and Phillip rode into sight.

He hadn't seen Allie since the soiree and, even under these circumstances, he gravitated to her. Just being in her company again felt good. He held Nephel by the bridle and offered his hand to help her dismount.

That felt right, too…

And yet there was the feeling that, once again, he'd destroyed the chance to have a life with a woman he loved.

"What's the damage?" Phillip asked, reining in his horse.

"I thought it best ye look for yerself, Master Gedding," Prenpas said. "Wicked, just wicked what's been done here. Come look at this."

The three of them trailed the blacksmith around the engine house.

"I told the two young fellas they could go home after they'd let ye know what'd happened. No point in them staying. We'll need to order some extra timber before we fix the sorting shed."

Soon, David and the twins saw the damage for themselves. The doors of all three outbuildings had been broken open. Inside the sorting shed, work benches had been smashed. And at the tool shed, equipment had been taken.

Phillip kicked the shattered timbers of the tool shed door in frustration and didn't restrain himself from uttering a string of curses.

David glanced sidelong at Allie. Her mouth was pressed to a thin line of barely restrained anger, but she had a little more self-possession than her brother – not that he could blame Phillip for venting his fury.

Worst of all, this was not the first time something like this had happened. No sooner had they started repairing the mine head and the engine house in preparation for reopening, strange little things started happening at night.

The ghosts of Wheal Gunnis had decided it was not enough to simply haunt. Equipment went missing, too. But it was nothing too much at first– a length of rope gone here, a spanner missing there. On the surface of it, it appeared nothing more than petty pilfering. Annoying but manageable.

This time, however, there had been serious theft as well as wanton vandalism.

"How much equipment has been stolen?"

"Thirty crow bars and roll picks; twenty of them boring hammers; a dozen shovels and all of the axes." Prenpas rattled the numbers off. "A good thing the order for the tamping bars and shooting needles weren't delivered yet."

"I find it hard to credit that any of the villagers would do this," said Allie. "All of them were thrilled to learn the mine would reopen. They know the money and jobs that will come with it."

"I don't believe it's anyone from Stannum either," said Phillip. "But if not them, then who are they? *Where* are they? No strangers have been seen to account for the stories of ghostly sights and sounds up here at night."

David felt a trickle of awareness travel down his spine. Lady Abigail's traitors perhaps?

If so, thus far, they'd been cautious enough to keep themselves hidden from sight. And why do this if it brought attention to themselves? Besides which, it must have been a bit of an operation to cart away all that equipment. What use would traitors have for it?

He left Phillip and Allie to join Prenpas inspecting the office building while he went into the engine house itself. He stared up at the fifty-foot tall iron monster. An involuntary shudder passed through him.

What if the damage extended further than smashing the sorting shed benches? If the engine broke down while in operation, miners could suffocate or drown in the pits below.

He didn't place any stock in the rumors of ghosts. The culprits were as much flesh and blood as he was. And there were enough odd coincidences for him to believe there was something strange going on that might include sabotage.

David started climbing the ladder up the Beast, as the pump was known.

He didn't know anything in particular about engines, but he was observant. If there were parts missing, it might be obvious, even to someone as untrained as he.

The salt-encrusted glass still let in light, but it was diffused, casting long shadows through the building.

He reached the platform and grabbed a post for balance to stretch out and touch the long thin plug rods. He gripped hold of one and shook it. It seemed firmly in place.

Far above him, another thirty feet away, was the cast iron bob, the thirty-three foot long beam that balanced in and out of the brick engine room on a central fulcrum – like a child's seesaw, but much, much larger and heavier.

If someone caused that to fall…

"Manston!" Phillip called out.

"I'm up here," he yelled down.

"Anything amiss?" Allie asked. He hated the sound of worry in her voice.

"Not that I can tell," he answered truthfully. He made his way back down the ladder.

"Julian will be returning in the next three weeks with the engineers to make sure the Beast here is in good working order before we begin," said Phillip. "I'll have them inspect it thoroughly. Until then, there's little we can do except keep people away from here. I've instructed Prenpas to organize a night watch."

"I can't see that we have any other choice," David admitted.

They walked out of the engine house to the brow of the hill. Billowing gray clouds like a giant ship in full sail sat out on the horizon. The afternoon had taken on a cold blue cast. A flock of terns, gleaming white, rose from its place in the cliffs and wheeled about in the winds, calling noisily to one another.

"Don't expect me home tonight," said Phillip to his sister, the young man's voice flat. "I'm going to Camelford and I'll stay the night."

He wished he could see Allie's face to read her reaction, but the stiffening of her spine told him as much as he needed to know.

ALLIE WATCHED PHILLIP mount his horse and ride away, shoulders sagging, without taking a second glance back. Her heart broke knowing there was nothing she could say to her brother other than empty platitudes.

Why was everything so difficult? It seemed every step forward they took was marred by another unforeseen problem.

She waited until he was out of sight before she turned to David, giving him a rueful smile. They hadn't seen each other since the party and memories of that night had never been far from her thoughts. But those thoughts ended with the resignation that the most she could hope for was friendship between them. Yet she'd hoped for so much more. She searched his face and tried to tell herself there was nothing personal in the sketch that she had seen, that hers was simply a convenient face to put on a fantasy…

She pushed the image from her mind.

"It always seems we take one step forward and two steps back," she said. "I know the thefts and the vandalism are costly distractions we don't need, but Phillip is taking this so personally."

"It *is* personal," David answered. "He sees it as a betrayal."

She conceded the point with a tilt of her head. Together, they walked back to their horses.

"I can't believe anyone in the village is behind it," she said. "At the meeting we had after the signing of the investors, everyone was thrilled."

"Clearly not everyone."

"Then who? I know times have been hard here for the past three years, and some were angry when the mine closed, but surely no one could hold a grudge so completely."

"Desperate men are not always known to be rational."

She offered him another small smile.

"I know," she answered. "I just want things to be better – not just for us, but for *everyone*. I want to see the cottages rethatched and filled with families again."

To her surprise, David put an arm around her shoulders as they walked. She accepted the comfort of it, even if it *was* only offered in friendship.

"Not everyone has your vision, Allie. They don't see what you see. They're rich in futility and poor in food. It's a combination that revolutions are born of."

She knew that. She'd heard the stories of homes being burned to the ground by desperate and vengeful tenants in other places. The fact it hadn't happened here at Stannum was nothing short of a miracle.

She shuddered. David stopped and pressed her closer to his chest. She accepted his embrace and returned it wholeheartedly.

"Come on," he said. "Come back to my cottage and I'll make you a cup of tea."

She turned out of his embrace and reached for Nephel's bridle.

"Why, Mr. Manston, think of your reputation," she teased.

"Believe me, I've been doing a *lot* of thinking about it."

Oh, that tone. She wondered if he had any idea what it did to her insides…

"And you deem yourself safe enough in my company?" she asked innocently.

"No. That couldn't be further from the truth."

She raised an inquiring eyebrow. "Perhaps I should refuse and spare your blushes."

"And risk losing a game of chess? Why Miss Gedding, I never thought you to lack courage."

"You've finished your carved chess set!"

David said nothing and returned an enigmatic look instead.

HE LEFT ALLIE in his warm little parlor, admiring the newly completed chess set while he poured them both a small glass of sherry from a bottle he'd forgotten he had – somehow that seemed more appropriate than tea.

Returning, he watched as she fingered each piece, running her thumb and index finger over the wood. He had designed the small figures as busts on a plinth. The black king, of course, was Napoleon, with his proud patrician nose and his bicorn hat.

His opposite number was King George in uniform. He did not wear a hat, but rather his chin was lifted regally, confidently toward his opponent. David was rather pleased with the queens. France was represented by Marianne wearing her Phrygian cap. For England, it could be no one else but Britannia wearing her Corinthian helmet, the Union shield at her side and lion at her feet.

The details were even more subtle. None but he would know it – both queens were modeled on Alexandra.

"These are wonderful!" she exclaimed. "The finest I've ever seen."

He grinned. "You exaggerate, but I thank you for the compliment, anyway."

She wrinkled her nose at him, accepted the glass from his hand and went to the window that faced the south. Was she ill-at-ease here alone in his company now? She had never been before. Until recently, she'd had her annoying habit of making herself right at home. He missed that now.

It was all the fault of Claire and of that damned meddling god-mother of Allie's.

Outside, a gust hit his cottage broadside, the howling wind sneaking in through the gaps in the windows and the doors.

Allie put her unfinished sherry down.

"The storm is coming closer. I should go."

Yes, you should, the little voice in his head echoed in agreement.

He closed his eyes and, once again, cursed the name of Lady Abigail Ridgeway for giving him hope that his past didn't have to destroy his future, the one he saw with Allie every time he closed his eyes.

I want what I saw in your books…

His body started to throb. It had been a mistake to ask her here.

He no longer cared.

David opened his eyes to see Allie looking out of the window with its view of the sea. The storm clouds that had still been touched with white a couple of hours ago were now fully black. The horizon was hidden by a thick gray curtain of rain approaching ever closer to the coast.

A peal of thunder followed a flash of lightning by some seconds.

The semi-darkness of the room, accented in the aftermath of the lightning's blinding light, emboldened him. He crossed to stand behind her and rested his hands on her hips.

"I think you should stay," he whispered.

He heard her sigh and felt her lean back against him. Wonderful, sensuous Allie and her passionate nature. If he could not appeal to her mind to stay, he would appeal to her body instead, and seduce her. She would know the full measure of his desire for her and she would return it tenfold.

"So, you think you know my secret, do you?" he whispered in her ear.

Her breath hitched.

He slid his hands around her waist, drawing her closer to him.

"Is that what you want?"

His hands roamed her body freely. He waited for the objections to begin.

Only, she didn't object. She raised her arms and, reaching back, placed her hands at the back his head which had the advantage of bringing his lips down to her neck while his hands got to know her further– the soft round fullness of her breasts, the slight swell of her belly, the edge of her hips where they met her legs.

Her responsiveness to him deepened his arousal. He felt her fingers splay through his hair then become fists. The slight tugging inflamed him further. How he'd love to see her naked in his bed, her arms raised above her head in a sensuous surrender where he could pleasure her endlessly, completely, until she begged for their joining.

He removed her hands from his head, then scooped her around into his arms. Large green eyes looked up at him. She needed kissing until those lips of hers were red and full.

He lowered them both together onto a cushioned settle, her upon his lap. Here, he could touch more of her. He ran his hand down long legs made strong by horse riding. How would they feel wrapped around him? The thought of her riding him filled his thoughts and stirred him further.

He kissed her deeply, giving himself completely to the desire, lust and want in him. How he wanted her in his arms, in his bed, in his life – and in his future.

Forever.

'Til death did they part.

He took advantage of her arms around him to begin loosening the stays of her riding habit. The temptation to rend her clothing was strong. No wonder lust was considered an animal, wild and untamed, but as much as he had given in to it, he'd had plenty of experience in mastering it, too, drawing out the pleasure until both were spent.

She shrugged her shoulders, seeming as eager as he to free her from the confines of her clothes. He would restrain his desires even as he would encourage hers, urging with his tongue and his touch to surrender to it. Surrender to *him*.

The rain arrived with a roar, beating the roof with a sudden, unrelenting drive.

Even the elements demanded their full submission.

ALLIE OPENED HER eyes. David was in silhouette, lit only by the fire, one low-burning lamp and the flashes of lightning from the storm. He looked dangerous and she was frightened and thrilled in turn. No timid, courtly lover could make her body burn as she did for him now. She wanted his experience and his mastery. She wanted him to teach her everything there was to know about full and unbridled sexual pleasure.

She would be his willing pupil and he her master in such things. There would be no girlish coyness from her. She already knew that, despite his physical superiority and experience, her desire could also rule him.

It would be a rather delicious battle to see who first surrendered to whom.

With the back of her gown loosened, Allie arched her back to aid him as he slid her dress and chemise over her shoulders, her breasts exposed for his delectation.

She felt his hardness beneath her, watched his eyes feast on her flesh, and her own arousal grew. Oh, the power there was in bringing out this side of him – her very body thrummed with it.

"Tell me how you know my secret," he said, only just louder than the teeming rain. His arms tightened around her.

Half-naked on his lap, she felt her vulnerability keenly.

"I came into the cottage to check it hadn't been broken into."

She looked for a response but could see none. "I didn't intend to go through your desk, but you had been away for so long without word. I was concerned."

"What did you expect to find?"

"I don't know. A clue to where you were?"

"And what *did* you find?"

He knew the answer. He wanted her to tell him.

After a moment of silence, he skimmed his hand over her breasts with the lightest of touches but it was enough to send lightning through her veins.

"I found your folio... and..."

His touch became firmer. She gasped and shifted restlessly on his lap.

"And you liked what you saw," he prompted. He leaned in and whispered. "'*I want what I saw in your books*'."

Memories flooded back of the illustrations of men and women coupling in all types of ways, along with the final sketch in that volume – the one of *her*.

"Do *you* want what you see in your books?" she asked in a fevered whisper. "How? How would you take me?"

He released her and eased her off his lap. He slid from his position on the settle down to the floor and knelt before her, his breathing ragged. He took both her hands in his and kissed them.

"Check and mate. I see I must bow to a more superior force."

She pushed herself up to a seated position.

"I'd thank you if I knew what on earth you're talking about."

"I love you and I've been a fool for trying to deny it."

I love you.

Before she could respond, he continued, "But what you see around you is all I can offer you."

She pulled her dress up to cover herself. The mood had changed. The intensity of just a few moments ago had softened. Without the heat of passion to warm her, she was cold.

"Do you think I want more?" she asked.

"You *deserve* more," he answered softly. "You also deserve to know all about the man you seem so determined to have, before you make a commitment."

"I know about a broken engagement with Claire and a… rumor about a place called The Olympus Club."

He winced as though she had actually stabbed him.

"Your godmother was right. I couldn't run from it forever."

He shook his head and took a steadying breath. He rose and crossed to a leather-bound chest in the corner of the room. He pulled out a blanket and returned to settle it around her shoulders. She pulled it tight to ward off the chill. He sat beside her.

"Even as a child, I was in love with Claire."

She breathed out to calm herself but she said nothing.

"Then I was to marry her, but she didn't want me. She wanted Thomas.

"The woman I adored was in love with my best friend and I was so caught up in my despair that I wasn't thinking straight. I didn't care what happened to me and I willfully made decisions that cost me *everything…*"

Chapter Twenty-Four

ONCE THE WELLSPRING of memory had been tapped, there was no stopping the images that played out before his mind's eye. David no longer saw Allie or his cottage. He was twenty-one once more and desperate.

He had been half-cut by the time dinner with his and Claire's parents was over. During the meal, he'd exchanged glances with Claire and Thomas. They looked nervous. Claire, in particular, picked like a sparrow at her food.

Earlier that afternoon, he'd sent a message to Thomas that everything had been arranged, but he hadn't dared commit the particulars to paper.

It was not until long after brandy and cigars that David and Thomas were able to make their way into the garden to talk.

They found Claire sitting alone on a stone bench by the fountain. She stood as she saw them approach.

God she was beautiful; an angel.

Her look of relief and adoration was enough to make his heart beat faster before tightening painfully, knowing the look was not for him.

The one *he* received from her was that of gratitude. He ought to be glad to have *that* and that alone.

Immediately, her hands were in Thomas'.

"Mother forbade me from receiving any visitors for the past two weeks," she said. "I am sure she is reading all the correspondence that comes into the house."

Claire then turned to him like an afterthought.

"The only reason she allowed me out tonight was to dine with your parents," she told him. "My mother and yours have arranged to have the first of the banns read next Sunday. What *are* we going to do?"

Her distress cut him deep.

"I've been trying," he began, but Thomas cut him off, his voice close to panic.

"Well, it's not enough, man. I thought being known as a member of The Olympus Club would fix it."

"I'm going to get myself thrown out tonight," he told his friend. "If being a member isn't enough, then..."

He cast a sidelong glance at Claire. He tried to imagine such a refined young woman in such a place but could not. Never would a well-bred lady, his golden goddess as pure and as perfect as marble –

Oh, listen to yourself!

He was drunk and rambling in his own head.

Still, he was sober enough to pull Thomas aside and tell him the plan he'd hatched with Chalmers that afternoon. His friend's eyes widened and his features slackened as he told Thomas the contents of the letter that would arrive tomorrow morning.

Part of him desperately wanted Tom to talk him out of this plan, to reassure him they would find another way, even elope to Gretna Green, *anything* – for a short-term scandal would surely be better than the drastic measures he intended.

But Thomas had not.

"You're a real friend, David, a real friend. You know if there was any other way to free Claire –"

David had looked away, unable to suppress a snort of contempt, and Thomas broke off his words of gratitude.

Claire glanced nervously up the path. She worried the kerchief in her hand, twisting and pulling at it.

"Maman will send someone to look for me soon."

David's Dutch courage was dissipating fast. There was one final piece he needed to put in place.

He recalled Chalmers' comment.

If your father doesn't cover it up...

That was why this last bit of theater was necessary. This was so he *couldn't* cover it up.

David approached Claire. She turned to him, her eyes hopeful. He stroked her cheek and she allowed it.

"I will always be grateful to you, dearest friend," she whispered.

Before she could say another word and ruin everything, he seized her and gave her a punishing kiss on the mouth. Behind him, he heard Thomas yell in objection. Now his fingers were under the shoulders of her gown, his mouth still on hers. He wrenched the fabric until he heard it tear.

Claire pulled her head away and screamed.

Just as he released her, Thomas put a restraining hand on his shoulder.

"What the hell are you doing?" he demanded but didn't wait for an answer. He swung a clenched fist.

David felt it connect with his jaw. The blow was hard enough to drop him to the ground.

Claire screamed. He caught a glimpse of her running toward the house. He staggered to his feet. Thomas bounced on his toes before him in a pugilist's stance. He tried to look menacing, but his face gave him away – he was confused, angry, sorrowful.

"You'd better go after Claire. Tell them what I did," he said around his swelling jaw. With just one glance back, David ran through the garden, hurdling over a low side gate out into the street.

He ignored the stares of passersby, startled at seeing a young man in evening dress and no cloak sprinting his way down the street. He didn't feel the cold as he made the familiar journey to the plain green door of the unassuming townhouse that was The Olympus Club.

The burly footman, whose remit was to toss out grossly unruly patrons, recognized him immediately. If the man noticed his attire lacking or his bruised jaw, he didn't mention it and, instead, handed him the silver-trimmed black silk mask that identified his membership status.

In return, David handed him an envelope containing the fifty guineas due to Zeus and stumbled into a former drawing room to take a whiskey from a servant's tray. He was numb inside, not recognizing the man he had become. Only the spirits he drank warmed him. The rest of his body was ice cold, outside and in.

After some time, the masked guest he knew as only Silenus called over to him. Somehow, he knew his young protégé's mind was elsewhere. The older man bade him follow to one of the private rooms. David drained his drink and followed meekly, not even knowing why he did so.

Normally, the mere sight of Daphnis, naked and laid out on the bed, would raise him to half-mast at least, but the inevitable pleasures of the flesh were not enough to ready him to perform with her tonight, let alone for their customary audience.

David stared at her unseeing, making no move to undress.

After a moment, Silenus spoke. "Arise my dear, it appears our young Ampelos is not of a mind to attend to you at present."

David saw the girl's moue of disappointment as she rose catlike from the bed.

"Do you have something on your mind, good sir?" she asked.

David could offer only the tightest of nods in reply.

"I'm sure we could *purge* that concern and help put him in a more suitable frame of mind," said Silenus. "I think now would be an appropriate time to perfect *your* technique with the flogger, Daphnis. After all, you've had enough experience on the receiving end. What say you?"

The girl's submissive manner melted away and the look she gave David was appraising.

"I should like that very much, sir."

DAVID WOKE FROM his half-doze alone. The heat and the stinging across his back had gone, leaving his muscles stiff. He sat up and mentally catalogued the aches and pains. He noted that the scourging had done nothing to remove his own shame.

"You wanted to see me, sir?"

The slim girl before him wore a simple shift. He could see the outline of everything including how her stomach was a little more full than one might expect on a woman of her build. He swallowed down his own self-pity.

Her glossy brown hair and softly colored cheeks suggested robust health. It was hard to believe she was dying and yet there was a melancholy in her manner that spoke plainly of it.

"I understand you're leaving, Jenny."

The girl swallowed and nodded. It seemed she knew the seriousness of her fate.

"I... I'm sorry."

"There's *nowt* to be sorry for, sir. 'Tisn't your doin', 'tisn't no one's. Just one of them things what happens. It's all right. Me mam'll look after me."

David felt his shame deepen in light of Jenny's quiet stoicism.

"I wanted to give you a gift... something I hope... for your future, for your family." He handed a cloth bag. She frowned, unsure of what strange request may be asked of her. "Go on, don't be afraid. Look inside."

She gasped. There was scrip for one hundred guineas.

"S...s...sir, I don't know what you want me to do for that kind of money!"

He shook his head. "Just go home to your family, Jenny. I understand from Chalmers that they love you very much."

Silent silver tears ran down her face. "No one has ever been this generous to me in London without wantin' somethin' in return…"

The desperation of his own circumstances grew the longer she wept. He hugged her to him to stop her seeing the tears roll down his own face.

"Remember me in your prayers," he whispered. "That's all I ask."

"BUT THAT WAS not the worst of it," David continued, pacing the room as he had done throughout his recounting, caged like a lion Allie had once seen at the Tower Menagerie.

It was just as well he looked away as it allowed her to dab a corner of her sleeve to her eyes to wick away her tears – for Jenny to whom fate had been so unkind and for David who deliberately ruined himself out of misguided loyalty to the woman he had loved and his best friend.

"I got lost in that world, became fascinated by it," he said. "Wherever I went on the Continent, I found myself in the same sorts of places doing the same sorts of things again and again until even the thought of the act itself became pallid. But somehow, I had a 'talent' for drawing it, and it was enough to keep me in funds."

The worsening storm filled the silence after he stopped speaking. Allie looked over the back of the settle to see him approach the east-facing window. He paused there as though something had caught his attention through the driving rain.

"The horses?" she whispered.

He shook his head. "No, they're well sheltered in the stable."

He turned to the room again. "I arrived here in Stannum intending to spend the rest of my days as the hermit you always joked I was. But the longer I stayed, the more part of the community I felt until, eventually..."

His voice trailed off but, this time, there was a hint of a smile. "I met you and Phillip. I suppose I felt a kind a kinship. You were a reminder of a world I once inhabited. Every now and again, I allowed myself to hope that my past wasn't all there was to me. That's why I offered to mediate when the mine closed down."

She got to her feet and stood before him wearing the blanket as a shawl about her. "You believed in us when no one else would. You were the first to put money into the mine when there was no certainty it contained enough copper to reopen. How can I not believe in *you*?"

He stepped away from the window and enfolded her into his arms. "Well, I hope the mine will make my fortune because no one seems interested in my art – well, the art that doesn't involve naked people, anyway."

"They are memorable, I do have to say." She giggled and felt him squeeze her.

"Oh, God, what would I do without you, Allie? The moment I fear falling into melancholy, you remind me there is always something to smile at."

He kissed her on the top of her head. "The printer tells me he's trying to sell my art but he keeps giving me commissions for the *other* work. Last time I was in Camelford, I sent him a letter to say the present commission was the last."

His hands cupped her face. She looked into his eyes as blue as forget-me-nots. She'd always loved this man, she knew it from the very first day she saw him. And now she witnessed the same look, that same love looking back at her. His mouth descended to hers in a tender kiss, one of reverence. He deepened it as a roll of thunder rolled across the landscape.

Except it wasn't thunder. It sounded like pounding hooves nearby.

They looked at each other with a frown.

David reached the window first. She got there in time to see the last of a dozen men on horseback gallop past.

"Who on earth would be out on a night like this?"

"Allie…"

She heard the note of warning in his voice.

"There's someone up at the mine."

She looked in the direction he indicated and saw light shining from the window of the engine house. David opened the door into the kitchen. Allie followed with a lamp to find him shrugging on his oilskin coat.

"You can't mean to go out in this," she said, but his expression brooked no argument.

"Get to the tavern in the village and send some men up. We've got a chance to stop these thieving vandals for good."

She swallowed down her objections and put the blanket on the kitchen table. "Help me lace up my dress."

David tugged the laces until the gown formed about her properly once more.

"There's another coat in the airing cupboard by the stove," he said. "Put it on. Otherwise, you'll be soaked."

Allie glanced at the cupboard and, turning back, saw him pick up a small knife and slip it in his pocket, its blade glinting gold in the lamplight.

"Be safe, my love," she said.

David gave her a wink in return, opened the back door and stepped out into the cold billowing rain.

THE KNIFE HE carried was not truly for defense. There had been a number of innocent occasions over the years where having a cutting implement was useful. He had once used his knife to free a frightened goat that had run away in a storm from brambles. He'd hacked small branches at times and often used it to remove stones from Jack's hooves.

But if it gave Allie a small measure of comfort to know he was armed, then so be it.

He glanced at Nephel in the stall and decided against saddling up his mount. He'd be faster going up the steep path directly to the mine. He'd also have the element of surprise moving in on foot.

But once he was underway, he almost wished he hadn't. The ground was slick and the narrow, worn path he followed was now a running stream. Everything below the knees was already wet through and he was only halfway there.

He remained in the bushes just on the brow of the hill along the western face of the mine buildings. The door to the engine house was open and a warm yellow glow spilled out into the rain. The windows were ablaze with light.

He looked up and shuddered as the wide brim of his hat tipped cold water down the back of his neck. A man stepped into the doorway for a moment, a thin blue-gray line of smoke rising then being gusted away in the wind as he sucked on a pipe.

David heard a calling voice from inside but was too far away to make out what was said. It attracted the other man inside. So, there were two there at least.

He looked up again at the tall engine house and wished he had a spyglass. There was what might be another man high up near the beam, though what he saw through the rain-washed windows could equally have been just a piece of the pump workings.

Although sure he'd be undiscovered here in the bushes, it was too damned cold to huddle in the downpour. He closed his eyes, trying to guess how long it would take Allie to get down to the tavern and how long it would take the men she raised to reach him up here.

During the day, it would be less than half an hour, twenty minutes if everyone moved with alacrity, but in this weather…

He couldn't afford to wait that long.

He made a run for the shelter of the building's eaves confident enough of getting closer without being caught.

Who the hell were these men? What on earth were they doing here? The "ghosts" of Wheal Gunnis had the engine house lit up like a beacon and that seemed to him a dangerous development. It meant they thought themselves unchallenged. And if they were saboteurs, the damage they could do to the pump didn't bear thinking about.

He edged closer to the door, hoping to hear them. Again, the heavy rain made it impossible to distinguish voices. His only choice was to sneak inside and hope he knew the layout better than they did.

Suddenly the knife in his hand didn't seem like protection enough.

Chapter Twenty-Five

THE COTTAGE WAS colder and darker without David in it. Allie pulled out the coat from the airing cupboard. It was a shorter length than the one he wore but, even so, it still fell to her knees.

She took a deep breath and followed through the door he had left by, slamming it shut behind her to run across the courtyard to the shelter of the stables. David's horse was there. He had decided to go on foot. Nephel whickered. Allie stroked her nose to calm her.

Lightning illuminated the sky followed by another crack of thunder. Both horses shied and stepped further back into their stalls.

"Then you stay here, my girl," she soothed Nephel. "Keep this big brute company."

No, it was far too dangerous to ride in weather like this. If she should bolt, the mare could take them both over the cliffs to their deaths. There was nothing for it but to run though the driving wind and rain.

The clifftop path was the most direct route to the village. It was only half a mile, but tonight it might as well have been three by the time she reached the inn. Despite the oilskin, she was soaked though to her bones and shuddering with the cold when she stumbled into the tavern.

She made a beeline to the fireplace and she didn't stop shaking even as she felt the heat from the roaring open fire.

"Eh-up, what ye be doing out on a night like this, lass? It's *pizendawn!"*

Allie turned and looked about. There was no one here where the tavern should be full of folks. She finished turning a full circle. The only soul in the place was Mrs. Angove, the tavernkeeper's wife, who stood behind the bar.

The shudders gripped Allie and she feared her legs would not hold so she reached for a chair and collapsed in it. The middle-aged woman moved quickly for a woman of her size and Allie found a cup of warmed cider in her hands.

She breathed in the spicy apple aroma and a single mouthful of the brew was enough to revive her. The violent shuddering slowed to just shaking again and the fire began to warm her. Mrs. Angove stood over her.

"There're vandals up at Wheal Gunnis. Manston's gone up there alone. Some men need to go up and help him."

The older woman's face became pinched. "There be no one here. All the men have gone down to the beach. There's been a *shipwreck*."

The chill returned, this time fueled by dread.

"When?" she asked.

"Uppards of an hour since."

"Any survivors?"

"Dunno yet, no one's come back." The woman leaned close and kept her voice low, seemingly afraid of being overheard even though they were the only two in the place.

"There's been a troop of soldiers come, *Revenuers*. Ye know what'll happen if any of our men are caught with salvage. They'll say it's theft and looting."

"Revenuers? The nearest garrison is twenty miles away. How did they get here so quickly?"

"I don't know, Miss Gedding. All's I know is I can't leave the tavern to warn them in case them soldiers come back."

Allie hastily finished the cider. "I need some clothes to change into," she said. "I'll go warn them and get a couple of men to go and help David."

Mrs. Angove concurred with a nod. She hurried to the tavern door and bolted it closed.

"Follow me upstairs to my room. Better get them wet clothes off and get yerself dry first. I got no clothes to fit ye, though."

"I need men's clothes," said Allie, trailing behind the woman up the narrow stairs. "Something I can run in. If I go on the beach in this storm, I'll drown in skirts."

"Aye, ye're right, Miss. Reckon my lad'll be about yer size. Ye can wear his togs."

Mrs. Angove opened the door into the bedroom. The room was smallish, but warm thanks to the fire burning low in the grate. Allie gravitated to its heat and immediately started on working the laces of her boots loose.

"There are towels in the bottom of the wardrobe," said the woman, then she left to get the promised change of clothing.

Allie's fingers were clumsy with cold, making removing her clothes a slow and laborious task. All the while, outside the wind rattled the shutters, demanding entrance. She was completely naked but dry, apart from her hair, when Mrs. Angove bustled back in with an armful of her son's garments. Allie felt no shame in her unclothed state. There was simply no time for it.

She immediately reached for a proffered shirt. It was already heated and warm. She shot Mrs. Angove a grateful look and was handed a pair of hose.

"Breeches are on the bed, Miss Gedding, along with a hat. I'll be downstairs with a tot of rum for ye."

Allie pulled her fingers through her long curls in an attempt to untangle them as her hair dried. Deciding there was nothing more for it, she pinned her hair in a knot at the nape of her neck and shoved the tricorn hat on her head, pressing it low over her eyes.

She saw her reflection in the looking glass, its silvering foxed with age, and decided it was passable. Her boots proved to be more difficult to get back on in their soaked state. By the time she had laced them, her feet were damp and chilled again even with the borrowed hose.

She accepted the tot of rum Mrs. Angove handed her and dashed it down before she ventured back out into the storm. Thankfully, it was now beginning to ease. It was another quarter of a mile down to the beach where she could see, among the lanterns and the occasional flash of lightning, men yelling over the wind which still howled a gale.

One of the first people she bumped into was Gerran Angove whose clothes she had borrowed. The young man shouldered a small barrel. Rum, if she had to guess.

The poor lad nearly dropped his burden when Allie tapped him on the shoulder.

"Miss Gedding," he stammered, his eyes wide at seeing the lady from the big house dressed in men's clothing.

"Gerran, look up at the mine." She pointed to Wheal Gunnis' engine house, its windows lit up.

"The *ghosts* are back!"

"No, not ghosts! Brigands. Manston is up there alone. Who knows how many of them there are. Take a couple of men and help him, I beg you."

Gerran nodded sharply and let out a piercing whistle. Two other men also shouldering small barrels emerged from the gloom.

Allie warned Gerran of the danger of Revenuers in the area and left the young man to relay instructions about mounting an expedition up to the mine while she slogged her way up the beach. She needed to find Angove and Prenpas and warn them about the soldiers.

DAVID LOOKED OUT over the brow of the hill that overlooked the beach at Stannum. In a flash of lightning that illuminated the clouds, he could see a large object where there ought to be none. Another flash of lightning revealed it to be a ship, listing on the rocks that sat off shore.

His heart sank. The engine house had been used to set a false beacon and lure the ship onto the reef.

He slipped inside the door cautiously and, seeing no one around, entered through the doorway into the pit head, staying in the shadows that hugged the walls. He heard the echoes of men seemingly down in the mine as well as some clambering up the pump ladder. There were more than two people here. There was a gang.

What could one man alone do?

Sadly, very little.

Come on, David, think!

If there was help coming from Stannum, they would arrive by the north path that came directly from the village. He could wait for them by the tool shed and they'd deal with these men by a force of numbers.

He slipped back out of the brick building. The rain had eased somewhat. Rising mist was taking its place. He shrugged his coat closer and jogged to the outbuilding. He reached the corner which gave him a good view of the path coming up the rise.

This explained the "ghosts" of Wheal Gunnis. More importantly, it answered why no one had ever seen anyone at the mine – the bastards were hiding underground! He had no doubt the "ghosts" and the saboteurs were one and the same. These men, whoever they were, believed the mine to be abandoned. They *needed* the mine to be abandoned for such a fiendish action as this.

Lady Abigail's rats... well, I just found the nest.

Phillip and Julian would have to check all the workings underground to make sure none of the shoring had been sabotaged. The engineers would have to be instructed to go over the pump with a fine-toothed comb.

Fury bubbled below the surface. This was his future, the future of

Stannum itself that these criminals were threatening.

He heard a sound beside him and turned, but by then it was too late. A single blow propelled the back of his head into the brickwork. He saw a flash of white light before his eyes. Then he felt nothing at all.

MEN SWARMED ACROSS the beach like ants, picking up anything of value. She warned everyone she came across about the danger of soldiers lurking about but most seemed more concerned about claiming their share of the salvage.

Allie noted she was not the only woman out here on this benighted evening either. Women and children from the village picked across the sand like crabs, risking their necks in more ways than one as storm-ravaged waves crashed on the shore.

She refused to stop and consider the moral and legal implications of such an act, even as she worried there were still men aboard the ship that lurched and groaned on the rocks. The people of Stannum had little enough to fill their bellies; she would not begrudge them an opportunity to improve their lots.

She trudged her way through the waterlogged sand until she found Prenpas among a cluster of men. He did a double-take at her attire. She ignored his astonishment and pointed up to the mine. "Our saboteurs!" she yelled.

Even in the lamplight, she could see the man's face turn grim.

"Do Master Gedding know ye're out here, Miss?"

Allie shook her head. "He's at Camelford. What of survivors?"

"We be counting twenty so far. The men over there are bringing as many to shore as we can before the tide turns."

Someone yelled Prenpas' name. Allie left the man to his work.

There was no sign yet of the soldiers Mrs. Angove had seen, so she ventured further along the shore until she could see the wreck of the ship for herself.

The rocky islet a couple of hundred yards out to sea was completely covered by the storm surge. Covered, but not deep enough to prevent this small ship from being caught on it. The vessel was aground fast and listing, no doubt holed by the rocks. The shroud and lines dangled uselessly from the crosstrees of the two masts.

She knew with a certainty it was not the villagers of Stannum behind the disaster. Smuggling was one thing, wrecking quite another.

Her heart sank. Those up at the mine were behind the wreck of the ship.

Lady Abigail's traitors.

Ahead, she witnessed a small group of men forming a human chain into the water, pulling out cargo and people.

Then two men caught her eye as they peeled away from the rest, dragging a half-drowned soul further up along the shore. Another approached and started searching through the man's coat as he lay gasping on his back. What were they doing? She began to walk toward them.

"Here it is! I've found it," the man yelled, waving aloft something rectangular. Allie was too far away to clearly see what it was. "Finish him!" he shouted over the crashing of the waves to the two with him.

The stricken man seemed to revive at this and started struggling against those who held him. His rescuers were now his captors. They dragged him backwards to the sea. The man's scuffling became more frantic. He bucked and kicked, nearly overthrowing the two men who'd pinioned his arms.

The one who held the mysterious prize aloft tossed it a little further up the sand and ran toward his compatriots to render assistance.

Allie slowed her pace, trying to make sense of the scene unfolding before her. If they were rescuers, why were they dragging him back into the sea?

The arm of the man who ran in came up and plunged down. The captive screamed. The man raised his arm again.

Oh, my God, they're stabbing him!

Allie wanted to yell, to scream at them to stop, but the horror had rendered her mute as the knife came down again and again. Knowing he could not be saved, she ran as fast as she could in the sodden sand to where the ringleader had stood. At her feet was an oilskin letter pouch.

She snatched it up and ran toward the cliffs which were only another hundred yards away. David's cottage sat at the top of those cliffs.

"Hey, boy!" one of the men yelled.

"Get back here, ye worthless tadger!" shouted another.

Allie ignored the threats and insults, and did not look back, though she knew they must be pursuing her. She stuffed the pouch down her shirt on the run, heedless how the cold and wet canvas chilled her skin – it left her hands free to clamber up the rocks. She did not dare look down, although she could hear the curses of the men blending with the shouts of people below as they swarmed over the wreckage of the ship.

The rain had gone when she reached the top. She glanced up to Wheal Gunnis. The engine house was completely dark once more. But behind it to the east, the sky had turned a blue-gray, announcing the arrival of a new day.

Allie looked back and couldn't see anyone climbing after her, though they could be hidden in the shadows of the cliff. She fled.

Despite her aching legs, she ran as hard as she could, praying she had enough of a start over the men who would ruthlessly murder a shipwrecked soul and would certainly kill her for whatever it was she now carried.

The temptation to give in to tears was nearly overwhelming. What of David? Had he made it back home safe?

There was a small yellow glow in the kitchen window where she had left the lamp burning. When she entered, the cottage was dark and silent.

"David?"

There was no answer.

She shut the door behind her and lowered the wick on the lantern until the room was in near darkness. The oilskin packet was warm as she fished it out of her borrowed shirt. She had to hide this thing which was important enough to take a man's life for.

David's drafting table. She entered the main room where the remaining embers of the fire still warmed the air a little. Going to the desk, she found the hidden catch, raised the lid and pushed open the slides to reveal the hidden compartment. She shoved the portfolios aside and laid the pouch in beside them then closed the desk.

At the sound of pounding hooves, she extinguished the lamp. The curtains were still open and, in fact, had not been closed the previous evening. A loud conversation outside confirmed her worst fears.

The soldiers!

She snatched the lamp and placed it near the fire so the guttering smoke from the wick would be drawn up the chimney, then ducked beneath the desk, bringing her knees to under her chin as someone attempted to open the kitchen door.

It wasn't the wisest place to hide but there was nowhere else to go.

Chapter Twenty-Six

THE DOOR RATTLED as it opened.

"I'm telling you, *I'm* the only one who lives here."

David didn't sound too pleased as he stepped into the kitchen. Allie turned her head, her cheek resting on her damp knee giving her a partial view into the kitchen. Another man accompanied him. She clamped her teeth against chattering from the chill, lest the merest sound give her away.

"I'm sure it is quite the inconvenience, sir, but I should tell you, the young man we're looking for is wanted for the murder of one of the passengers from the *Zelos*."

She recognized him! It was the *naturalist*, except now he wore the uniform, and had the bearing of a junior officer in His Majesty's Army – gray trousers fitted into black Hessian boots, a fitted red coat with gold epaulets.

"I'm afraid I can't help you." David sounded increasingly annoyed. "I was nowhere near the beach tonight."

He came right toward the desk. Allie held her breath. He stopped before it and turned on his heel to face the man who had followed him into the parlor. "I suggest you start investigating up at the mine. There were lights up there."

"Ah, yes, the infamous ghosts of Stannum," said the man mockingly.

"Well, it was no ghost who hit me, you can be sure of that! Look up there if you want to find your killer."

"We'll take that into consideration. But the fact doesn't change that a man was seen taking the cliff path up to the headland. Yours is the only cottage within a half a mile, so you'll understand why we need to look around."

David shifted his weight onto one foot, but otherwise remained planted where he was.

"Do you *see* anyone else here?"

The officer stepped further into the room. Allie could no longer see his face, only the trousers and highly polished boots that didn't even look like they had been out in the weather much at all.

There was silence a moment before a creak of leather told her he had moved on. She listened to the clomp of boots as the man climbed to the attic bedroom. David remained in front of the drafting table. Allie considered letting him know she was there but was afraid that any action would give her away.

The footsteps presently returned.

"*Satisfied?*" Sarcasm dripped from every syllable.

"We apologize for the convenience, Mister..."

"Manston... and you are Lieutenant...?"

"Smith. We'll take a look at the mine site as you suggest. Good morning."

The man left the way he came – through the kitchen. David followed him, standing by the kitchen door waiting for him to leave. Allie heard the hooves of more than one horse, possibly up to three riders. The kitchen door closed with a bang. The bolt rasped into place as David locked it.

The sun had risen a little higher in the sky, spilling light through the window.

"You can come out now," said David, still in the kitchen.

Allie tried to move, but she was cold, stiff and so very, very tired.

"I can't."

David approached the desk and squatted down. In the early morning light, she could see exhaustion written large on his face also.

"Come on, let me help you."

She placed her hands in his and allowed him to half-heave her out from under the table and helped her to her feet. She fell into in his arms, heedless of the fact they were both soaked through.

He took in her appearance. Allie looked down at herself. Her guise as a man would never have borne close scrutiny.

"How did you know I was here?" she asked.

"I saw drips of water from the kitchen to the desk and knew it could only be you. I followed them to cover your tracks."

She tried to chuckle but it came out as a shudder instead.

"Please don't send me home," she whispered.

His arms tightened around her. He dropped a kiss on top of her head.

"What am I going to do with you?" he whispered.

At this moment, she didn't care as long as she remained in his arms. She shuddered once more.

"Come on, we can't remain in our wet things. Let's set the fire in the bedroom."

She considered all the things she wanted to tell him – of the killing of the man on the beach, the pouch, the lieutenant who wasn't a lieutenant, but the effort was too much. He escorted her upstairs to his room with the oversized bed.

Despite her overtiredness, or perhaps because of it, Allie started to giggle and once she started, she couldn't stop, unable to protest as David pressed her down into a chair and started working on removing her boots.

He raised his head, his eyebrows raised.

Her giggle became hiccoughs as she fought to control herself. "I was thinking about all the times I dreamed of you taking me to your bed," she confessed.

David's long-suffering sigh didn't fool her a bit. She found a hint of a smile. "Unfortunately for you, the only thing we'll be doing in this bed is getting warm before you catch your death."

She sighed as one boot, then the other was removed from her feet. She rose to her feet.

"Let me help with your boots," she said.

He nodded over toward the fireplace. "I'll manage these, you light the fire."

She did so, thankful it was set and only waiting to be lit. She reveled in its warmth a moment. He pulled a shirt from a drawer and placed it over a chair by the fire.

For the second time in a night, Allie began removing wet clothing. But this time, she was conscious of doing so in front of the man she had loved for so long. He left her by the fire and closed one of the bed curtains. He remained on the other side to undress himself.

"Let me know when you're dressed and in bed," he said.

It was distracting to think of being in that soft, extravagant bed, wrapped in David's arms with only two layers of fabric between them but it was clear they both craved sleep over amorous activities.

"What happened up at the mine?" she asked. "You told that man you were hit."

She pulled the warm shirt over her head. It was tempting to leave her borrowed clothes on the floor but she found a reserve of energy to drape them over the chair to dry. She climbed into the bed but the sheets were cold and she forced herself to stop shuddering again. She closed her heavy lids.

"Are you in bed?"

"Uh-hmm."

"In answer to your question, 'tis nothing, my head is hard enough."

Allie willed warmth into her body. She listened to David don his shirt and move around to the other side of the bed. He climbed in beside her. She snuggled close for warmth. He released the other cord and the bed was shrouded in a cocoon of curtains. His arms wrapped around her and she felt warm for the first time in hours.

They lay silently. Within moments, she felt herself slip toward sleep, but she had to tell him before she could let it claim her completely.

"I saw them kill a man… and the soldier who came to the door… I've seen him before. He's not really a soldier…"

She thought David heard her, but too far gone in his own exhaustion to respond beyond enfolding her further into his embrace. Then she was asleep, too.

DAVID'S DREAMS VERGED on nightmares. One moment he was at vertiginous heights atop the engine house, the next plunging into the darkest depths in the mine. Now being washed out the other side onto the rocks, then being marched along by soldiers who were not soldiers.

By the time he emerged from sleep, he was once again warm. He opened his eyes, head pounding from the blows that had knocked him unconscious. The parting between the curtains was bright, telling him he'd slept for hours. He moved and the woman in his arms moved closer. His hand fell across her breast covered only with the linen of his shirt. Still only half-awake, he palmed it and heard a satisfied sigh in response.

He didn't imagine it.

Allie…

He slowly drew back to look at her, hoping not to wake her. She was beautiful like this, dark curly hair an unruly tangle around her face, elegantly shaped brows over an ivory complexion, her eyes closed in slumber. Her mouth drew his attention, soft and full.

He hesitated then stroked her hair, overwhelmed by the tenderness he felt for her.

It was too late.

He was lost.

If Allie was too stubborn to heed his good advice and chose to love him anyway, then how could he do less in return? He would propose properly and let the chips fall where they may. He closed his eyes and wondered what Phillip would make of it. Not best pleased, he imagined – especially learning Allie spent the night in his bed – but, he suspected, not angered enough to stop his sister doing what she really wanted.

His soft snigger was enough to wake the sleeping beauty. Green eyes framed with dark lashes looked up at him in wonder.

No. That's not right. Sleeping Beauty was awoken by a *kiss.*

He leaned down and captured those sweet lips. She opened her mouth to him and they savored a long, unhurried exploration. He might have continued except there came a mighty pounding on the door.

"We've never had the best timing, have we?"

Allie frowned. "If that's my brother making such a racket…"

David grinned. "You will defend me from him, won't you?"

She snorted inelegantly. "I'm sure a big fellow like you can manage."

As much as he enjoyed joking with her, the events of last night were too recent to ignore. What if the hammering at the door was those soldiers returning? Suddenly, he became aware of something odd Allie said just as he was losing himself to his exhaustion last night – that the man who searched his cottage was not really a soldier?

"Stay there," he said, all levity gone from his voice.

Wearing nothing more than a nightshirt and hose, he went downstairs and was almost relieved to find it was, indeed, Phillip pounding at the door with the side of his fist. In his other hand he carried a small bag.

Phillip looked David up and down but said nothing as he entered, his face grim.

"I take it my sister is here?" His question was asked without inflection.

"I'm here."

David saw Phillip's eyes glance up and down at Allie. She was halfway down the stairs. The shirt she wore fell above her knees.

"Make yourself decent," he told her and threw the satchel in her direction. She caught it easily.

David exchanged a glance with her before she went back upstairs without saying a thing. He turned back to her brother.

If Phillip wanted to confront him, then let him say his piece. He was not going to apologize or explain anything anymore when it came to his love for Allie.

He thought he could anticipate Phillip's words.

He was wrong.

"Four men died in that wreck last night," he said, "but only one of them was stabbed to death."

David closed his eyes a moment.

I saw them kill a man...

"Allie witnessed it. It's something to do with the so-called 'ghosts' of Wheal Gunnis. I saw the operation for myself up at the mine last night. That ship was deliberately lured onto the rocks."

He expected some kind of reaction from Phillip, of anger or outrage, but his temper was even.

"I was told you went up to the mine to investigate the lights. But when Gerran Angove and his friends got there you were nowhere to be found."

"Someone knocked me out," David explained. "When I came 'round, some soldiers were there. At least they appeared to be soldiers. They brought me home. Allie was here by then."

Phillip shook his head. "There's going to have to be a coroner's hearing. In the meantime, we have a murderer in our midst."

David directed Phillip into the kitchen. They sat down at the table as he relit the fire and set the kettle to boil.

"Do you think the killer could be one of the surviving crew?"

"Perhaps. The crew is a mix of French and Irish; who knows what they're thinking?"

"The men I heard were English."

Both men turned to Allie who was wearing a summer dress, her hair loosely worn.

Phillip nodded, his face grim. "Prenpas told me about the wreck as soon as I got into Stannum. He said you came down to the beach and warned everyone about the Revenuers. Mrs. McArthur was beside herself with worry. Tell me about the man you saw stabbed."

"There was a group of three men. They appeared to be helping with the rescue of those stranded on the ship but then they dragged this man aside and up the beach."

"They've already identified the other three killed," said Phillip, "but no one knew the murdered man. He must have been a passenger but he wasn't on the passenger list."

"That's odd," mused David.

"Well, whoever he was, they were searching him for something," Allie continued. "As soon as they found it, they dragged him back to the water and…"

Allie drew a deep breath. Phillip took his sister's hand and squeezed it.

"Do you know what they were searching for?" David asked.

Allie nodded. "I do. Because I *took* it."

She removed her hand from Phillip's and went into the parlor. David heard the squeak from the mechanics of his drafting table riser. A moment later, she returned with a small oilskin letter pouch bound with a leather thong.

He and Phillip made way for Allie to sit down between them at the table. She worried at the knotted thong with her fingernails.

Phillip loomed beside her. He seemed fairly itching to take the pouch and see to its untying himself but managed to restrain the impulse.

What emerged appeared to be a small journal. It was lightly water stained and the leather cover creaked as she opened it. Careful not to tear pages still damp, she leafed through them until she reached the center of the book. Drawn there was a map of two islands and the coast of a much larger land mass. And an inscription.

Saltee Islands

"They're just off the coast of Ireland, not far from Wexford," said David.

Allie turned over the next page. It was the map again but this one featured a large set of annotations.

"What do you make of these?" she asked.

"They look like navigation coordinates," answered Phillip. "They're the types of observations one might see in a ship's log. But why would a passenger be making entries like these?"

"I can't read them," said Allie. She looked at David and Phillip. "Can you?"

David shook his head; Phillip did the same.

"Keep going, Allie," David encouraged. "I want to know what's so important about this journal that a man lost his life over it."

The next page held illustrations of wicker baskets of various sizes and shapes along with their dimensions.

"These are too big for a man to carry," said Allie. She turned to the next page. The baskets here were even larger.

Phillip laughed. "That looks big enough to hold a horse."

A bolt of ice went down David's back. "Or hold several men."

Phillip looked up at him and frowned.

Allie turned over another page, and found a double page of illustrations of curved shapes to be made of either linen or silk, their dimensions listed in exacting detail. She shook her head. "I can't begin to describe what this is for. Or how someone could buy so much fabric. This would have to be produced to order."

The next page was turned.

"What the hell are those?" said Phillip. "They look like –"

"Yes, that's *exactly* what are," David interrupted. "They're hot air balloons."

Chapter Twenty-Seven

The Queen's Head Inn
St. Sennen

"HOT AIR BALLOONS."

Adam was aware Lady Abigail's protégé expected ridicule, or a little incredulity at least from Sir Daniel. But he received neither.

David Manston looked exhausted. Dark shadows beneath his eyes confirmed it, although he radiated tightly-leashed nervous energy.

Hot air balloons...

Adam didn't laugh either, nor did Nate Payne. That didn't stop a snigger arising from Bassett who remained head down at his drafting table across the room.

The book, marked as belonging to Dermot Flannery, now sat open in front of Ridgeway. The detailed schematics of hot air balloons filled the page.

The very notion of it should seem fantastic, but it did not. It made a horrible sort of sense.

"Of the man who had this..." began Ridgeway.

"He was murdered, sir. It was witnessed by my... *fiancée*." There was a hesitation here, as though that part was too new to be used to – or not quite the truth.

"Miss Gedding, I presume?" said Sir Daniel, his tone serious. "My congratulations. Lady Abigail will be delighted by the news of her goddaughter's betrothal. She's not yet missed the opportunity to ensure her league of ladies get their man."

The double entendre was too much for the young apprentice, Joe, who burst out laughing beside Bassett. His inappropriate response was met by a cuff on the back of the head from his superior.

Adam had to own he was impressed by Manston. He completely ignored the distractions coming as they did at his own expense. His focus remained solely on the peer before him.

"And the dead man was this Dermot Flannery?" Ridgeway asked, turning over the journal to its inscribed flyleaf.

"That I could not say. He had no identification on him when he was found."

"You saw him?"

"Not alive. I saw his body the next day."

"Describe him," said Adam.

Manston turned to him and spoke without hesitation. "Five foot, eight inches, I'd say. Thin build, black hair."

Not Flannery. *O'Brien.*

Adam could not hide the dismay from his face as he shared the news with the others. The young Irish patriot who'd bravely came forward wouldn't be making a new life in Boston or New York with his girl. And she'd never know he died on an English beach trying to win that prize for them, just that he'd disappeared one day and never came back.

Worse still was the realization that Bickmore must have learned O'Brien had turned informant after the ship left Ireland and organized the wrecking of the ship on its return solely to stop him handing over this journal.

Bickmore must also know of their plans to abduct Flannery.

"There's more you need to know," Manston continued grimly. "Your traitors have been using Wheal Gunnis as a bolt hole for months – that's why you've not be able to find them. They've even evaded the miners who are working on reopening the pit."

Nate looked to Adam. "Now that Bickmore has dealt with O'Brien, he's moved on, surely."

To Adam's surprise, it was Manston who answered before he could. "They've been committing acts of sabotage in recent weeks to try to slow down the reopening, I think. I'd say they have more use for the mine than just a hide out."

Sir Daniel slowly nodded. "That makes sense to me."

Manston continued. "My most pressing concern is for Miss Gedding. She's spoken with this man you call Bickmore. She confronted him and another man outside my cottage and he passed himself off as a naturalist called Silsbury. She also saw him when he was dressed as an army officer on the night of the wreck. I believe she is under watch.

"I hadn't known it before but I'm certain the man she described with 'Silsbury' is the same man I caught trailing her down the streets of Camelford a few months ago."

"I won't give you false comfort," said Adam. "You're right to be concerned. Bickmore is not averse to using women to ensure he gets his way – my wife was among them. I would urge care to the both of you."

A curt nod of acknowledgement was all Manston gave. "Then by your leave, Sir Daniel. I don't believe I have time to waste. If I leave St. Sennen now, I can be back in Stannum by dark."

Ridgeway got to his feet.

"Then you must go, by all means," he said. "We will review all of this and, rest assured, we will do everything in our power to deal with these traitors as quickly and effectively as possible And, needless to say, for my wife's sake as well as yours, we will do everything we can to keep your fiancée and her family safe."

His hand was extended. Manston accepted it.

Thank you, Manston," said Ridgeway. "You've done your country a great service."

Manston shook his hand firmly. "If Lady Abigail can perform a miracle for me as she insists she can, then I would consider any debt more than amply paid."

Ridgeway's face split into a grin.

"I've learned to never underestimate my wife," he said. "I'd recommend with confidence you shouldn't either."

WHEN MANSTON HAD gone, Sir Daniel handed the journal over to Bassett who examined it with the eagerness of a boy receiving a new toy at Christmas.

"I want a copy made of this," Ridgeway instructed. "With key details changed. We're going to use it to bait a rat trap."

Adam left the others to begin to decipher the book. He walked to the window and watched the glint of sunlight on the Pengellan estuary in the distance.

He drew his mind back to a conversation he'd had with Bickmore in France where he was apparently determined to leave a breadcrumb trail of clues instead of being forthright – another reason why he hated the man.

"Do you remember a shore leave two years ago? We stayed at a tavern in Corsica and we caroused with one of the local men."

"We were dicing as I recall."

"You won a particular bet."

What bet? Adam had turned it over again and again in his mind, trying to dredge up the recollection of a matter which had meant little to him at the time.

What could that bastard have meant by it?

As he looked out through the window, he saw Manston ride by on his way back home.

Everything within Adam wanted to be riding out as well. The fact that Bickmore was so close nagged at him. If he closed his eyes once more, he could see the man before him within touching distance.

Adam wasn't a naturally patient man, but he knew better than to ask Ridgeway for permission to go to Stannum without a plan.

The request would only be refused – and with good reason. Charging in with no plan at all would ensure Bickmore would always be two steps ahead; after all, Bickmore knew Adam's temperament and habits as well as Adam knew *his*.

He listened to Bassett, Ridgeway and Payne talking as they studied the journal. "Hot air balloons as troop carriers... I do have to say, what a novel concept," offered Bassett.

"I heard Napoleon used them as aerial observation posts in Egypt, but never as a means for transporting men and weapons," said Payne. "What an idea."

Adam rejoined the conversation. "We were all given to understand the French Aerostatic Corps was disbanded three years ago."

"Evidently not," said Bassett. "Remember the names O'Brien gave you – Fouché and Blanchard?"

"We already determined Fouché is Joseph Fouché, Napoleon's Minister of Police," said Sir Daniel, "but who is this Blanchard fellow?"

Bassett gave a slow, sly grin as the little man was apt to do when he knew something others didn't.

"The *fellow* is, in fact, *la femme*. She is Sophie Blanchard. I'm surprised you hadn't worked it out before now."

Nate didn't seem inclined to indulge their quartermaster. "So, when did *you* work it out? It would have saved us a hell of a lot of time if you'd told us earlier."

Bassett shrugged indifferently. "As soon as I heard that hot air balloons were involved. I thought it must be her and here's the proof – her instructions for the construction of the balloons. And those 'baskets', I'll have you know, are 'gondolas'."

"Well, call me slow on the uptake," said Nate, glowering at Bassett as if daring him to make another snide comment, "but I've never heard of this woman. Who is she?"

"Madame Blanchard is the famous aeronaut, of course. She and her husband put on aerial displays and Napoleon has taken a particular shine to her. He named her Chief Air Minister of Ballooning. Although as far as anyone knew, her role was to advise on the best use of balloons as observation posts."

Adam frowned. "Remember Felix's letter? *'Pyroeis wanders closer'*. Were we wrong to think he meant Congreve rockets?"

"An aerial invasion of Britain? Surely such a thing is impossible," said Nate.

"A whole army? Certainly," said Sir Daniel. "But I believe we're still on the right track. Consider this, using balloons to carry small squads into England with arms and resources to foment discontent and riot."

Ridgeway went to the back wall and examined their large map of Britain's west coast from Land's End in Cornwall to Cardigan in Wales.

"Do you remember the last time there was a military invasion of our country?" he asked.

"The Battle of Hastings was a *very* long time ago," quipped Adam.

"Ah, then you'll have forgotten about the Battle of Fishguard," Ridgeway said, dropping his finger on the map just south of Cardigan. "The village has a long and venerable history, but a most curious part of it took place in 'Ninety-Seven."

Adam moved closer to better see the map. In black and white were outlined two countries, which ought to be as close as cousins, but were close to war instead. The coast of Ireland filled the left-hand side. The Saltee Islands were illustrated off the south coast.

"To keep the United Irishmen onside, Napoleon approved the plan to send an expeditionary force into England to make contact with the Jacobins and encourage the population to rise up against the *bourgeoisie*."

Nate crossed his arms across his chest. "Well, you have to say this for them, they're certainly original."

Sir Daniel acknowledged the joke with a smile and a nod of his head. He continued. "The plan was ill conceived from the beginning. An Irish-American Colonel, William Tate, first chose Liverpool and then Bristol to come ashore, but bad weather forced them to make the landing at Fishguard. The town was hopelessly ill-defended – the fort had only three rounds for each of their eight nine-pound cannons. The French had with them three ships and fifteen thousand troops, although only fourteen hundred men landed."

"You seem to know a tremendous amount about this, sir," added Bassett, his thick eyebrows furrowed.

"I happened to be part of the group of agents assigned to question them. My hair was a little less gray then, so I passed as an Irishman. My French is superb, so I also passed as a Frenchman," he said.

"But these were not well-drilled or disciplined soldiers. Most of them were malcontents and criminals pressed into service. The local militia did a fine job rounding them up…" Ridgeway chuckled, recalling a detail. "There was a rather imposing shoemaker by the name of Mistress Jemima Nicholas who brought in twelve Frenchies on her own, armed only with a pitchfork!"

"In all seriousness," said Nate, "do you really believe Napoleon would try an attack on the mainland again?"

"With a more disciplined group's than Tate's, certainly. He has the funds to do it. The Americans have paid him fifty million francs for the colony of Louisiana. And it's more than possible if Thomas Emmet is involved. The Irishman has amassed a strong group of sympathetic backers in the Americas. As for the will, we know only too well they can turn good men into agents right under our very noses."

Adam felt a tightness in his gut – the end was near. He could feel it. The thought of finally addressing this unfinished business nipped at his heels.

"What about their 'tinkerer', Dermot Flannery?" he asked. "Have we cocked up? We were supposed have been informed about which ship he'd be on and when ahead of time. Was he on the *Zelos*, or is he still on the Continent? Where is he?"

"Let's find out," said Ridgeway He returned to his desk and scribbled a quick note. He called Bassett's apprentice over.

"Give this to one of the footmen and tell him to go to the signal station at Tintagel with this message."

Young Joe took the message and rushed away.

"Hopefully, we will have an answer by tomorrow morning," said Ridgeway, "but I don't trust us to have such good fortune. I wasn't expecting either O'Brien or Flannery back until August. I suspect the man is still on the Continent."

Bassett cleared his throat to draw their attention. "Well, what I can tell you right now is that Madame Blanchard is, indeed, the real brains behind this," he said, a small magnifying monocle in his eye. "Her initials are on some of the diagrams. She has given Flannery everything he needs to ensure the flying army will get off the ground. Her preference is for silk over linen. She includes information on the quality of silk required.

"And in addition to information about the hotness of the coals to create the hot air, the good madame has also provided a formula for making hydrogen as the elevating agent."

"Hydrogen is extremely flammable if I recall from my Cambridge chemistry classes," said Ridgeway. "Any indication how soon they intend to launch?"

"It says here that the most favorable winds are in September," the man answered.

Suddenly, it all made sense. The prevailing winds traveled from the west. Under no circumstances could a fleet – *a flotilla* – of balloons be carried across the Channel from France to England. Ireland was the only place such an outlandish plan would work.

Adam mentally calculated the date and considered the likely late summer weather.

"That's less than six weeks away. We have to get Flannery before he arrives in Ireland. Once he reaches the Saltees, it will be too late to stop him. We need to find out what ship he intends to return on and whether she is under escort. I suspect not since they've been particular about not drawing attention to themselves thus far."

"What do you propose? Another change of plans?" asked Nate. "If Bickmore knew O'Brien had turned against the cause, then he's bound to know we'll be after Flannery."

Adam gave them a broad grin.

"We keep the plan as it is. After all, we don't want to disappoint the man."

Chapter Twenty-Eight

THE MOOD AROUND Stannum was positively carnivalesque. The sound of fiddles, tin whistles and squeeze boxes filled the air, competing with the half-drunken laughter of villagers enjoying the spoils from the wreck of the *Zelos*.

Earlier, Allie had looked down from the cliffs and noted the small ship was still held fast on the rocks, but every hour that passed saw the vessel list even further, buffeted by the waves and tide.

Now Allie urged Nephel onward toward the noise emanating from the village.

Phillip and Julian rode beside her.

"You'd think the salvage fee had already been paid, judging by that racket," she said with good humor.

"As long as the men aren't too worse for it come the morning," said Julian. "We're going to do the first tests with the pump engine."

Phillip shrugged. "Be happy to leave it another couple of days, man, if it means everyone is in good spirits and refreshed. There's been little enough to give them joy over the past few years. Getting the mine back in operation should also put an end to the sabotage."

Julian abruptly slowed his horse, then dismounted. He examined the beast's right hoof and pulled a small knife from his pocket "He's picked up a stone," he told them. "Don't wait for me – make sure you get a taste of that brandy before it's all gone!"

Riding on, Allie was happy to have a few minutes alone with her brother.

She had barely seen him in the two days since the shipwreck. He'd been occupied with his duties as head of the local community – contacting the authorities, sending for a coroner, speaking to the survivors of the wreck, and arranging for the burial of the poor souls who'd died – including the man who'd perished under unnatural circumstances.

So far, he had said nothing about finding her at David's cottage wearing nothing but a shirt. Did he think they were already lovers? She knew her brother had hopes of finding her a suitable husband among acceptable society. Her hoydenish behavior was enough to make him despair of her. But this? No man wanted a first-time bride who had known another.

The louder the music from the village, the more Allie knew their time to talk was limited. Should she broach the subject herself? The mood between them was tense. She feared she didn't have the courage to begin the conversation, so perhaps not saying anything at all was her wisest course of action.

They reached the village. Allie dismounted. Phillip did likewise and handed the reins of both horses to Gerran Angove to lead to the stables at the tavern.

They smiled and shared some words with the villagers but not between each other. Allie trailed behind him. He did not continue down to the revels on the beach. Instead, she followed him along the grass on the crest of the dunes.

Phillip glanced at her out of the corners of his eyes.

"I need to speak with you."

Allie let out a breath and waited for the lecture.

There was an awkward hesitation before Phillip spoke. "Why did Manston hare off to see Sir Daniel in such a hurry yesterday?"

It was not the question she expected and the answers she'd prepared in her mind did not cover it. She considered how she should answer her twin. Did he not know the Ridgeways were spies? Lady Abigail had confided in both her and David. Allie had taken it as read that her godmother would have spoken to Phillip as well.

Obviously, she hadn't.

"Well... Sir Daniel is an influential man and..."

"The *truth*, if you don't mind!"

"I thought you *knew*, Phillip..."

"Knew what?"

How to phrase it?

"Lady Abigail and Sir Daniel are... spies... of a sort."

Phillip stopped in his tracks. "I asked for the truth!"

"Don't shout, Phillip!" she hissed, looking about. "It *is* the truth. They're agents of the Crown and they're pursuing someone who's in the area."

Although the summer's day was bright about them, Phillip's face grew more thunderous. Allie watched him try and master his anger.

"*In the area?* Why the deuce wasn't *I* told? I *am* the squire of Stannum." He paused and she saw the thought come to him. "The sabotage at the mine? You know the men behind it?"

"I know only as much as you, Phillip – that they are the ones who set a false beacon in the engine house to lure the ship onto the rocks. I don't know all of it, but Cousin Abigail says they are spies and traitors."

"And what if the insurance men believe it's not mysterious ne'er-do-wells but *our* villagers who turned *wreckers*?"

"Then Sir Daniel can put them to rights. And *you*, of course."

Phillip folded his arms, another barrier between them. "You seem to have an answer for everything."

She frowned and laid a hand on her brother's arm. "I swear to you it's the truth. I'm not deceiving you."

He gave her a sharp look. "So, what am I to make of you emerging half-dressed in Manston's cottage?"

"You *know* how I came to be there," she said softly, hoping her gently delivered words would ease his anger. "Mistress Angove and Prenpas told you all, I'm sure."

Each response to his questions, no matter how reasonably answered, seemed to strike him like a blow. Phillip's head sank, his chin nearly on his chest.

"No man likes to learn he has no idea what is going on in his own household, Allie. What must Julian think? I'd hoped…"

His words trailed off and he sat wearily on a tussock of grass.

Allie gathered her skirts and sat beside him.

"Julian is a dear friend and no more. We spoke at the soiree and we understand each other. Our affection is no more than between sister and brother."

Phillip reached down and plucked a grass stalk. He twirled the seed head in his hands. The annoyance that had plagued him a few moments before had gone. Instead, he seemed resigned.

"I just want you to be happy, Sis. Is Manston truly the one? Even after everything that is said about him?"

"You know of that?" Her voice was strained. "I only learned when Abigail told me…"

Then she could say no more without her voice betraying her completely.

"I was told the stories about Manston by others in Bodmin when he assisted us with the business of shutting down the mine," Phillip confessed. "I'd not known what to think when he first arrived in the village, why a man of his obvious breeding would hide himself here. But since he seemed to want for nothing but his own company, I said nothing.

"I continued to say nothing when I accepted his help, and nothing when I heard the awful tales about him. I mean, at least he seemed to have left that behind. But knowing what I did, I was ill-at-ease for the longest time knowing you visited him often, even if it was entirely innocent on your part.

"Still, the more I got to know him, the higher I regarded him and I came to see him as a friend. Now, well… I don't know what to think, Allie."

She waded through the shifting sands of her emotions. First came irritation that Phillip knew about David's past but had said nothing, then dismay that her brother believed the worst of a man without knowing the truth. Eventually, she felt respect for Phillip that he'd come to judge David on his deeds and character rather than his past. This was the heart of the matter as far as she was concerned.

She nodded, accepting Phillip's explanation. "If I'm not the only one who has been keeping secrets, it is unfair to censure me for mine."

"Then consider us even," said Phillip. "Just as we were as children."

"And yet even seeing David as a friend, you do not consider him to be a suitable match for me?"

"That's not fair," Phillip entreated. "Your welfare is my responsibility. How is he going to support a wife? Would you be content leaving Stannum House and the life you have known to live in a tiny cottage, eking out a living?"

"He's never once given me any encouragement to think of marriage. I –"

"And that's *exactly* the issue, Allie. I know you love him – are *mad* for him – but does he feel the same way about you? Has he ever once proposed marriage?"

Allie frowned.

Had he?

David had told her he loved her but he hadn't mentioned marriage – nor had they had a chance to talk since the morning after the storm…

"He will," she averred. She tried to inject confidence into her voice but she was no more certain of it than Phillip was.

Of one thing, she *was* certain – David loved her. She knew it to the depths of her soul. Was it enough to overcome his past?

Phillip took her hand and turned it over, pouring the stripped grass seeds into her palm. She frowned at him and received a gentle smile in response.

"I think he will, too."

He nodded over her shoulder. She looked back.

Up on the ridge, lit by the last of the summer afternoon sun was a rider on a large black stallion. Even in silhouette, she knew the horseman. Phillip closed her hand around the seeds holding her fist as he leaned in, giving her a meaningful look.

"Tell David I expect him to call on me tomorrow."

AN IMPROMPTU BONFIRE was lit on the beach sometime during twilight and the more garrulous continued drinking and dancing. Among the thinning crowd, there were only familiar faces, people he considered friends and neighbors.

Allie seemed in no hurry to leave. David admitted to himself that, despite an exceptionally long day, he, too, was in no hurry to leave her side.

He was content to watch her as she laughed with some of the villagers. She was beautiful outside and in. His heart swelled with undeserved pride knowing this woman knew his darkest secrets and yet still loved him.

They had yet to speak formally of marriage, but he determined they would on the morrow. He fell deep into his own thoughts. He would arrange to give Allie a token, his grandmother's diamond and emerald ring, the color of her eyes. It would be a promise – a promise that he would court her properly and pledge his devotion and constancy, not just in love but in all things, that every day he would be a valorous man, the worthy man she believed him to be.

The ring was also a promise to himself. He had far outrun and outgrown the callow youth of his past. No longer would he be the servant of what was gone, nor would he rely on Lady Abigail Ridgeway's schemes to reclaim what was his by rights.

In his mind, he'd already drafted a letter to the family solicitor. *The Baron of Carreg requests a meeting with the viscount to assume his rightful place.*

It was well overdue.

As for Thomas and Claire, it was time for them to more publicly acknowledge their involvement and make amends for *their* sin – the sin of omission. They could do that by making his new bride welcome into society – not just in Cornwall and Wales, but also London. Allie well deserved a Season among the Beau Monde.

Prenpas and Foggett wandered over and, soon, David was drawn into conversation with them about preparation for testing the engine pump after so long idle. His thoughts drifted again.

There were fortunes to be made in Wales. What he learned here in Stannum might also bring prosperity to the land of his birth.

As the evening wore on, a slight chill entered the air, reminding him how late it had become. He squeezed Allie's hand, indicating they ought to leave. He noticed the knowing look Mistress Angove gave him as he and Allie walked off hand-in-hand, but he didn't care. Within a month they would be wed.

Young Gerran Angove brought their mounts from the stable already saddled, but the evening was still mild and far too lovely to bring to a premature end. They led their horses for the mile-long journey up to Stannum House.

Before they walked down the drive under the spreading canopy of elms, David paused, drawing Allie to his side.

"Have you ever stopped and looked at the stars in the heavens above?" he whispered. "Examined the constellations, considered the vastness of the universe?"

"They're beautiful tonight with the sky so clear." she answered in an awed hush. It seemed appropriate here although there was no living soul they could disturb by their conversation.

"No matter where I went in those days, I would look up at the sky and see the same stars looking down as though telling me I couldn't outrun what had happened in the past. It took me more years than it should to have the courage to put things to rights."

She rested the back of her head on his chest as she looked up and he took advantage of the intimacy to wrap his arms around her.

"Now the stars have brought you to me," she said.

He took advantage of the exposed pale column of her neck to drop kisses down along its length. Allie's satisfied sigh stirred him. A reminder to himself that they would soon have a lifetime together made it a simple decision to stop his lovemaking.

How remarkable that at the ripe old age of thirty-one, he was actually *courting* a woman. There was something really quite satisfying in it, a tenderness and consideration that went beyond the expression of physical desire.

With no false modesty, he knew he was an accomplished bedmate. But there had been times too many to count that he'd coupled with a woman without being entirely sure of her name, let alone her feelings for him.

But this... this was different; *remarkable*, even. Before he could give it rational thought, he turned Allie in his arms and went down on bended knee. The bright spray of stars in the sky could not hope to compete with beauty of her face. As far as he was concerned, she was the stars, the moon – the whole damned universe.

He had to say the words before his heart burst from his chest.

"Marry me, Allie," he said. "I can't promise you an easy life or a certain one. I can only promise to give you the best of me and hope that is enough. Whatever is left beyond that can live up to who you want me to be."

Two additional stars glittered above him, her tears in the moonlight. Her hands squeezed his tightly.

David's throat ached with the tension of controlling his own emotion. "I hadn't realized how lost I was until I met you."

"I thought you didn't like me." She smiled and there was no disguising the tease in her tone through the thick emotion of the words.

"I didn't at first. I resented you."

Allie gave a tearful giggle.

"I'd grown rather comfortable in my bitter and cynical little world and you were determined to pull me out of it. Now, I'm asking you to take mercy on me."

"Mercy?"

"I need an answer, Allie, I'm kneeling on gravel."

She laughed warmly and tugged at his hands to encourage him to stand before her. She threw her arms around him in a full embrace.

"The answer is *yes*," she said. "It's always been yes."

He kissed her hair and face over and over.

"My darling, I'm sorry it took me so long to get to the right question."

They talked as they walked down the drive to the stable.

"Will you call to see Phillip tomorrow?" she asked.

"Yes."

"There's something else you should know. I had to tell him the truth about Sir Daniel and Lady Abigail, I mean what they do and that they were looking for the saboteurs. It was unavoidable, I'm afraid."

David shrugged. "No matter. Phillip would have had to be told eventually anyway."

A couple of lamps dotted the windows of the house beyond – one in the study where Phillip and Julian were no doubt talking, another belonging to Mrs. McArthur's room.

David removed the saddle from Nephel's back and placed it on the rack. Allie led her mare into her stall for the night.

"It's late. You'd be welcome to stay overnight at the house."

Her words were softly spoken, so as to not wake Harry Watt whose quarters were on the other side of the stable wall.

"The offer is tempting and so are you," he replied, "but your brother will rest easier knowing you sleep in your own bed and I in mine."

There was no artifice in her smile, no deliberate effort at seduction, yet she tempted him anyway.

"Then a kiss to last me the night until we meet in the morning," she demanded.

He pulled her to him. "Are you always this bossy?"

Her arms twined around his neck "You'd better get used to it since you're marrying me."

"You might discover I'm not easy game either," he whispered before he kissed her thoroughly, tasting her lips, her tongue, and the slight flavor of the apple cider she had been drinking.

Yes – in addition to the courtship, there was the seduction, and he was a master at it.

Her body shifted restlessly against him as it seemed her own passion grew.

A wife, a help-meet, a friend, a true lover... Alexandra was all of these things, all of these parts of his life he never knew he needed until he met her.

DAVID LEANED FORWARD on the stirrups, adjusted himself on the saddle, and allowed Jack to run at full gallop along the headland where his cottage lay silhouetted against an indigo night sky filled with the silver stars.

He glanced over at Wheal Gunnis. The mine was quiet and still, as it ought to be. He was tired after his long ride to St. Sennen and back, and the evening on the beach with Allie. But accompanying his weariness was a deep satisfaction that not only was his body near home but his heart was also.

His bed beckoned and, with the pleasant arousal of Allie's kiss no longer sustaining him, he concentrated on the task before him. The final canter into his small yard. Unsaddle Jack. A quick brush down before giving him his oats.

If David hadn't been so tired he might have paid attention to the shadow that filled the entrance to the stable before he heard the cock of a pistol.

"Mr. Manston. We've been waiting for you to come home."

Fatigue vanished. David straightened and turned around slowly. Before him was the young "officer" he'd seen two nights earlier, the man called Bickmore.

Except he was not in uniform tonight.

Behind him stood another three men, their faces too dark to make them out clearly.

"We have business we need to discuss."

Chapter Twenty-Nine

D AVID FELT HIS heart beat faster but forced himself to maintain composure. Still, he kept his eyes on the man and the weapon he held in his hand.

Idly, he wondered if Allie would be surprised to know this was not the first time he had been held at gunpoint. There was that time in Venice when a man demanded satisfaction for cuckolding him. The poor woman screamed at her husband to stop and, fortunately, he did. It was just as well, because David was not the man with whom she was having an affair. Apparently, all Englishmen looked alike in the dark.

"What kind of business has you and your men bailing me up outside my own house?" he asked.

Brazen it out, but make no sudden moves, David told himself.

"There is a book I want, and I'm certain you have it."

David considered his answer. He could pretend to know nothing about it and they might believe him. Then again, they may not. He thought of Allie. Her safety and protection was his paramount concern.

"It's no longer here," he said.

The man nodded thoughtfully, as though he had already considered that answer.

"I thought as much, but I thought you might know where it is now. Is it with that rather fetching Miss Gedding? Quite a spirited thing, isn't she? We spoke once, and it was her horse in the stable with yours when we chased our thief to your cottage."

If the idea was to goad him into losing his temper, then it was an effort made in vain. Although not naturally a gambling man, David knew enough of gaming to know when to raise the stakes. The best way to protect Allie was to keep his *sangfroid*.

"The document is at my bank at Camelford... Lieutenant Bickmore."

Bickmore's face first registered surprise that slid into a sly grin.

"Bravo, Mr. Manston."

David inclined his head in acknowledgement.

"May I ask how you know of my name?"

Without waiting for him to answer, Bickmore waved the barrel in the direction of the cottage and stepped aside. David hesitated a moment and two of the other men quickly stepped forward. He recognized one of them – the mustachioed scarecrow he'd discouraged from following Allie at Camelford.

The next moment, he and the other man pinioned David's arms, turned him round, and, if he was not mistaken, the point of a blade touched his back at his kidneys to direct him to the door of the cottage.

Exuding confidence was the best way to keep himself alive, so long as Bickmore thought him useful.

"Surely not false modesty, Lieutenant?" he answered the man. "You are, in equal parts, famous *and* infamous."

"Only to one person," Bickmore added breezily. "Now open the door, sir. It would be polite to invite us in for refreshment."

David unlocked the front door and received a shove in the back for his trouble.

"Do come in," he said sarcastically. "You'll be sorely disappointed. I have nothing stronger here than tea."

"I'd quite enjoy a cup of tea, actually."

There was something off-putting about performing chores with an audience. But nevertheless, within a few minutes, the parlor was ablaze in candlelight and the fire was lit. All the while, Bickmore whistled, low but cheerily. It took David a minute to place the tune then he had it. It was that children's song. *Polly Put The Kettle On.*

David didn't really imagine Bickmore wanted tea.

Satisfied with the growing fire in the grate, he turned his back to the heat, his ankle brushing against the fire irons, and folded his arms.

"Well?" he said, giving Bickmore a level stare. "Even though I've told you the book isn't here, I take it you intend to search regardless? If you do, all I ask is that you don't damage anything."

"My, my, my... for a man I could kill and dispose of before day-light, you seem to be making a *lot* of demands. How about I ask my friend here to start slicing bits off and see how smart your mouth is then?"

The tall, thin man with the sunken face and the voluminous mous-tache held up the silvery blade of his knife. David calculated how quickly he might be able to snatch up an iron poker to brandish as a weapon. He could take on one or two of them and pray Bickmore misfired with the pistol.

He discounted it.

"You could, but it would do you no good if the answer is the same. As I told you, it is with my bank."

The scarecrow-looking man didn't look impressed. He snarled and brandished his knife once again.

"Well, ain't that just too bad for you then? Perhaps you might need more persuading."

David spared him a glance of ill-concealed contempt and returned his attention to Harold Bickmore. He also ignored his colleague's threat.

"That is going to cause us a great deal of inconvenience," Bick-more continued affably, "because we really *do* need it back."

David decided to match his captor's tone. "Tomorrow is Saturday and the bank is closed. Sunday, too, obviously. We could still go over there tomorrow and plead an emergency, but that would result in a lot of questions being asked. I suspect that would not do."

"Perhaps you should be our guest until Monday."

"Ordinarily, I would oblige. But I have appointments both tomorrow and Sunday. If I am absent, my future brother-in-law will have the garrison swarming by the afternoon. They are, of course, concerned about finding the men who wrecked the *Zelos*…"

Because he had shown himself unafraid but still cooperative, Bickmore seemed to regard him with a bit more respect.

"Why not send a man for me on Monday morning? I'll be here. I give you my word as the Baron of Carreg."

David had no idea what prompted him to use his title, but it was worth it to see the expression on Bickmore's face. It had the desired effect.

"Very well," the man announced. "You have been a gentleman and, under ordinary circumstances, I would simply take your word as a gentleman, but these are not ordinary times. I will require some kind of surety before we conclude for the evening."

"What are you considering?"

Bickmore's pleasant manner evaporated and David was under no illusion the man before him was desperate. That made him unpredictable, *dangerous*.

"I shan't take anything. I'll make you a promise instead. Failure to live up to your end of the agreement will result in something swift, devastating, and terribly unpleasant happening to the Gedding family."

David felt the weight of exhaustion. He hadn't slept more than five hours over the past two days. He closed his dry and aching eyes a moment. His concentration as well as his patience was ebbing.

"We have an agreement."

He found himself holding his breath, wondering what might happen next. If he'd been jumped by these three unsavory looking men in London, he had no doubt he would be lying dead tonight. It was only Bickmore who held them in check.

"Rest assured, your every move will be watched."

Yes, yes, yes, of course you will be watching. David nodded wearily. He sagged against the door frame and stifled a yawn. This intrigue was becoming more wearisome than worrisome.

Bickmore waved his men from the room, paused at the door and bared his teeth. David was utterly unprepared for the punishing blow to his gut.

Drawing in breath was painful. He reacted to the blow with a violent shove of his own, but before the matter could escalate, Bickmore had the pistol aimed, this time at his head.

"There will be time enough to settle our business. In the meantime, I advise you to take heed of our bargain."

With a salute of his free hand, Bickmore even shut the door behind him. David threw the bolt home with a curse before giving in to the agony of the blow.

FOR MORE YEARS than Allie could remember, she preferred to keep country time. Despite the fact it was so terribly fashionable in town to drink and dance until the wee hours of the morning and then not rise until noon, she preferred it this way. Country folks would dance only until nine or ten o'clock, knowing that chores came with the first light of dawn.

At Stannum House, Allie awoke just as the first light of the new day prompted a chorus of bird song. She lingered in a half-world of new light, savoring the dreams of being held in David's arms, the memory of his proposal last night. She cared nothing of his past, they would navigate whatever remained of that storm together.

Morning sunlight shone like tiger stripes through the aged and rotted lining of the gold jacquard curtains at the window.

Not so long ago, she would have found the evidence of their poverty dispiriting, but not today.

She dressed and drew back the curtains, looking out across the cove. The wrecked ship was still held fast on the rock. It had not shifted in the night. Now at low tide, villagers were swarming over the wreckage like ants on a carcass, each taking a little more of what was useful until, she suspected, only the ribs of the vessel would remain.

Wheal Gunnis cast a morning shadow down toward the village. Today, Phillip and Julian, along with few of the men, intended to finish their examination of the Beast and fire up the boiler. Should that be successful, the mine could reopen as soon as next week.

From down within the house, she heard a knocking at the front door and a short while later it being opened by Mrs. McArthur. A smile spread across her face. She didn't need to hear the caller's voice to know it was David.

She took the stairs two at a time, reaching the landing with a large smile on her face. It faded on seeing him.

He looked no better rested than he had done the evening before. His cleanly shaven face served to highlight the dark shadows under his eyes and his look of exhaustion. Only the fact that those blue eyes brightened when he saw her eased her concern a little.

"David? What's amiss?" she called down to him.

He held out his hand toward her just as Phillip opened the door to his study.

"Manston! Good to see you this morning," he said brightly, stepping out into the hall. He glanced up at Allie and offered her a smile before turning his attention back to their guest. "I understand we have business to discuss. And I'm glad to see you about it so early."

David didn't respond to the jest. Allie finished descending the stairs and went immediately to David's side, taking his hand. He gave it a

SPY ANOTHER DAY

squeeze but it didn't bring her any comfort.

"Is Winter here?" David asked Phillip.

"He's up in his room. Shall I call him?"

"No, I think what I have to say is best kept from him for the moment. We can decide what to tell him later."

The tone of his words brought home that David wasn't here to tell her brother about their engagement.

Phillip directed them into the study.

"I have deadly serious news that concerns us all."

Allie listened as David told them of his encounter with the traitorous Harold Bickmore last night, his lie about the journal being at the bank, and the threat to her and Phillip.

Phillip clenched his fists, his face tightly drawn. "I will *not* let these bastards threaten me and my sister in our own home or endanger our business. We've worked too hard to let them stop us."

"I agree," said David. "But we need to exercise an abundance of caution."

"Now that their hideaway is known to us, do you think the men are still there?" Allie asked.

David shook his head. "We've seen them on horseback. I suspect they're only at the mine from time to time. There must be somewhere else nearby where they hide out."

Allie shook her head. "Lady Abigail and Sir Daniel's men never found it. If they had, she would have told me."

"It would take more than just a handful of agents to successfully search all the abandoned houses and buildings in these parts," said Phillip. "It could take an entire division and, even then, if men don't want to be found, there are plenty of places to hide."

"Then what do we do?" asked Allie.

"There is safety in numbers," said David. "We carry on as we usually would, keeping in mind that Bickmore's men will be watching us."

Phillip nodded in agreement "I'll ride down to see Prenpas now and arrange for some of the men to accompany us up at the mine today. They won't be needed for the work, but I'd be happier with extra eyes watching over us," he said.

"And I, too, Brother," said Allie.

"Does Sir Daniel know about this?" Phillip asked.

David shook his head. "No, not these latest developments. I wanted to warn you first. But I need to get to Camelford as soon as possible and arrange a messenger."

"How? If we're being watched then how do we get a message out?"

"A group of villagers from Stannum are making the journey to Camelford for the Saturday markets today," said Allie. "If we are being watched, could we not get someone we trust to deliver a message to Sir Daniel?"

"It doesn't give him a lot of time to help us," said Phillip.

"Some time is better than none," said David. "My bluff is only good for two days."

Allie frowned, giving more thought to the problem. "We could tell him to arrange a return message to us at church on Sunday. Surrounded by people there, we would be safe enough."

"I agree," said David, then his manner changed. He gave her a look that started her heart pounding.

"This grave news is not the only reason why I've come so early this morning," he said. His eyes never left hers as he raised her hand to his lips for a lingering kiss.

"I need to speak to your brother about a matter of importance to us both. And an additional reason to be at the church service on Sunday."

DAVID FOLLOWED PHILLIP into the library.

He had shared his most urgent news and was drained. He hadn't realized how much until he found a glass of brandy being pressed into his hand.

"Sit, before you fall down, old man," Phillip instructed.

He didn't have to be told twice.

Phillip saluted with his glass which forced him to acknowledge it and take a measure. The heat of it sent a line of fire down his throat, reviving him.

He shook his head clear to find Phillip watching him patiently, and with faint amusement.

"Life around here has ceased to become dull, you'll agree – spies, wreckers, speculators, incognito barons…"

David inclined his head in acknowledgement.

"How long have you known of my identity?"

Setting his own glass down on the little round mahogany wine table, Phillip took a seat opposite and stretched his legs out.

"When you agreed to help me negotiate my way out of the debts when the mine closed."

"And you still invited me into your home, even after learning of my reputation, and again after learning of Allie's interest in me. Hell, I'm sitting here now asking for her hand and you've not tossed me out on my ear."

"I've learned not to take anything at face value." Phillip offered him a wry smile and picked up his glass once again. "For two years, you were simply the village hermit. I was content to let sleeping dogs lie, as long as you caused no trouble. You earned my gratitude and my loyalty when you successfully mediated with my creditors. The man I knew was not the man with the evil reputation I'd been told about. I figured everyone deserved a shot at redemption. I know I did, and you deserved no less."

David nodded his understanding.

"I've lived too long with past regret," he said. "It would be a greater regret to not reclaim my life, my title, and begin a new future with Allie. I love her and spent far too long denying it."

He rose to his feet and Phillip did likewise.

"You have my solemn vow that Allie's protection and happiness are all I seek. You will never have to wonder about my care and my love for her. Do I have your blessing?"

There was a play of a smile around Phillip's mouth. David was relieved that Phillip wasn't making this as difficult as he might have done.

"Your word as the Baron of Carreg?" he asked.

David squared his shoulders and thrust out his hand. "My word as a gentleman, as your business partner, as your friend – and, God willing, your future brother-in-law."

Chapter Thirty

THE CARRIAGE TILTED as it rounded a bend. Allie reached for the leather strap to keep her balance.

The old Nancarrow conveyance was not exactly comfortable. It was old and needed repair. It had not been used for more than six years and it showed, despite Harry Watt's best efforts to keep it maintained.

During fine weather, she and Phillip usually walked with the villagers to the church in Camelford. It took nearly an hour each way, but it somehow did not seem right to be riding in a carriage, an obvious sign of wealth and privilege, when so many people were deprived.

But bringing the vehicle out today suited their purposes. They could not be overheard, nor seen by Bickmore and his men. And they *were* watching – she had seen the man who had accompanied Bickmore at David's cottage outside the church when they arrived.

They had revealed the whole situation to Julian yesterday after much discussion. The fact was he needed to know and he'd reacted with about the same level of incredulity as David himself had when he was first made aware of Sir Daniel and Lady Abigail being involved in espionage for the Crown.

"You mean they didn't just come here to help us find investors?" he'd asked.

"Not entirely," David had responded with a wry smile.

Now, he and Allie, Phillip and Julian rode back from church in grim silence. It should have been a happy day, even with tomorrow's trial ahead – they had spoken to the priest and arranged for the first reading of the banns. But the vital matter of contact with Sir Daniel remained unanswered.

Their message had gone out to him yesterday; today there was no reply.

"Stay with us tonight at Stannum House, Manston," said Phillip. "I don't like the idea of you being out there on your own with this traitor about."

David shook his head. "On my own, I can draw attention away from you and Allie. If the book is what Bickmore wants then that is what he shall have."

"Somehow, it doesn't feel right to give these blackguards exactly what they want," Julian observed.

"Worse than that, I don't actually have the journal to give them. I gave it to Ridgeway."

Phillip forced brightness into his voice. He leaned forward, slapped David's knee and squeezed Allie's hand.

"Well, at the very least, we ought to have a celebration when we get home," said Phillip. "It's not every day your sister becomes engaged."

David let his disquietude recede to the corner of his mind.

HARRY WATT DREW the phaeton up by the front door which immediately opened. Mrs. McArthur came out before anyone had had the chance to climb down from the carriage.

"There's visitors, Master Gedding," she said. "Sir Daniel and Lady Abigail with Lieutenant Hardacre."

Allie felt her spirits lift.

Sir Daniel was the first to greet them in the drawing room. He, Lady Abigail and Adam Hardacre were all dressed in plain riding habits.

Allie caught a look that immediately passed between Ridgeway and David. It seemed to take in both Phillip and Julian as if questioning their presence.

David explained how they had brought both men into their confidence. A hushed discussion between him, Ridgeway, his wife, and Hardacre followed. Finally, Ridgeway seemed satisfied to speak openly.

"First of all, forgive me for not sending a message to the church to reassure you. We made the assumption Bickmore's men would follow wherever you went," he said. "So, I decided to let them trail you to church and see nothing amiss, and trusted the house would not be watched in your absence. We eschewed a carriage so as not to draw attention and came on horseback."

Mrs. McArthur entered to announce an informal meal had been served in the dining room.

Phillip took in the party.

"I'm not sure how I feel about my sister being caught up with all of this," Phillip said at length. "It's a dangerous enterprise for a woman."

"It's a dangerous enterprise for anyone," said Lady Abigail. "But your sister was in no direct danger. Her job was simply to report what she saw to me. The complication was she saw more than she should have done. With luck, by this time tomorrow, Harold Bickmore and his gang will be in irons where they belong."

David filled his plate from the sideboard and found a place at the table. "Would someone care to explain the plans for tomorrow? If there is a role to be played, I'd feel better if I knew my part."

"Just do as you're instructed and no more," said Hardacre.

"I'm not sure I feel comfortable with that. It's my life on the line and I've recently found a good reason to be more mindful of it."

"I share your sentiment, but the less you know about the whole plan, the less you could reveal to Bickmore and his men if things took a bad turn. It's enough for you to have him accompany you to the bank. Be there at nine –"

"It doesn't open until ten."

"Be there at nine. It will be open. One of our men will be there. He will take you to the room with the strong boxes and you'll open your box with your key."

"And when they see there's no journal in it?"

"There will be. You will find the journal in your lockbox exactly where you told them you put it."

"How on earth...?" Phillip exclaimed.

Hardacre shook his head. "The fewer explanations the better."

"A counterfeit?" said David.

Hardacre said nothing.

"I don't know how you could create something convincing in just a few days," said Phillip.

"You've heard of fairy godmothers?" said Lady Abigail. "*We* have a troll who can whisk up a bit of magic when the time calls for it."

Hardacre gave a half-shrug. "Just give the journal to Bickmore's man and let him leave with it. Sit tight for a minute to let him shove off, then you can go, too. Job done."

Allie thought she ought to take some comfort in the fact that the plan seemed straightforward. She reached for David beside her, putting her hand on his leg. So much could go wrong. The thought of something dreadful happening to him now, when their lives seemed to have righted themselves after so long...

"What are we to do while David is at Camelford?"

"You are to go about your day," said Sir Daniel. "I understand congratulations are in order. Abigail will keep you occupied with wedding plans, I'm sure."

"It's times like this a girl needs her mother," said Abigail. "And in her absence, I will indeed fulfill my long-neglected duties as your godmother."

Allie frowned. "How did you know about my engagement?"

David squeeze her hand.

"I may have described you as my fiancée when I met with Sir Daniel the day after the shipwreck."

Allie quirked an eyebrow. "Before you asked me? You must have been very sure of my answer, Mr. Manston."

He was not fooled by her mock affront. David brought her hand up and grazed it with his lips.

"Very sure."

Phillip rose from the table with a glass of white wine in hand.

One by one, everyone at the table stood also, their glasses charged.

"To the engagement of my sister Alexandra to the only man I know who is up to the task."

Allie raised an eyebrow at the affectionate dig and proposed a toast of her own.

"To the reopening of Wheal Gunnis, may she prosper as never before to the betterment of Stannum."

WHILE THE REST of the guests readied themselves for dinner, David found himself in the library on Lady Abigail's invitation.

On the desk was a folder.

"As you can see, Manston, I keep my promises."

Did he actually want to know what was in it? Did it even really matter anymore? Did he need the Carmarthan title to make himself complete?

With his beloved Allie at his side and the partnership with Phillip soon to bear fruit, he could be content without it.

Assuming he survived tomorrow's outing to Camelford, of course.

He'd been a fool to let his future be dictated by his past, and he was glad Allie had been the one to call him out on it.

Seeing Claire and Thomas at the soiree all those months ago had made him realize he was no longer the person he was at the age of twenty-one – a callow creature subject to the whims of emotion, battered by the wind and tide of events.

It was time to put away the regrets that had him living only half a life.

"Aren't you going to read it?" asked Lady Abigail. "I went to such great trouble to get it."

David looked back over his shoulder to where the woman sat.

"Is there a point? After all, I'm convinced you're already aware of its contents."

"I've read the report," she admitted without the least bit of self-consciousness. "I think it would do you a world of good for you to read it as well."

The truth of the matter was that his own self-pity was as bitter as rue compared to the one who rightly deserved his pity.

Jenny.

Dear God, he didn't even know the girl's surname.

He'd had wealth and position and little else. She had no advantages, but she had a family who loved her.

Who was the richer then?

He preferred to think of Jenny as he last saw her – a pretty young woman not yet succumbed to the ravages of a disease that all the money in the world could not cure.

With a shake of his head to clear it, David opened the cover to find a charcoal rubbing of a headstone inscription.

Virginia Carpenter
(our girl Jenny)
1779-1797

SPY ANOTHER DAY

He closed his eyes but it was too late – the imprint in his mind's eye was indelible.

"She did not linger long," he observed in a whisper.

"It is said she died peacefully in February of that year."

Lady Abigail's voice was sympathetic, which only served to make it worse. The ghosts of self-pity drifted their way back into his mind but he fought them. *He'd* been given a second chance in *his* life. That had to count for something, right?

"There is something else, if you would care to see. Jenny had a very specific request recorded with the priest of the little Catholic church her family attended in Leeds."

David turned the page over.

… that on the first day of each March, a candle be lit and prayers said for David (no surname given), a man who in his own struggle had shown me great kindness…

"It is a tradition the family has carried on ever since."

David heard the rustle of fabric behind him as Lady Abigail stood. The scent of her gardenia perfume accompanied her to the desk.

"Did her family know… what she did for the money she sent home?" he asked.

"She told them she was a parlor maid in a big house in London."

"And when she returned home with the promissory notes?"

"As far as her family was aware, it was a token from a kind employer."

There was a final document in the folder, a statement signed by Reynold Chalmers testifying to the true nature of the events ten years prior.

"As you can see, you are absolved."

David turned to Abigail.

"I don't know how to thank you," he said. "This is more than I could have hoped to find. If it were for myself alone, I would not have bothered, but I don't want Allie to be subject to any rumors should there be the chance of reclaiming my title."

The older woman took his hands and squeezed them.

"I didn't do this solely for my goddaughter's benefit," she said. "I know what it is to be accused and shunned. It is a lonely business, indeed, if you have no one to stand beside you. I also know what it is to be given a second chance."

The creamy sweet perfume filled his nostrils as she leaned forward to kiss him on the cheek.

"Consider this my engagement present to you both," she said. "Go, share this news with Allie. You will find a no more loyal woman as your bride-to-be."

"I know it." David allowed himself a smile.

"Then we look forward to attending the wedding next month."

Chapter Thirty-One

D AVID SLEPT POORLY, but well enough to be up and alert at dawn. He was dressed and ready when Pockmark came to the door. He had dubbed the man that for the pitted scars that marked his face. The henchman pulled out a small primed pistol from his pocket – small but lethal at close quarters. He said little other than to give the instruction to saddle his horse.

He didn't dawdle, neither would he let the man dictate the pace.

"Where's Bickmore?"

"None of your business," said Pockmark. "Just get to Camelford like you've been told and nothing bad'll happen."

David looked up at Wheal Gunnis. A thin line of smoke rose from the chimney stack. Before too long, the pump would be in operation and Stannum's industry would begin once more.

He hoped he lived to see it.

Despite assurances that Sir Daniel's men were within calling distance, he saw no one. Pockmark seemed strung tighter than a bow. It transmitted itself through his horse that shifted restlessly until they were both on their way.

They followed the path along the headland. Below on the line of rocks, the *Zelos* was proving tenacious. Although keeled over at a sickening angle, the mast and spars still held firm. Waves crashed over the gunwales and white foam slithered down the decks.

They met no one when they reached Stannum. The fishermen

were still abed after a night at sea, while those able-bodied men who worked on land were most likely up at the mine. They passed the entrance to Stannum House. David resisted slowing down and looking along the drive.

He was glad Allie had the company of Lady Abigail – he knew of no one else who would be able to curb Allie's desire to join him on this enterprise. As it was, he felt like a man who was heading to the gallows. Despite his own desire to live and enjoy the life he knew there would be with his beloved Allie, he was equally prepared for things to go so much worse.

The journey to Camelford dragged out in such miserable company, since his traveling companion was in no way loquacious. The nearer they got, the more concerned David became.

Camelford was a picturesque market village with whitewashed wattle and daub buildings gleaming in the early summer sunshine. The river which gave the habitation its name ran through the center of it.

On any other day, David might have slowed his pace and admired the view. But not today.

The bank did not typically open before ten o'clock. But on this morning, as promised by Hardacre, the blinds of the imposing building were up although David estimated it was only a little after nine.

David tried the door. He was half-surprised when it opened, the little bell above it tinkling. He swung the door wide and stepped in, trailed closely by Pockmark, hand in coat pocket, no doubt grasping a weapon.

He expected to see Mr. Hillier, the usual banker. Instead there were two men seated at a table, an older man and an apprentice, heads down, apparently absorbed in studying the ledgers before them.

Despite the fact that the bell had announced their presence, the man before him did not raise his head.

David recognized them as Ridgeway's men from The Queen's Head, but they hadn't been introduced and he didn't know their names.

He coughed loudly. The "banker" slowly raised his head and peered over his thick glasses.

"May I help you?" he asked, his voice on just this side of peevish.

"I wish access to my strong box," he said.

"Your name is Manston, is it not, sir?"

"It is."

David attempted to keep his face neutral. It was imperative that this pantomime go without a hitch.

"Browne, fetch Mr. Manston's strong box if you please. Number fifty-eight." The young man immediately went back to the strong room. The older man rose to his feet and held out an arm. "This way, gentlemen, let me show you to a private office."

Pockmark was doing his best to quell his agitation. He kept his hand in the pocket of his coat.

Seconds ticked away with the swinging pendulum of the wall clock. Ridgeway's man stood, silent and stone-faced, just inside the door. A minute passed and David could see Pockmark was becoming agitated again. Then the young man brought in the box and placed it on the table.

"Gentlemen…" said the "banker" and withdrew from the room, closing the door behind him.

Pockmark's chair scraped on the floor as he sprang to his feet, full of tension and nearly bouncing on his toes.

The King's Rogues might enjoy the theatrics of all this but David did not. He feigned calmness as he turned his key in the strong box lock and opened the lid.

The water stained journal sat on top of his pouches within. He picked it out and gave it to Pockmark.

The man opened it carefully on the table and quickly scanned page after page. As each was leafed over, David held his breath waiting for the man to declare the document fake.

Pockmark closed it without comment.

"There – you got what you came for. Tell Bickmore I never want to see his face or yours again." David stood up and faced the man. "And if you *ever* threaten my friends or my family –"

"Threats don't mean nothing to me, Manston. We'll see how brave your talk is when Frenchie soldiers are walking down the street."

Pockmark slipped the book in his pocket and walked out of the room. David heard his boot steps on the wooden floor and the tinkling of the front door bell as he left.

As instructed by Hardacre, David waited a full minute. He needed the time to bring his breathing under control. Before closing the strong box, he opened one of the pouches and withdrew the diamond and emerald ring. It would be on Allie's hand before the end of the day.

He locked the box and rang the little bell which was the only other object on the table. The young man returned and took the box back to the strong room. David went out into the bank.

"There, wasn't that a bit of fun," said the older man with a grin from ear to ear.

"If you say so, but there wasn't a pistol pointing at your gut," he said.

"Pish, there was never any real danger to you," the man replied.

"There might have been if Bickmore's man had realized he held a forgery in his hand."

Ridgeway's man raised himself up to his full height which didn't look more than five foot, three inches. "Apart from the alterations requested by Sir Daniel, that book was completely identical to the original right down to the water stain on the pages. As far as forgeries go, that was one of my absolute best – and completed in record time."

"Where has our man gone?"

"He's traveling south. He's being watched. You don't need to concern yourself any further."

"Thank you, but I'll wait for Sir Daniel to provide me with such assurances."

The little man responded to the snub with a shrug of his shoulders.

ADAM HARDACRE HAD never been fox hunting. Such sport was for a group of society in which he would never be a member, but he imagined a manhunt was much the same thing.

He recalled a time onboard the *Andromeda* when they'd played cat and mouse for three weeks with a French frigate off the coast of Barbados. In the end, they discovered the vessel in shallow water, battle scarred and its crew exhausted, ready to surrender.

It was a hollow victory and, as a younger man, Adam had felt cheated out of the opportunity to fight.

Now, with the maturity of a decade past, he would welcome the opportunity of such an easy resolution to *this* pursuit. However, he knew Harold Bickmore would never surrender.

But soon, the hunt would come to an end at this abandoned farmhouse on this isolated part of Fowey Moor.

For the past few days, he and Nate Payne had camped on the large hill with the improbable name of Brown Willy that overlooked the granite-strewn landscape below. Out of the landscape – and indeed made from the very same stone – was a two-story farmhouse, abandoned but habitable. Indeed, it was inhabited now.

A slide of small stones behind him alerted him to Nate's return.

"Anything new to report?" he asked. "Sir Daniel will want an update before the sun goes down."

Adam put down his telescope and took the proffered water canteen from his friend's hand.

"Nothing. Same as yesterday and the day before yesterday." He didn't attempt to hide his frustration. "Ever since Rickards returned with the journal, they've been holed up there."

Nate picked up the telescope to look for himself. "Well, you know the orders. Do nothing unless they look like they're ready to move or we confirm that Bickmore is amongst them. Then it's act at one's own discretion."

"So, you know the coded message to send." He did not hide the bitterness from his voice.

Nate shrugged and moved back up the rise to where, on the other side, out of view of the farm, they'd made an encampment within the foundations of the ancient round house that once had a commanding aspect of the moor.

Their location was less than ten miles away from Camelford; seven if one wanted to be precise about it. Yet it might as well be in the middle of the wilderness.

He and Nate had agreed to take it in turns to keep watch. Adam knew how long it would take for Nate to reach the semaphore station and return. Two hours. After that, the sun would go down and thus would begin the long night watch.

To occupy his time and quell his resentment at remaining here on the wind-swept hill, away from his wife, Adam marshaled every word of profanity he knew and arranged them in alphabetical order – going back to the beginning each time he recalled another one.

He remained at his vigil as the late afternoon sun cast dark shadows across the vale. A golden glow from a lamp filled the window of the stone farmhouse below. A thin stream of smoke rose into the pale gray sky, he resentfully observed, a privilege denied *him* as a result of his surveillance.

There would be no fire to warm him until nightfall, lest smoke give away his position. Adam shrugged into his coat and stretched out his legs.

Bickmore *was* in that house. Adam hadn't seen him but he knew it as certainly as he knew his own name, as though he could actually look through the stone and see him walk around inside.

It is easier to forgive an enemy than to forgive a friend.

He didn't know where he'd first heard the phrase but it was apt.

Harold Bickmore had been like a brother to him, a brother-in-arms. He'd once trusted the man with every important part of his life. How much of that friendship had been genuine? Any of it? How long had Bickmore lived this double life?

He couldn't shake the idea that their "friendship" was cultivated for Harold's own ends from the beginning.

A new thought struck him suddenly, like a shove off a cliff, his stomach plunging as though he were falling from a great height.

Had Bickmore been in some way responsible for his failed promotions?

The idea brought back a flood of memories both good and bad, trying to fit things together like scattered jigsaw pieces. He closed his eyes, trying to make sense of it all.

Had there been anything *about the man that had been true?*

Adam shook his head and opened his eyes. A movement caught his eyes and he snatched up the telescope. He straightened. A man on horseback approached the farmhouse. A figure from within emerged.

Harold Bickmore.

"You bastard," Adam muttered under his breath.

The rider dismounted smartly and saluted in the French military style. Bickmore returned the action, right palm displayed outward instead of the Royal Navy salute where the palm was always face down.

A visceral part of him reacted, snarling at the man he once called friend.

Adam rose to his feet and checked the bandolier across his chest, feeling for the flint and striker and the small pouch of powder before heading back to the round house camp. He put together a backpack filled with several flasks of black powder, all the while raining down all the curses of heaven on the man he vowed to destroy.

He carried a pistol on a loop on his belt, along with a knife. Adam pulled out a belt from another pack and donned it, then hesitated over his cutlass. He left it, also considered taking his horse, then decided against that, too. He would be quicker and quieter on foot.

The rational part of his mind that told him to wait for Nate to return was overruled.

This ends today.

DAVID SWUNG THE axe and struck the wood. The deadfall split cleanly. Over his shoulder, he could hear the sound of hooves. The gait of the horse was so familiar that he knew without looking that it was Allie's mount.

He swung the blade once more. The axe bit into the chopping block and held. David wiped a hand across his brow and looked up, ready to greet his fiancée.

Their wedding could not come soon enough. It marked a new beginning for him, a place where past and present came together. And with the woman he loved at his side, there would be a new future together.

He'd made another step in reconciling the past with the future by sending a letter to his parents telling them of his marriage plans and his intention to reclaim his title. Ten years in purgatory – even one of his own making – was long enough.

David took in her form, framed in the riding habit of blue which was his favorite. His eyes reached her face and any frisson of arousal died at the sight of her grim expression.

He jogged over to meet her.

"Phillip and Julian are missing," she said as she dismounted. "I'm worried. No one has seen them since the day before last."

Allie accepted his embrace. It was the only comfort and answer he had to give her.

He glanced up at the mine. It was still. Perhaps that peace was a deception hiding something malevolent. He led Allie into his cottage and pulled back a chair for her to sit down at the table.

Her hands were shaking. Allie noticed his observation and curled her fingers into fists that she set in her lap.

She took a deep breath as if to prevent the worry he saw clearly on her face, spilling over into tears.

"The day before yesterday, when you went to Camelford... Phillip returned home to say he and Julian were planning to spend overnight at Wheal Gunnis. They wanted to be sure none of the wreckers came back and to get an early start on testing the pump."

She watched him fill in the gaps. It was too much of a coincidence for them to believe that Bickmore was not involved.

"Prenpas and Foggett haven't seen them?" he asked.

Allie shook her head and fought to stop her voice from shaking. "They didn't know about the plans. Yesterday, they worked above ground and didn't see them. When Phillip didn't come home for supper last night, I thought he and Julian might have decided to stay overnight once more. Then, about an hour ago, Prenpas came by to ask for Phillip..."

David's hand covered hers, giving her time to recover.

"... I knew then something was wrong."

"And Lady Abigail, what does she say?"

"She's ridden directly to Camelford to see Sir Daniel. I didn't know what else to do, so I came here."

David drew to her side and placed a soft kiss on her forehead. She rose to her feet.

"I can't just sit here and wait," she whispered.

Chapter Thirty-Two

A
S THEY RODE up to Wheal Gunnis, Allie was grateful that David did not raise an objection. The fact that he did not spoke volumes about his concern for her brother also.

They reached the brow of the hill. She sheltered her eyes from the glare of the setting sun.

"Prenpas is raising a search party from the village. Should we wait for them?" she asked.

"Let's take a walk around up top first and see what we can find out ourselves."

Allie let David lead the way. She noticed he skirted clear of the engine house, instead heading to the outbuildings. He said nothing and neither did she. Allie listened. The sound of the wind was constant, making it difficult to isolate other sounds, other than the shrill cry of a red kite searching for prey.

"If Phillip and Julian are not up here, then they must be below ground," she said.

"If they planned to inspect the pump workings starting from the bottom of the pit," said David. "I imagine there's more than a day's work in it, so there's still every chance that Prenpas simply missed them."

Allie didn't believe that, and she suspected David didn't either, but she appreciated his attempt to allay her fears.

The sorting shed was the next building they searched.

There! In the back corner of the shed.

She might have missed it, if it not for the angle of the light through the door. A piece of fabric hastily stuffed under a bench caught her eyes.

David reached it before she did. He squatted down, reached in and pulled it out from its hiding place. It was a large satchel – Phillip's. Allie bobbed down beside him. She did not need to tell him who it belonged to. He nodded his understanding and, to her surprise, stuffed the bag back in place.

"I'm going to send you home. I'll wait for Prenpas and his men to get here," he said.

"Why? As soon as the search party arrives, I'll be in plenty of company."

He had no answer for her logic, but his eyes told her of his fears. Did he not realize her concern for *him* was no less acute that her concern for her brother? He answered her question by reaching for her. Allie had no choice but to fall into his arms, letting him support her weight as he kissed her.

She ran a hand through his hair, feeling for the lump he sustained only a week before. They stayed like this a moment.

David stood and helped her to her feet. He hesitated just inside the doorway and glanced about, then held out his hand behind him. She took it, and he turned back into the shed swiftly, away from the open door. He took her into his arms and held her close.

"There's a man walking about outside," he whispered in her ear. She didn't need to be told that the man David had seen was not anyone they knew from the village.

"Where did he come from?" she whispered back. "Why didn't Prenpas see him?"

She felt David shrug his shoulders in response.

He shifted, leaning around the corner.

"Come on, let's go."

Outside, they quickened their pace to a half-run toward the engine house on the southern side of the mine. She guessed his plans. He was going to tell her to take the steep path that would take her directly to down to his cottage.

She took in a deep breath, ready to raise an objection, when she heard a crack. A second later there was a sting as though something bit the flesh of her upper arm. Yells behind spurred them onward.

She bit her lip against the pain, knowing if she cried out David would stop and the man who pursued them would soon be upon them. Instead of crossing the well-tamped grass that led to the path, David now veered to their right toward the tailings dump on the southern side of the hill.

"This way."

He released her hand. She followed him over the edge of a steep slope, sliding a few feet down to a ledge. He urged her forward along the narrow path cut into the rock face. She gingerly patted her arm where it stung and her hand came away smeared with a small amount of blood.

"Don't slow down! Keep going! We need to make it to the opening over there. Do you see it?"

She nodded and moved as fast as she dared on a ledge that was only three feet wide at best on a rock slope that was now very steep. Ahead was an opening into the mine. She knew what it was. It was the adit for the main drainage channel. When the pump was operating, it would draw water up from the depths of the pit and spew it out into the tailings pond far below.

The entrance was not quite high enough to allow them to stand up straight.

"Where are you hurt?"

She looked at him uncomprehendingly for a moment before she realized he was talking about her arm.

"It's nothing, a scratch," she said. David insisted on looking for himself. She looked down. The short sleeve of her dress was stained. A thin trail of blood stopped at her left elbow.

"That," he gritted out, "was a musket ball fired at us."

"I don't think it was that which hit me. It felt more like a sting from a wasp."

"A ricochet then, it really doesn't matter because I'll kill the bastards who did it."

ADAM KEPT WITHIN the long afternoon shadows. Boggy areas that might have impeded his progress were nearly dry thanks to several days of sunny conditions while the large granite outcrops were tall enough to hide him should anyone think to look his way. The fact that this was a godforsaken moor and his enemies thought themselves safe out here made him feel confident no one would look his way.

He had advanced two hundred yards before he considered that he didn't actually have a plan, only that he wanted this hunt over and his world set to rights again.

He thought of his beloved Olivia. He did not want to leave her a widow and he would do his damnedest to ensure he didn't, but he would not be a coward about it either.

A time to live, a time to die.

Adam prayed it would be the former.

He found himself within fifty yards of the farmhouse, squatting behind a rock and angled in such a way that he could see the Frenchman who had arrived. He and Bickmore lingered outside, clearly unafraid of discovery.

The rider appeared to be unaccompanied and was taking a great deal of interest in the journal Bickmore gave him. Snatches of their conversation reached him, but his French, although much improved, was not good enough to understand the spoken words.

But the sharp metallic click of a pistol hammer being cocked meant the same thing regardless of the language.

Adam looked behind him to a tall, thin man with a full moustache pointing a pistol at him. The man flicked the nose of barrel. He didn't need a translation for that either. He rose to his feet slowly.

With arms raised, Adam stepped around the rock. He locked eyes with Harold Bickmore who regarded him with only the mildest surprise.

"I suppose I should be more surprised than I am to see you here," said Bickmore as Adam came closer.

Adam shrugged his shoulders. "The student and the master must someday meet."

It was odd, Adam considered. He ought to feel afraid. But he was not.

He knew his life could be forfeit at any moment, and yet there was a strange feeling of inevitability about this whole situation, as though everything was preordained. And he felt quite calm about it, all things considered.

No matter what he did or said, today would end with one of these two indisputable truths – either Harold Bickmore would be dead, or Adam Hardacre would.

Bickmore addressed the Frenchman. *"Allez directement à Bristol. Mes hommes vont vous accompagner."*

Then he spoke to the man with the pistol. "Go and wake up Padgett and escort this man to Bristol."

"You not coming with us, Guv?"

"Not yet. I have some business to take care of here. The important thing is you get to Bristol and arrange for this man's passage back to France. You'll go with him. Our mission continues. Make sure the journal gets into Dumphrey's hands and tell him to get everything ready for Flannery's return. Tell him we stand ready on this side of the Irish Sea for word on when the operation will begin."

The man who held the pistol at Adam let it waver a moment before handing it to Bickmore. He went inside the farmhouse. Bickmore held Adam at gunpoint and continued to speak in French with the rider until two accomplices emerged from around the back of the farmhouse, mounted on horseback.

Adam forced himself to stand at ease, watching everything but without drawing attention to himself. He estimated it was not quite an hour since Nate left to send the signals to Sir Daniel. That would mean nearly another hour before he returned to their encampment. Adam hadn't left a message. He didn't need to. Nate would know exactly where he was and would kindly provide some backup.

He hoped.

With his men on their way, Bickmore turned his attention back to Adam.

"I think you'd feel more comfortable indoors. It seems we have a lot to talk about."

Adam allowed himself to be shepherded toward the front door of the farmhouse. He kept his movements as easy and unthreatening as possible as he considered and discarded various courses of action.

The door of the farmhouse stood open and Adam entered, Bickmore at his back.

As the man closed the door, Adam removed the heavy backpack and placed it on the table in the center of the room, then staked his position at one end of it.

Before them, a cheery fire of logs burned atop andirons within a stone inglenook. The fireplace served to warm the whole house. To the left of the fireplace was a door that probably led to the kitchen and the stairs to the second story.

Without asking, Adam removed the pistol and put it down grip toward Bickmore who watched him from the other end of the table. For good measure, he surrendered the knife from his belt also.

Let Bickmore think he was entirely cooperative, a puppet, a tool to be used. There was something to be said to being underestimated. It was something he'd lived with for his entire career. No one thought much of a youth pressed into service. No one expected anything of a poor Cornish man who rose through the ranks. And yet each and every time, he proved them wrong.

Now was his last chance to prove Harold Bickmore wrong.

"There's no other choice for it," said Bickmore, "I will have to kill you."

"In your situation, I would have thought you have no other option."

Bickmore nodded. "You can be assured that I do so with great reluctance."

Adam was aware of the absurdity of engaging in chit-chat with a man who intended to kill him.

"That brings me great comfort."

Bickmore barked out a laugh at the jest before sobering.

"It's nothing personal, Adam."

"Was it *ever* personal?

Bickmore regarded him more thoughtfully.

"Was our friendship a joke?" Adam asked softly.

The question seemed to catch the other man off guard. He lowered the pistol and placed it on the table.

He continued. "We served together for ten years. You get to know a man. To trust a man. You go on with your life relying on certain things being true. To learn it was a lie..." Adam shook his head gravely.

"And that's what you want to know? That's what matters to you so much that you would come here to your death to find out?"

Bickmore's eyebrows drew together. He seemed suddenly more like the uncertain, inexperienced young officer Adam had befriended aboard the *Andromeda*. For a moment, he wondered if Harold was really so far gone that he couldn't be brought back. He dismissed the thought.

"I looked up to you, Adam. You were confident, strong, respected. You may not have had education but you were wise in all the ways that mattered. I admired you at first, then I came to scorn you. Again and again, you tried to work within the rules. And time and time again, they tried to keep you in your place. I resented them, so I started listening to the Revolutionaries. Burning the whole world down seemed the only way forward, but *you* never seemed to see it, so I came to resent you, too. But when you quit at last and came to join us, I genuinely thought you'd become a true believer at long last."

Bickmore's boyishness disappeared, replaced by a harder, more cynical expression. He glanced down at the pistol.

"You think yourself aggrieved?" said Adam. "As far as I'm concerned, you betrayed *us*."

Bickmore reached for the gun.

"Tell me about the bet in Corsica."

The man's hand hesitated over the weapon, then withdrew.

"You honestly don't remember that night?"

Adam shook his head slowly. Bickmore burst out laughing.

"Neither do *I*! I only said it to wind you up. Dear God, you're even more contemptable than I imagined. You're about to die and you're worried about whether we were friends and a piece of nonsense I invented to keep you off guard!"

Bickmore picked up the pistol.

Adam snatched up his satchel and tossed it toward the fireplace. It landed in the middle of the burning logs, smothering the flames as one firedog toppled and the logs fell to the floor of the inglenook.

"Then in that case, you won't care for the information I carry."

"What information?" said Bickmore, sharply. "What have you brought with you?" He was torn between taking his shot and recovering what might be of use. Curiosity won out. Keeping the barrel pointed in Adam's general direction, Bickmore went to the fire and reached over it.

"What the hell?"

As he lifted the backpack, the canvas charred by the hot coals fell away. Loose black powder ignited. Orange flames leapt up the chimney.

Adam threw himself to one side as the powder flasks inside the bag ignited like a mortar. He covered his ears but it was not enough to stop the deafening roar. The heat from the explosion rolled over him like a wave intense enough for him to fear that his very clothes might ignite.

Then he felt cold as if all the heat had gone from the world.

After a moment, he struggled to his feet, his stomach roiling and ears ringing. The air was thick with white smoke. He coughed once and sank to his knees, crawling on his hands and knees toward the cool air from the broken front door. Little spot fires burned around the room.

Blocking the door was the crumpled shape of a man. Adam had seen enough charred and broken bodies in his time on board ship. When a cannon misfired, the poor boys who served as powder monkeys usually bore the brunt of it.

He rose unsteadily to his feet again and looked down. Embedded in Harold Bickmore's chest was one of the firedogs.

Adam stepped over Bickmore's corpse and stumbled a few paces outside, coughing furiously before sinking to his knees, unable to hold his own weight.

Part of his mind tried to force movement into his legs. He felt a thrumming urgency to run. Bickmore's men could not have gone any further than a mile, two at most. They would undoubtedly have heard the explosion. If they returned, they would find him here and kill him with vengeance. He'd only had one trick in his bag and he'd used it.

Even now, they could be upon him and he wouldn't know it because he still couldn't hear a damned thing.

Adam flinched when a hand touched his shoulder. He raised his head to see Ridgeway and Payne looking down at him, their faces a mixture of wonder and concern. One of them said something, but the roaring in his ears prevented him from hearing it.

He shook his head. Ridgeway repeated himself. This time, Adam could guess the question being asked.

Where's Bickmore?

"He's gone to the dogs."

Chapter Thirty-Three

ALLIE TURNED AWAY to stop David from observing her injured arm.

"We can't stay here, those men will still be looking for us," she said.

Through the afternoon light coming through the adit, she saw his lip curl in frustration.

"Then further into the mine we go. We'll have to play cat and mouse until Prenpas gets the men up here, unless your fairy godmother can pull off another miracle."

Allie looked down at her clothes. Her riding habit was ruined – and her best one at that. The mine had better be as profitable as Julian said it could be because she intended to extract her share and spend it on a new wardrobe fashioned by the most expensive modiste in London.

"Pass me your knife," she said. David obliged, handing it over hilt first. Allie gathered a handful of the skirt, took a deep breath and plunged the blade into the fabric. She started cutting. Soon, a puddle of fabric from the knee down fell to the dirt.

"I don't intend to be hampered by skirts climbing up and down ladders," she told him as she handed the knife back.

He simply shook his head and grinned.

"Your brother is going to think I'm leading you astray."

"He already thinks that, so it's just as well you've properly proposed marriage. Let's go find him and he can tell you himself."

David glanced back to the entrance then nodded further into the channel.

"Time to move."

The adit narrowed toward the mine shaft until they could only traverse it in a crouch. The light from the entrance was fading fast. "What are we going to do for light?" she asked.

"The sluice should be just ahead and there are lamps there. I've got a flint and striker with me," David assured her.

She thought of the men who spent twelve hours a day in these cramped, black conditions.

Julian had told her that women, too, worked below the surface in the coal mines of Yorkshire. Children, as well, walking and crawling for a mile before they even reached the coalface for their day's work to begin.

She said a silent prayer for her brother and their friend, missing somewhere below.

Allie knew how the pumping system worked and was surprised the channel wasn't wet from the testing of the pump. Perhaps it hadn't run for long and anything drawn up never made it past the cistern on the lower levels.

They climbed the upward slope of the adit. Ahead was a dim glow from an opening partly hidden by a structure. As they drew closer, she saw it was a channel fashioned from tin – the sluice for the water pump.

David squeezed around it and took her weight as she scrambled up and around, too.

A voice suddenly echoed behind them.

"D'ye think they're so daft as to go all the way into the mine?"

"I tell ye, that's where I seen them go."

"If that's how they got in, that's how they can get out then. Stay at the entrance. We don't need to do nothing but to keep all four of them below ground 'til Bickmore says we can go."

Allie couldn't hear the other man's reply, but she knew it was a grumble. He didn't seem best pleased by the order.

She released a breath as the voices moved back toward the entrance to the adit.

David stepped to where the passage opened into the main ladderway. Grasping the edge of the sluice, he looked down the shaft then up.

"I don't like this," he said.

Allie could think of a dozen reasons but decided not the voice them aloud.

She knew the sense of it. She was ill-prepared to climb ladders and traverse underground through narrow spaces with precipitous drops hundreds of feet below the earth. But her brother was down there – more than her brother, her *twin*. If anything happened to him, it would be as though part of her had died.

"Where do you think Phillip and Julian might be?"

"They said they were going to examine the pump's balance bob which will be in one of the side openings between galleries seven and eight." He gave her an appraising look and seemed to realize what she was thinking. "You are not coming down there!"

"You have to take me with you," she argued. "We don't know if Prenpas and the miners have arrived or whether they've dealt with the men who were following us."

Allie watched his face as David considered how to proceed. "We can climb down to the first gallery, it's only six or seven feet. I'll find you somewhere safe to hide, while I go down to look for your brother and Winter."

"I want to come with you," she protested.

"Sorry, Allie, that's not a risk I'm willing to take."

David was right, she *knew* he was right. Wheal Gunnis was more than seven hundred feet deep and a difficult climb.

Moreover, it was not just the main shaft to worry about. Among the levels were winzes which connect one gallery to another and to the best of her knowledge, there were any number of those.

You lose your way or your footing, and you lose your life.

Knowing that, it didn't stop the restless fear for her brother. If something dreadful had happened to Phillip, she would feel it, *wouldn't she?*

Allie felt David caress her wet cheek. She looked into David's eyes.

"Courage, my love, we haven't come this far to fail."

She swallowed against a lump in her throat and nodded once before stepping forward to the opening on the ladderway. It was surprisingly well lit by several lamps that burned from pegs down the drop.

David went first and climbed confidently out onto the ladder, dropping a few rungs below her to guide her as she clambered cautiously out into the ladderway.

"Keep a good grip and go slowly. Make sure your foot is firmly on each rung as you go. And just look forward, don't look down. When we get to the gallery, I'll help you in."

They climbed down and David exited into the gallery before her. His hands were firm on her hips as she stepped down the last few rungs to where she, too, could cross the gap into the first level of the mine.

After a few steps in, David turned suddenly, his finger to his lips in warning. Whispered voiced echoed along the passage. They were indistinct at first. But after a few seconds, she recognized the speakers – Phillip and Julian.

She drew breath to call out to them but David closed in, swept one arm around to pull her close and clamped his other hand across her mouth. He brought his lips close to her ear. "Don't," he breathed. "They may not be alone. Stay back."

He released her and began to advance in the direction of the voices. She followed a little behind – he'd not told her to stay where she was, just to stay back. Within a few yards, the gallery opened on one side into a low stope, its roof barely above head height. About twenty feet in, lit by a single lamp turned low, sat Phillip and Julian on the floor.

She rushed past David to her brother who leapt to his feet on seeing her.

"Allie!" he said in a low voice, "what are you doing here?" He embraced her in a bear hug.

"Is it safe to speak?" she whispered to him.

"Better keep it down, Sis – I don't know if the 'ghosts' are about. They know *we're* here, but I'd rather they don't learn *you* are, too." Phillip looked to David. "What the hell's going on? Why have you brought her down here?"

"There was little choice," said David. "We were up top looking for you and were pursued. It was come in or be captured."

Allie knelt beside Julian who struggled to sit upright with a groan of pain.

"No, don't move, you idiot!" Phillip hissed at him. Julian sagged back into his seated position against the wall.

Allie knelt beside him. His clothes were covered in dirt and his face was deathly pallid. One leg was stretched out in front of him, bound to a piece of old timber with torn rags to keep it straight and still.

"Took a tumble, I'm afraid," he gasped.

"It was hardly a tumble," said Phillip. "It was a six foot fall down a winze further along the level. His leg's not broken, but it's bad."

"I think I put my knee out," Julian offered weakly. "It twisted badly when I hit the bottom. Hurt terribly. Couldn't even straighten my leg at first…"

"Are you in pain now?" she asked.

"Not as much as it was…"

David squatted beside her and clasped a hand on Julian's shoulder. "We'll have you out of here very soon, my friend. Prenpas and the miners are on their way. They'll see to the gang."

He stood and turned to Phillip. "You said they know you're here? What happened?"

"We were coming up the ladder yesterday when we heard voices so we just hung on and listened. They were back in level two, talking about their orders. They'd been told to stay here and await further instructions. From what we could glean, they meant to stop the mine reopening at all costs. They intend to use Stannum as a base for a gathering of troops before they move inland. They were talking about how surprised the locals would be when Frenchies started dropping out of the sky."

Allie reached across Julian to take Phillip's hand and squeeze it. "How did they catch you?"

"We tried to climb past them and actually managed to, but then they heard the ladder creaking and fired a shot up at us. So, we got off the ladder on this level and ran. That's when Julian fell through the winze. After that, there was no option but to surrender."

David shrugged. "At least they let you live."

"To be honest, I thought we were done for. One of them is completely demented. He was all for killing us on the spot, but the other two calmed him down. Instead, they decided to light lamps in the ladderway so they could see if I was trying to escape, and the madman said if I got away, he'd kill Julian."

Allie shuddered at the story of their close call. She rose and embraced him again. "Thank God you're alive."

David clapped Phillip on the back. "Look, Prenpas and the miners must surely be here by now. You and I need to go up and arrange a litter to get Julian up the ladder."

"Allie can't stay down here."

"She'll be safer here looking after Julian until we *are* certain Bickmore's men above have been dealt with."

"COULD YOU PLEASE get me a drink of water?" Julian asked after David and Phillip had gone. "The canteen's over there. There's a cup fastened to my rucksack."

Allie looked where he pointed. The canteen and his pack stood on a pile of rocks. She untied the cup and brought it and the water over. She settled herself down beside Julian and poured him a little water. He accepted it gratefully.

"We were going easy on the Adam's ale," he said. "We didn't know how long we'd be down here. Haven't eaten since yesterday either."

She shook the canteen and estimated it was still a third full. "Want another drink? You'll be back above ground soon."

"Yes, please."

She poured a full cup for him this time then looked about the stope for anything left of the rags used to tie the splint to Julian's leg, intending to bathe his grubby face. All of it must have been used, however. The only cloth she could see was a dirty old sack with a scattering of rusty tools on it. Oh well, she thought, the habit's ruined already...

She tore another scrap of fabric off her skirt, wet the cloth with water from the canteen, and sat back down with Julian to wipe his face.

He laughed weakly. "Now you really are treating me like a brother. A little brother!"

She smiled at his good spirits despite the pain she knew he must be in.

He suddenly frowned. "What's that?"

She saw him looking at her bloodstained sleeve. Both sleeves were so grimy from brushing against the walls of the adit that one had to look close to see the dried blood that had soaked through. "It's nothing. I scratched myself on the way into the mine."

"Must have been a deep scratch to bleed that much," he offered with concern.

To distract him, she told him how she and David had run from the two men into the drainage adit that led out to the tailings pit, and how David had helped her climb down the ladder.

"I'm so glad you and Manston managed to work everything out," he said. "I'll be sorry to lose you though – how will I fend off Lydia when you're wed?"

Allie let out a giggle that was half a sob.

Julian took her hand and squeezed it. His eyes revealed the depth of his pain despite his attempt at humor.

"I just hope I can find someone who loves me as completely as you and David love one another."

"Well, ain't that sweet?"

Both Allie and Julian started at the rasping voice as the man emerged around the corner. She recognized him instantly. His was a face one didn't forget quickly – he was the man who Bickmore called Bert when she found them snooping around David's cottage.

Allie scrambled to her feet. The man's eyes gleamed speculatively as he stepped forward. His head bowed beneath the low ceiling, his pockmarked visage that of a devil in the flickering light from the oil lamp.

The light also caught something else – the long thin blade in his hand.

Julian tried to scramble to his feet but cried out in pain from his damaged knee. He fell back to the floor with a gasp.

"Don't give me any trouble either of you if you want to keep breathing," he hissed. "You!" He pointed the knife at Allie. "Clever enough to get in the drain adit, you're going to show me how to get out."

"Leave her alone," Julian yelled.

The man turned the knife toward Julian. "Shut it or I'll cut your tongue out." He turned his attention back to Allie. "You're going show me the way out of here and, if we meet anyone along the way, you're my ticket to pass."

Allie backed up several paces. "I will not!"

The man snorted with disdain and, ignoring her, immediately walked over to Julian and kicked his splinted leg. Julian's shriek of pain cut through Allie's ears and echoed about the passages. The man then dropped to his knees, grasped Julian's hair and pulled his head back, pricking his neck with the tip of his cruel blade. "Tell her to do it or I'll cut your throat right now," he snarled.

Julian made no sound other than huffed out sounds of pain through clenched teeth.

The devil was so confident, he had his back to her. Allie cast her eyes desperately about the space for anything to use as a weapon. One of the tools on the old sack was a short crowbar.

She picked it up. But as she raised it above her head to bring it down on the man's back, it clashed with the low roof. He let go of Julian at the sound and tumbled to the side, out of the way.

Maintaining her grip on the bar, Allie sought to use it like an epee, thrusting it one handed at her adversary as he scrambled to his feet, but the weight of it was too much on her wrist. Her thrust dropped and the end of the crowbar prodded him in the thigh.

The man brought up the hand that held the knife.

Allie took the bar in both hands and swept it crosswise at an angle. It connected with his wrist. Now it was the man's turn to yell in pain. He grabbed at his arm, the knife clattering on the ground.

Still holding the crowbar in both hands, Allie swept it back and forth in front of her, driving the man back. He cursed her with almost every awkward, stumbling step he took, but she ignored him, heard only her fencing instructor's words...

Feint, deflect, parry, lunge. Feint, deflect, parry, lunge...

The man swore vilely as his head first grazed, then bumped painfully against the lowering roof in the gloomy wall of the stope.

He was in full fury now. He lunged forward with a roar, arms outstretched toward her.

Allie ducked below his grasping paws and swept the end of the crowbar across both his shins.

With a cry of pain, he staggered back two or three paces, went to stand up straight to regain his balance, and smashed the top of his head into the rock above. He fell on his bony backside with an *"oof"* and put his hands out behind himself to stop from falling further back.

Allie saw the sudden shock in his wide eyes. His hands found nothing but air in the split second he tumbled backwards into an open shaft. His scream echoed upwards for several seconds then stopped abruptly with a sound remarkably like that of a sack of potatoes dropping on a flagstone floor.

She rose slowly to her feet, still holding the crowbar, and stepped cautiously forward to the edge of the winze into which the man with the pockmarked face had fallen. It wasn't very wide but it was obviously quite deep – there was nothing to be seen peering into it but blackness.

Allie backed cautiously away from the edge and returned to Julian.

He'd dragged himself several yards face down after her with his elbows. She dropped the crowbar and knelt beside him.

"What happened?" he asked. "That scream…"

"He fell into something a bit deeper than you did," she replied, her voice trembling on the edge of hysterical laughter.

She let herself fall onto her seat and stayed there on the floor next to Julian, lying on his front, until David and Phillip returned with news came that three men had been captured and no one else remained below.

Now came the tricky matter of bringing an injured man to the surface. Julian wasn't the first man who'd injured himself down a mine and the practice of getting a man to the surface was one well known to the most experienced of the miners. They had lashed him firmly to the wooden litter and hauled him upright back to the surface on a thick rope that disappeared up the ladderway.

Now, the rope hung down without the litter but with a large open loop.

Allie stood in the edge of the gallery and raised her arms above her head for David to lower the loop over them. He snugged it firmly under her arms and over the top of her breasts.

"Are you sure this is necessary? I'm not sure this is what they mean when they talk about tying the knot," she quipped.

"Humor me," he replied dryly.

She dropped her arms around his neck and hugged him tightly.

"Now I have you where I want you," she whispered.

David pulled her closer still for a languorous kiss, their tongues teasing and tasting, a kiss born of passion but also of relief.

"Perhaps it is I who have you exactly where I want you," he countered, his hands roaming freely around her waist and across her back.

"Ready down below?" Phillip called.

"On our way," David yelled up.

Allie began her ascent, David only a few steps behind her.

"Don't worry, I won't fall," she told him.

"You have it wrong, my love," he said. "I am the one who's fall-en."

Chapter Thirty-Four

October 1806

THEY SHARED AN unhurried kiss, long and full. The stroke of his hand over the silk of her robe was arousing. David let the kiss linger a moment before he left her to set up his easel.

Through the window, the afternoon sun filled the bedroom with light. In concession to the warmth, the window was open a couple of inches, letting in fresh air from outside that smelled of fresh grass and the sea.

They might have gone anywhere for their honeymoon – Lady Abigail offered as much as a wedding present, but she and David declined. What more could they need but a secluded place of their own in the most beautiful part of the world?

"Are you sure?" he asked.

"It seems only fair that since you drew me from memory you ought to draw again with the model in front of you," she answered, knowing how much her sexual confidence stirred him.

"Trust me, the reality far surpasses the imagination," he said, drawing closer once again.

The feeling of his hands running over her satin-clad form was arousing, building in her a need that was yet to be satiated despite being wed for several weeks now. She felt the belt of her robe loosen about her waist, his hands touching bared flesh as they rose, following the parting up to her shoulders.

Not once did his eyes leave hers, warm blue eyes watching her intently. His thumbs rubbed small circles across her shoulders as he slid the fabric away. The room was silent but for the whisper of silk as it fell to the floor and the sigh from her lips.

It was not the first time Allie had been naked before him, but that had been simply as a prelude to their lovemaking. This was something different. A foreplay that could last for quite some time before their mutual desire demanded their joining.

David, still fully clothed, stepped back and beheld her as though she was already a work of art, a sculpture he admired. That, too, was arousing, Allie decided. She liked him looking at her as he did now. Any self-critical thoughts she had about her body disappeared as David taught her to see herself through his eyes.

He approached once more, his eyes hungry. The kiss this time was full of urgent but restrained passion. The feel of his clothed body against her skin ignited sensations everywhere.

She nearly begged him to stop and make love to her immediately but she held her tongue. There was also intense pleasure to be found in the delay, and if the bulge in his breeches was any indication, he, too, found this play to his liking.

Tenderly, as though she were made of gossamer, he led her to the west-facing window, the one that looked out to sea.

"The light is perfect here," he whispered. Allie allowed David to pose her to his satisfaction. The right arm on the windowsill, her body angled so that the stream of light fell over her breasts, down her stomach; the rest of her body a play of shadows.

"You're beautiful," he whispered, brushing a lock of her curly black hair over her ear, before artfully leaving a tendril to fall across her breast.

Once more, he ran his hands down her body as though committing her form to his fingers in order to bring her image to life on paper.

David stepped back to examine the view. He adjusted himself. She gave him a knowing look. Apparently satisfied by what he saw, he stepped behind the easel and picked up a pencil.

"Keep your face in profile… just a little more to your right. Stop. Perfect."

There was no need for words between them. Allie focused her attention out to sea for a while, watching the endless roll of the waves as they came into shore. She was more aware of her senses than she had ever been in her life. She breathed in deeply and let the cool air fill her lungs while exposed skin experienced sunshine for the first time.

She listened to the quiet scratching of pencil on paper and the call of the terns and gulls over the headland. After a while, she closed her eyes and enjoyed a daydream of his caresses bringing her earthshattering ecstasy. Even her memory of this caused her to sigh.

David chuckled as though he knew what she was thinking.

Soon, she felt a touch of his hand. Allie opened her eyes. "Finished?" she whispered with surprise.

David shook his head. "The light has changed. I want at least another four hours before I can get something I'm satisfied with."

The double meaning of his words caused her to sigh with longing.

He kissed her once. Again, it was a slow and leisurely mating of their tongues, his hands sweeping across her body before she found herself swept up into his arms and then on the bed while he stopped to admire her once more.

She stretched, arching her back, as confident as a courtesan while he undressed but not fully. He untied the cravat and let the ends drape over his neck. She followed the twin lines of fabric down to where an impressive erection waited for her.

David climbed onto the bed, drawing his body over hers. The hairs of his chest tickled her skin, raising gooseflesh and causing her nipples to stand proud on her breasts. Allie took hold of the linen and used it to draw him closer.

"Why have you a need for anything other than yourself in our bed?" she asked. It was a disingenuous question. She had seen copies of sketches he had drawn of the brothels and bordellos and saw how such bonds were employed.

"You expressed a particular curiosity," he said, giving her a cock-eyed grin that made her heart beat a little faster. He sat up on his haunches, her legs spread on either side of his thighs.

She pitied the women for whom bedding was a chore to be endured instead of a mutually satisfying union, one where give and take was explored in equal measure until both experienced the delight of surrender.

He slid the cravat from his neck and folded it over twice, before swinging it, pendulum-like across her body, the ends tickling her ribs, the underside of her breasts, then lower to her hips and lower still where she was open to him.

"Some people use alcohol or take a stimulant to bring them to this point," he said. "But I've always found it a lot more satisfying to simply use time and touch."

He leaned forward for a kiss then leaned in to whisper in her ear. "Sometimes, there is nothing more arousing than anticipation..."

He draped the linen across her eyes. It smelled of peppermint, cinnamon, and him.

"... not knowing where the next stroke..." He ran a flat hand lightly across her breasts, skimming her nipples, teasing them. On his next pass, she strained up to him, his hand cupping her breasts more fully.

"... or kiss..." This one was on the planes of her belly.

"... or taste will come from."

She cried out as his lips touched that most sensitive part of her, his tongue darting into her folds, circling her bud. Her hips shifted and rocked beneath him.

"David! *Oh!*"

She could not bear it, the sensation was too much, but oh, how she wanted more. She spread her legs further, granting him deeper access, and ripped the linen from her eyes to watch him.

Her orgasm took her quickly, rising up her body with tingles until the sensation erupted in pleasure. She called out his name over and over. He raised his head, the satisfied look on his face turned almost predatory. He settled himself between her legs, poised at her entrance. She needed him, craved him. She shifted her hips, drawing her legs over his until her heels pushed at his buttocks in an attempt to draw him closer. But his superior strength held her away from him.

Allie groaned her disappointment and received a chuckle from him in response.

David lavished kisses on her breasts, his hands stroking and rubbing while her own fingers slid through his hair to hold him to her. After a moment, he pulled her hands away from his head, their fingers joining as he stretched out her arms.

His expression turned serious for a moment. "Every day, I count how fortunate I am to have met you."

"Beloved… darling… husband," she whispered.

"I love you so much, Allie."

She used the distraction to shift her hips beneath him, seeking his body, silently demanding that it join with hers.

"Is it your intent to torture me?" she groaned.

He chuckled. With a thumb and index finger circling her wrists, he gathered his cravat with the remaining fingers of his left hand, before drawing her arms up over her head. She held them there as he tied the length of cloth around them.

She was not truly bound. She knew she was free to move as she wished, but there was something arousing about allowing herself to be at the mercy of such a masterful lover.

"If it will keep you where I want you," he said and began stroking that smooth flesh between her legs. Her arousal grew once more. She was slick and hot and more than ready for him. He entered her and she knew another orgasm was not far away.

She squeezed him, causing him to groan. After demonstrating so much restraint, he could not be too far from needing to seek his own release. His mouth descended on hers, plundering it. She writhed beneath him, matching stroke for stroke as they sought the summit of pleasure together.

In the end, she could not keep her arms above her head. She brought them over his head and onto his back, trapping him in her embrace. He rolled them together onto their sides, and drew her leg up over his hip. The slightly different angle of his penetration brought her to the peak immediately.

She cried his name over and over. Then his own movements became erratic as the throes of his own release overtook him.

Afterwards, he whispered words of endearment followed by a rain of kisses until their breathing returned to normal.

They lay content in each other's arms, watching the play of shadows on the wall and the changing color of the daylight from yellow to pink, and then to softest purple.

"For too many years, I sought pleasure as a release from being rejected," he said. "As a man craves drink, the more I needed to partake before the pain was numbed. I knew if I continued, I'd be dead by one means or another."

Allie remained silent during these half-light confessions in which he answered the deepest questions about himself without her needing to utter a word. She had bared her body to him, giving him her complete trust; now he was baring his heart and soul in no less a way, exposing his own vulnerability.

The sacredness of the moment, this union of mind and body, was the true intimacy between husband and wife.

"There's something else," he said a little later. "I received a letter from my father's estate at Carmarthan."

She held her breath. She knew he had written to his father seeking an audience but, after so long an estrangement, neither of them were hopeful for a satisfactory outcome.

"What did it say?"

"I am no longer the Baron of Carreg."

Allie sat up in bed, tugging a sheet over her breasts against the cool of early evening. "Oh, David, no. They can't possibly take your birthright from you. That's not fair, it's so unjust!"

She was silenced by a kiss and it was only then she saw the twinkle of amusement in his eyes.

"It would seem I am now the third Viscount Carmarthan and my mother is eager to be reunited with her son and to meet his bride."

He pulled her into his arms and pulled the sheet up until it covered them both.

"When would you like to go? It would mean leaving Stannum. How do you feel about that? I know you are close to your brother and it is said the bond between twins is particularly strong."

"He has plenty to distract him now that the mine is running again," she assured him.

She pushed at David's shoulders and he gave in, allowing her to roll on top of him. "Besides, we will all be together soon enough in London. I have shopping to do. It's not every day one is invited to dine with the Prince of Wales and The King's Rogues."

David's strong arms surrounded her, holding her close, and she felt the stirrings of another erection.

"A royal summons is not to be disobeyed," he answered with mock gravity. "But I implore you to be kind on my purse until we know the true *state* of my estate.

She nuzzled her cheek against his chest. "According to Julian, as of next month, you could buy all the jewelry from Garrard's twice over from your royalties from Wheal Gunnis."

"I'm sure the man exaggerates just a little."

She considered how she loved the rumble of his voice through his chest.

"We've been through so much in a year," she whispered. "I can scarcely believe it. People are moving back to Stannum and, thanks to assistance from Susannah and Peggy from St. Sennen, the monthly markets are back. Phillip talks of a school! Someone ought to pinch me because I'm still afraid it's a dream – *ouch!*"

She raised her head. David raised his eyebrows. "Your wish is my command, after all."

She decided to take her revenge by lightly running her fingernails down his flanks. As swift as lightning, he rolled over, trapping her beneath him, raining kisses down her neck and then her mouth with the same passion she recalled from their kiss back on that cold November day.

She broke the kiss long enough to tell him, "Make love to me again."

His touch grew bolder, his hands roamed across her possessively.

"T'would be my pleasure – and yours."

Epilogue

December 1806
London

IT WAS EXTRAORDINARILY busy at the St. James' Square townhouse of Sir Daniel and Lady Abigail Ridgeway. Indeed, it was a *full* house.

Adam and Olivia Hardacre were there. So, too, were Nate and Susannah Payne.

The Viscount and Viscountess of Carmarthan, with the viscountess' brother, Phillip Gedding, and their friend, Julian Winter, were also there.

In a few hours' time, they would all travel to a Mayfair ball at Carmarthan House, where the guest of honor would be the Prince of Wales himself.

It was to be the first official duty performed by the third Viscount Carmarthan. He and his bride opening up Carmarthan House for the Christmas ball was the most sought-after invitation of the Season, made more prestigious by the attendance of the Prince of Wales.

But first, there was to be a private royal audience.

Prinny was here at St James' Square with Major-General Arthur Wellesley in attendance.

The prince greeted each guest in turn before clearing his throat. The room fell to silence.

"I would like to thank you, my loyal agents – my *rogues* – for your service in these difficult recent years. You have thwarted Napoleon's most audacious plot and we are now confident the threat of invasion is over.

"With this, I declare your organization is officially disbanded. You may retire to your lives secure in the knowledge that you have done your country a great service in keeping its borders safe from those who would overturn the heritage of this green and pleasant land.

"Rest assured, your contribution has been recorded for posterity but, by necessity, they must be held secret under seal. As such, I deeply regret there can be no public honors and, with our country still at war, the reward for your efforts must be discreet.

"Nonetheless, it is to you I propose a toast."

The Prince of Wales raised his champagne glass.

"To The King's Rogues."

Eleven other glasses were raised enthusiastically in response.

"The King's Rogues!"

THE PRINCE OF Wales and Wellesley left shortly after. They would be at Carmarthan House later in the evening.

The initial excitement in the Ridgeways' townhouse became a little more subdued. Sir Daniel and Lady Abigail spoke with David and Allie as the young couple prepared to leave to ready themselves for their guests. Phillip and Julian chatted with the Paynes about the trials and tribulations of running a family.

Adam remained apart, alone and deep in thought. It didn't go unnoticed by Olivia who came to his side.

"Is anything wrong?" she gently inquired.

He shook his head. "No, not really. It's just... oh, I don't know."

She smiled sympathetically and touched his arm. "It's always the same at the end of an era. Our old lives are over, but new ones are beginning. I certainly won't be sad to leave behind the worry of your being away so much – and the worries of what might happen to you."

"You're right, of course," he said with a rueful smile.

SPY ANOTHER DAY

"What were you expecting?" she asked.

"I'm not sure – but I'm certainly glad to be retiring on a captain's pension. I just hope that one day the war will be over and England and France can finally live in peace."

DAVID AND ALLIE were ready to leave. The entire party followed them out into the hallway. In the middle of it was a large crate that had not been there before. Atop the crate was a letter addressed to Lady Abigail.

She looked at the handwriting and passed it to her husband. Sir Daniel opened and read it.

"Well, Captain Hardacre," he said, looking up, "you'd better see what's inside."

The Ridgeways' butler fetched a chisel, and Adam prized apart the planks. Inside the crate was a barrel.

"This is a whole hog's head of brandy!" he exclaimed. "Who on earth could get their hands on such an amount?"

"I have the answer here," said Sir Daniel. He handed over the note for it to be passed about the group.

The importance of the letter writer was evident in the quality of the paper which featured, printed and embossed, a gold crown over a black shield with fifteen golden discs – the Duke of Cornwall's own coat of arms.

Underneath, in a flourishing script were written the words:

From the Duke,
with love.

The End

Do not be afraid; our fate cannot be taken from us; it is a gift.

– Dante

About the Author

Elizabeth Ellen Carter is an award-winning historical romance writer who pens richly detailed historical romantic adventures. A former newspaper journalist, Carter ran an award-winning PR agency for 12 years. The author lives in Australia with her husband and two cats.

Made in the USA
Coppell, TX
25 July 2024

35180886R00193